THE
LOST
CODEX

HEATHER LYONS

PRAISE FOR THE COLLECTORS' SOCIETY SERIES

"The most unique, fascinating, wondrous book I've read in a very long time! I was glued to every page."—*Shelly Crane, New York Times bestselling author of Significance and Wide Awake*

"So unique and different, the first thing I thought when I finished. . .Man I wish I would have thought of that! Buy this book, you won't regret it!"—*#1 NYT bestselling author Rachel Van Dyken*

"This book should come with a handwritten tag that says 'Read Me'. And you should. Right now. One of my favorite reads of the year. Loved it! I want to live inside Heather's brain."—*Daisy Prescott, USA Today Bestselling author of Modern Love Stories*

"This fantasy was a breath of fresh air. It was unique, inspiring, and obviously a five-star read. If you enjoy romance, adventure, and traveling through worm holes go get this book ASAP!"— *Jennifer Foor, author of the Best Selling Mitchell Family Series, The Kin Series, The Bankshot Series, The Twisted Twin Series, Diary of a Male Maid, Hope's Chance and Love's Suicide*

"One of the most inventive stories I've ever read. Brimming with sexiness and romance, magic and lore, it's a modern-day fairytale adventure that is not to be missed."—*Vilma's Book Blog*

"THIS BOOK WAS EPIC! . . . I wanted to escape into a story that held not only romance, but also mystery. And that's exactly what I got when I read **The Collectors' Society**. I got a riveting, refreshing, and unique plot that was not only driven by a beautifully sweet romance, but also a thriving story filled with suspense and unbounded mystery."—*Angie and Jessica's Dreamy Reads*

"Alice is the new standard that I set for all heroines."—*BFF Book Blog*

"Deserving to be a new classic for the modern day, **The Collectors' Society** should be on your must read list."—*The Paisley Reader*

"If you love classic literature, and you love fantasy and fairy tales, this is a must read book for you."—*Book Briefs*

"This is one of those books where you have to sit back and question an author's sanity because how the hell did they ever come up with this amazingly insane and totally unique idea if not for a bit of insanity on their parts. All I can say is thank goodness for Heather Lyons and her crazy thoughts, **Collectors' Society** is. . . . . .I can't even explain it, just know that it IS…"—*Reads All The Books*

"…A unique tale that will leave you breathless, enthralled and begging for more. If you thought you knew classic fairy tales, think again!"—*Resch Reads and Reviews*

"I'm finding it almost impossible to put down in words the love I feel for this story. It was nothing like I expected and yet everything I wanted."—*The Book Hookup*

"I'm not exaggerating when I say that **The Hidden Library** has everything you could possibly want or need in a book: laughter, heartache, romance, action, adventure, mystery, suspense – the list goes on and on. If I could've dreamed up a book that would satisfy my not-so-secret love of fairy tales as well as my never-ending search to find exciting and inventive storylines, I wouldn't have come close to dreaming up **The Hidden Library** because it's completely and delightfully unique. Not only does it have a nostalgic feel that beckons my inner book lover, but it's also refreshing in a way that kept me guessing as to where the narrative would go next. "—*Nose Stuck in a Book*

"Beautifully crafted settings, gripping plots, and enough emotion to satisfy even the coldest of hearts, Lyons has taken elements from some of the greatest novels in history and fashioned them together to create *herself* a spot on the shelf of future "Great American Classics". Heather Lyons has woven together a story that transforms history, bringing a new-found love of classical literature to a whole new generation of readers."
—*One Guy's Guide to Great Reads*

"I was completely entranced with the first book of this series, **The Collectors**

Society, and **The Hidden Library** is no different. This is a highly entertaining and well-written series that I hope doesn't go away any time soon."—*Books She Reads*

"This series keeps getting better and is a must read. A rare 6 star rating from this picky reader!"—*A Literary Perusal*

"I've never, never, never EVER read a book with such extraordinary characters in the fantasy genre."—*Melissa Reads Books*

"A mystically fantastic read that takes you on a magical fun journey. . ... Start this series now!!!"—*TSK TSK What to Read*

"This book has everything, everything. A beautiful romance. Wonderful friendships. Some love sacrifices. Broken hearts. An evil genius."—*Lost in a Book Blog*

"Sequels don't always live up to the original books but let me tell you Heather has knocked it out of the park with **The Hidden Library**. . ."—*Book Starlets*

"This is why I love reading!!! This. Series. Right. Here."—*Maria's Book Blog*

"If I could give a book a million golden stars, this would be the one. **THE FORGOTTEN MOUNTAIN** has upped the Collectors' Society game and once again, captured my attention with its incredible heart, valor, passion, and creativity! In years to come this series will be one I recommend to young and old alike. The brilliance of this story and series is one that should be savored and adored by all the world over."—*Typical Distractions*

The Lost Codex
Copyright © 2016 by Heather Lyons
http://www.heatherlyons.net

Cerulean Books

ISBN: 978-0-09908436-9-6

First Edition

Cover design by Whit And Ware
Editing by Kristina Circelli
Book formatting by Champagne Formats

*This one is dedicated to
Evelyn Torres and Samantha Modi,
two amazing, supportive women
I am lucky to call friends.
Brom officially welcomes you
as honorary members of
the Collectors' Society.*

THE JABBERWOCKY

ALICE

A GNAWED-UPON BONE SHARD PROTRUDING from a patch of trampled, jaundiced grass pokes at my boot whilst others haphazardly adorn the loamy forest floor. No dread pools in the pit of my belly upon such a gruesome sight, though. It is the intoxicating rush of anticipation that courses through my bloodstream.

According to my Grand Advisor, I suffer from a constant thirst for adventure.

When I draw it out, my vorpal blade hisses from the sheath hanging upon my back. In the distance, a scaled tail, mottled and greenish-purplish-black in the dappled sunlight filtering through the tulgey trees, crushes a thornbush in a cantankerous thump, but the destruction is likely due to a wild jubjub bird daring to taunt the beast than anything else.

Tracking this particular Jabberwocky posed no problem. Although its dam was vanquished years before, the younger beast's favorite haunts are well known to Wonderlanders far and wide. Remembering its dam's ferocity and proclivity toward death and ruin, most leave the heirs to their own devices, although there always are those addled enough to dare to attempt be the latest to best one of Wonderland's most fearsome monsters.

And here I am, attempting to do the same—only, I do not wish for this Jabberwocky's death. I do not covet the glory some may bestow upon such a feat. I simply desire a scale from its hide.

If only Jabberwockies were known for their reasoning.

I glance away from the tail, toward a stately tree several yards beyond where the beast dozes. Tall and silvery-golden, adorned with velvety, plum-colored leaves that glint like cut amethysts in the thin shafts of light streaming through branches, the tree offers protection to my favorite hunting companion. We two are not so foolish to believe our combined might will prevail against a Jabberwocky without better tactical planning, even against one as young as this. Instead, we employ an old standard: we shall conquer and divide.

I give the signal. The White King of Wonderland tilts his crossbow toward the grove just beyond the beast's scaled belly. An arrow laced with jubjub feathers is fired. The Jabberwocky rouses, its attention no doubt captured by the sight of common feathers, but as expected, it does not abandon its prone position. I use the opportunity to sprint closer, ducking behind another large, twisted tree carved by scarred strokes of talons.

I've cut the distance between myself and the Jabberwocky in half.

A few minutes pass before another feathered arrow soars through the air. As before, the Jabberwocky does little to investigate, but its attention diverts just enough for me to finish my approach. While not the most intelligent beasts within Wonderland, or keen of hearing, Jabberwockies rely instead on aromas to lead them to their prey. Indiscriminate about food sources, Jabberwockies are known to eat all sorts of animals, including humans.

In order to counter such a quandary, my Grand Advisor, the

Caterpillar, concocted a noxious concentrated oil for the White King and me to bath in in order to allow the stench to permeate our pores and hair. Naturally, we were thoroughly repulsed at mimicking decaying woods, fungus, and feces, and we involuntarily wept from the fetor. I reminded Jace there was no need for him to go through with the hunt, that it was my responsibility. His response was as stalwart and familiar as always. "The beauty of free will," I was told, "is that we can choose whether or not to do what we wish. And I wish to go with you today."

Thus, here we are, reeking in such a way that renders us invisible to the Jabberwocky.

To many, our mission would be superfluous. Plagued by dreams I cannot fully recall or understand for the past two mornings, I've woken disconcerted, aching for a man whose name or face I cannot conjure. Once daily reality emerges and the dreams fade, I am left with unexplainable, heartrending emotions I refuse to allow myself to dwell upon, and yet manage to do all the same.

Jace and I are to be married on the morrow. The White and Diamonds kingdoms will unite in such a way Wonderland has never seen before. Peace, prosperity, and stability will be assured for half of our land's inhabitants. It is a dream he and I have lovingly planned for years, one that even the White Queen has officially, albeit grudgingly, sanctioned.

I am baffled how, for the past pair of days, each brush of his skin against mine feels erroneous rather than blissful. When our mouths touch, the urge to pull away overrides our history and what we mean to one another. A niggling, deep-seated tug in the confines of my soul insists he is not the man I wish to be with, that my heart impossibly belongs to someone I cannot recall except in remnants of pure emotions and desires.

I cannot allow this. I love him, this kind, honorable, wonderful man. My heart and future have belonged to Jace since the age of eighteen. No—he possessed it long before then. We met when we were children, verbally sparring on a battlefield over words beginning with the letter H. I adored him near instantly. For the scant years I returned to England, I daydreamed about the handsome, young king to the point of distraction. My sisters swooned over potential suitors, yet I rebuffed any who dared to court me. I pined for a Wonderlander with nearly colorless eyes.

When I returned to officially claim my throne, and we came face to face for the first time in years, he greeted me with, "Hail, harridan." It was accompanied by a deliciously naughty smile.

Years of fanciful daydreams were easily displaced by a far superior reality.

I countered his salutation in kind. "Hello, hapless hedonist."

The Caterpillar's loud snort of disapproval failed to lessen my delight. Neither did any of the gasps from my ladies-in-waiting. The White Ferzes' eyes nearly popped from their exceptionally large sockets. I was utterly besotted by a widening smile from a handsome boy now grown into a beautiful man.

In the days, weeks, and months that followed, the connection between us deepened, solidified. While there was no doubt I found the White King physically attractive, it was his sense of self as both a man and a ruler that drew me in like a bee to a premier singing Flower's garden. We shared similar ideals, similar hopes and dreams for a better, more prosperous Wonderland for all. Our politics aligned just as smoothly as our hearts.

He is everything I admire in a partner, a man, a friend, and a lover.

Something as meaningless as dreams cannot be allowed to derail our future together. If I must battle a Jabberwocky to ensure our happiness, and Wonderland's future, then I will do just that.

A good minute stands as a test to whether the Caterpillar's poisons are enough to mask my smell before a third feathered arrow soars overhead. As soon as the Jabberwocky lifts its head, Jace fires a poisoned arrow into the base of the beast's neck. The Jabberwocky roars as the liquid-filled tip digs into its flesh. It pushes itself up on its two legs, stumbling instantaneously, just as the Caterpillar promised it would. Another howl rattles the trees before it collapses in a clumsy heap upon the sawdust corpses of trees.

"Jabberwocky blood is acidic," my advisor informed me just this morning. "Anything injected will be neutralized fairly quickly."

"Define fairly quickly."

His smile was thinner than normal for one without substantial lips. "For most concoctions? Seconds." I was offered a tiny bottle with a cork stopper. "With this? A minute, if you are fortunate."

I peered into the iridescent lavender liquid. "What will it do?"

"Temporarily weaken muscles." To Jace, he said, "Use a crossbow. Aim for the small space at the base on his neck, to the left. There is an inch or so of unprotected skin. Do not miss."

The White King's ability to strike any object, even at vast distances, is legendary throughout the Courts. And now he once more proves the validity of such praise, as his arrow pierces the Jabberwocky exactly where ordered.

My window is opened, tiny as it may be. I dart forward, the vorpal blade firm in my hand as I mentally count down seconds. The beast releases a mournful gurgle of frustration, its elongated whiskers and scaly jowls limply sagging around massive teeth. When I skid to a stop, the tips of my leather boots collide with its tail.

A groan ripe with helpless ire nearly blasts my feet from the forest floor.

I throw my satchel to the ground before prying thick scales off with the end of my blade. "My apologies," I gasp as I wrench off bits of its tough hide. "I promise, I'll depart momentarily."

Its body shudders, as if allowed, it would quake with indignation. Once I reach the count of ten, I shove my treasures into the satchel and sprint out of the jabberwocky's lair.

Seven.

The earth beneath my feet rumbles.

Six.

Jubjub birds explode from the trees at the sheer intensity of the beast's wrath.

Five.

Rumbling turns to assured quaking.

Four.

I curse the forest's messiness.

Three.

I barrel over broken branches and bushes, my hair snagging upon greedy twigs.

Two.

I shift my sword, holding aloft a free arm.

One.

Jace grabs hold, lifting me up. I settle between his chest and his stallion's withers, claiming hold of the reigns. Laughter burbles forth from the both of us as we gallop through the remaining thicket. Bursting into the Dark Meadows, sunlight warms my face. My cheeks hurt, my grin is so broad. My lungs sting, my breath heaving in exhilarated bursts.

We slow three-fourths of the way across the clearing, allowing the stallion to munch on the bittersweet black grasses of the meadow. Just beyond the tree line, the Jabberwocky's bellows send hordes of outgribing toves scurrying to safety amongst the indigo and pumpkin Flowers. Around us, those Flowers burst into delighted songs that taunt the bested beast.

Strands of hair are brushed intimately away from my cheek as we watch the Jabberwocky stomp around in stymied outrage. "It is a shame he won't leave the tree line," Jace murmurs wistfully.

A young Flower calls out, her voice tinny amongst all the chatter, "Oh, Your Majesty, do not wish such a thing! He would trample us!"

He holds back his amusement. "My apologies, madam. I most certainly would never wish for such a travesty."

I twist in the saddle, repositioning my legs so we face one another. "The true shame lies in how uneventful this hunt was. We might not have even needed the poison."

"And to think this Jabberwocky is feared." Gleaming, black hair tilts toward the snarling, raging beast. "The Cheshire-Cat's tantrums are more frightening than he. How many scales did you confiscate?"

A tree collapses, its splintering sending yet another swatch of jubjubs soaring toward safety. While the flowers around us scream, the stallion barely twitches, its mouth too full of grass.

"Three." I shrug. "Perhaps four. I cannot understand why it's

raging on so. There was a minute amount of blood. It isn't as if it requires a bandage."

His lips curve higher, and I chuckle.

"Do you remember that time during the Serf Uprising?" I trace the
length of one dark eyebrow until I feel a bump and then a small dent.
"When you were bleeding profusely, and you scandalized the poor
healer by insisting there was no time for bandages. Even I marveled at
how it was possible to see through such a waterfall of red."

His head ducks toward mine, lessening the already slim space
between us. His warm breath is soft and welcome upon my lips.
"Humble."

"Hubris."

I feel, rather than see the strength of his smile. "Hostile."

"Hopelessly."

"Henpecked."

"Hardly."

His chuckle is smothered when our mouths press together. Without
coming up for air, he urges his stallion forward, toward home. The
Flowers call out their farewells, offering a song of safe travels. For a
small, lovely time, I allow our kisses to consume me before guilt roars
to the forefront of my heart and body and mind.

A thought, swift and sharp: *This isn't right. This isn't whom I
desire.*

Jace must sense my change of emotions, as he tenses a hair's
breadth before I break away. I am a coward, for I shove my forehead
into the crook of his neck rather than face his hurt.

A warm hand strokes the back of my neck; although I cannot see
it, he cannot hide the entirety of his disappointment. And now I am the
one with acidic blood in her veins, guilt-ridden, acidic blood, only for
entirely different, befuddling reasons.

I am gifted a lingering kiss upon my temple. "It will be all right,
my heart. Your answers are coming soon."

I pray a solution arrives at the same time.

POTIONS AND DREAMS

ALICE

BEYOND THE WINDOW, WHITE and blue tents rise between the trees surrounding our house in the tulgey woods bordering the White and Diamond lands. Guests, dignitaries, and courtiers have arrived in preparation for the morrow's ceremony. I spy Jace amongst a grouping of our Ferzes and Nightriders, acting, upon my insistence, as host for the both of us. He wished to remain with me while I willingly succumb to the Caterpillar's dream poison, but propriety cannot tolerate such rudeness, not where guests are concerned. It is insufferable enough one monarch is absent, but to have both abstaining from the night's festivities held in their honors is unconscionable. We've explained my absence away easily enough—I am readying myself for our union.

In many ways, it is the absolute truth.

The Caterpillar is nearly finished with his concoction. Whilst the White King and I hunted the Jabberwocky, he prepared the rest of the ingredients for a poison that will uncover and eradicate my mysterious dreams. The whole upstairs of our abode stinks with its potency. I must maintain shallow breaths in order to still my stomach. I have great faith in the Caterpillar's skills, though. His knowledge of poisons is unrivaled throughout Wonderland, even if some mimic rotting flesh left out in the sun on an overly balmy day.

"You mentioned the need to take a symbolic object within the dream." I hover over his work, curious as to what I will be ingesting. "One I must destroy. Yet, you have given no instruction on what that object must be."

He nudges his half-moon glasses up his bulbous nose, barely sparing a glance as he waves me away. "I did."

Which means I must figure it out myself. I do not bother asking how one even brings an object into a dream, as I can already predict his answer.

What, then, would sufficiently constitute symbolic for a series of dreams I cannot remember? In place of images, all I possess are entrenched sentiments that refuse to relinquish their hold on me, including a maddening sense of love for a nameless man whose face I cannot invoke.

Why does he remain faceless?

His face . . .

Perhaps a blank mask will do? Destroy the mask, destroy the passion for an imaginary person for whom I have assigned preposterous feelings for.

I own no such object, though. Therefore, as the Caterpillar fiddles with beakers and bubbling concoctions, I call for a maid and request scissors and parchment. Not even batting an eyelash at the request, she returns mere minutes later with just such items. I immediately set to work.

The clearing of a throat draws my attention. "Tick-tock, Your Majesty."

I glance up, startled, the hairs on my arms rising at the unnerving

9

sense of familiarity.

Tick-tock.

Tick-tock.

The Caterpillar dangles a vial of glowing, bluish liquid at the same time an uproarious cheer resonates from outside. I nod, sweeping the scraps of my artistic efforts to the side of the bed as he undulates his way over to where I am.

"Is this truly what you wish for, Your Majesty?"

I do not hide my irritation. "Yes."

Isn't it?

If I thought the stench of the concoction terrible, its taste is the exact opposite: *Roast chicken, followed by lemon curd.* I settle down upon the soft blankets and place the mask over my face, glad for the small boon.

"Be vigilant with your observations, Your Majesty. Ensure that, when the time comes, your decisions are true to yourself."

I assure him that I will, that I have always acted in just such a manner and would continue to do so. Within seconds, smoke from his hookah stings my nostrils, and seconds from that, the cotton of silence stuffs my ears.

When I open my eyes, mask still upon my face, I find myself in my sitting room, one floor below my bedroom. Golden, dying rays of daylight stream through the windows, casting shadows across the furniture. Before me is . . . *another Alice*, her shoulders convulsing. Jace's arms wrap tightly around her, his shoulders a perfect mirror of hers. I wander closer, close enough to discover wet cheeks. Close enough to spy his fingers turned white as they twist the silk of her dress. Hers are the same as they grip his fine coat. It is as if both fear if they were to let go, the other would dissipate like dew lapped away by a thirsty sun.

Ribbons tighten the corset constricting my lungs until I can hardly draw breath. Melancholy suffocates the room, stealing away all hope.

Could this be part of the dreams plaguing me? None of what I'm witnessing feels like a dream. Nerves stretched raw and taut insist upon something . . . different. Something more meaningful than a mere dream.

Something akin to a . . . a *memory*.

Beyond the walls and panes, Begonia's voice lifts in mournful melody. The lead Rose's chorus joins in, the swell rendering an ache in my bones. I reach back to grab hold of the settee, to steady myself as I drown in sorrow, but the fabric beneath my hands swirls away like the Caterpillar's smoke.

Cowardice rears its jaundiced head. I cannot endure watching this scene unfold before me. In just these few moments, a piece of my heart rips away from the muscles and bones within my chest. I turn away, only to find myself still facing the other Alice and Jace. Each rotation brings me to the same sight.

There is no escape. Even closing my eyes illuminates the same event.

The truth is not always easy, the Caterpillar warned just this morning, as I saddled my horse to ride out to find the Jabberwocky. *Be sure that this is what you want.*

"I do not know if I can do this." Jace's whisper to the other Alice cuts the very air. I am sure if I were to look, it cut my skin, too. "I know I must—*we* must—but. . ."

A heartrending cry disintegrates from her lips before she desperately presses her mouth against his. "Do not fail me. I need your strength right now." Her voice is nothing but shards of broken porcelain. "I—I cannot—"

He lovingly kisses away her tears, even as his own stream freely. "Forgive me." His voice matches hers, and my knees give way. I sway, a tree no longer moored by roots. "I vowed to be strong, and instead I am. . ." He closes his eyes. Murmurs her—*my*—name.

A pair of syllables breaks the both of our hearts. Wounds rip open, ones whose pink, tender skin is still all too fragile.

Still?

How can a dream cause such palpable pain?

As grief leaves me gasping, Jace curves his hands around her cheeks. "Allow me to accompany you. Just to the end."

The request intensifies the shudder wracking her overly taut body, and the suffering disintegrating me. "I want nothing more, my heart." So much anguish saturates each word. "But if you were to, my chances of leaving peaceably would be much diminished. How could I follow through if you stood there as sentry?"

A knock on the door fails to pry the pair apart. The other Alice calls out, "Enter," even as my beloved's head lowers to the slope of her neck.

Crimson blooms across his tunic. Rubs against the silk of her dress. Drips until it stains the floor. I have no doubt the other Alice's chest would do the same if it could.

As would mine.

The door swings open. The Caterpillar and the Cheshire-Cat are illuminated in hazy, late-afternoon sunlight. Both are weighted by a somberness that defies gravity.

My Grand Advisor coughs into one of his many gloved fists. "It is time, Your Majesty."

A keening choking consumes the White King of Wonderland. The other Alice draws in shuddery breath. She says, she whispers, "I cannot wish for a better person to take care of my peoples and lands. You honor me, my lord."

His answer is a kiss filled with emotion stripped so bare it saturates the room. He forcibly pulls himself away, putting distance between their bodies. An arm crosses his bloody chest. "To this I avow: I will defend the Diamonds' lands until my dying breath, my lady."

The other Alice unclasps the golden necklace ringing her neck, the one bearing a meaningful H. The same one around mine. She transfers it to his neck, tucking it beneath his newly scarlet shirt. "Heartbroken."

He whispers in kind, "Hollowed."

Her back straightens in just a way I am all too familiar with. She readies herself for battle, even if it is the last thing she wishes for. There is nothing else to say. She does not collapse, she does not weep hysterically. She does not cling. The other Alice collects a traveling coat draped across the settee and swiftly exits the house, the Caterpillar and myself unbidden upon her heels. She does not look back, not even when furious crashes and howling sound within. She marches past the Diamonds' guards lining the path from the house to carriage, her head held high as they intone my crown's song.

I attempt to return to the house in effort to calm Jace's rage, but I possess no free will. I am tethered to this Alice. Within a split second, I am within the Diamonds' carriage, alongside my doppelgänger and the Caterpillar, watching as broken remains of a chair careen through a window.

The carriage lurches forward. "Do you have the second dose?" The other Alice is wooden as she addresses our Grand Advisor.

His hookah remains untouched. "It will not be pleasant."

The Flowers take over for the fading soldiers, taking up the Diamonds' song. The tulgey woods fill with the melody I once found so stirring but now painfully melancholy.

My doppelgänger maintains her focus upon the Caterpillar. Her eyes are glazed and red—but from more than crying, I suspect. "None of this is."

Of that she is correct.

"This will be the worst yet. Have you felt any effects so far?"

The twist of her lips is ugly. "The Queen's Council still stands, does it not? There are no charges of regicide, no matter how much I might have wished it differently." After a pause, she adds bitterly, "I somehow walked through the door, much like I just did."

He says nothing more, instead proffering a bottle filled with black liquid. She uncorks it and, without hesitation, throws her head back and drinks it in one gulp. New shudders wrack her limbs, ones not crafted from heartbreak. Her fingers dig into the blue velvet lining the seat we rest upon until tears spread beneath her nails.

Long minutes pass as she spasms, spittle frothing at the sides of her lips. The Caterpillar puffs away at his hookah, offering no assistance whilst his beady eyes never stray from her person. Finally, after blood joins spittle, the other Alice stills enough for small twitches to be spaced between seconds.

Upon reflection, she has gone through battle, and I vicariously. Can sleep or poisons truly bring about such fanciful delusions? And if so, how is it that it can strip my feelings until they are utterly raw? The pain consuming me is too deep. Too familiar.

I blink and am no longer in the carriage. Instead, surrounded by the Caterpillar and a small squadron of Spider soldiers, the other Alice and I face a rabbit hole.

I glance around, trying to pinpoint our location. We are outside . . . Nobbytown?

My Grand Advisor motions one of his feet-hands toward Ferz Marish, an enormous elderly Arachnid who serves on my council. "I would have your report."

"Guards are in place, sir." The Ferz straightens its body, graying, bristling hairs swaying gently in the wind. "I can assure you that there is nothing amiss. The area has been swept thrice. There are no civilians or enemies within the radius you outlined."

The Caterpillar grunts. "And the White Rabbit?"

"Effectively neutralized, sir. Spies are in place to ensure he remembers nothing of construction."

"The moment a singular word is spoken of it, he is to be dealt with." The slant of the Caterpillar's small mouth is grim. "Is that understood?"

"Yes, sir." The Ferz scuttles closer to the other Alice. "Your Majesty, you honor myself and my squadron by entrusting us with the hole's defense. We will not fail you."

A closer look at the rabbit hole reveals that it is swarming with Spiders.

The other Alice places her arm and fist across her chest. When the Spiders quietly sing the Diamonds' battle song, fresh tears fill both of our visions. My doppelgänger places a hand upon the equivalent of the Caterpillar's shoulder, which is a risky endeavor. I, myself, have often found the endearment too intimating to attempt. She says, voice rough yet still measured, "Ensure my people and lands safe."

He shrugs off her hand. She does not take offense. "Until my dying breath."

Her pupils nearly expand the entire width of her red-ringed irises as she strides unevenly toward the hole. Despite her obvious imbalance, her shoulders roll back. The Spiders at the mouth retreat as she climbs in. And then—

Then I blink, and the other Alice and I are in a padded room with no windows. She dons a jacket that restrains both arms and movement. Her hair is stringy, matted, even; her eyes are demented. Her bottom lip bleeds. Nearby, reddish-pink lines streak the dirty linen walls. My doppelgänger is shrieking and then sobbing and chortling all in the span of mere minutes.

She head-butts a cautious yet optimistic orderly in a white uniform who attempts to feed her soup. He is rendered unconscious, saved from her wrath only by a portly, soft-spoken gentleman bearing a syringe. As she staggers backward, the other Alice groans, "The toves gyre at midnight."

Our combined cries are mournful and fearsome all at once when her cheek slams against the padded floor.

I stare just as unabashedly as she does at the gentleman when he murmurs kindly, "It will be all right, Alice. Rest now. Someday, these will all be nothing but memories."

Memories.

I blink, and the padded cell disappears. I am in in a bizarre room with glass walls and a long table, shaking hands with a handsome gentleman who makes the damaged muscle in my chest find strength enough to sprint. A warm feeling, bright and strong and . . . *familiar*, seeps comfortably into my pores as the pair awkwardly talk with one another.

Who is this man? His clothes are foreign, his accent American.

I blink, and the glass room dissolves. The other Alice and the gentleman are next to one another on the floor of what appears to be a hallway. My doppelgänger wears an obscenely short dress, yet the gentleman does not seem to find it scandalous. He is kind to her, respectfully attentive.

My pulse beats faster.

Another blink of the eye, and we are sitting within a surreal, coffee-scented room filled with wondrous sights and peoples. The other Alice—no. *I* am drinking hot chocolate, appearing as if I belong in such a whimsical place. Once more, the gentleman is kind as we talk.

I sway closer to them, to him, a flower reaching for sunlight.

I blink, and the scene changes once more. We are at the seashore. I dip my bare toes into the gentle waves lapping the sand, reveling in how the briny breeze curls my hair. I am wearing another outrageously short dress that barely grazes my knees, gauzy and white and beautiful all the same. The sun slowly sinks into the ocean's embrace.

I am smiling, no longer an incoherent beast snarling in her cage and chains.

The handsome gentleman approaches the other me, shells and colored bits of smooth glass filling his gift to me. I take him in, this man, and Bread-and-butter-flies swarm beneath my ribcage just as surely as they do within the other Alice's.

A name surfaces, one instantly, infinitely precious and meaningful. *Finn.*

He has a name now. This man, this one I am certain has haunted my dreams.

"I like it here," my doppelgänger tells him.

Tells Finn.

A smile curves his full lips, one that weakens the structural integrity of my knees. He deposits the shells and colored glass into her—*my*—hands. "Are there beaches in Wonderland?"

The other me hesitates, as if such a question came at the end of a blade. "Not like this." A quiet piece of laughter wrenches away from her. "There is a legend in Wonderland that attributes one of the lakes near where I lived to my tears."

"You must have cried a hell of a lot to make a whole lake." It's said teasingly, though. "What's it called?"

"The Pool of Tears."

"Just not your tears?"

Her head tilts back as she inhales sharply. Pain slashes across her—*my*—face.

Hands stuffed into his pockets, his own toes dig into the sand as he gazes toward the horizon. Gorgeous shafts of orange and purple ripple across the vast cerulean.

She and I stare at the trinkets he gifted us. "I suppose the Twenty-First Century isn't so terrible."

He chuckles, and it's so lovely I wish to bottle the sound and uncork it during my darkest times. How I would delight in being drunk on this man.

They converse for long minutes, Finn and the other Alice, until the moon crawls into the sky and the air chills. And then we are in a fantastical moving vehicle, and I listen to them—*us*—discuss everything and nothing all at once. A tangible ease wraps around us, one I wish to knit into a blanket to circle my shoulders.

Sparks, undeniable and sharp as lightning against sand, sizzle between Finn and the other Alice. Between us.

In a blink of an eye, I am in a lush park, standing before a bronze statue of a young girl perched upon a mushroom. A rabbit in a waistcoat and a gentleman in a tall hat stand next to her. The other me is dressed in the most scandalous garb yet: skintight pants and a sleeveless top. Sweat unattractively drips from her brow as she glares stonily at the monument. Finn jogs up to where she—I—*we*—wait, his own breath uneven from exertion. He wears a damp, dark shirt and trousers cut off above the knees, and I am inexplicably attracted to the peculiar sight.

"Oh, shit." Self-loathing colors his hushed epitaph. "I totally forgot about this."

A child nearby shouts, "Mama! Tell me all about *Alice in Wonderland* again!"

Alice in Wonderland.

What had the other Alice said upon the beach? *The Twenty-First Century*.

The other me tears her attention from the bronze monstrosity, eyes impassive. "Is there one like this of you?"

"Yeah." He clears his throat. "Not here, though." One of his hands curls around our arm before he leads us away from excited children. At a discreet spot beneath shady trees utterly unlike any found within the tulgey woods, I cannot help but notice how my doppelgänger leans in toward him.

He is kind when he talks to us. He does not push. There are no expectations. Instead, there is an irrefutable connection between us, an undeniable chemistry I cannot deny. It is an attraction that rivals what is between the White King and myself. It wavers in the air between man and woman, shimmering and tangible. How is this possible?

I love the White King. I have loved Jace for years. Yet . . . I cannot deny what is before me, what coils low and hot as I observe these events and conversations.

Another blink brings about another location where the blaze between Finn and myself turns into wildfire. Each additional blink brings with it new scenes, new conversations. They bring about an Alice who gradually softens and succumbs to the gentleman at her side whilst accepting the foreign world around her. There are places and peoples populating these scenes who breed familiarity, ones who take root within my bones and the soft folds of my brain.

There is a sharp-tongued woman. A doctor. A distinguished gentleman with piercing blue eyes. A petite, sophisticated woman who deftly pricks my nerves.

I know them. I know the building in which they—we—live and work.

I know Finn. *I know him.*

These are no dreams, no illusions the Caterpillar created. These are my memories.

Another blink of the eye has me crammed in a cramped armoire. Racks of clothes poke at me as I watch Finn and I kiss. The sparks that fly between our bodies, our mouths, our souls, are brighter than all the stars in the sky.

I ache for this man. My body burns for him now.

Another blink has us in a bedroom. We are making love, and it is beautiful and erotic all at once. If I thought I ached in the armoire, now I willingly succumb to the intensity born in these moments.

I drift down the river of time, each second, each moment more precious than the next as I find my footing and purpose outside of

Wonderland. Just as importantly, I fall wonderfully, fully, magically in love with Finn.

I love him. I love this kind, intelligent man. He understands me. I understand him, too. He is my partner. He is more than that, though. He is my equal, and he does not even wear a crown.

Another blink. We are in Wonderland, alongside Jace. Jace . . . who somehow no longer weakens my knees or hatches Bread-and-butter-flies like Finn does. More blinks bring more scenes, more colors and memories, more emotions to fill in the gaps. I witness events astounding and terrifying, dangerous and significant all at once: Timelines, catalysts, and the Society. The Piper. The Queen of Hearts providing a villain a boojum in an effort to assassinate me from afar. Finn saving me, only to be stabbed shortly after. I rip apart the worlds until I find him, and then save him as he saved me.

He and I move heavens and earths to ensure one another's safety. This gentleman, this non-Wonderlander, is my true love. We are not bound by prophecies, but by choice. How could I have forgotten such a miracle, such a gift, for even a singular moment?

Another blink illuminates the danger we face in a mountain, of how desperately I cling to him but fail as a dissonant melody that lifts the hairs on my arms fills my ears. A murderous rage blossoms within my chest as I helplessly watch Finn and myself succumb. Children armed with weapons dance around our prone bodies, cheering and chanting as the other Alice's eyes drift close. Before they seal shut, a beautiful, cold woman approaches the Piper.

I have seen that face before. This is a woman of dark magic.

I blink and find myself in a room of pure white light. Before me is the Piper himself, holding a blank-faced bust with my mask on its face. Worse, the Diamonds' crown rests upon the bust's head. I instinctively reach for my vorpal blade, but there is nothing but the villain, the crown, the bust, and myself to be found.

My fists will have to serve as my weapons instead. I rush him, but as with the settee in my house at the beginning of this journey, the Piper blurs in a swirl of smoke.

"Why would you wish for all of this pain? This misery? You were exiled from your beloved homeland," he says, as if I did not just attempt to strangle the life out of his body. "Take my hand, Alice. Listen to my music, and I will make it all go away."

I lunge again, only to grab handfuls of nothing. He dares to trick me, to hypnotize me with his melodies and words? This is yet another of the Piper's insidious games, and I refuse to play. Instead, I will destroy him and his kin, and then salt the earth they inhabited afterward.

As if the Piper can hear my thoughts, pity fills his infuriatingly handsome face and eyes. "I will take your pain away. Your exile can lead to something better. Help usher in a new day. All you have to do is listen." He fondles the crown upon the bust. "Destroy this relic of the past and allow the rapture take you."

He lies. This villain lies. Even as he oozes sympathy, he lies.

A pedestal materializes, and the Piper carefully positions the bust upon its gleaming surface. "Do you choose happiness or pain? A new day or exile? Do you have the audacity to reach out and shape the world?"

I do, actually.

"You are nothing." His image wavers before me. "I will never allow myself to become corrupted by your foul music. You will never use me as a puppet for your malevolent deeds."

"You cannot fight me forever." His body is translucent, nothing but faded stained glass in an abandoned church. "The world is changing. You can live in the new order or die in the old."

My fist shatters the glass.

As blood drips down my arm, down upon colored shards, my vorpal blade appears propped against the pedestal. I wander closer to the bust, pressure building within my chest.

The mask no longer is blank. It is Finn's face—gray and lifeless, eyes hollow.

No.

I crumple the paper. This isn't Finn. This isn't his fate. I won't allow it.

I take my crown and place it on my head. I am the Queen of Diamonds. And I will never forget that again.

ALICE

I WAKE AT DAWN. JACE sleeps next to me, a heavy arm across my chest. The mask is nowhere to be found. Temptation beckons, as a beloved, warm body presses against mine, to close my eyes and revel in blissful oblivion.

I don't, though. I cannot. Instead, I quietly slip from beneath the covers to search for something sharp.

Sitting at my vanity, I scratch four letters onto my arms as I desperately cling to retreating visions. I chant the name in my mind. I fervently whisper the single syllable.

Jace appears in the mirror. I watch as he kisses my forehead, and savor the ones that linger against my neck's pulse. The scent of forest and man curls around me. Warmth from his hands seeps into my shoulders.

I tug my sleeve over my physical reminder.

"Today is the best of mornings." Another kiss finds its way to the corner of the mouth, and I shiver at the streak of bittersweet pleasure that infuses me. "For today, all of our dreams come true."

I hunger to hold him tight, to cry or rage at the unfairness of it all. Better yet, to confirm his assertions, to hold them just as dear as he. Instead, I kiss his hand curved around my shoulder, fumbling for meaning or reason.

Once my silence stretches too long, he claims my hairbrush from the vanity. "Did the poison work?"

I gaze at myself in the mirror as he drags the bristles through my hair. There is so much heartache written all over the face of the lady who stares back. Who is this person that sorrow has claimed on a day promised to joy?

My answer is soft. "Yes."

"The Caterpillar assured me it would," he says evenly, "but poisonings are tricky at best."

A shiver of pleasure takes hold as the brush slides through my hair and down my back. The cuts grow deeper. I ask, "What is reality?"

He's thoughtful. "I assume it is the same answer as the riddle the Hatter constantly taunts us with. The one about the raven and the writing desk."

I cannot help the smile that itches my lips. "Helpful."

"Honest."

Honest. The White King and I, we have only ever been as such to one another. Even now, as wounds reopen and weep, I battle to stay the course. "I must talk to you about last night."

A sharp knock rattles the door. "Your Majesty?" It is one of Jace's squires. "The Cheshire-Cat bade me to fetch you. The White Queen's standards have been spotted."

My soon-to-be counterpart groans. "Allow me a few minutes." He returns my brush to the vanity. "Why am I surprised she shows with so little time left before the ceremony?" I watch the reflection of Jace, rather than the man. It is easier this way. "I suppose it ought to be me who welcomes her. Or at least warn her that any public or private tantrums will be swiftly dealt with. Let us hope she has no dolls with her."

Snatches of a vision of the two of us in one another's arms while tears streak our cheeks knock the breath clean out of me.

"I swear to you, she is only here as a witness, nothing more." His kiss is tender, familiar. I refuse to watch it. "I will take my leave so you may finish getting ready." Another kiss lingers against the inside of a wrist. "I cannot wait until all our dreams come true today, my lady."

Dreams.

"Jace. Wait."

Another series of raps nearly knocks the door off its hinges. "Sire? The Cheshire-Cat is most insistent you come down immediately."

"We will talk more on the morrow. On this day, let us usher peace, joy, and love into Wonderland." He winks. "Despite the White Queen's insistences over how lovely we will look as dolls that will undoubtedly come from the front row."

Jace departs, either uncaring of my requests or oblivious. Was I a coward for not pushing the discussion? In his place, several ladies in waiting join me, ready to style my hair and help me into the most beautiful of wedding gowns.

I clamor for courage, for strength. I ask myself, over and over: *What is reality?* More importantly: *What does my heart say?*

As I am fussed over, my fingers brush across the red lines upon my arm. I continue to trace the word as my hair is carefully arranged. As my corset is laced and tightened. As my gown is smoothed. As comments are made about the strange markings on my back.

Reality is what I choose it to be. I know what I want, even if my heart breaks and bleeds and no one is able to see it happen.

The Flowers are signing, the trees swaying. Tiny, perfumed Dandelion wishes float upon soft breezes. Revelers form a semi-circle around Jace and me. It is beautiful, this wedding. I could not ask for a more lovely setting. We are in our garden, a beloved location. Everything has been perfect, down to the readings and songs. The White Queen has held her tongue. Jace is the epitome of a handsome king in his white suit. The way he looks at me, with such blatant adoration, has guests swooning. And yet, a question now hangs in the air between us, one I've fantasized answering in the affirmative for years.

"Do you take the White King of Wonderland for your husband?"

I cannot speak the words, though. I do not allow myself this daydream, even here, even now. Instead, I cut the thread between self and question. Between reality and dreams. My bouquet tumbles to the ground, petals spilling like the abandoned hopes and desires they are. Shock dims the garden's joy.

Nearby, the Caterpillar lounges on an ornately tufted pillow. The hookah slips from his lips, and for the first time in a long time, all that pours from his nostrils and mouth is simply smoke. No sly pictures, no meaningful depictions. His beady eyes are fastened on me, though, as if he knew this would happen all along.

When Jace utters my name, bewilderment coloring those pale eyes of his, there are a hundred questions stashed within two syllables. I fear I might collapse in on myself, the pain is so visceral.

Not once, not twice, but now three times I must lose this man.

I gaze down upon my arm, at the letters I'd scratched upon my skin: *F-i-n-n*. Four letters that, even now as they solidify and ring within head and heart, accelerate the very beat of my heart.

Slivers of golden-brown hair and blue-gray eyes haunt me. He is here, this man from my dreams, hovering on the edge of my consciousness. I refuse to lose him again. I concentrate harder, sharpening the edges of Finn's face. The feelings infusing every pore, every nerve in my body, are real. They must be. I cannot accept the depths of my emotions for him are figments of an overactive imagination.

What I saw last night were memories. The truth.

I love him.

The blueish veins lining my hands sparkle and glow beneath pale skin. I shove the beautiful lace sleeve of my wedding gown up and flip my arm over. There, from wrist to elbow, I marvel at the same phenomena, sure that the same decorates my lower back.

His love is so visceral, it marks my skin.

Behind me, the subject of years of dreams, hopes, and immense, intense love whispers my name again. When I suffocate in agony, it is all too familiar.

Highs and lows, so closely woven together.

I close my eyes and inhale deeply to steady myself. I must trust my instincts. They have yet to fail me. Slowly, carefully, deliberately, and yet loudly all at once, I give life to the contents of my heart and mind.

I say, "This is not real. None of this is real."

When I open my eyes, the wedding guests have vanished. So have the Reverend and the Cheshire-Cat. All that remain are the Caterpillar, still puffing away on his hookah, and Jace.

"None of this is real," I say once more. "I am not really in Wonderland. *This* is the dream, and it is far past time for me to wake up."

A tidal wave sucks me under, drowning me in what was previously hidden: the prophecy; the Pleasance Asylum; Van Brunt; the Institute; catalysts; Timelines; the Piper. Most importantly, my choices—and Finn.

I remember. I remember them all.

The Caterpillar abandons his pipe. "I wondered how long it would take for you to come to."

And yet, here I am still, at my home in the tulgey woods. I wear a wedding dress. The White King of Wonderland stands beside me. My Grand Advisor speaks to me.

Grief, strong and swift and cutting, tears another piece from me. The Caterpillar is deceased. The Queen of Hearts struck his head from his body. His beautiful, iridescent skin was callously fashioned into a clutch for her amusement.

"How can this be?" I gesture around us. "I've felt things. I cut myself. I bled. I hurt. I—" I turn to Jace. His pale eyes watch me carefully. "I've loved."

I love.

A bittersweet smile curves his beautiful lips, yet he says nothing. Nor does the Caterpillar.

I fumble with pieces of my puzzle. "Is this dream courtesy of the twelfth Wise Woman's gifts? Whatever she did to me must have countered any curses the thirteenth Wise Woman laid upon me alongside the Piper's music."

The music. "He has attempted to wake me with his infernal melodies, hasn't he? I have not given in, though. I withdrew into my dreams to. . ." It is all so clear now. "To protect myself." More softly yet resolutely, "Somewhere safe. Somewhere they couldn't break my spirit. Somewhere I allowed myself to believe was real because reality was too much to bear."

"You could stay." Jace clasps my hands. His are beloved and familiar, and it hurts all the more. "You *are* safe here. You are not at risk of rapture while you stay, no matter how hard they continue to coax you. Your mind is untouchable."

My mind, yes. What of my body? What about Finn?

"All your dreams of years past are coming true." His thumbs stroke mine. It feels so real. "Our marriage. Our Courts uniting. Wonderland at peace. It is yours for the taking. If you want, you will forget any other reality. This will be all that there is."

For so many years, this is exactly what I wished and planned for. But dreams and hopes and roads and stories and seasons change, as they are oft to do, whether we wish for it or not.

My road diverged from Wonderland. From the White King. From formerly precious dreams. I hold tight to new dreams, new goals, and purposes. My heart willingly belongs to another.

It is past time to once more let go of Wonderland.

"You are not really the White King." I release his hands. "The Jace I know and cherish would never ask me to back down from a fight. I cannot subsist in a dream world, no matter how alluring it may be, not when there are those in the real world who need me."

The Jace before me fades to translucent. Once more, I ask myself how it is that, after everything he and I have been through, after everything we've meant to one another, we arrive at a place where we are only what might have been, rather than what should be. Only, as these words fill my soul, I no longer mourn quite so deeply.

True love encourages you to live.

I do not doubt or resent my choice. Given it a thousand times, I will always make the same. "I thank you for the safety given these last few days."

His arm crosses his chest in farewell. Soon, the White King of Wonderland no longer stands beside me.

The Caterpillar remains, though.

"Do you know what has happened to me?"

Two of his leather-clad feet absently rub together. "I know no more than you."

"You are my conscience, just as you were in life." My lips lift in the barest of ways. "Or my subconscious."

"I am always with you. It is what those who touch lives do, Alice. Hearts are not solid, not really. They are mosaics, cobbled together from pieces we take from life and others. Sometimes, certain pieces fall away. Sometimes, we fill them in with new bits of emotions and life. Sometimes, what is there remains, even if the people we took them from are no longer with us. You see, some pieces are more stead-fast than others. Those are the ones that will remain the longest. I am in your heart. You were in mine."

"You say that because it is what I wish to be true."

"I say it because you know it to be true."

"You wanted me to see the truth—"

He holds up a singular hand. "*You* wanted the truth. Your stubbornness forced the memories."

I mull this over. "The Piper was in my visions. Only, when he spoke to me, it was not a memory. Perhaps he was with my body in the real world."

The Caterpillar blows a question mark.

"He had my crown." I reach up, but the heavy gold and diamonds symbol is not upon my head. Instead, flowers weave throughout my hair. The last I'd seen of the Diamonds' crown was in my flat back at the Institute in New York City. The Librarian placed it in a protective case within my rooms so I could hold on to a piece of Wonderland. "He encouraged me to destroy it."

The Caterpillar blows a replica of my crown. As I wave away the smoke, I muse, "The Piper wants for me to destroy Wonderland's catalyst."

My Grand Advisor's long body shifts upon his pillow. "If he even has the crown at all."

If he was even with me at all.

"Anything is possible." The Caterpillar fiddles his pipe. "You won't know until you wake up."

"When Finn was attacked, my love protected him. It kept him in a stasis of sorts, where any transformations were delayed."

A thin stream of smoke pours from his lips, shifting into the pattern that I know to wrap around Finn's torso.

"Over the last few days, a pattern grew upon my back, one I originally attributed to a bruise. And now there is this." I peel back my lace sleeve once more to reveal glowing, sparkling lines beneath my skin. "His blood is in mine."

The Caterpillar's smoke morphs into stars.

I remember a conversation between the twelfth Wise Woman and myself. *As long as you live, as long as your love holds true, he is safe.*

Alarm bells sound. I am alive, yes, but for days I forgot Finn, believing the man haunting the outskirts of my dreams to be nothing more than a dream himself. The Wise Woman's spell protected me, yes, but at what cost?

"I must awaken. I must find Finn."

"What are you waiting for?"

My mind whirls. "I wonder if there is a rabbit hole out . . . Maybe a looking glass?" I search for the house, but it, too, has vanished. Nothing remains except for the Caterpillar and myself.

However will I escape such a dreamland? I must find Finn. Victor. Mary. Jack. The Piper must be dealt with. Too much is at stake.

Panic seizes hold until the Caterpillar says calmly, "Alice, haven't you long realized the impossible is possible?"

I believe in the impossible.

I rip the circlet of white flowers from my head. As it drops, bits disintegrate and float away like ash in a storm until nothing remains. None of this is real, but Finn is. So are our feelings for one another. The Piper is, too, as are his terrible crimes against Timelines.

I can no longer stomach this dream world. My soul aches for reality, even when it is beautiful and ugly all at once.

I straighten my shoulders, resolute. The Caterpillar before me wavers, a mirage in a desert, fading upon approach. My own skin does, too, all except the sparkling blue running through my veins. "Will I see you again?"

"In dreams, perhaps. In memories." He rises, crawling over to where I stand. The tufted cushion he sat upon disappears. One gloved hand gently presses against my heart. "In here. Always in here. Now awaken, Your Majesty. You have much work to do."

And because I believe in the impossible, I do exactly that.

REALITY

ALICE

I AM IN A DANK stone cell, lying upon a pile of filthy, moldy straw. My hair is matted, my dress is stained, and my skin is no better off. Crust outlines my eyes; corset boning replaces bones and muscles. There is no furniture within my blurred field of vision, no windows, no conveniences other than a bucket. Before me is wall of rusty bars. Beyond that is a large, heavyset man.

Shrieks of agony pierce the stale air.

The jingle of keys catches my attention. I still, closing my eyes. A child's voice, honeyed and lilting, inquires in German, "Is there any change?"

"Last I checked, no," a man answers, most likely the one I saw. "I checked vitals a few hours ago."

"Heartbeat?"

"Still slow yet regular."

"Brain activity?" Frustration sours her youthful sweetness.

"Still comparable to REM sleep."

"What about eye color?"

"Same as before."

A string of curses no child ought to utter burst like gunfire. "If this keeps up, heads will roll."

"They already are." Something heavy clatters upon wood. "What with the chaos over the codex missing, and the convergence near upon us—"

Another distant scream punctuates his explanation. *What codex is missing?*

"If you value *your* head, you will shut your mouth. If the Lady were to overhear you. . ." Fear tightens the girl's warning, but I suspect it has nothing to do with the cries.

In my mind, images of a large, leather-bound book resting upon a golden stand stationed between two thrones surface, ones that remind me of an order issued by Finn to Jack and Mary: *"Get that book."*

When the man clears his throat, the sound is wet and thick. "Any word from the Lord?"

"None. He vowed to not return without success."

A pause. "How does the other fare?"

The other? Does he refer to Finn?

The girl says, "There have continued to be setbacks."

"What kind of setbacks? The last I saw, he was in rapture."

No. My love protects him. Finn is too strong to allow this to happen.

"There are minutes where we are certain rapture has begun. But then his eyes will clear. It never lasts." Something clanks against the metal bars before the girl continues. "The last time he resisted, blood from three of our brethren was spilled."

Fierce pride suffuses my achy limbs. Finn is still fighting. He has not fully transformed. *Hold on, my love. I'm coming.*

"He should die for such insolence!" Another wet cough rattles from the man. "I cannot understand why the Lord and Lady desire these infidels. I could do pretty things with their guts."

"You dare to question the Lord and Lady?" A stinging slap rings. "It is not for you to understand, you imbecile. If it was, you would be the Lord, instead of a pig who tends the unworthy."

The man grunts like the pig he'd just been called. "My apologies." More contritely, "As the other is not down here, I assume he is being dealt with?"

"The latest punishment will be swift and vicious." Sadistic pleasure coats her promise. "He will undergo a much more intensive immersion round. I'm to join shortly. He will either embrace rapture or die trying."

Pride transitions to horror.

"In the Lord's absence," the man asks, "has the Lady made comment?"

"She has yet to emerge from her chambers, and there are precious few willing to disrupt her."

The man grunts his piggy grunt.

"If I were you, I would focus on ensuring this one wakens soon, and in rapture. The Lord was quite specific that she was to be in attendance at the convergence."

"Of course."

The light patter of boots upon stone fade until I am certain of the girl's departure. A clang and scrape of metal against metal precedes a deep groan of rusty joints. Wheels rattle against stone as the stench of uncleanliness fills my nostrils.

My muscles are tight and sore, but I brace myself anyway.

"The sooner you transform, the better," the man mutters. Coarse cloth brushes against my arm. "You have work to do."

I scissor kick the man, knocking him off balance. A cart filled with medical supplies clatters to its side, its contents spilling across the floor. His body thuds onto the moss-covered stones next to the straw pile, and I quickly roll over until I am atop him. I twist until one of his arms is pinned beneath him; the other is trapped as I use my body weight to control his pathetic attempts to shake me. This jailer is older than he sounds, the oldest of the Piper's minions I've seen yet. Wispy white hair tufts in uneven, thin patches across a freckled scalp. An entire map's worth of latitude and longitude designations crease his craggy face.

Just as prior battles with child soldiers did little to faze me, neither will one with the elderly.

I shove an elbow against his throat. "I must respectfully disagree, as there will be no transformations today or any other day."

He continues to struggle beneath me, a bloated slug desperate to wiggle back into a dank hole. Bony fingers fumble for contact with a nearby medical instrument. Such pitiable efforts are not worth even rolling my eyes over.

"How long have I been asleep?"

A head butt is attempted, but it is clumsy at best. He is no match for youth, let alone me.

The wicked grin shaping my lips only grows more pronounced. "Cat got your tongue? Shall I break bones, one at a time, until it loosens?"

Anxiety widens his irises, but he clings to silence.

Very well, then. I twist my legs to pin him more securely and then, with one fist, land a solid punch against an eye socket. His cry of pain rivals those peppering the dungeons. I do not worry over his comrades rushing to his aid, though. To these murderous fiends, what is one more wail within these walls?

"Are you one of the Piper's original children? Did he allow you to age? Or perhaps force? I image that, at seven-hundred-plus years, your bones resemble a bird's." The blooming contusion on his face grows before my very eyes. I prod it a few times, eliciting another cry. "Ah, it does feel broken. Now, then. How many days have I been asleep?"

He gasps. "Three!"

Unacceptable. "Outside of myself and the one with me, were there any other captures?"

It is then he realizes I'd been listening in on his conversation for some time. My jailor has the audacity to be aggravated by my eavesdropping.

"How loyal of you, holding on to your silence. What did the

fiendish little girl say? Perhaps you require '*a much more intensive round.*'"

I lift a fist.

"Wait!" Spittle clings to the wiry whiskers circling his pale lips. "There were none others captured!"

Grymsdyke escaped, as did Mary and the A.D.—with the book, from the sound of it. I do not allow myself any relief, though. Not with Finn still at risk. "What is the convergence?"

His mouth clamps shut, even as tears trace paths down the grooved lines of his ancient face.

"Naughty, naughty cat," I murmur, "holding on to your tongue so tightly." My fist meets bones until a satisfying crunch sounds.

His lips move. Jumbled whispers emerge.

My bloody fist lifts. He mumbles, "Meeting . . . of . . . Chosen."

I lean in. "I already figured that part out for myself. What makes the convergence so special? Why is the codex required for such a meeting?"

The man beneath me openly weeps as he shakes his head in defiance. "They . . . will . . . kill . . . me."

"What is worse, I wonder?" I muse viciously. "Die at their hands, or mine?"

Pupils black, not from rapture, but terror, tell me that any death I offer is the preferable of the two.

A large Spider lands upon my shoulder, thin, silken threads flying behind him. He scuttles down my arm until he's mere inches from the man's face. One hairy leg, wrapped tightly with silk, protrudes from his body at an awkward angle.

The sight of such an injury increases my fury tenfold.

"You!" the man burbles, staring up at my Wonderlandian assassin.

"Me," the Arachnid hisses in return. "Allow me to take care of this brute, Your Majesty. Although, considering the sins he has committed, death may be too generous a gift."

"Might you perhaps wish to elucidate upon the convergence?" I inquire.

All of my jailer's anger toward Grymsdyke weakens into tears and rattling breaths. "I don't know. Even if I did, I wouldn't tell you."

So be it.

The Spider's fangs sink into the man's broken cheek. I roll away. His distorted body flops about on the stone and moldy hay like a fish whose water has been stolen, his skin gradually darkening to purple. I watch in apathy as pustules bubble and erupt.

Soon, screams morph into gurgles, and then fade away entirely until glassy, unmoving eyes gape at the ceiling. I rise to my feet, my legs tight and my back even more so.

"I would have your report," I tell my assassin. "Beginning with the moment I lost consciousness. Let us be quick, as we have Finn to locate and quarry to hunt."

The Spider bows before me. "I barely managed to escape after you and Prince Finn collapsed. The Piper called for my immediate execution, and I have spent the last several days evading the mountain's residents."

Prince. Finn is more than my lover, more than my partner. He is also, by my own decree and that of the White Court, the Diamonds' Prince of Adámas. My love for him is so strong I fashioned a way to tie him to my exiled home.

I shove a sleeve up; the bright lines from my dream no longer paint my arms. I have no doubt, though, that if I were to look at my back, I would find the proof of our love darkening my skin. Just as mine stains his.

I must find him.

Grymsdyke continues, "I overheard more than they would undoubtedly prefer. While this tomb of a residence is well fortified with both futuristic and magical wards, there are still those places one such as me may find shelter. I am a Spider, after all." A barking cough rattles the hairs of his body. "It was imperative to the Piper, prior to his hasty departure, that you and Prince Finn be separated until you both became Chosen. I made the decision to follow you, at a discreet distance, of course. When it became clear that none could rouse you, not even with their dissonant instruments, I hunted for Prince Finn. It took me most of the night before I determined his location."

Time abandons me. "What did you witness?"

"He was awake, Your Majesty." The Spider's voice is gruffer than normal. "And his eyes reminiscent of when you brought him back to the Institute—black as the Clubs' banner."

My assassin might as well have crawled down the length of my spine, my shiver is so strong.

"He was most unlike himself when his eyes were like that," the Arachnid continues. "The fight had left him. It was most disconcerting. I wondered more than once if it would be a kindness to use my fangs to release him from such a fate."

Culpability tears at my insides.

"I was quickly spotted. Although I took care of several of the childlings, I was forced to retreat. I have been unable to gain further access to his location."

"You did what you must." A hint of a tremor strains my voice. "We will find him together."

The Spider dips into a bow of sorts.

"You spoke of the Piper's departure?"

"He hunts for a codex."

"Did Mary and Jack escape?"

"If they were apprehended, word of the deed has yet to reach me."

At least there is a bit of confirmed good news.

"And Victor?" The last I saw Finn's brother, he was beaten senseless by a creature and dragged into a room safeguarded by a disappearing door.

"Alas, I was unable to determine the Doctor's location, Your Majesty."

Finn will never depart this mountain without his brother, of this I am sure.

"What do you know of the thirteenth Wise Woman?"

Another cough wobbles his body. "You must always be on your guard around her, Your Majesty. She is not right in the mind."

If my most feared assassin fears the lady in question, she must be formidable, indeed.

"I beg forgiveness that the information I am to present you is incomplete." Grymsdyke bows the best he can, considering his leg, and I wave off the gesture, assuring him it is unnecessary. "Once Prince Finn and Your Majesty were apprehended, word quickly spread that a codex was missing. This sent both the Piper and the Wise Woman into rages. The Piper gathered a group and departed to track the stolen item." He rubs a leg against his injured one. "The Wise Woman left a trail of victims in her wake. She is in her room, conjuring, while orders are sent through lieutenants."

I creep to the edge of the cell and peep past the bars. No one in sight. "Are we to assume the codex to be the book Finn asked Jack and Mary to take back to the Institute?"

"I believe so, Your Majesty. No book rests between the thrones any longer."

Which means the Institute is now under threat.

I glance around the cell. "Weapons?"

"There is an armory one floor up, toward the southern end of the structure. It is constantly guarded."

"What about security monitors?" When he offers a Spider's equivalent of a blank look, I clarify, "Moving pictures that are recorded by machines hung in corners. The Institute utilizes them."

"If they are present, I have yet to see them, Your Majesty."

I rifle through my former jailer's pockets for anything of use. I am rewarded with a small blade and a set of keys. Something akin to a cell phone is also discovered, although I am unsure of how such a device would work in a land such as this.

I do not risk it possessing tracking devices similar to those my own possess. Best to smash the device with the heel of my boot.

"Very well. We must push forth and pray that we do not come up against such preventatives."

Grymsdyke settles upon my shoulder. "Where you go, I shall follow."

"Let us show these fiends what it means to come up against Wonderlanders."

I do believe that if spiders could grin, Grymsdyke's would be most fierce, indeed.

N⁰ MERCY

ALICE

THE WIND IS STRUCK clean from my lungs when my back slams into the wall. No reprieve is given, as the child who barreled out of one of the cells charges me once more, his teeth blackened and body blanketed by the stench of death and rot. I duck just in time, rolling to reclaim a blade lost far too easily.

Days of sleep do not do a lady any favors in battle.

A guttural growl tears from the child a split second before ragged nails shred the back of my dress. Son of a Jabberwocky! He's carved uneven lines into my flesh. Swallowing the unexpected sting, I give no outward satisfaction. Instead, my arm swings, my blade digging into a soft belly. Growling transitions to pained grunting and then to soft cries. I scramble to my knees, and when I face my attacker, purpling skin greets me.

The child writhes on the ground as blisters form. His lips form an "O" in a silent scream before all light fades from his eyes. "I have scouted ahead," Grymsdyke announces from his perch on the child's neck.

Standing is more painful than I would prefer to admit. Breathing, as well. Staring down at my attacker, I harbor no pity. He may resemble a child, but chances are, as one of the Piper's minions, he had lived through seven centuries, making him far older than myself. "Any other surprises ahead?"

Grymsdyke eases off the still-twitching corpse. "I ceased the suffering of one prisoner with a perchance toward shrieking. She was clearly insane from torture. Her eyes were black, her skin riddled with poxes and open sores. My apologies for failing to identify this particular threat beforehand."

"Apology unnecessary. There are two of us and hundreds within the mountain. It will be impossible for us to ascertain the locations of all beforehand." Careful exploration informs me that my dress is torn scandalously low and my wounds deeper than I'd initially estimated.

Frabjous.

I am disheartened to discover only a teeny gun upon the child's body. Finn is the sharpshooter, not I. My talents lie with blades, not bullets.

"The childling is stupid for not using the gun against you," Grymsdyke remarks.

The little fiend had emerged from a foul-smelling room, wielding a bloody scalpel. I shudder to think what we might find once we peek into the chamber.

I spin the gun's barrel open and look within to find a sufficient reason for its lack of use. "No bullets." I return the weapon to his body. "What I would do for a decent blade."

Inside the nearby cell is a young man, his body riddled with missing strips of skin. His stomach is torn open, his intestines strung into a filthy bucket below. He is strapped upon a scarred, bloody table. I wander closer, only to find his eyes, swarming with fear, trained on me.

German is not my best language, but I give it a go anyways. "Have no fear." I stroke the youth's sweaty, matted hair. "We are not here to harm you."

And yet, he whispers, he chokes in English, "Kill me." Blood bubbles from his lips. "I refuse to—to be one—" Pain leaks from his eyes.

My heart hardens as I take inventory of his wounds. What is the purpose here? Why such malicious torture? Is this what the Piper does to those he cannot control?

From the nearby wall, Grymsdyke murmurs, "Time left the lad behind long ago, Your Majesty."

My fingers sweep across the youth's stained cheeks. "Sleep, then. Know no more pain." Grasping his head, I quickly snap it.

Although unnecessary, I unbuckle the straps. I wish there was time to properly take care of his body. To sing a farewell song, to find flowers and soft earth to welcome him to sleep. Shaken, I rub my forehead. What if this is what was done to Finn?

"We are clear to move on," Grymsdyke says.

I nod, and we leave the youth behind. My assassin is meticulous when it comes to scouting ahead, ensuring no further surprises. But our journey is akin to crawling when all I wish to do is storm.

Forever and a day passes before we make our way to the end. I dispatch a child guard with little difficulty, as this one reeks of strong ale. He, however, possesses a switchblade, and I am delighted to relieve his corpse of the burden.

And then Grymsdyke and I begin anew across another floor.

Her braids are brown and smooth, as if she spends much time lovingly tending them. The ribbons binding the ends are velvet—rich, midnight blue to match her extravagant gown of lace and velvet. She is pretty, this girl no older in appearance than ten or twelve.

And she is the fiend from the dungeon, the one who gleefully spoke of Finn's punishments.

She is currently in a heated discussion with an older youth with a chin covered with downy scuff. Between them is a much older man, bruised and nude and on his knees. A satiny pillow bearing a sleek whip rests upon his back. From my position just around the bend of a corner, I watch them warily. Intently.

When the girl departs, she snatches the whip from the cushion and storms away, spewing in her wake words no child ought to know.

The youth vents his frustration on the man, who squeals and collapses against the slick floor's tiles. Grymsdyke does not wait for me to rectify the situation. Silken threads fly past my face as he swoops forward, a blur of brown and blue bristles. I wait until fangs meet flesh before addressing the injured man.

His eyes are brown and filled with all that is wrong in a society that abuses people in just such a way. I hold a finger before my lips, asking for his silence. And then I throw my body upon the youth's purpling one, clamping a hand over his mouth just as his maw opens to scream.

As his life drains from his bite and the fight evaporates, I drag his corpse into a nearby room. I am pleasantly surprised at how it just so happens to be meant for storage. I shove the body behind trunks and barrels and make my way back out to where Grymsdyke and the naked man are waiting.

I crouch down, my hands raised in goodwill. I ask in broken German, "Are you all right?"

Defeated eyes widen. "My—my lady?"

He thinks me one of them. "What is your name?"

I wonder if anyone has ever asked him this question, he is so taken aback. "Har-Harry, my lady."

"We have little time to chat, Harry. We must find our friends, but I wish to assure your safety first. Is there anything we might do for you?"

Wariness keeps his muscles taut alongside fragile emotions ready to form hairline cracks. "You are . . . one of the prisoners." His attention flicks toward Grymsdyke. "And you are the spider they hunt."

They. Not I, not we. There is no disgust. No hostility. No call to arms. His eyes are clear. A bit dull, but not black.

Perhaps there are still those within the mountain, outside of the dungeons, who do not fanatically follow the Piper.

I throw my dice and pray my odds are good. "We are, yes. Do you perhaps know where our friends are? There was a man with me when I was taken. He has golden-brown hair. There is another man with much darker hair, who fought with a creature who appeared to be stitched together."

Harry's gaze darts around before mopping his blood and the youth's pus up off of the floor with the satiny pillow. When voices surface at the end of the hallway, he ushers us to the room next to the storage closet. The walls are rock, the floor is dirt.

It is a true piece of the mountain.

I glance around the area. There is little but wooden barrels stacked upon one another. Harry shivers in the cool air, his bare, sagging skin riddled with scars and pockmarks. I wish I had clothes to offer him. "I have not seen the dark-haired man you speak of," he whispers, "but if he is with whom I believe you speak of, I urge you to not seek him out. He will be forbidden, protected. The other one, yes. I know of his fate. He is not too far—Frau Magrek is on her way to where he is now."

Beneath my skin, my blood boils like oil readied to pour over walls during a siege.

"My lady. . ." He trembles, his attention shifting to the assassin perched upon my shoulder. "Even if you were to liberate your friend, they will never allow you to leave. No one leaves this mountain, not even in death."

Grymsdyke hops off my shoulder, onto a nearby barrel. Harry steps back, wringing his hands.

"Do not worry for our safety," I gently assure him. "And do not worry about my Arachnid associate. As long as you mean us no harm, we offer the same in return. What can you tell us of the room our friend is in and those within it?"

Hesitation stretches between us, sticky with long held fear. But Harry tells us what we wish to know.

Grymsdyke lifts a leg out of a crack running through one of the barrels. "This powder is meant for warfare, Your Majesty."

I pry one of the lids off. Glittering black powder fills the barrel. *Gunpowder.* This container's contents alone could wreak devastating havoc upon a battlefield, destroying hundreds of lives.

"Did you know this?" I ask Harry.

"No, my lady." The stringy muscles tying his bones together tense. "The debased are not allowed to touch what is not ours without permission." His gaze flickers toward the door. "The consequences for disobedience are never slight."

"Who are the debased?"

When his chin lowers, the fight leaves him. "Those who are unworthy to be Chosen."

"Do you wish you had been so?" I ask. "Chosen?"

Now his chin lifts. "I would rather die as myself than anyone else."

I turn this over as I scope the contents of the room. By my estimation, there are nearly two-dozen casks.

"Check what barrels you can," I tell Grymsdyke. "Discover if they all hold the same contents." As my assassin does as requested, I ask Harry, "How many so-called debased are within Koppenberg Mountain?"

He knows what I ask. *How many are held against their will?*

"I do not know the exact number, my lady."

"Are the so-called debased constantly monitored?"

"We are constantly in service, my lady. But there are times during which we must leave our assigned masters in order to fulfill their wishes."

Questions pile up faster than answers. "Do you serve more than one master?"

"While our lives are given to a singular master, we are never allowed to disobey any of the Chosen."

He is more than a mere capture. Harry is a slave. The contents of my stomach roil unsteadily. In Wonderland, slavery is outlawed and considered barbaric. "Are all of the Chosen gifted one who is supposedly debased?"

My stark disdain is all too evident. Although the Caterpillar taught me to hide my emotions well, I do not think that even he could contain his horror over such a situation.

"No, my lady. Only those who are in the Lord and Lady of the Mountain's inner circle."

Grymsdyke calls out from the other side of the room, "The malodorous powder fills many barrels."

A plan curls into existence. According to the conversation I overheard in the dungeon, the Piper may not be present within the mountain . . . but the thirteenth Wise Woman is. And so are a vast number of the Chosen, all to come together for the convergence. I may not know what the convergence is, but I cannot assume it innocent.

The Piper is no longer within my immediate reach, but there are many others just as capable of destruction who must be dealt with.

I turn to the bowed man unfairly labeled as *debased*. He is still strong. He still strives to be himself, which is all any can ever do in the face of such adversity.

"Do you know the time?"

"The morn is still upon us, my lady."

I offer a slight incline of my head as I process that. "You say that you wish to die as yourself, Harry. But I ask for you to consider to fight to *live*. Dying is unfortunately too easy. Let us, instead, fight for your freedom, for the opportunity where life may be lived as you desire. You are not debased. You are a man, a soul who deserves respect and dignity."

He chews upon a flaky, blood-crusted lip as my face, my seriousness, is all thoroughly, slowly examined.

"The Chosen within this mountain have done more than enslave people," I tell him. "They have eradicated the existences of trillions of souls over the last year. Blood stains all of their hands." My step forward produces a small flinch, a furrowed brow, but he does not withdraw. "I cannot allow this to continue. I must do everything I can within my power to cease these unforgivable acts. I would ask for your help."

He says nothing, but he still does not withdraw. The plan within me finds sunshine and spouts through the soil taller and stouter.

"You have no allegiance to me, no reason to believe or aid me if you do not wish. But if you are the man I think you are, the man you cling to in the face of such depravity and despair, I ask that you gather as many of the non-Chosen as you can." I glance about the room, relieved when I find what I am looking for. A kind fate, perhaps, has not abandoned me yet. There are strands of rotting rope on the dirt-packed ground several feet away.

"Fill pouches with powder within these barrels—as much as you can without being caught—and take them to important rooms within Koppenberg Mountain. Strategically place them where they will not immediately be seen, and lay lengths of rope in the powder so that they stretch a good distance, hidden. An hour before dawn, you and your brethren must light the ends furthest from the pouches and then hurry back to this room. Start on the furthest floor and work your way here. I will find us a way out by then. You will not die in this place, Harry. Not if there is still breath within my body."

His eyes settle upon the still open barrel. "What does the powder do, my lady?"

When I tell him, the first smile I have witnessed upon his face surfaces.

"You do not ask for my allegiance, my lady, but," his knees creak as he lowers to the floor, "I offer it anyway."

When I touch him, another flinch rolls across his loose skin. I take no offense, though. Not when the scars and scabs across his flesh inform me he has good reason to shy from contact. "There is no need to kneel before me. All I ask is that you hold firm to yourself this day and night. And know that there are those who now stand beside you."

He rises, and the dullness that once glazed over his eyes has been buffed away. "My lady, if you truly seek the man I think you do, you must hurry. Frau Magrek is not kind to those who fail to bend to her will."

"I thank you for your assistance." I incline my head. "You will leave Koppenberg, Harry. And when you do, it will be as yourself."

It takes several minutes for Harry to pull himself together. He rubs at his face so that any trace of tears disappear. All of the youth's blood is scrubbed away. A breakdown of what we might expect from Frau Magrek and her compatriots is delivered. When the man departs, Grymsdyke comments, "Pain governs many a soul."

"So does hope."

"If he turns, I will bite him."

"I would expect nothing less," I tell my assassin.

Between the two of us, we have fangs and a switchblade. Inside the room Harry believes holds Finn, there ought to be at least three Chosen: a master torturer, an apprentice piper, and Frau Magrek, who is well known for her love of pain. Considering her whip, I do not doubt the rumor.

I tear small strips of my dress off and pass them to Grymsdyke. He quickly wads the cloth, spinning silk around them until they are sticky balls. He grumbles as he toils, "I am the assassin, Your Majesty. Allow me to assassinate these fiends for you."

I do not bother responding such a ridiculous statement. He knows better than to urge me to stay behind. "Attend the musician first. I cannot risk the music affecting me again."

I accept his offering of the silken balls. He grunts, adjusting the threads around one of his legs.

I stuff one pair of my makeshift earplugs into my ears, shaping the pieces until they contort to my canals and I lose all sense of proper sound. I place the extra pair in a pocket.

"It is a good day to fight," my assassin declares.

The door we seek is unlocked. A menagerie of instruments crafted for pain and death, illuminated by torches, line the walls of a filthy room.

Excellent. I stuff the switchblade into the bodice of my dress and quietly select a pair of curved, serrated daggers, all the while eyeing the hallway on the far side of the room. Dim light spills from an open doorway at the end; a man garbed in all black lands on his arse, forcing Grymsdyke and I to press up against the weapon covered walls.

Dare I hope?

Once the man in black is on his feet, I waste no time making my way down the corridor. A peek into the new room presents an ugly picture. Bile and blood splatter the walls, floor, and tables; the stench from such gore is incalculably worse than anything in the dungeon. There *is* a fight in progress, although now dwindling, and my pulse leaps as I take it in.

An apprentice piper hovering in a far corner continues to play, face red and sweaty, as Frau Magrek and the hooded, black-garbed man wrangle with the man I am in love with. They have him backed up against a maroon-crusted rack, a blade pressed against his neck. The Frau struggles to clamp restraints around Finn's left wrist as he lands solid kicks on both assailants.

The pair are wounded. A scalpel is gripped in one of his hands, its blade slick with fresh rebellion.

The hooded man's blade draws blood as he smashes a fist against Finn's face. The scalpel clatters to the floor. My love sags, allowing the torturer to resume his attempts at restraint. It's then that I am given a good look at my partner. Finn's torso is bleeding in multiple places. Like the youth in the dungeons, skin has been stripped away. His face is battered.

Fury, white hot and unquenchable, demands vengeance.

Grymsdyke leaps, fangs bared. I fly, madness wrapping around me like the old friend it is. Within, blood blue and glowing surges anew. The Frau's shriek of anger is muffled, just as the piper's melodies nothing but the buzz of bees on a lazy spring day. A whip is claimed, and the sleek leather flashes before me. Madness ensures I do not care. I duck, hitting the floor stained with misery and torture, and roll, kicking out at her pretty, stained dress.

She collapses at the same time the apprentice piper does.

The tiny Frau struggles beneath me, stronger than any child ought to be, all sinew and deception beneath lace and velvet. Painted nails tear into my skin and I laugh. Is this the girl who loves pain? This is child's play. This is nursery foolishness. This is a quarrel over a dolly.

I bash my head against hers, until stars flutter and spark before me. And then I repeat it for good measure until the stars bloom red. We roll down an imaginary hill of grass, down, down, kicking and squabbling over our dolly, clawing and scratching and seething.

I covet the dolly more.

She yells, dull hums against spider webs, and I laugh all the merrier. She fumbles for her pretty whip. Perhaps it is time to be the bully in the nursery, to simply take the dolly and push her to the ground whilst doing so. A jab of elbow ceases her pathetic fumbling, and I roll off of her, toward the whip.

I think back to a time in Wonderland, in which the White Queen and the Queen of Hearts quarreled over whose bakers made the better tarts at a monarchs' luncheon. A battle-axe, formidable and capacious, appeared, as did a slithery whip. Honestly, if one was to put a fine point on it, the tarts from my kitchens were superior, but I enjoyed their spat immensely.

I scramble to my feet as the piper's pustules fester. The torturer is locked in a game of cat and mouse with Grymsdyke, although I believe he wishes to advance on the Frau and me.

I feel rather than hear the crack I issue, delighting in the gleaming brilliance of this whip. She must polish it regularly. I'd always shunned whips, finding them uncouth, but I suppose I owe the White Queen an apology. The girl who enjoys pain ought to be delighted right now, because her hand must be welling with plenty of it as scarlet splatters decorate the tile.

Another crack, and the girl herself rests next to her unintentional artwork. Alas, there is outrage facing me instead of pleasure.

Perhaps rumors painted her character incorrectly.

I kick her outstretched hand before slamming the pommel of the whip down upon her forehead. Her blackened eyes no longer focus on me or anything else. I waste no time whipping the man in black. As he arches his back in distress, Grymsdyke makes contact with the strip of flesh between mask and tunic.

I drop the whip, throw off my cloak of madness, and rush to Finn. He sags against the rack, half propped up, half beaten senseless, and yet my arms go around him, careful of the wounds carved into his skin.

"I'm here." I remove one earplug to allow sound to return. "Finn, I'm here." I kiss his forehead, his cheek, and his bruised mouth oh so softly. I touch his face, will his eyes to open. I press my forehead against his and breathe him in. "I am here."

His weak cough warns of broken or bruised ribs. When eyelids slowly flutter open, his irises are the color of cool English mornings, just before the rain rolls in. There is confusion clouding them, irritation, even. I do not allow myself any tears, or even the hair plucking clamoring for release over the knowledge that all too recently his beautiful eyes were black. Not now. Not when there are still miles to go.

Not when I have a mountain to destroy.

"I've taken care of the girl," Grymsdyke announces. His voice is a harsh whisper with his threads still stuffing one ear.

I press my mouth against Finn's once more, willing the strength of my heart to be conveyed in such a gentle touch. He jerks away, a sneer tainted by disgust wrinkling his nose.

A sharp, unfamiliar sting shoots through me.

I clear my throat. Ask, "Can you walk?"

The once bright pattern my love and blood created for him is now pale. His face is far too purple and black. There is too much blood everywhere. These are not Finn's colors.

Tick-tock. Tick-tock.

His focus settles over my right shoulder. "I *know* I need to hurry."

"We all do." I stroke his face, but he does not look at me.

He says, "The music has stopped. You can let go now."

The sting sharpens all the more. "Finn—"

"Did you finally locate where she is?"

"Who?" I tear a piece of my sleeve off with my teeth and press it against the shallow cut on his throat, whether he wishes for my hands on him or not.

Suddenly, he convulses, eyes rolling back until all that is visible are the whites. I steady his head, terrified he will slam it against the rack. His hands clamp around my arms and we are spun around. My back slams against the crusted wood and metal as an elbow shoves against my windpipe.

Grymsdyke leaps upon Finn's shoulder, fangs bared. I rasp, "Do not harm him!"

I refuse to fight back. Instead, when Finn leans in, fury darkening his dear face, I kiss him. I kiss him with intent. I suffuse all the love and adoration and respect I have for this man in the simple act of my mouth on his.

He gasps and tears away. The fury melts like ice on a hot day, until confusion is all that remains. "Alice?"

I heave in a trembling breath, which is not easy whilst one's windpipe is restricted. "Yes, love."

He stumbles backward, regarding at me as if I am a stranger, or worse, a ghost. Grymsdyke leaps upon my shoulder, assuming a defensive stance.

Finn holds out his hands, still bloody and dirty from his fight with the Chosen. "I—" He swallows, shakes his head.

I remain where I am, although desperate to touch him, to assure him of my love, of my presence.

His attention shifts to the left, where the Frau's body lies, but his focus hovers several feet above her. "Did I black out again?" A finger points my way, although he continues to stare at nothing. "Is this—is she real?"

Coldness seeps into my shoulders. *Who is he speaking to?*

I answer him anyway. "Yes, Finn. This is very real. *I* am real. We are once more together."

His unshed tears gut me. I close the distance between us, but it is his arms that curl around me even as he gasps in pain from the contact.

Grymsdyke has sense enough to take refuge on the wall.

Fingers twine into my hair. Anguished words warm my cheek. "I couldn't find you. I have never been so scared in my whole damn life."

His voice breaks, and I break in return. "Thank God you're alive."

I cling to him, and my own emotions breach the dam I've tried to hide them behind. I press my forehead against his neck, soaking his skin with the unstoppable escape of relief and terror.

It is Grymsdyke's cough that rouses us. "Forgive me, Your Majesty, Your Highness, but it would be wise for us to leave this place of death before these miscreants' fates are discovered."

I first dry my face with a sleeve. Again, I ask, "Can you walk?"

"Yeah." Finn straightens, stretching his neck. He fails to hide his wince quickly enough, and it only adds fuel to the raging fire stoked within my belly.

I find a tattered, bloodied shirt nearby, one they must have torn away from him in order to carve away pieces of his beautiful skin. I pass it over, lamenting I have nothing better to offer.

I am lamenting more than that.

Grymsdyke and I inform Finn of what we know. It's not enough, though. Not for him, not when it comes to his brother. And it is not enough for me, knowing the Piper is no longer within Koppenberg Mountain.

The others will pay for his sins, and the cost will be heavy, indeed. But when the time comes, I will extract payment from the Piper, too. Of that I have no doubt.

CONVERSATIONS

FINN

"**L**ET HER HELP YOU, darling. There's no shame in needing help."

As Alice grabs a pair of daggers off the floor, I glance at my mother. Katrina is standing guard at the door leading to the hallway, her bright eyes flicking back and forth.

On the floor between us lay the bodies of dead Chosen.

Every inch of me aches and burns. I might as well be underwater, my head is swimming so badly. My breaths are shallow, my moves minimal. My ears ring. I honestly worry if I will be able to walk out of the room on my own two feet.

As if she could hear my internal doubts, my mother continues, *"You aren't safe here. You know they rotate in and out like clockwork."*

I do know this. Everyone in this damn mountain wants their piece of flesh.

"I don't know if you can survive another go around." Color has leeched from her face. *"I also don't know how much longer we can keep the effects of these monsters' ministrations at bay. The mind and body can only take so much, Finn. Even yours. Let Alice and the spider help you. Don't keep her in the dark."*

I can't tell Alice. She has enough to worry about.

Worse, I fear I don't have the strength to finish the mission. Another trip to the Lady of the Mountain and I am positive I won't make it out—or at least, make it out as myself.

How I've survived as long as I have, I have no idea.

Before I can ask, Katrina adds, *"He still hasn't located your pen, let alone your gun. You'll have to make do with something from in here. But, darling, only fight if necessary. You must conserve your strength."*

"Forget the gun." Even talking hurts like a sonofabitch, but I won't admit that out loud, either. "He needs to focus on finding Victor."

Alice passes me a wicked-looking knife she's pried off the wall. There's a hesitation to her that I haven't seen in months, not since her early days in the Society. I'm not entirely easy with the way she's looking at me. "Of course we'll find him. But I truly believe it is best that Grymsdyke stays with us, though." She pauses, wincing as she once more scans my body. "At least for the time being."

Huh? Oh. Of course. She can't see Katrina, either. And because of the promise I made my mother and Jim, I can't tell her about them. No one can know, not until I'm home.

If I ever make it home.

"I meant—"

Katrina steps between us, cutting off my words. *"Promise me you'll take your brother home, darling. Don't leave him to rot in this hellhole."*

She doesn't have to ask this of me. I give her it anyway. "I promise. You can trust me."

"I always have, and always will." She steps to the side, her focus shifting to Alice.

"Always." I try to refocus on Alice, now standing before me, but she's still far too blurry. "Just as you can trust in me."

"I'll go ahead and see if Jim has found anything. Stay with Alice and the spider. Do not die, do you hear me? It's not your time. Listen to your mother for once, will you? I'll be back as soon as I can."

Hell, even swallowing is painful. I wish we had more time for introductions. "Be careful."

Katrina nods before ducking down the dark corridor and disappearing around the corner.

"Finn." Alice sucks in a long, quivering breath. "I am—" She gently touches my shoulder, her eyes glassy. "When it comes to you, I will never be careful. I will not fail you again."

The room suddenly spins so viciously, I fall to my knees and retch before I can take another breath. Alice drops next to me, her grip tender yet insistent, but the moment I look at her, I'm on a roller coaster, going a hundred-and-fifty miles per hour on a series of loops.

I vomit until I'm dry heaving, until I fear my stomach is ripping pieces of itself off its walls just to throw up. Until I'm positive the thirteenth Wise Woman is finally getting her way. My muscles cramp and spasm before the room darkens.

"Don't fight them," Sara begged just last night. She snuck me water after the worst visit. "And don't fight *her*. It'll only makes it worse."

But I did fight. I kept resisting, and will continue to do so until she, Alice, and Victor are out of this mountain. And in my fighting, I took down my fair share of the Chosen, even if they repaid me tenfold for every ounce of blood spilled.

Even when they dragged me in front of that bitch.

Even when she momentarily broke me.

"You're burning up," Alice is saying. "We need to—" Her voice wavers, and it scares the shit out of me. Alice doesn't waver. Alice is the strongest person I know. "Grymsdyke, were you able to ascertain the location of either of our sets of pens and books?"

I continue to dry heave as the Spider tells her no. A discussion arises as Alice lights a nearby lantern, but it's too hard to focus on what they're saying. Eventually, when my gag reflexes calms to a mere quivering, Alice slings my arm around her shoulder to haul me to my feet. "You must try to walk, Finn. We need a safer location to regroup in."

There is nowhere safe in the mountain, I want to tell her. And there is no one who can be trusted. But I will my feet to move, and, somehow, they actually do.

THE SAFEST PLACE

ALICE

UNFAMILIAR TENDRILS OF INDECISIVENESS and help-lessness claw their way through me until my stomach and nerves are nothing but shreds. Finn is in no shape to fight, let alone hunt down the Piper. Red lines bloom across the back of his tattered shirt, ones too easy to surmise came from the end of a whip.

He does not complain, though. Since departing the torture chamber through a hidden door Finn noted the man in black moved in and out of, he has been silent, as if each step requires the sum of all his thoughts and focus. The heat of his fever soaking into my clothes and skin demands my immediate attention, consuming *my* thoughts and focus.

While I lay slumbering, dreaming of a peaceful Wonderland, what horrors did Finn face? Why didn't he, too, retreat to the shelter of his mind, somewhere the damned inhabitants of this mountain could not touch him? The twelfth Wise Woman and goose's gifts came to my aid—why not his? I cannot bear to imagine what he has gone through, and yet I also cannot stop myself from doing so. Finn was alone, fighting against these villainous fiends, and the knowledge breaks both my heart and sanity.

Perhaps the goose's strength did aid him after all.

He requires medical attention. To do so, I must locate Victor, and it must happen before dawn.

I fervently pray Finn's brother is in one piece. He, too, must be in torment, as days have passed without any doses of the medicines required to stem the tide of his madness. Once he is recovered, and if we are lucky enough that my plan is enacted, a retreat will be mandatory. I loathe the thought of licking wounds rather than reveling in victory, but I am not foolish enough to doggedly insist we continue to hold advantage when we do not.

That does not mean I still do not have a hand to deal, though.

Grymsdyke has scouted the twisting, unfamiliar hallway we find ourselves within. Without warning, though, a door opens, and a woman close to my age emerges. Most of her blackened teeth are long gone, replaced by sharpened silver monstrosities. She bites me several times as we tussle, and I want to tear the fangs from her mouth. I have just slammed her head against the floor when Grymsdyke sails in with his own fangs.

In order to mask her screams, I quickly drag her body back within the room she exited from. As I clap a hand across her gnashing, foaming mouth, Finn struggles to shut and lock the door.

We are in a bedroom. Small, unadorned, and possessing two beds, a singular armoire, and a washstand and a pitcher, the space still lit by a sole candle will do nicely for the time being.

Once the body beneath me ceases its twitching, I tell Finn, "You ought to sit down and rest." To Grymsdyke, I say, "I'll take first watch. Get some rest, as we have a long day before us still."

My assassin scuttles to the top of the armoire, coughing as he constructs a web.

Finn motions toward one of the beds. "There are straps both on the head and foot boards."

I dust off my skirt as I peer more closely at the items in question. "I promise not to strap you down." I force a naughty grin, even though my stomach churns at the thought of such confinement. I get to work on lighting the remaining two candles in the room. "Unless, of course, you want me to."

His laugh is little more than a soft burst of air, punctuated by a wince.

I hurry to his side, herding him toward the bed. It isn't soft, but the sheets are clean and tucked in neatly. Whoever sleeps within this room may require restraints but also possesses a sense of discipline. "Let me look at your wounds."

He brushes off my concern like a bothersome Gnat buzzing about. "We—"

"Finn." I adore him dearly, but I refuse to allow senseless ego to override common sense. "Although I would love to admit my concern for your health is purely due to the strength of my feelings for you, I must also selfishly admit I am not the only person depending on you today."

Resistance melts into curiosity.

I carefully peel off the tattered shirt as I recount my meeting with Harry and about the gunpowder stockpile. Too many pieces of cloth stick to his wounds, and the urge to simultaneously weep and rage at the destruction wreaked against his beautiful body nearly drives me back into madness' arms.

His back is nothing but slashes of angry lines. His front is a puzzle missing several pieces.

"We have to find Victor," he snaps as I rummage through the armoire.

I select a plain cotton shift hanging within and begin ripping it into shreds. "All the more reason you're needed in decent fighting condition."

"I won't let you blow this damn mountain up until I find him."

I take no offense to this, either. Instead, I wet some of the strips with water from the washbasin and gently dab at his wounds. He hisses, and I wish oh so much that I could strip all his pain away.

I can no longer hold back the tears. What must he have endured while I slept?

I clean the dirt and crusted blood covering and surrounding the cuts littering his body. Winces erupt as I methodically, gently, make my way across this new map. Each bit of pain I uncover stokes the fire within me, until I am certain that if another of the Chosen, let alone the Piper or the thirteenth Wise Woman, were to stand before me, I would shred their heads from their necks with my bare hands and jagged, dirty nails.

When I am finished, he wipes the traces of my anger and helplessness away with his thumbs and sweet kisses. "I'm okay," he whispers, but I know this is a lie.

I set aside a bloody rag and pick up a clean one. He asks, "What about you?"

Soft snores drift down to us from the top of the armoire. At least one of our party sleeps. "I am fine. Lift your chin, please."

"Alice. . ."

Beneath the stubble are yellowish bruises that claim days of residency. "Hush. I'm almost finished cleaning. Afterward, I'll need to wrap your wounds until we obtain medical attention."

My stubborn Finn fails to do as requested. "Where did they keep you?"

I stare ahead, into the darkness encroaching upon us. "The dungeons."

I can feel his eyes trace over me. I am filthy, and a bit worse for the wear from the day's altercations, but it is starkly obvious that I have not been abused like he has.

Nonetheless, he asks, "Did they hurt you?"

My conscience throbs. "Please, do not worry needlessly about me."

"I worried when I couldn't find you." He presses his forehead against my cheek. "No one would tell me about you. Not that I expected them to answer, but still. It was like you disappeared. I was so damn terrified that something bad happened."

"There is nothing to tell." My truth is brittle. Resentful. "From what I gather, no one could wake me from whatever sleep the Piper lured me into." *Or the twelfth Wise Woman.*

His breath heaves. "Thank God."

With my teeth, I tear new strips of cloth from the shrinking shift. "Did you also sleep?"

It is a plea, to be honest. A fervent wish.

"A bit." He shifts upon the mattress, and one of the wounds bleeds anew. "I wanted to continue sleeping, to be honest, but . . . I had to keep my promises."

I motion for him to lift his arms so that I might begin the bindings. "Did you dream? Or . . . perhaps believe all of *this* was merely a dream?"

The sound of his uneven breathing is all I hear for several beats. But then admits, "Yeah." The ghost of a laugh runs its transparent fingers against my neck. "Thought I was back at the Institute, and everything was like it used to be. I wanted it to be real. Letting go wasn't easy." Another pause stretches between us as his words resonate all too strongly. "You?"

I knot the end of two strips together. "The same, only I believed I was in Wonderland."

"Our safe places," he murmurs.

I shake my head, my golden strands mixing with his. "We are safer together. Wherever that is, is our safe place."

He grabs one of my hands. Kisses it.

I tie off an additional strip of cloth. "Get some rest before we head out to find Victor. You will need your strength."

Praise Wonderland, he does not fight me when I urge him down onto the mattress. "Sara, too."

Sara? It takes a moment before the name resonates. Sara Carrisford, Finn's former partner. We saw her amongst the Chosen shortly before our capture.

I keep my tone neutral. "If she's here, Finn, it may be too late."

"She helped me. Risked getting caught to help me when. . ." His swallow is audible. "She's fighting it. She's not one of them, at least, not fully. I won't leave her behind."

I wish I shared his optimism.

"Stay here, with me?"

I'm relieved to hear that the onslaught of drowsiness has settled in.

"Of course." I press my hand in his as I sit next to him. "Sleep. I'll keep watch."

"Don' let me sleep too long." His childhood soft twang emerges. "Gotta fin' Victor an' Sara."

I brush aside sweaty, golden-brown curls from his forehead. "I'll wake you in an hour."

I snuff all candles save the one lit when we entered and then wait by the door, a knife in hand. One occupant lies lifeless beneath a mattress, purple and covered in dried pus, but there are two beds within this room.

I am not one for surprises.

Fatigue worms its way into my muscles and eyelids, which makes little sense, considering I spent the better part of the last several days sleeping. I refuse to wake either Grymsdyke or Finn until they have had enough rest, even if I wish for their counsel.

Neither Finn nor I have our editing pens in order to depart this Timeline. In addition to finding Victor (and apparently Sara), we must track down one or the other's device in order to escape this infernal mountain, unless Harry or one of his comrades knows of an exit.

My plan was a poor one, built upon desperation and fervor. I conscripted the help of an equally desperate man who has little to no experience in such matters. For all the good it may do, I may be sending innocents to their grave come dawn.

I may be sending Finn and Grymsdyke to the same graves.

I would happily sit at the Caterpillar's feet once more, if only he could offer me sarcastic, at times belittling, yet always sage counsel.

The door latch depresses, and the fatigue so freshly plaguing me retreats. I swiftly step to the side of the door, knife bared, as it swings open. I waste no time grabbing hold of the visitor, kicking the door shut. My blade rests against her windpipe.

"Move," I whisper, "and you will have savored your last breath."

Bristled legs appear on top of the dark hair facing me. Grymsdyke must not have been sleeping as soundly as I hoped.

"Say the word, Your Majesty, and I will take care of this villain."

"Not yet," I tell my assassin. "I possess questions that require answers."

"A-Alice?"

Her voice is familiar, and while hesitation sets in, my blade presses more firmly against her throat.

"Oh, thank goodness." The woman I'm holding does not move, nor does she struggle. "You found Finn. I have been in a tizzy, wondering how to get to him tonight."

I'll be damned. There was no need to search for Sara Crewe Carrisford, Finn's former partner, as she has gone and found us.

"We don't have much time." While she remains still, urgency hurries her words. "Check-ins begin in twenty minutes. Strap me to the bed if you must, but please, they cannot find him here. Or you."

My options are rapidly dwindling. I spin her around, knife still at the ready. Sara obliges by continuing to remain docile.

Her eyes are green, not black.

"You are not in rapture."

Her lower lip tugs in between her teeth. "I fight it best I can. Sometimes there are moments of clarity, and I cling to them as one would a piece of driftwood after a boat capsizes. I am not always successful, though." Her attention shifts, settling upon Finn's still sleeping form. "My worry over whether or not he would live this day has kept the rapture at bay today."

"Grymsdyke, you may leave her person," I begin, but Sara turns her head, slowly but assuredly.

"Is your spider poisonous?"

"Venomous," Grymsdyke answers. "The one we met coming out of this room now lies lifeless beneath the bed we stand before."

A shuddery breath lifts Sara's chest. "Then do not leave me. If I fall prey to rapture, give me the same fate."

The assassin settles in, twisting his legs into strands of her hair. "Your hair will make a decent nest."

"You need to leave," Sara says, and my laugh is just as quiet and bitter all at once. "Get Finn back to the Institute. He needs a doctor. They took him to—" Words clog within her throat. "He needs to see the Librarian. She'll know."

"I would like nothing more than to immediately exit this place," I tell her, "but as neither of us are in possession of our pens, and Victor is still missing—"

"I don't know where Victor is. No one has mentioned him." Her hands, lacing in and out of one another, tremble. "You're wasting time. They're coming for check-in. If they find you, if they take you to the witch. . ." She sniffles loudly. "If he goes back to her. . ."

A blizzard of questions nearly weighs me down. I settle on the most pressing. "Will you assist us?"

"I cannot promise to remain myself. I've tried so hard, for so long, to resist the music. I am nothing more than a bomb waiting to explode. Leave me behind." She wipes angrily at the wetness staining her fair skin. "Better yet, have your spider bite me to guarantee my silence."

In Wonderland, perhaps, I might have considered such an action merciful. But I know Sara's story, I know the strength of her heart, of her convictions and love for her colleagues within the Society. She is a victim, used badly by the Piper. Sara Carrisford is yet another reason he must pay for his sins.

I roll my shoulders, stretching my still-stiff muscles. "Finn will not leave without you. He has made that clear."

I will not leave without her.

"Tell him I was in rapture. Better yet, tell him I attacked you."

"You have yet to attack anyone," Grymsdyke mutters.

"This is not who you are, Sara. Rather than give in to the Piper and hurt your colleagues, you ran far away, back to your Timeline. You remained vigilant. You fought for Finn when he showed up at your house. You continued to fight for him here. Fight for yourself, too. Do not give up so easily." I take her trembling hand in mine. "You are not alone, Sara. Your life has value, it has worth—not to the Piper and the Chosen, but to all those who know you. To all of the Timelines you have aided over the years. But most importantly, to yourself."

Her breath is a cross between a hitch and a hiccup. "You make it sound so easy."

"I wish it were. I have long learned that life, itself, is not easy. It just is. Death is easy, though. There are times when death is necessary, when it is the right choice. And there are other times when it is the coward's way out. Help us, Sara. In turn, we will help you. There must be someone within all of the Timelines who possesses the ability to remove this festering so-called rapture from your and Wendy's minds."

Her hesitation is small, the span of a heartbeat, maybe two, before she offers me her silent agreement.

There is no time to take pause and enjoy relief, though. "What will happen when they find one bed empty, and the body of another occupant dead beneath the frame?"

"I don't know." Her whispered words tremble just as badly as her limbs. "They confine those of us who are not elevated to our beds."

The elevated . . . "Do you mean the original children the Piper kidnapped?"

"No one has clarified, but that is my guess."

Frabjous. Undoubtedly, an alarm would be triggered, and a search.

I make my way over to Finn. "Well then. I suppose we must find a secure location so that I can fill you in on the rest of the plan."

I gently shake Finn's shoulder. Sara asks, "You have a plan?"

She does not hide her hope as he slowly wakens, even if it is all too evident she shares none of it for herself.

"It is mimsy and riddled with more holes than a butter-sieve, but yes," I admit. "I have a plan."

"Plans are good," my love murmurs, sand still clinging to his voice and body. And then, "You found her."

"She found *us*." I hold Sara's eyes. "And she's coming with us, too."

A ROOM WITH NO DOOR

ALICE

HAVING ONLY BEEN A resident of Koppenberg Mountain a single day before us, Sara's knowledge of its layout is incomplete. Grymsdyke abandons his perch upon her head in order to scout, and it is clear Sara suffers from an internal argument over whether or not he must return in order to prevent her from going rogue.

She refuses all weapons, even when Finn argues the necessity.

Twice, we are forced to retreat within shadowy recesses when footsteps and voices come too close for comfort. Keen to prohibit any undue attention drawn to us, especially when Finn is in such delicate condition, I allow the Chosen to pass by without bloodshed.

We descend two floors before entering an eerily unoccupied corridor, one that drowns in neglect. Long-abandoned webs covered in dust and neglect drape the scant amounts of visible furniture, and assumed electrical lighting gives way to dying torches.

"Do you know this place?" My voice is little more than a whisper to Sara.

Her response is even quieter than my own. "I was warned to never come down here, on pain of death."

My teeth are once more in danger of turning to powder.

Finn groans and stumbles; I catch him before he falls. Fresh red stains bloom upon his tattered shirt. "Are you sure?"

His eyes are not focused on me, nor Sara, but on a nearby door as he asks this.

Sara hesitantly tries the closest door's latch. "I've heard it at least two or three times now."

"There." He winces as he gestures weakly at the painted black wood and rusty handle bearing a large lock. "We need to go in there."

Sara shares in my surprise, but immediately makes her way toward the door.

I fumble for reason. "Finn, we don't know who might be within. Let us—"

He jerks away, brandishing the blade I'd given him. "I hope you're right about this."

Sara attempts to grab hold of him as he nears the door. "Finn? Are you all right?"

He does not respond to her, either.

Is he . . . hallucinating? From the fever? A quick glance shows his eyes beautifully blue-gray, not black.

I am not quick enough to prevent him from slamming the butt of his blade against the lock. A peal rings out, followed by a second attempt. I drag one of my own daggers out, wary of visitors curious of suspicious sounds.

But the lock gives way, clattering to the ground. Finn pushes the door open, collapsing across the threshold.

Both Sara and I dart forward; she snatches a torch from the wall, I kick the lock within the room. Grymsdyke scuttles in a mere second before I shut the door behind us.

I set the lantern down and bend down to assist Finn. I tell my assassin, "Scout the room to assure we have no surprise visitors."

"I will help." Sara motions for him to climb upon her head. Together, woman and Spider need no further instruction before disappearing into the darkness.

"Where is—" Finn's swallow is audible as he struggles to stand. "I can't. . ." And then he retches once more as I hold him in my arms.

I am smoothing his sweaty hair back, murmuring words of love and encouragement, when the door and wall behind us begin to shudder. In firelight, we watch in stunned silence as seams stitch together and disappear altogether, leaving behind a room with no apparent exit.

Finn's inhalation is audible; mine is the same.

We have seen such a door before. Victor disappeared behind a vanishing room the day we entered the mountain.

Perhaps, once more, luck is smiling down upon us after abandoning us for days.

"Victor?" Finn's call is hoarse, a strangled pant. "Victor!"

"Sara and Grymsdyke are searching," I whisper. "They will find him if he is here. But if the creature is, too, we must not bring attention to ourselves."

Gleaming, wild eyes glance around the area around us. "We need to—help us find him. *Please*. I can't—" He swallows once more. "He's afraid of the dark. Always has been."

"I will do anything I can to aid Victor. You know this." My squeeze assures him that I am with him, that no matter what we find within, I will always be with him.

Our new surroundings is a showcase in dichotomies abound: rough, stone walls but gleaming tile floors; wooden tables whose better days are now ghosts, littered with a mixture of both modern and Victorian medical equipment; bottles and jars filled with liquids and specimens crowd shelf after shelf; lightbulbs smashed upon metal carts but no signs of lamps.

"Have you been in here before?" I ask quietly.

He shakes his head, wincing afterward. Both hands grip his forehead as his breath quickens.

"You need to rest." I continue to gently stroke his hair as I take in our environs. "I'll have a look around while you do so."

An argument touches his lips, but dies before it goes anywhere.

As I have heard no screams or sounds of struggling, I assume our companions have not unearthed any surprises. I place a blade in Finn's hand before shoving a table against the wall where the door once was. Then I cautiously make my way through the shrouded chamber.

When I have located a simple cot, Grymsdyke and Sara materialize out of the gloom. "The room is clear, Your Majesty."

I flip through the stack of books propped on a chair next to the bed. Medical texts mix with poetry. "Anything of note?"

The Spider coughs, fluttering Sara's glossy black strands. "The reek of death haunts this space."

That it does. The faint undertones of decomposing flesh, of alcohol and blood and bleach, sting with each breath drawn.

He continues, as Sara continues to survey, "There is a door at the end of a hallway, hidden behind a curtain. A solid, proper door. As it is closed, and there are no visible cracks, let alone light shining through, I was unable to look within."

"Any sounds of note?"

"Yes," Sara says, "but they are more mechanical than anything else."

"Show me."

I follow the pair down a narrow hallway, also obstructed by a dark curtain. My grip on the stolen dagger is tight as I push aside the second bit of dusty cloth. Grymsdyke's description of the door is apt.

Oh, what I would do for a proper Wonderlandian doorknob right now.

I press my ear against the cool wood and listen. Vivid memories surface, of the time I rode within an ambulance, of when I was attended to by medical professionals after the Piper destroyed a catalyst within the Institute's walls. Quiet hisses of *whoosh-thump, whoosh-thump,* alongside a steady yet faint blipping, accompanied me during the drive to a local hospital. I focused on the audible patterns, willing them up and down, in a meaningless effort to hold back the madness and grief born from Finn's supposed demise that threatened to swallow me whole.

Whoosh-thump. Whoosh-thump.

Might there be modern medical equipment behind the door, in a hellish place such as Koppenberg Mountain? Something that could aid Finn?

I grip the curved metal handle of the door, and slowly depress the latch. The door, unfortunately, is locked.

"I also tried it," Sara whispers. "I listened for sounds of active life, but there were none to be found."

We retreat back into the main chamber. "Do you know of this place?"

"Not really. Before he was dragged away to the dungeons, one of the others said there is nothing but death beneath the mountain."

We find Finn standing, albeit unsteadily. The sight of him wicks my breath clean away, but not in the way it normally does.

The blood upon his shirt has tripled.

"Gotta find him, Alice." His voice is raspy, once more painted with twang. "I promised."

I pass the lantern to Sara. Bearing both torch and lantern, she is both past and present personified. I loop an arm into Finn's, steadying him. "And we will. But before we go further, I need to tend your injuries."

"I—I'm fine."

"Of course you are," I lie, I pray. I lead him across the room, with Sara trailing all too closely. "Applying fresh bandages cannot hurt the cause."

"A lantern—there, on that table." Sara waves the torch in its direction. "And another, nearby."

"Light them, please. And look for anything that can help."

She nods and immediately sets to task.

I ease Finn onto the bed. "Rest a moment while we find something that can be used for your wrappings."

He is wise enough to not argue, especially as his body agrees with me. The moment his head comes to rest upon the thin pillow, sleep beckons. "Just a few minutes," he mumbles. "Victor. . ."

I press a kiss against his forehead and promptly search the newly lit room for something, anything, that might aid him. I estimate nearly a hundred bottles and jars present in the large room, but many are unlabeled. Body parts, both human and animal, float suspended in pinkish liquids, curling my toes and stomach. Glazed, unseeing eyes stare through the glass, unable to recount any horrors they might have faced.

Those bottles which are labeled are done in a neat, elegant script—and in English, not German. Scraps of crumpled sheets of papers litter the floor, all bearing the same handwriting. Many recount poems, or Shakespearean quotes, rather than medical notes, leaving me wondering exactly who the mysterious doctor or scientist who works within these walls might be.

"Do many of the Chosen speak English?" I ask Sara.

She considers this as she sorts through the papers. "Not many. There is a woman with purple-pink hair who does." Her lips tug between her teeth. "Sometimes, when it gets unbearably lonely, I talk to her. She likes books, and is from modern-day New York. Her name is Jenn."

I let out a small laugh. "We are acquainted. When Mary and I attempted to question her about the Piper's association with the New York Public Library, she took offense and shot at us for our troubles. I must admit, it did not go well for Ms. Ammer." I pause. "Much like you, she was confined before journeying here. Last I was updated, she was in prison, awaiting trial for both attempted murder and destruction of public property."

Sara does not laugh, too, though. Instead, unnecessary guilt cloaks her, as if she is not allowed to find comfort and companionship in a hellhole, even with a murderous woman like Jenn Ammer.

Sara rolls a corner of one of the papers into a mini scroll. "You and Mary seem to get along well."

I sort through several bottles on a shelf. "I suppose we do."

"Over the years, I tried so hard to get along with Mary. It never happened, though. And it wasn't so much that she didn't like me—she

despised me, true, but she never respected me. And it cut so deeply."
Sara's eyes glitter like emeralds in the lantern light as she gazes, un-
focused, at the words curling and uncurling beneath her fingers. "I can
see why she would like you, though. You're so stubborn. You don't
care if anyone likes you or not. You probably argue with her all the
time, and tell her when she's wrong. I never did that. I tried to make
myself as agreeable as possible."

I place a bottle back on the shelf. "There's nothing wrong with
being agreeable."

My assessment draws pained lines on Sara's forehead. We continue our search in silence. Several minutes later, she whisper-calls
my name. I hurry over to her side.

"It is not much," she says, handing me a squat jar marked *Comfry
Salve*, "but it is better than nothing."

Praise Wonderland.

She rips off the bottom half of her skirt. It is cleaner than mine,
and thus more sanitary. As she tears the fabric into strips, I once more
undress Finn.

Never have I wished to sob more over the sight of a damaged
body.

The majority of his wounds are festering; some are puffy, both
white and red in anger, some weep more than blood. Infection has set
in. A hand to his forehead informs me his fever rages.

Our escape has become all the more time sensitive.

I gently spread the salve across his skin, and he is stronger than
most, for he shows us nothing more than mere winces as he awakens
from the pain. Sara passes me the strips, and as I wrap them around
his abused torso, I tell her both of Harry, and of my pitiful plan.

"Do you know any exits?" Grymsdyke asks from his perch on
Sara's head.

"They are all well-guarded now." She is once more chewing on
her bottom lip. "Gabe . . . the Piper." Her eyes hollow. "Whatever his
damn name is . . . He knew you were coming. He let you in. I wanted
to stop it, to warn you, but . . . the music was too strong."

I refuse to allow her to go down a path the Piper would delight in.

"How did you get here?"

"I don't know." She drags a chair closer and drops into it. "I was in a bathroom, chained to the sink, when the music in my head turned deafening. I blacked out. I was strapped to the bed within the room you found me when I awoke." Shame dampens her lashes. "I am so sorry for all of the havoc I wreaked upon the Society. More sorry than you will ever know."

"You are not to blame, Sara. You must understand that. The Piper and the thirteenth Wise Woman possess powerful magic." I rub my forehead, as a nasty headache has found a new home. "Let us focus, instead, on finding Victor and then a way out before the mountain's servants set off their explosions, lest we all perish."

"She won't let that happen." Sara's warning is little more than a whisper as she glances furtively around. "She knows everything."

"Which *she* do you refer to?"

"The Lady of the Mountain." Fear seizes her to her chair. "The one you call the thirteen Wise Woman."

"Let her dare and try to stop me."

"My money's on Alice." I glance down, surprised that Finn has yet to fall back asleep. But no, his eyes, although glazed with fever, are wide open. "Hell, she can take down giants and batshit-crazy people alike without a needing a second wind."

A genuine smile fights its way onto my face. "I may have been out of breath after my interactions with the giant."

"Interactions? Is that what you're calling them?" His cocky grin weakens my knees. "Alice Reeve: modest to a fault."

He is rallying, and I fear my heart may burst over it. "You believe me to have faults?"

My hand is claimed and kissed. "I love them anyway."

Amused, Sara smacks her forehead. "I never thought I would see this day. Finn Van Brunt actually allowed someone into his heart."

Finn weakly reaches up and swats at her, but it done with great affection. "There are lots of people in my heart. You, for example."

Her grin reaches me. "Not like this."

"I'm a prince now, you know," he mumbles, and I want to laugh at the stodginess he attempts to feign. "You ought to assume a more respective tone when talking to me now."

When she giggles, I almost forget our circumstances.

Almost.

A FAMILY'S SIN

ALICE

MY FINGERS DIG INTO the tightened muscles of the back of my neck, but it does little to alleviate the tension threatening to snap my spine apart in multiple locations. The Piper is no longer within the mountain, and thereby out of our reach. Even if he were here, current events have shown he holds the advantage. With Sara paranoid she is on the brink of rapture at any moment, Finn assuredly injured, all but Grymsdyke vulnerable toward the Piper and his minions' infernal music, and the possibility of the thirteenth Wise Woman's magic a very valid threat, the odds of our success are minimal at best.

And yet try we will.

Finn is on his feet, stubborn as always as he wanders the room. Despite the fever, he is miraculously steadier than when we entered.

Could this be the result of the goose's gifts? Or the twelfth Wise Woman's? Nevertheless, threads of worry tug at the anxiety stitching me together. "You ought to rest and let Sara and I figure out our next steps."

"There isn't time for that." He taps the wall, which once held a door.

His point is valid, and in normal circumstances, loafing would not be tolerated. These are not normal circumstances, though. Since meeting this man, I have nearly lost him too many times for my comfort and sanity. His bravery, so alluring and admirable, can also be more than a bit discomforting.

I chose him. I *choose* him. He is my heart, my north star.

I move in front of him, in front of the hallway leading to the curtained door, now guarded by Sara and Grymsdyke. "*I* will pick the lock."

Irritation flashes across his handsome yet battered face. "I'm completely capable of picking a lock."

Fair or not, I shove a stolen blade his way. "You are also capable of standing watch and holding a lantern."

The irritation marring his features grows more defined. He stares at me so intently that the weight of his displeasure presses against the tender walls of my ribcage.

I dig four sticky, silk-covered balls out of a pocket and offer him a pair. "These dull any music we might encounter."

He does not accept the makeshift earplugs, nor does he even acknowledge them. "What's going on right now? Why are you acting like this?"

"Like what?" I ask coolly.

"Like I'm fragile, or that I'll break." When I refuse to validate or refute, he continues, "I haven't broken yet, Alice."

Yet. It's a word I fear all too much lately. "They tortured you." I loathe that my syllables crack, thin ice splintering beneath heavy boots. "Even the strongest need time to heal."

"There isn't time—"

"Finn." He ceases arguing at the raw voicing of his name, the same one I scratched into my arm in my dreams, in order to break free. "Please."

The angry lines on his forehead soften.

"I cannot—" Attempts at swallowing the large jubjub egg that has found its way into my throat fail. I pull my wrist out of his grasp only to claim his hand in the tightest of grips. "*Please*."

I simply cannot articulate the fear and concern threatening to consume me. It clutches my tongue, my reasoning too tightly.

Finn's exhalation is quiet, resigned. "All right. I'll hold the damn lantern."

There is no relief to be had, though. No savoring of victory. I simply place the earplugs Grymsdyke crafted into his hand before inserting my own and then make my way to the curtained door. Sara once more rejects any weapons or earplugs, as she claims she constantly hears the music, anyway. It takes very little time to pick the lock.

A shroud of gray and black looms before us. Shadows crawl about stealthily, desperate for the light from the lantern in Finn's hand. The stench of decomposition is strongest here, so much so that the contents of my stomach reach my throat.

Slabs filled with near a half-dozen hacked-up corpses in various stages of decomposition resting in vats of ice line the walls.

Finn stills as he stares at the shells of what once were.

I wish there were words of assurance I could offer, but as I trace each face, each hand, each scrap of remaining clothing, none come. Together, we search for the one face we undoubtedly both pray will not appear.

When Finn removes the earplugs, I follow his lead.

Whoosh-thump, whoosh-thump.

My prayers turn feverish when I spot a small table at the end of the slabs that holds a pen, an open copy of the Institute's book, and a familiar bag.

Finn angles the lantern toward the darkest corner of the room. Cold radiates from it, but when I shiver, I am certain it has nothing to do with temperature.

Grymsdyke whispers in just the way spiders can, a Diamonds

military prayer. *"Allow us to go forth into the unknown and know that our day, our lives, change, and that we have made our peace with our fates."*

Finn pushes forward into the veil. Sara, Grymsdyke, and I follow, my blades at the ready.

Another slab appears, titled at a forty-five degree angle. Upon it rests a rectangular metal box packed with ice and another mangled body attached to dozens of tubes.

I close my eyes. Order myself to steady my breath, to cling to strength and reason.

Sara whispers, "Sweet, merciful God in heaven, no." And Finn . . . His voice shatters into a thousand shards when he says his brother's name.

The person before us is not entirely Victor Frankenstein Van Brunt, though. His face, yes—hair shaved haphazardly, some strands long, some missing entirely; stitches unevenly lining his forehead and neck. I cannot be certain that it is his torso we see, but I know one of the arms is not. Victor bears tattoos on both biceps; the body before us has one arm completely bare of any adornments. One leg is dark-skinned. Thick, black thread embroiders jagged lines across the body, and I am reminded of the White Queen's dolls.

I catch Finn's lantern just before it smashes into the ground. He has two fingers pressed against Victor's neck, just below the ear. I hold my breath. Sara openly weeps.

Whoosh-thump, whoosh-thump.

There are machines next to where Victor rests, their parts beeping and moving up and down. Green lines blip across a screen that should not belong in this Timeline.

"Victor?" Finn shakes the patchwork man. "Victor, wake up."

The elder Van Brunt sibling remains still, his face pale blue.

Finn snaps, "Do you know what's wrong with him?"

I set the lantern on a nearby table. "No—"

He hushes me. Sara attempts to answer, but he does the same to her while focusing on a spot across where Victor lies.

There is nothing there, but when he nods, it's as if he is responding to someone . . . or something.

An uneasy glance passes between Sara and myself.

I join him next to the icebox. "Finn—"

My love leans his head down against his brother's chest, over where the heart lays. "Don't do this, you sonofabitch. Don't give up. Don't you go and think death is the easy way out. I'm here now, and we're going to take you home."

Helplessness replaces the blood in my veins. I send Sara to fetch the other lanterns.

Nothing Finn does rouses his brother. He continues to carry on a discussion that I am apparently not part of, nor Sara after she returns. Minutes tick by, and eventually, his administrations cease. I circle my arms gingerly around his waist, and in the safety of my embrace, he struggles to maintain his composure.

"I don't think we can unhook him from the machines." He keeps the diagnosis calm and logical, as if this weren't his brother we were discussing but a stranger. "We'll bring them with us. I'm sure there is someone from some Timeline that can . . . fix him."

As I hold the man I have grown to know and consider family over the past year, I loathe the doubts that creep in. There are true miracles to be found within different Timelines, but can anyone successfully rouse from being stitched together with pieces from the dead?

"I won't." His head lifts from my shoulder. "Dad won't, either."

Over my shoulder, Sara's brow furrows considerably.

I jam steel rods into my spine. We now have a pen. It is not mine, nor Finn's, but it is a Society pen, and that means we have a way out, even though our miracle is accompanied by a curse. No matter what the outcome, Victor deserves to come home, be it for burial and peace or miracles and recuperation. "Is there any way to override Victor's pen? Allow us to use it?"

He disentangles from me. "No."

"Are you su—"

He holds up a hand. "I can try, but I've never heard of that working."

"Of what working?" Sara asks, but he hushes her, too.

"Maybe the three of us, though? Our intent might override it?"

"You want Sara and I to help?" I query.

"No, no." He strides over to the table with the pen. "It can't hurt to try."

A blast of light illuminates the room of death. A shadowy outline of a man appears momentarily in a new doorway before melting once more into darkness. "Who dares to intrude in my workspace?"

The voice is hauntingly memorable. The same baritone belonged to a sallow, dark-haired man with shards of blackened teeth who wreaked vengeance upon Victor.

Grymsdyke hisses from atop Sara's head.

This beast of the Piper's will not escape us a second time. Not now, not after Victor's fate.

It repeats its question. Footsteps squeak on polished tiles. Finn grabs what appears to be a bone saw off of a nearby table.

"This is *my* sanctuary." The shadow emerges in the gloom, closer toward our lantern light. "You three are trespassers, and your lives now belong to me."

I toss Sara a blade. She is smart enough to catch and then hold on to it.

Finn tests the weight of the saw in his hand. When the glint of lustrous, dark hair appears, he says flatly, "A family's sin is a stain that cannot be washed away."

Victor's manic cries of the same punishment buzz in my ears.

The creature grins. "So this is where the missing assets are. How fortuitous. Mother is livid." It jerks its jaundiced, marred face toward Victor. "Do you like my latest creation?" Rubbery lips peel upward, revealing his abysmal set of ghastly teeth. "Not my best work, but the current crop of parts to choose from is lacking."

Its lips are black, its teeth rotten. This is not the creature from Victor's Timeline, though. This is not the creation his biological father birthed. This is nothing more than another of the Piper's minions.

Finn holds out the saw, as if it were a gun. "I will have my retribution."

"I would expect nothing else. After all, a family's sin is a stain that cannot be washed away. Not even if I cut it into pieces and sew it into something new."

Finn launches forward at the same time the creature snatches a scalpel off of a nearby table. I dart into the darkness, circling toward the back whilst Sara and Grymsdyke attack from the side. The creature laughs merrily, as if the taste of a multi-pronged death means nothing, and soon I realize why.

The room elongates, much as the hallway we lost Victor in did. Grymsdyke, Sara, and I are left behind, hastening to catch up with Finn and the creature but never truly gaining ground. The pair clashes, blood emerges, and hysteria brings forth blessed madness.

"Stay with Victor," I order my companions.

I failed Victor during the last battle with this monstrosity. I failed Finn whilst I slumbered. I refuse to fail either now.

I believe in the impossible. I live the impossible.

The room ceases growing, and I am within throwing distance. No creature is invulnerable—not the Jabberwockies, not the Queen of Hearts, not boojums, not this stitched-together man. I hurl a dagger. The blade sinks within the flesh just north of its kneecap.

The creature staggers and roars.

Finn kicks the beast, sending it sprawling against a wall. Somehow, a scalpel still rests within a raised, grayish hand, and that is unacceptable. I send the second dagger flying. The scalpel clatters to the floor as its hand fastens to the wall.

Finn wastes no time. The saw within his grip slashes; the creature's gurgled roars splatter against the walls. A jagged red line replaces black stitching before a scarlet bib soaks its shirt.

Finn yanks my blade from its knee and shoves it deep within its heart. Glazed, defiant eyes are now empty.

I catch Finn as he staggers back. Warmth seeps against my hands, sending jolts of fresh worry throughout my veins. "You're bleeding again."

His voice is nothing more than a shuddery wind through autumn leaves precariously clinging to a tree. "I don't care."

The urge to sob and alternately rage clamors up my throat, but I swallow it back. The room rights itself. "We must—"

"He's dead."

"Do not grieve for this monstrosity." My hold on Finn tightens. *My love will keep him safe. My love will keep him safe.* "Who knows how many have suffered at his hands in the past? The world is better off without such a homicidal fiend."

"I know." An uneven breath expands his chest. I shove a wad of my dress against a bleeding torso wound. "I—how do I. . ." His swallow is audible. "I couldn't protect my brother. He knew this was going to happen, Alice. Even when he was little, he had reoccurring nightmares about becoming. . ." More quietly, "How do I explain this to my father? To . . . Mary?" His focus shifts. "I let you all down."

I press my cheek against his hair, still soft despite sweat and blood and violence. "Do not be silly. You have not let anyone down, especially me. There is breath still in Victor's lungs. His heart still beats. Do not give up on Victor, love. He will need you in the days to come."

Despite his fever, Finn's teeth clatter together. He whispers, "What if that isn't my brother's brain in his head?"

As I kiss his forehead, I catch sight of Sara's face gleaming in the lamplight. Her eyes remain green. "Let us first take him home and we will deal with the rest of it together."

A MOTHER'S LOVE

FINN

ACROSS THE ROOM, SARA tells Alice, "He'll have to use the pen."

Alice turns away from the wall she's been running her hands over for the better part of an hour, searching for the door the creature came in from. The two overly opinionated women relegated me to a chair after the fight. I'm not sure if I like them being in such well-regulated collusion.

Thank God Mary isn't here, or we'd be doomed.

Mary.

My brother's girlfriend's name is a fist straight to both my kidneys and balls.

What the hell am I going to tell her?

"Pardon?" Alice is asking.

"There's no way out," Sara continues. I won't tell her, but her hair now looks like a nest, and Grymsdyke a bird perched within it. Hell, the Spider has even gone and spun some webs to make it all the more comfy. "The room is sealed. Even if we could find a way out, there is no way for us to employ any stealth while hauling a heavy, ice-filled box and numerous machines alongside us. Since they're brothers, Finn will have to try to use Victor's pen to open a doorway into the room you found. And then he will need to immediately open another door to the Society."

I call out, "*He* is right here and can hear you. Did you forget that we're both adopted, so our blood type is different?"

My comment doesn't faze either woman, but it does bring them back over to where Victor and I are. "Is it even possible to open a door within one Timeline to another location in the same space?" Alice asks.

"Granted, I am not Wendy," Sara says, "and I do not have any technological working knowledge of how editing pens function, but I cannot help but surmise that, if one can open up a portal between time, space, and dimensions, which seems pretty damn impossible, it can do something as small as open a doorway between a much smaller amount of space."

Alice considers this. "We do not have a book with a photograph of that room."

"We have you and Grymsdyke." Sara motions to her new friend, as if none of us can see that a giant Spider isn't acting as a hat. "That will have to suffice."

Alice rests a hand upon my shoulder. "Do you think this is possible?"

I want to say no, but then I remember the Cheshire-Cat babbling on about how he believes in the impossible. And Katrina thinks it's possible, so. . .

I muster my remaining shreds of confidence. "Give me the pen."

Sara quickly grabs it and Society book off the table and passes them over to me.

"The room was on the same level I found you upon," Alice says. "It was carved of rocks and dirt—there was no sign of civilization save the two-dozen barrels of gunpowder within."

"What color was the door?" Sara presses.

Alice gives as much detail as she can. Grymsdyke adds his own impressions, and then I have them repeat it all until a firm image surfaces in my mind.

I rub a hand across my face, sweat beading on my brow. It's then I notice my mother hovering near the creature's body.

"You did good, Finn."

Her praise is vicious, and in turn, it viciously pleases me.

"Put it in his hand, and then place yours directly over it. Tell him what we're going to do. You two have forged enough notes in your time that you ought to be able to replicate his handwriting."

I do as my mother says. "I need you to help me edit, Victor." I shift the pen a bit. "We need to save a lot of people before we leave, so you're going to have to work with me here."

Not even a damn twitch answers me.

"Keep going. Don't give up."

I write out the directions for Alice's room, but nothing happens.

"Try again."

Victor's hand, the one I know for sure is his, is cold. Too cold. I know he's been packed in ice, but I have no idea how anyone's hand can be so cold.

I readjust his fingers around his editing pen, ensuring mine seamlessly overlap his.

"Talk to him. Tell him what to do. Don't let him give up, either. We Van Brunts don't give up."

Katrina now hovers behind a very quiet, strained Alice. It's getting harder and harder to hold on to her, though. And Jim hasn't returned since he left the torture chamber.

I'm losing them again, aren't I?

I take a deep breath and try to sound calm yet forceful. "Think about home. Think about how we need to save all these people and take them back with us. You're a doctor. You know that they need a safe place."

Does he even hear me? Is my brother even still here?

I lift the pen. Victor's handwriting is terrible, a doctor stereotype that perfectly fits. Mine isn't much better, but nonetheless, they are not remotely alike. I still try to mimic his style, though, as I write out the order to return to the medical wing.

And then. . .

Nothing happens.

The room tilts, and before I know it, Alice's arms are around me. She hasn't been talking much lately—or maybe she has, and I'm just not hearing.

Or noticing.

I won't tell her, but I'm worried. I can feel the thirteenth Wise Woman roiling around inside me, insidiously burning her way toward my soul. It's getting harder to see straight, harder to focus on anything but continuing to breathe in and out.

I have to get Alice to safety. Get Sara and Victor back home.

"Why do you resist, when you know that, in the end, you'll transform?"

I think I did transform, though. Once or twice. I don't feel like myself anymore—not entirely.

"Don't listen to her," Katrina snaps. She is now next to Victor and me. *"Don't even think about that bitch. Right now, the only other voice in your head is mine. Is that clear?"*

I wish I couldn't, but the thirteenth Wise Woman's influence is fighting to be stronger than even my mother's.

"Perhaps we ought to take a break," Alice is saying. "Try again in a bit."

No break. I shake my head too fast, and the room spins once more. "There's no time. If it's as close to dawn like we think. . ." I grip the edge of the box holding my brother, fumbling for his hand and pen.

Explosions are coming. Too many innocent people dead in an effort to wipe out the guilty.

Alice cannot die. I won't let her. Victor or Sara either. Hell, I can't even let the Spider die.

I'm friends with a Spider. How—

"Focus! Pull yourself together."

"Finn—"

"We need to get Victor home," I bite out more strongly than I ought to.

Alice does not release me. Instead, she becomes a strong backbone, holding me up. For his part, Grymsdyke says nothing from his perch on top of Sara's head. Sara, either. She and I are in the same boat, having been the thirteenth Wise Woman's playthings. Sara's trying so hard to keep herself together that, right now, I doubt she has the ability to talk.

I readjust the pen in Victor's hand and carefully overlap my fingers with his. Katrina bends over, her hand pressing down over mine. *"Together, then."*

"Think of a room filled with barrels of gunpowder," I tell my brother. "Help me save these people and then kick the asses of the ones we've been chasing."

Katrina kisses his forehead. *"Help us, my sweet boy. Don't you give up."*

This time, when I write out the instructions, a door appears. Beyond the frame lies a room filled with rock, dirt. . .

And barrels of gunpowder.

A naked man, cowering and covered in welts, peeks his head through the doorway.

Alice's relief is audible. "Harry!"

Terror and confusion fill the man's eyes. Thankfully, they are brown, not black. He answers in German, "My lady?"

New faces appear behind him, ones abused and covered in wounds. They're slaves, aren't they? Humans treated as nothing more than chattel.

Oh, hell no.

The fire in me stokes until the flames burn high.

Alice rushes to the doorway, urging the others to enter. "Did you light the fuses?"

It's done warily, but Harry and the others—a good dozen or so—step through, ashen as they take in their surroundings. "Yes, my lady," Harry says.

I want to pound my fists against guilty flesh at how these folk still cower, even now, even here. When I was a kid, I saw this kind of pain all too often. Blowing this damn mountain up is too generous an ending for the Chosen.

"Is this it?" Alice glances about the small crowd. "Are there none others?"

"No, my lady." Harry's shoulders droop. "There are not many of us." A bleakness sags his jowls. "The debased do not last long in our positions."

"Do you know if there are any other innocents present? Any that are not Chosen?"

The men and women shuffle their feet. Stare at the ground. No one answers.

These people are scared—no, terrified. It's plain as day, and yet, here they are, walking through glowing doorways, naked as jaybirds.

Trusting us to keep them safe. Trusting us to take them to freedom.

I can practically taste Alice's frustration, and share it. Technically, we have no guarantee all captives and slaves are accounted for. It eats at me that we can't assure that every last innocent is saved from this cursed place. But, as shaky as it is, Alice's plan must go forth.

We cannot allow the Chosen who remain here to escape.

We cannot allow the thirteenth Wise Woman to leave Koppenberg Mountain.

We cannot allow any more Timelines to perish.

I grab the Institute book, ready to open another door, when an explosion rocks the room. Our new companions cling to one another, openly screaming and weeping.

It takes three tries and a quartet of explosions before Katrina, a still-unconscious Victor, and I are able to open the second door. Beyond the glowing doorway lies the quiet medical wing of the Institute. Something feels wrong, though. It looks . . . dirty? Shit is strewn everywhere.

Alice ushers the group of naked, shivering servants through the doorway; Sara grips my arm. "Cover my eyes. Tie my hands together, behind my back. Quickly. I can't let them follow us."

She's angled her body away from the door. Kept her back to the other door, too.

Sara Carrisford is as close to a sister as I am ever going to get. I *know* her. Her heart, her soul—no matter what that asshole did to her—are good, and I will argue that to my last breath.

I do as she asked, but I make sure she knows it's under protest. "I trust you."

Her sad smile hurts. "Don't."

Another pair of explosions collapses part of the roof as I'm scrambling to find something to tie her wrists with. Stone crumbles down around us. "Put the earplugs in my ears, too," Sara says as she yanks off the sash that loops around her waist.

"This is insane. You know that, right?"

"Your safety is not insane. Man up, Finn. Think with your brain, not your heart."

When I push her into the Institute, I do a double take. It looks like a bomb has gone off. *What. The. Hell?!?*

Apparently on the same page as me, Alice says, "We shall figure it out later. Let us bring Victor home before it is too late."

I fear I am more hindrance than help as Alice and I push Victor and all the equipment he's hooked up to through the door. The walls and ceiling back in the mountain completely disintegrate. It's then that I hear *her*. Feel her wrath in my blood.

The Wise Woman knows I'm leaving. She knows what we've done.

Sara thrashes, fighting her way back toward the glowing doorway. She gnashes her teeth, yet Alice barks at Grymsdyke to hold his ground and keep his fangs retracted. Harry steps forth and grabs hold of my friend, wrapping his bony arms around her.

He's surprisingly strong for someone so scrawny.

One of the slaves yells in German, "She is one of them! She will kill us!"

Another man and woman step forth to help Harry. I need to get the door closed before any of the real Chosen find us.

Katrina hovers on the other side of the frame. Jim now stands behind her, his hand on her shoulder.

"I can't keep it open much longer." I motion them forward. "They're coming. *She's* coming."

"It's okay," Alice is saying from behind me. "Close it. We're all through."

"Stay strong." Tears shine in my mother's eyes. *"I love you. Take care of your brother and father."*

Jim's lips thin as he says, *"Don't give in, Huck. Don't let her win. We'll do what we can on this side. Take care of those people. They need you."*

The hell they're staying in Koppenberg. "I can't lose you two again. Please, just step through the door, okay? Just—"

The door winks away, leaving nothing but a damp, burned medical wing behind filled with a bunch of people who have only ever lived in medieval Germany.

It's then that the thirteenth Wise Woman's fury explodes within me.

ARSON

ALICE

FINN DROPS TO THE ground, the whites of his eyes visible as violent shudders wrack his body. I barely catch him before Finn's head slams upon wet, dirty floor that once shone.

If that were not bad enough, the woman who was screaming about the Chosen snatches a scalpel off the floor and rushes Sara, still held tightly in Harry's arms. She jabs the blade deep into Sara's chest. In German, she snarls, "I will die before I allow you to steal my soul!"

Sara cries out. Grymsdyke hisses and leaps from her head, landing on the perpetrator's. Harry pleads, "Please do not kill her! Ilse is just scared!"

It is then that I begin to scream—and pray that someone within the Society is still present that will hear me. Finn convulses in my arms. Sara is now on the floor next to me, bleeding profusely, the scalpel still in her chest. I have one hand on her, assuring her that I am present; my other arm is wrapped tightly around Finn.

The woman who stabbed Sara is hysterical.

What happened here in New York? Where is everyone?

"Push the red button on the panel next to the door," I beg in German to the woman standing closest to me. She is young, too young to have been abused so badly. "Please!"

She does not hesitate to do as asked. Once the button is depressed, a deafening peal fills the air. Chaos consumes the people I have brought back to the Institute; many drop to the ground, their hands covering their ears as they rock in fear. I continue alternating between shouting for help, begging Finn to wake up, and holding on to Sara.

How doth the little bird go mad. . .

A voice barks, "Put your hands up!"

As it is uttered in English, none of the company present follows this order. The A.D. skids into the room so quickly that when Grymsdyke leaps from Sara's all-too-still body to his, he slips upon the wet floor, landing on his arse whilst shrieking. A shotgun wavers in his grip as the assassin climbs up his chest. "BLOODY HELL, SPIDER. Are you trying to give me a heart attack?"

"My leg is sore." Grymsdyke gingerly motions his wrapped appendage. "I am merely using you as a means of transportation. If your heart chooses to battle you, that is of your own doing."

Van Brunt's assistant's focus finds Finn, Sara, and me several feet before him. "Alice?" The firearm lowers. "Jesus! When did you get here?" He glances around. "Who the hell are all these people? Is that Sara? Is that . . . was she *stabbed?!* Where did she come from? I left her in a motel, chained up!"

I cannot even appreciate the swift, yet fleeting breath of relief over discovering that the Piper did not locate nor slay the Artful Dodger. "Help them," is all I can say, plead, as his weapon clatters to the ground. He scrambles toward us. "Whatever is happening to Wendy is now afflicting Finn. And Sara. . ."

The A.D.—no, he is more than that now. He is more than a smarmy thief who thinks only of his own creature comforts. He has proven himself. My trust, for good or bad, has been gifted. *Jack* grabs hold of Sara. "I think Finn's having a grand mal seizure. Roll him to his side." He rips off his sweater, bunching it into a ball. "Lift his head so I can put this under it. Don't restrain him." And then, his eyes widen near comically as they glance upward, toward the ice-filled box nearby. "Holy shit, is that *Victor?!*"

Now that Jack is assisting Sara, I wrap both arms around Finn.

Grymsdyke kindly answers for me. "It is mostly the good doctor."

More footsteps sound seconds before a rumpled, crossbow-toting Marianne Brandon appears. "Jack, did you—" Her footing upon the slick floor is also unsteady, but she manages to right herself before meeting the same fate Jack did. Tears fill her bloodshot eyes. "Thank goodness you have all returned. Although, apparently under terrible circumstances. And with so many people. . ." Her cheeks blaze scarlet as she ducks her eyes. "Who are in dire need of clothing."

As she enters a code to cease the alarm, I round on the thief hovering over Sara. "What can we do to stop whatever is happening with Finn?"

"Nothing." Dark circles ring his eyes; soot smudges his face and hands. He yanks off his T-shirt before carefully tugging out the blade from Sara's chest. She cries out, a keening, pathetic sob before she stills. Did she pass out? Jack presses his shirt against the bleeding wound. "We have to wait it out; most seizures only last a few minutes. What triggered it? I've known Finn Van Brunt a long time, but I've never heard of him experiencing something like this." To Marianne, he says, "We can use some of our meds here, but Sara needs a doctor. Call an agent in—we don't want to risk the Piper getting hold of her again. But first, help me untie her."

Our colleague still averts her eyes. "Sara?"

"Crewe. Carrisford. You know, Finn's old partner?" Impatience snaps between them. "The lady who is hogtied and bleeding out beneath me? The one who had a rusty scalpel in her chest?" He waves it over his head.

"Don't take off the blindfold or ties," Grymsdyke warns. "It is her wish to remain constrained until the rapture fades."

Jack scowls. "I don't think now is the time to keep her tied up."

Grymsdyke's hiss sends shivers down even my back. "It is her wish, and we will respect it."

I grapple with my shreds of sanity, attempt to piece together the insanity of the last day as Marianne places a quick call to a Society doctor before excusing herself to fetch medicine. On her way out, she coaxes several women to accompany her. "His behavior has been erratic," I tell Jack. I pause as cords of anger and helplessness constrict my lungs. "He is in need of medical attention. He was tortured. He requires stitches and antibiotics."

I am rambling, and am well aware of it.

Jack glances around at our guests. "Did they do this?"

"No." It's a shotgun blast of a denial if there ever was one. "Well, to Sara, yes. I think it was out of fear for her quasi-Chosen state, though. These people were enslaved by the Piper and the Chosen. They aided us and deserve shelter and aid."

The A.D. accepts this, and the oddest urge to hug him for not arguing for once surfaces. I repress it, though. He will only get ideas. "And Victor?"

The spasms holding Finn hostage slowly lessen. Sara, too, is still, but that offers no relief whatsoever. Grymsdyke once more fills in the gaps more coherently than I. He informs Jack of what occurred in the laboratory between Finn and the creature, and of what actions toward Victor's person it gleefully claimed.

Marianne and the ladies return, bearing armfuls of random clothing from various Timelines that must have been raided from the Society's dressing room. Our technology savant shoves clothes at a shivering woman. "Please dress yourselves." Her eyes are anywhere but upon their bodies, and if I wasn't so on edge, I might very well laugh.

I had thought Mary quite prim once upon a time, but I fear Marianne might be even more so. If only she could meet the Hatter and the March Hare.

She hurries over to us. A bulging tote clinks as Marianne lowers it next to Jack.

The A.D. motions for her to maintain pressure on Sara's wound so he might sift through the bag. "Ahh, you brought the remaining cans of the healing spray. Excellent job, M!" To me, he says, "I'm no doc, but it'll be a good start."

"My lady, is there something I might do for you? Or any of us?"

I glance up to find Harry standing over me. He is wearing jeans and a button-down shirt, and looking very much like a small boy wearing his father's clothes. Others stand near him, wearing equally ill-fitting garb, but I take comfort in that they are warmer than they once were in a cold mountain. All bear matching expressions of expectation.

The woman who stabbed Sara is in a corner, in another's arms, still weeping. What must she have lived through in Koppenberg?

"A queen never allows her personal feelings to trample her duties to her people."

I swallow, squaring my shoulders as I remember this piece of early advice from my Grand Advisor. There are people here counting on me, ones I offered my protection to. "I apologize that you have been brought to a safe house that appears to no longer be quite as safe as I remember."

"We are out of the mountain," a man whispers. "We never thought such a day would happen. A place such as this surely must be heaven."

Jack pushes his smudged glasses back upon the bridge of his nose before he gently begins tearing Sara's dress away in order to access the wound. He says in German that is much better than mine, "Blimey. You all look as if you need some solid food. Wish I could offer you some right now, but I'm afraid it's going to have to wait a bit."

My eyes meet Harry's. "You are not in service to anyone within this building. All I ask of you is that you give us time to deal with whatever has happened before we arrived before we return you to your families."

"Some of us do not have families." It is a young man who says this, one far too young to bear the scars riddling his face. "The Lord and Lady of the Mountain and their kin ensured that. We have no homes, nowhere to go."

If homes are needed, I am certain the White King of Wonderland will allow these refugees to find sanctuary. Both the White and

Diamonds lands have long welcomed those fleeing other Courts. "Have no fear. I promise each and every one of you that we will not abandon you in your time of need. There is food here, shelter. When our colleagues return, we shall all come together to decide what is best for each and every one of you. It will be your choices, naturally."

I recognize the can in Jack's hand from Mary's laboratory. Not too long ago, Mary and Victor confiscated miraculous medicines from a futuristic Timeline in order to heal Van Brunt's injuries. Their handiness is unparalleled in situations such as these.

"Alice, you'll have to let me know where you think the majority of the injuries are," Jack says, "lest I strip them both naked right here and now."

"The floor is filthy." Marianne warily surveys the space. "A sterile area must surely be preferable to conditions such as these."

"Won't matter. This stuff," he shakes a canister, "kills all infections." There is no labeling upon the bottle, no ingredients or directions other than a simple name. "At least, that's what Mary's report said. Didn't bother to read the story myself."

"Perhaps I ought to be doing this?" Marianne squeaks as Jack continues to tear away fabric. "I am sure that she would appreciate her modesty, considering your reputation."

"It's not like I'm ogling her!" Jack cries. Sara's chest is fully exposed. "And it's not like it's the only pair of boobies I've had a gander at this day!"

The very air around us cramps as feet shuffle and eyes flit about, gleaming with the sheen of all that comes with having one's life upended, whether for the best or not.

My to-do list grows longer, heavier.

Finn's body finally, blessedly ceases shaking. Madness continues to grip my shoulders, though, whispering alluringly in my ears. I ask, "What happened here?"

Jack hovers close to Sara's chest, spraying in bursts before rifling through the bag for a different canister. "That musical, manipulative bastard somehow got ahold of Wendy." My colleague's voice cracks. "He convinced her to set fire to the Institute."

Dear God.

"She didn't know what she was doing." The protestation tilts more closely to threat, to warning of retribution should I choose to pursue vengeance rather than mere explanation. "She has no memory of those hours."

The crocodile smiles as it lures in its prey, swallowing them whole, doesn't it?

"How fare our colleagues?"

He mists the second spray across Sara's wound. "Some suffered burns, but nothing that couldn't be easily treated. We were able to stop the blazes before the fire department was notified." A grim line slashes across his mouth as he dabs the blood away from the injury. "The Institute wasn't so lucky, Your Majesty. Most of the library was destroyed. Labs, too."

I awoke from pleasant dreams to descend into one nightmare after another. "Any catalysts?"

Jack shakes his head, and his black-framed glasses dislodge from the brim of his nose. He applies a second dose of the first spray. "The Librarian has long assured that fire or explosions can't damage any of the cases. And nothing reached the Museum. Wen's clearance had already been revoked, so she couldn't get down there." He clears his throat, motioning with the can toward Finn, whose eyes have now closed. "He'll sleep off the effects of the seizure now. Don't be surprised if he's disoriented when he wakes up, or if he has a bit of amnesia."

Although Finn's golden-brown strands are sweaty and caked with blood, I savor the ability to run my fingers through them. "How is it a thief knows so much about seizures?"

Jack wipes at Sara's wound once more. Satisfied at whatever he sees, he glances around the room, at the people huddled together, disoriented by lack of orders for the first time in too long. He motions for one of the men nearby to toss him a stray blouse. "I read up on 'em after Wen started having 'em." He extracts a syringe out of the bag and wags it at Marianne. "Clever girl! I could kiss you."

Marianne smiles weakly. "Please don't."

As he injects the serum within into Sara, Jack explains it will put Finn's former partner to sleep. Once they are assured she is dozing, she is untied and the fresh blouse put on.

Jack smacks his hands. "Let's have a look at Finn. We need to get these two somewhere more comfortable, though. These folk, too."

The beds nearby are charred, more metal and springs than comfort. "Any damage to living quarters?"

"Some. Cleanup has been a bloody nightmare. My flat is tolerable, and it's closer than either of yours. We'll take Finn there. The others can find comfort in some of the flats around mine." He glances up at Victor. "Has he woken up?"

"No." And then, more quietly, "Where is Mary? Van Brunt?"

"Hunting for the Piper. They're all out there searching, except for me, Marianne, and the Librarian. We're the only ones still in the building. Well, and now you all."

"He was looking for the book. The codex." Jack's blue eyes widen as I say this. "The one Finn asked for you and Mary to steal. As it is missing from the mountain, I am assuming you were successful. Did he reclaim it—or rather, Wendy?"

"No. It's down in the Museum. The Librarian has been pouring over the damn thing." As Jack folds his gangly legs beneath him, Marianne removes everything from the medical bag, sorting the items into neat piles. "Everything happened so fast that we really didn't stop to think that it could be tied to the book instead of me and Mary. Shall I take off his shirt or you?"

His touch was surprisingly gentle with Sara, but I choose to meticulously peel away bloodied, tattered pieces of cloth from Finn's skin. "Have you learned anything about the book yet?"

"Other than it's enchanted? Not yet."

Once the shirt is removed, along with my makeshift bandages, Jack whistles. "Oi! They did a real number on 'im, didn't they?"

My fury, my agony, leaves me mute.

Marianne's emotions get the better of her, and part of me envies how open she is with them despite the restrictions of our similar Timelines. "What type of person can inflict such trauma upon another soul?"

The people in the room with us know the answer to that all too well.

Eventually, skin is mended, wounds are closed, and infections are calmed. The bluish-purple markings decorating Finn's torso return to their vivid, comforting state I have become accustomed to.

"We couldn't edit back into the mountain." My focus snaps back to a grimmer-than-usual Jack, now cleaning his glasses with his shirt. "I tried. Everyone did. The boss man was singularly focused on sending a team to extract you guys before the fires broke out. But we couldn't edit into 1812GRI-CHT no matter how hard we tried, let alone 1816/18GRI-GT."

I have no answer for his unasked question, though.

Rocking back, Jack swipes sweat and grime away from his brow. "What happened during the last few days? Were you able to escape the horde of Chosen?"

My answer is as brittle yet raw as I feel. "No."

Grymsdyke bursts into a flurry of coughs. "Your Majesty, as my ward is sleeping, I request permission to scout the Institute for further threats."

I give it, asking Jack and Marianne, "Might there be?"

"I rather doubt it, as we have been able to ascertain Wendy was behind the fires." Marianne repacks the medical bag. "Nonetheless, Jack and I have searched the building from top to bottom to confirm our suspicions." She zips the tote shut. "We haven't slept in. . ." Her laugh is more hoarse than joyful. "I honestly cannot recall the last time my head found comfort upon a pillow."

I must admit, I, too, find the allure in a pillow and bed. "Where exactly is the Librarian?"

The shifty woman's absence is puzzling, as her habit of appearing whilst spouting mysterious information is well documented within the Institute.

Jack's yawn is infectious. "She hasn't left the Museum since the fire."

A hitch unsettles my lungs as the muscles holding my bones

together lose their fight when Finn shifts in my arms. Blue-gray eyes leisurely come into focus; a reticent exhale of consciousness flutters across my hand still cupping his face. And then I laugh thickly when the man I love asks, "Why am I on the floor?"

AFTERMATH

FINN

THE INSTITUTE, THE ONLY place I've never wanted to run away from, no longer feels like the haven I once thought it, even though Alice and I offered it up as such to a group of terrified former slaves.

Marianne takes them to the mess hall and shows them rooms where they can clean up and rest. Some of the folks break down at the sight of beds, bathrooms, and pantries free for their use. Some maintain stoniness, shifting from nightmare to dreams, and I can only hope that, when they finally give themselves permission to wake up, we'll have resources available to them.

But for now, resources and manpower are severely lacking.

I have to give it to Wendy: she rained down hell within these walls. While some floors bear only minimal scarring, all are damp from sprinklers and novice fire fighters christened within split seconds. The musty scent of charred mildew permeates just about everything.

One of the world's greatest, albeit secretive, libraries is now unrecognizable. Ashes, blackened pages, and spines replace carpet and neat rows. Ladders that once curled to reach upper shelves are newly scorched. Couches and chairs are gutted. Lumps of melted stained glass form hardened puddles across the floor. Only the catalyst cases remain unscathed, their surfaces eerily gleaming amongst the gloom.

All of the main labs are useless; so are the weapons rooms. Outside of a handful of items stashed away in bedrooms, the majority of our weapons have smelted into misshapen, useless lumps of metal and charred slivers of wood. I have never been an armaments aficionado, despite my proficiencies, but taking in the remnants of antiques from across the Timelines is a one-two punch.

The Piper was able to gut us from the inside, using one of our own.

I want to put a bullet between his eyes, and name it Gwendolyn Peterson, AKA Wendy Darling.

From the A.D.'s report, Wendy used explosives set on timers. It no longer matters how she got them, or if they were ours or the Chosen's. As I tour the damage, I can't help but think that her actions weren't so much of an attempt to bring the Institute to its knees, but rather served as a message: the Piper and his ilk can get to us at any time they wish. They can pull Sara from an unknown Timeline, where she's incapable of accessing any kind of communicator. He can convince Wendy to betray the people she considers family and torch the only place she's ever considered home. He can instruct his minions to destroy catalysts, robbing people of their families. Destroying countless lives and legacies . . . and for what?

Marianne launches into a thorough report of the building's renewed security system once we reach the control room. On the surface, I'm impressed by her tenacity and creativity with newly developed, highly sophisticated security protocols and firewalls, especially considering the brief implementation timeframe. She's damn good at her job, which makes her misplaced, lingering sense of culpability all the more frustrating.

This isn't her fault. Hell, it isn't even truly Wendy's.

I send a message to Brom, informing him we've returned and that Sara is in our custody. That we've got a bunch of folk who require medical care and help. I don't detail Victor's state because there just isn't a good way to relegate the severity of the situation in a text. I can barely grasp it myself—what's been done to my brother, or whether he's still Victor. If he'll even wake up.

I might as well as be walking through nightmares and dreams, too.

Eventually, as we survey the wreckage of my father's office, Marianne quiets, as if she knows I'm on system overload. The Collectors' Society's symbol, which has loomed over its leaders' desks for centuries, now lies ruined upon the floor.

When I return to the medical wing, Alice and the A.D. are making some headway cleaning up. Victor remains in that grotesque icebox, the machines attached to him continuing to beep steadily. My hands unconsciously search for weapons I no longer have on me.

I killed the sonofabitch who did this to my brother, but there is no satisfaction to be had.

"Anything coming back yet?"

The A.D. is dumping a dustpan of blackened medical supplies into a trashcan. While his tone is neutral, even bordering on friendly, his beady eyes latch onto me like handcuffs.

Needles rake up and down my spine—at his legitimate question, at my inability to figure out what in the hell happened from the moment the door opened, at how other memories are hazy, like dreams, at the knowledge that I'm going to have to explain all of this to my father and Mary.

At how I let Victor down.

The shake of my head is a quick bite of irritation. Before I remind him he needs to mind his own damn business, Alice sidles up next to me. Soot streaks her cheeks. Her hair is disheveled. There is dried blood on her dress, the same one she wore when we entered the Grimm's Timeline. She moves in just a way that it's like she fears she'll shatter at the slightest wrong turn.

She offers me a broom. "Perhaps you can assist in sweeping up some of the mess?"

I accept the broom, wondering if I might actually cave and fall apart. We weren't even here when the chaos all shook down, and yet Alice and I are just as charred and weakened as the medical supplies and books that now lie in ruins upon the floor.

A yawning hole within me exists, one whose event horizon pulls everything in its wake like pieces of taffy. And yet, my skin is smooth; I bear no gaping wounds. There are no broken bones. While my pants are crusted with dried blood, I'm currently wearing one of the A.D.'s T-shirts. I have at least twenty pounds of muscle on the guy, so I'm constantly tugging the hem and sleeves down.

Victor calls these sorts of shirts smediums. He and I don't wear smediums. We mock the smediums.

Jesus. My brother is unresponsive. In a box. Stitched together like something out of a horror movie.

My brother.

So many nights, he'd wake up drenched in sweat from night-mares constructed around his biological father's creature. Sometimes the damn thing watched him. Sometimes it hunted him. Sometimes it would taunt him, in great detail, exactly what it would do if it ever got ahold of him.

Victor's mania and borderline schizophrenia were blamed for the dreams, even though Katrina insisted she never allowed him near the *Frankenstein* book or movies. Any representations always came from Halloween, of a green monster with bolts on the side of its head and oversized, clomping feet. His blood knew the truth, he insisted. He could describe the creature with eerie accuracy that matched Mary Shelly's: dark, lustrous hair; pale skin; black lips; cultured voice. When I was a senior in high school, I found the book in the library and skimmed it until I found his descriptions.

Shelly's creature looked nothing like Boris Karloff's.

Voices haunted Victor during the daylight and dark alike. He saw things no one else could. At times, he raved incoherently, unable to articulate his fears or excitement to any of us. He was paranoid more often than not, often of inconsequential matters. There were times when he would hide, or even become violent with those he loved. Worse yet were the times no one could get through to him, when he barely blinked and spoke no words.

Victor was deeply ashamed, even thought my parents and I constantly reminded him mental illnesses are nothing to be embarrassed about. What he suffered from was genetic. It was an illness, a disease. It was not self-inflicted.

It was not his fault. It was never his fault.

That explanation was not good enough for him. He kept researching until he discovered a protocol in a Timeline where medical advancements are closer to miracles than science. The treatment stabilized Victor to the point there were no hallucinations or voices. But there were—are—side effects, even when the benefits are extraordinary: skipping doses will lead to an unknown, terrible fate. It was explained to us as thus: a cancer patient might receive a medication that did away with carcinoma, but if regular dosages ceased, the malignant growths would come back and nothing could counter it again. The cancer would, in fact, transform into something worse than before, like cancer on steroids mixed with advanced AIDS and Ebola. Something unpredictable, something insidious and different for each person who fails the protocol.

With such possibilities looming, Katrina was adamant about Victor not taking the protocol. She begged him to trust that he could manage his illnesses with other treatments alongside the support of his family and counseling, but his embarrassment and fear of failure deafened him. He wanted a shot at what he thought was normalcy, but the thing he never understood is that normalcy is nothing more than an illusion we try to fool ourselves with. That he, just as he is, is *enough*.

He extracted promises from all of us to never allow him to forget his dosages, even if he argued or resisted. And, because we love him, because we believe in him, we gave those vows.

He didn't take the protocol when we were stuck in 1905BUR-LP. Too many days stretched out between doses. He bounced back, though. But now, with even more days gone. . .

My replacement phone beeps, dragging my blurred focus away from the jagged line running across Victor's scalp. It's a text from Brom. He'll be home in the morning. A numerical code follows, signaling the implementation of a silence directive.

The A.D. chugs a cup of cold coffee. "Why don't you and Alice go get cleaned up? I just got word that a handful of agents are en route. They're bringing in a fancy-shmancy cleaning crew and some medical personnel to look over Victor and the ladies and gents you brought back. Speaking of the Doc, I'll cobble together a list of specialists within associated Timelines."

My surprise must show, as there's a bit of hurt shading his eyes, although I'm positive he'd rather walk across coals than admit it.

"I'll stay in order to debrief." I'm not overly comfortable leaving Victor alone.

"Look." The A.D. rubs the back of his neck. "I din't want to have to say this, but you've left me no choice. You don' smell too pretty right now, or at least like how your pretty self normally does. And while some of us may have grown up around such delightful scents, others haven't." He leans in. "Even Her Majesty is a bit ripe, although I am not goin' to be the one to tell her."

"You're an asshole."

His grin is rubbery and wide. "Why, thank you, gov'ner."

I really don't have time for a shower, even though it sounds like heaven. "I ought to head down to the Museum to talk to the Librarian."

The A.D. whips out his phone. He scrolls through his texts before showing me the screen. "She's triggered a silence directive for the next five hours."

An irritated sigh builds up within my chest. "Brom, too."

The A.D. glances toward the open doorway leading to a recovery area. Alice is within, sweeping up broken glass. "She's got some injuries, too." His voice drops so low that there's no way she can hear him. "You ought to have a look at 'em. Her Majesty is doing what she does best, acting like nothing touches her, but she's moving slower than normal. Her back ain't so smooth."

Annoyance flares. "Why didn't you use the sprays on her like you did me?"

"And have her slap me for impertinence?" He snorts. "You know the lady."

When I say nothing, he crosses his gangly arms across his chest. "Get some food in your bellies. Fix up your pretty girlfriend so she can kick arse at one hundred percent again. Get some rest while you can, because you two need to hit the ground running in the morning. We ought to have the Institute back in fighting condition by then, and we need our top players ready to go. This is no longer a marathon, Finn. We're in a bloody race to the finish, and I'll be damned if we let that arsehole win."

It's almost like I don't know the person standing before me, his fire is so hot.

"If anything comes up—"

"Yeah, yeah. I'll come and get you. Now, get the hell out of here. I'll stay with Victor until the docs come."

I almost want to hug the bastard.

I find Alice in the other room, broom and body leaning against a wall. Her eyes fly open at the sound of her name, her cheeks flushing.

"I was simply considering how best to tackle this room." It's offered defiantly.

I don't argue, even though we both know differently. "I'm told I smell terrible. Want to come upstairs with me so we can take a shower?"

She glances around at the mess, and I fill her in on what the A.D. reported. Like me, she's reluctant to leave, but the weight of the last week is too heavy to ignore. I bring the tote filled with medicines. As the elevator was another of Wendy's targets, we are forced to climb stairs, and Alice slows down even further. Miraculously, both of our apartments are only minimally damaged, more likely from the aftermath of nearby explosions and sprinklers rather than being epicenters.

I grab a clean change of clothes and my razor before heading back into Alice's. She's already in the bathroom, peeling off layers of medieval clothing. It's then I notice the darkened slashes in her gown, and of how she winces with each movement.

I am such an asshole for not noticing beforehand.

My hands stay hers. "Allow me?"

In the mirror before us, I watch the flash of relief sweep across her lovely face. I ask her to hold on a minute before rummaging around in one of her desk drawers for a pair of scissors. I carefully cut off the dress, corset, and chemise from her body, ensuring the blades go nowhere near her injuries.

I miraculously stay calm when I ask where all of the wounds come from.

She shivers when air meets skin. "I fought my way out of the dungeons."

My warrior queen.

I dig out the bottles of healing spray and make sure each and every scab, bruise, and cut marring her body is attended to.

"I've suffered worse. These are nothing but scratches." She holds perfectly still for me, head held high, and I marvel, once more, at her resiliency.

When I'm done, and all that's left is crusted blood and dirt, I lead her over to the shower. Beneath the steam, warm water, and soap bubbles, all of the physical reminders of the mountain spiral down the drain.

Too bad memories can't follow.

Her mouth finds mine, her tongue demanding entrance. The kiss isn't gentle, or soothing, but desperate. It's matched in kind, because even though its dirt has left my body, the mountain's darkness crawls within me. I press her against the cool, white tiles, deepening the already blazing kiss, desperate to lose myself in her light. Her hands leave my chest, traveling lower until she swallows my gasp. She strokes me until I no longer see straight, until every nerve ending in my body focuses toward a singular need.

"I want you in me." Her hot breath weakens my knees. "Now."

I reach over to turn off the water, but she knocks away my hand. "*Now.*"

I lift her up; her legs curl around my waist. She grips my shoulders before pushing downward, until I'm fully seated. Both of us groan, the rhythm of our bodies and feelings instinctually shifting into drive. I have one hand curved around her gorgeous ass, one planted firmly against the tile as I pound into her. She nips my ear, my neck, kisses me until I fear I'll unravel. She clenches so tightly around me as I move in and out, like if she had her way, our bodies would never separate.

I'm down with the idea.

An earthquake rattles her body as she cries my name, and seconds later, a quake of my own rocks my balance. I dig my face into her neck, her wet hair sticking to my face as I spill the strength of my feelings for this woman into her body.

Once we've caught our breaths, she turns off the water and leads me to her bed. We don't bother drying off before her mouth claims mine and the dance is started anew.

No more words are said. There is no need. When my eyes finally drift shut, my emotions and body temporarily sated during a wartime reprieve, I know we said all that was necessary without a single syllable uttered.

A MYSTERIOUS BOOK

ALICE

THE LIBRARIAN FAILS TO chide me for being late, and it triggers warning bells. I'm offered a cup of tea that smells and tastes suspiciously similar to my favorite strain from Wonderland, alongside an apology for the lack of proper seating.

An apology . . . from the Librarian?

A number of agents, including myself, have gathered in the Museum. Hidden by copious amounts of security and located deep beneath the Institute, countless catalysts housed in gleaming, glass cases stretch out as far as the eye can see. Peppy music pipes through hidden speakers throughout the secretive location, utterly inappropriate melodies for the Museum's current inhabitants or their moods.

For the first time in our association, the Librarian appears, dare I say, frazzled and even unkempt. Her normally glossy, long black hair is piled high into a messy chignon; her clothes are rumpled. And . . . is that a tea stain upon her blouse?

The sight of her in such a state is far more unsettling than any of the damage wreaked upon floors above.

Jack bounces on the edge of a metal folding chair stationed across from mine. He yanks off his glasses, massaging the bridge of his nose. "Had to sedate Sara awhile back. She was behaving in a very unprincess-like manner."

Finn's eyes narrow, prompting Jack to clarify, "She's restrained in a bed, so at least now she's not rolling around on the floor like a hog tied before transport."

Hanging from a newly constructed web in the corner of the Librarian's office, Grymsdyke's cough sounds more ominous than practical. "You are disrespecting her wishes by releasing her from such bindings."

Jack slips his glasses back on. "She was banging her head against the wall, and now she's got an ugly gash across her forehead. Traitor or no, she was always kind to me. I'm not going to stand by and watch her bash her brains out in the name of that arsehole."

Henry Fleming, one of the Society's best field agents, stretches his legs out in the small space afforded him. He and a few others arrived at the Institute only an hour before, weary after their combined missions. Unfortunately, there is still no word from Van Brunt or Mary. "I'd read the reports on Sara, but. . ." Fleming brushes a piece of lint off of his military-style pants. "It's as if she's possessed. She's better off in the bed."

Jack glances toward the corner, at the large assassin hovering there. "Don't worry, my spider friend. Our princess is still blindfolded and deaf to the world, as the lady requested."

"Sara Carrisford risked much in order to assist Finn when I was in the dungeons, and then again when we sought a way out." My fingers curl into the fabric of my dress as I dare anyone in the room to contradict me. "She is not Chosen, nor the Piper's—at least, not fully. She continues to fight against the Piper's influence, and we must do whatever we can to aid her in the battle for her soul."

Seated behind her desk, the Librarian observes me over the rim of her teacup. I return the action in kind. Does she have no snide instructions or mystical insights to offer?

"Of course we're going to help her," Finn is saying. "She's family."

"All that's well and good, but what about Wen? Doesn't she deserve our help, too? Isn't she family?" A dark flush steals up Jack's neck, across his fair cheeks. "What she did—that wasn't *Wendy*, and you all know it."

Seated beside him, a laptop perched on her knees, Marianne pats his arm. "None are blind to such a fact, Jack. Lest you forget, Brom ensured Gwendolyn is receiving the best possible care. She is—"

"Alone." His lean frame shoots up like beanpole in the sun. "Somewhere far from everyone who loves her."

"It was her choice, freely given during a moment of clarity." The Librarian reunites her cup and saucer. "Wendy insisted upon a placement where we could assure the Piper could not touch her. And that is exactly what Brom did."

"Where exactly is she?" Finn asks.

The Librarian waves a hand. "By design, only your father knows the exact location in an undisclosed Timeline. Be rest assured, though. Every precaution has been taken to protect Wendy."

"I have no doubt that Brom did his best." Finn leans forward, elbows propped on legs, arms dangling between in between. "But the Piper and/or his Chosen were able to get to Sara, even though only the A.D. and Alice knew what Timeline she was in. What's to stop him from getting to Wendy again?"

The Librarian fingers a small sugar biscuit on a nearby plate. "Faith."

Well now. If that isn't a patently shoddy Librarian answer, I do not know what is.

Franklin Blake arrives, dropping a satchel just beyond the doorframe. His clothes are rumpled; dark circles ring his normally cheery eyes.

"Any luck?" Fleming asks as he passes our colleague several sheets of paper.

Blake settles into the last free chair, running a hand through mussed hair. "All leads have disappeared. I can't guarantee it one hundred percent, but I would gladly place a wager insisting there are no Chosen left in this New York City, let alone this world."

"What about Connecticut?" I press. "At the John and Paul School for Gifted Children?"

Van Brunt, Jack, and I investigated the mysterious school shortly after a conversation with Sara revealed a connection between the institution and the Piper. There, we not only captured one of the Piper's lieutenants, a rather crazed woman by the name of Grethel Bunting, but encountered several of the Chosen as well. It was shortly afterward that we learned the John and Paul School for Gifted Children served as a local base for the Piper's minions.

"We raided it," Franklin is saying. "There wasn't even a single piece of paper found upon the premises." He jerks his chin upward toward Finn. "Brom enacted Protocol 11."

"What is Protocol 11?" I inquire.

"We have a reserve squad of agents, built up of members from across various Timelines," Finn explains. "The team can function in a variety of ways, including as a military unit, if necessary." He brushes his forefinger across his upper lip. "Until now, we've never used them as such, though, especially since we aren't officially a military body." His attention reverts to Blake. "Did local authorities pose any problems?"

"None. A local contact intervened on our behalf. After we left, the FBI assumed control over the case and is now investigating the school for alleged child abuse."

Which is, ironically, a truth of the complicated situation.

Fleming peers down at a copy of the report Finn and I submitted two hours earlier. "How certain are you two that the explosives set off in 1816/18GRI-GT were successful?"

When lines form between Finn's brows, and his focus blurs from continued confusion over the last hour before we left the mountain, I say smoothly, "Not at all. Although, considering the room we were within prior to departing was demolished, I figure there must be a level of some success."

Fleming considers this. "Think any of the folk you brought back with you might be willing to share what they know about the inner workings of the Piper's organization?"

"That is a question you must ask them."

Fleming nods. "After we're done here," he says, "I'll go round and see if anyone is willing to talk."

Blake glances up from his copy of the report. "I'll go with you."

I turn toward the Librarian. "Jack informs me that you have been examining the book he and Mary stole from the Piper's lair. Is there any progress in determining its nature or importance?"

She pushes aside her tea in order to slide a heavy, leather-clad tome toward the middle of the desk. Taut lines form around her eyes and mouth. "No."

I wait, but nothing follows. "No?"

The lines become more defined. "No."

"Is it written in a language that you do not know?"

She snorts, inelegantly so. "There are no languages I do not know."

Her ego is astounding. What nonsense. "Is it in German?"

"No."

I wait once more, yet she offers no further response. I no longer hold back the rude burst of agitated air that shoots through my nose. "I do not particularly feel like playing any of your games today, including having to pry each and every detail of this book out of you. If you would just—"

"I do not tell you anything," she interrupts tartly, "because I do not know anything." She flips open the book and holds it aloft. The pages facing us are blank. She turns a gilded-edged, yellow-brown page; the next sheet of parchment is blank, as well. A chunk of pages is skipped, only to reveal more empty sheets. She does this several more times before displaying the cover and spine. There are no words, let alone symbols, to be found.

I leaf through the book myself, frustration mounting. "I am certain this is what the Piper is looking for. *This* is why he was no longer within the mountain once I broke free from the dungeons. There was much terror in my jailer's voice when he mentioned how *'the codex is missing.'*" I face Jack. "Was it as thus when you absconded with it?"

"I din't exactly flip through it when Mary and me were running away from hordes of psychotic kids," he says, frowning. "Staying alive was a bigger priority. I handed it over to the Librarian as soon as we edited back into the Institute."

"Perhaps it is like some books in other Timelines, ones that require light from moons, fading sunsets, or other certain times of significant days," Blake muses.

I run the pads of my fingers across the pages. The pulp within is thick and textured, not entirely smooth. It is not parchment, as I originally believed.

"This is papyrus." And possibly Egyptian?

"Perhaps." The Librarian takes the book from me. "Or something similar."

"If I am not mistaken, papyrus is the oldest type of paper, dating as far back to the. . ." I dredge through long distance memories from a childhood spent in Oxford offices and classrooms. "Fourth millennium before Christ."

"In this world, yes, this is true." She settles her small frame back into her oversized chair. "But it is not for other worlds."

"Do not all Timelines find their origins in this one?" I ask. "From authors who live here?"

The corners of her lips nudge upward a small tick. "That is the hypothesis the Society has worked under for some time."

She is utterly maddening. "Why only a hypothesis?"

"It has not yet been proven." She leans forward, folding her well-manicured hands. "This book does nothing to verify that idea, either."

"Could we not test the paper? See if it originates from the papyrus plant?"

"And potentially destroy its secrets?" Tendrils of black hair spill from her chignon as she shakes her head. "It matters little, anyway. I cannot access this book because it is enchanted."

A tiny scoff escapes Marianne. Blake nods sagely, as if this is confirmation of his suggestion.

"You think it was the thirteenth Wise Woman who enchanted it, don't you?"

Finn's voice is emotionless as he says this, but the tic that ripples upon his jaw does not escape my notice.

"I would very much like to talk about her with you." The Librarian's head tilts as her vivid blue eyes narrow upon him. "Provided you are willing to do so after all that she has done to you."

Her careless yet paradoxically carefully placed words seize all of my nerves, paralyzing me. I . . . I knew that Finn had been tortured, I knew that the Chosen attempted to bring him to rapture, but I did not have confirmation the thirteenth Wise Woman personally dealt with him.

I know little of the magical fiend, other than she is one of thirteen sisters who once guided 1812GRI-CHT. Slighted by a king's negligence to include her in attendance at a banquet honoring his newborn daughter, the thirteenth Wise Woman cursed the child to a hundred year's sleep that could have lasted much longer, had a prince not arrived with true love's kiss. Coupled with her relationship with the Piper, and the assumption that she is in love with a murderer, I cannot help but assume that she, too, is a psychopath.

I reach for Finn's hand, uncaring that everyone in the room is witness to my dread. My grip is tenacious, too firm to be soothing. But then, terror does not allow for tenderness.

Finn tolerates my hold, though he does not return in kind. There are no assurances offered, no comfort. He simply nods, his mouth an ominous slash of a line.

Word arrives, via Jack's phone, that Van Brunt and Mary are expected by nightfall. When the meeting adjourns, all depart save the Librarian, Finn, and myself. Even Grymsdyke hops upon Jack's shoulder, insisting he will once more scout the Institute for anything nefarious.

I refuse to vacate unless Finn demands it so. Part of me wants to, though. Desperately. Part of me wishes to find the sharpest of blades and find a way back into 1816/18GRI-GT, for if the thirteenth Wise

Woman truly invoked magic upon Finn. . .

There would be no Timeline she would be safe in, not if she still draws breath.

"The report from the doctors is encouraging." Clearly broaching a safer topic, the Librarian presents Finn with a folder. As he peruses its contents, she continues, "Victor's heart is strong and brain functionality is within normal ranges, considering. According to their diagnoses, though, he is in a medically induced coma."

How is it that a creature in a Timeline such as 1816/18GRI-GT would have access to medicines that can do such a thing?

Finn holds aloft a translucent black, gray, and white sheet of plastic that has outlines of human bones upon it. "How is this possible?"

His question, muttered beneath his breath, is for the Librarian, not me. I peer at the plastic sheet, curious as to what it is he sees. His brows pull together as he holds aloft another sheet similar to the first. This one features the outline of a skull. "Are you sure these are Victor's?"

The Librarian rises from her chair only to perch upon the desk, one leg crossed over the other. "I cannot think why the doctors who have examined him thus far would deceive us."

He tugs out yet another black-and-white sheet. "Are the wounds superficial, then?"

I can no longer bear it. I ask, "To what is it you're referring?"

He runs a finger across the outlines of bones from the first sheet. "There are no signs of fractures, no indications of bones being cut or sawed." His frown deepens. "Victor broke his arm when he was in college. A friend dared him to jump off a building. Even though it healed, there'd still be evidence of it in these x-rays. But there's nothing. Not one bone looks as if it has ever been broken."

"It's most intriguing, is it not?" the Librarian posits.

Alarming is more like it.

"Read the rest of the report, Finn, although I fear you will have more questions than answers."

As he does, I slide a photograph of Victor out and tap upon one of the arms. "Victor had matching tattoos ringing both biceps. This skin is now bare."

"He got those as a dare, too," Finn murmurs. And then his face pales as he pinches a handwritten report so tightly wrinkles form.

I come closer "What is it?"

His eyes are bleak when they meet mine. "They did a biopsy on his different limbs. The arm. . ." His throat bobs as he swallows. "It's not biologically the same. Neither is one leg." He rubs his upper lip. "Part of his scalp is different." More quietly, hoarsely, "But there's an eye that isn't his, too."

Dear lord.

Finn shoves the paper toward the Librarian. "How is this possible? How do the bones show no signs of grafting? One of his legs is black now, so unless the creature knew how to change pigment, it's a given that leg is different. How is it that my brother's blood type went from AB to *unknown*?"

I take the paper from him as she says, "I wish I had the answers to give you, Finn. I do not, though. Not yet."

Finn tugs both hands through his hair, swearing quietly. Before I can peruse the page, he says, "I need a minute to take this in," and then exits the office.

"Leave him be," the Librarian tells me. "Finn, like most people, requires time to process the unimaginable when faced with it."

An eyebrow lifts. "And I do not?"

"Only those found within the Twenty-First Century," she says mildly. "Although you did an admirable job of doing so in short time." She stands, brushing her hands together. "I'm glad for the few minutes alone with you."

"Are you, now?"

Bold as bold can be, she says, "As you well know, things are not always what they seem."

"Are you referring to Victor?"

"Unfortunately, no." Her attention flits toward the office door, still propped open. "Although time will tell if he is the Victor we know and love. No, I am simply reminding you that you must be ever vigilant in your quest."

"I have long tired of your riddles," I say coolly.

A sense of weariness sags her physically tiny yet always metaphorically giant shoulders. "Do not allow your suspicions of my loyalties to dissuade you from doing what is right."

Fine. I will then start with, "Who are you?"

Her smile is fragile, less smug than the standard I am accustomed to. "I am someone who believes in the Collectors' Society and its agents."

My chin tilts upward. "You refuse to answer, even now, even when so much is at stake."

"You wonder if I am an ally or an enemy, friend or foe." Her neck cranes so her eyes can meet mine. "You wonder how so many within these walls come to me for guidance and help without asking the same question. Shall I tell you that you are right in wondering these things? I will, if that will ease your conscience."

My pulse escalates until the dull roar of its beat in my ears.

"Allow me to answer this one thing for you today. Know that I am freely offering you this, because I respect you and your suspicions, Alice. Many have known me as an angel; many more have known me as a monster. It is always intent that makes the difference."

Something flashes in the depths of blue still rooting me to this spot, something infinitely, primitively menacing. I am taken back to nights spent as a child, when every sound was followed by worries over beasties or ghouls beneath my bed or within my armoires. My screams would be soundless, fear would strangle me so. And now, a graveyard sprouts across my skin, hundreds of tiny tombstones rising out of nowhere. A ghost's hand traces the length of my spine.

I ask carefully, "What is your intent within the Society?"

She clucks, amusement replacing the ghastliness I just witnessed. "I already answered that question for you long ago. You should know by now that, while I may not always give you all that you wish for, I am no liar. Lying does little for my complexion."

She laughs then, merrily, loudly, and the goose pimples upon my arms double.

Finn reappears in the doorway, sheepish yet exhausted all at once.

"I'm still worried about my memory or if I'm seeing things right. I wanted a moment to take it all in."

The Librarian brushes past me, toward him, the scent of her floral perfume strong. "Apologies are wholly unnecessary in this instance. You are merely human. Now, shall we discuss the witch you met?"

I make my way over to where they stand, unnerved on several fronts. "You think of the Wise Women as witches?"

"It is a broad term that has long painted women of magic." Her shrug is elegant, dismissive. "It will suffice for the time being."

Finn chooses, like I, to remain standing, his body drifting closer to mine. "I don't remember a lot of our encounters, to be honest. What I do. . ." He bites his lip. "The images blur together, like watercolors left out in a rainstorm. Like dreams, I guess."

"How many times did you see her?" My question is hoarse, tainted with too much trepidation.

A weighted minute or so passes. The Librarian slowly loops around him, us, her eyes slits as she traces every inch of his body. His, not mine, although it feels as if her sight passes straight through my skin and bones so that it can find his. "No, don't try to answer." She ceases pacing. "You won't be able to."

A small flinch shudders across his shoulders. "Why not?"

Rather than answer him, the Librarian wanders back to her desk for her teacup. "Remember what we discussed, Alice. I'll see you two when Brom returns tonight." Then she pivots and heads into the catalyst stacks.

"What did you two discuss?" Finn asks as she disappears around a corner.

I tell him the truth. "I honestly have no idea."

TWO DIFFERENT-COLORED EYES

FINN

THE COMMUNAL DINING HALL is busy—not with Society agents, but with folks still shook up from a swift exit out of their original Timeline. Up until the day before, while many witnessed various advanced technologies brought back into Koppenberg Mountain, none had personally visited worlds where society advanced beyond slavery. There are still lots of tears and many folks who drift hesitantly, as if fortune will change in the blink of an eye. Too many stoop when standing or shy away from those who do not share the bonds of Koppenberg slavery. I don't blame them, not after what I experienced in that hellhole. All we can do is give them space and as much comfort as possible. We've brought in a translator to help erase the wall erected by language. Our guests are clean and wearing new clothes. They are under the care of excellent physicians. Their bellies are as full as they wish them to be.

It's a start.

"We ought to officially present ourselves," Alice told me after our meeting with the Librarian. "Especially you, as the standing official representative for the Collectors' Society."

It was the queen in her, thinking about the concerns of others. And it's the same now as she benevolently commands the room, inquiring about health, sleep, and necessities. When men and women drop to their knees before her, offering their names and clutching her hands as they press kisses against her skin, she soothingly reminds them that they owe her no service, nor should they bow before her. Their days of service are done, if that is what they wish. More tears flow, along with gratitude. Harry, the de facto spokesman of the group, talks briefly about the hope of new mornings. Strangers wish both Alice and me well, thanking us for risking much to ensure their safety. Prayers are offered in our names, and I cannot help but wonder if this is what Alice's life was like back in Wonderland.

As lunch of pizza is served, which is met with both suspicion and then delight. Harry joins us in passing out drinks and napkins. Alice encourages him to sit down and eat, but he stubbornly insists on helping out. "Too many here have only served. None know what it is like to *be* served."

Once everyone has what they need, Alice ushers Harry to a table. I bring him a couple slices of pepperoni and some salad. As he pokes at the melted, greasy cheese, Alice asks, "Did two gentlemen by the names of Henry Fleming and Franklin Blake come to speak with you?"

"Indeed they did, my lady. I was happy to talk to them and answered as many questions as I could." A black smudge of defeat appears. "And yet, I feared what would happen if they were to discover my betrayal."

"You have betrayed no one," Alice assures him. "A person belongs to themselves, and no one else."

It's not entirely true, though. I hold no illusions or grudges that my heart belongs to her. Willingly, though. Consensually.

She continues, "Allow me to promise you and the others that we will do everything within our powers to ensure your continued safety."

When he gazes upon her, it's with adoration. It's another thing I can't blame him for. I look at her the same way, like she's the brightest star in the sky.

As they discuss the definition and merits of psychological counseling, especially in light of the risk of rapture, I focus more on Alice than what she's saying. On how her shoulders remain straight and strong when she speaks to others, only softening in private. On how her voice changes, too—how she is so self-assured and steady in any public situation, yet when she pushes past the queenly veneer, there's a heartbreaking quality to everything she says. Her hands, elegant and pale, can alternately serve as weapons and yet deliver kindness and bliss.

Before Alice, the concept of love was nebulous. I grew to love my family. There were friends I loved, like Jim. Attraction and lust ruled intimate relationships. Once upon a time, I thought I might be in love, but after a month of hot sex and little else, Avery and I decided we were better off friends. I wasn't broken by the transition; in fact, I was relieved when we shifted gears. There were no tears on either side and neither of us argued about the switch. When Avery and I get together nowadays, always as mere friends, that month never comes up. One night, after too many beers, Victor insisted that was how one knew if it was love or not: if it left a mark, a hole, if it lingered . . . it was real.

I trace the curve of Alice's lips, the bow that forms at the top, with the paintbrush of my mind. If she were to walk away from me today. . .

I wish that we'd met under different circumstances. If only life and death weren't commonplace occurrences. That, instead, we could debate restaurants and movies rather than ways to bring down a mass murderer. I want us to go dancing, rather than travel to distant lands in order to find ways to save one another. I wish that guns and swords and homicidal maniacs were not the norm.

But I would never wish her away.

When I was in Koppenberg's torture chamber, I held fast to a daydream. If I lived through a minute, an hour, the day, I promised myself, I would be that much closer to finding out whether or not my hopes would ever become realities. Alice and I were older, in my dream, and were at a kid's birthday party. My arm was around her; her head was on my shoulder. Someone who looked an awful lot like Alice, but had my hair color, bent over the child, reminding them to blow out the candles on their cake.

I want that. I want that pretty damn bad.

I want her. Forever. She owns me as much as any person can own another without the chains of slavery.

Brom and Mary arrive ten minutes after sunset. They come up from the garage, indicating whatever mission they were on most likely meant car rather than editing pen.

We convene in the conference room, which will have to serve double duty as his office until the other is officially renovated. He claps me on the shoulder but rethinks the action, pulling me into a bear hug. "Glad you made it home, son." More loudly, as he pulls away, "You worried us by staying away so long."

Mary says nothing, but there's no need to. Her questions are written plain as day across her pinched face.

Brom tosses a rain-slicked wool coat onto the back of a chair. "Where is Victor? Call him and let him know that we must debrief the past week's events."

I can do this.

Only, as I open my mouth, I can't. Any coherent words are themselves sucked into the event horizon of the black hole inside me.

Alice shakes out Brom's coat before hanging it on a nearby coat rack. "Victor is currently within the medical wing, under the care of a number of physicians and specialists."

Mary bolts for the door, but the A.D. swiftly blocks her from barreling through.

"Let me out lest you wish to become a eunuch." It's as sinister of an order as Mary has ever issued.

No matter how hard she shoves, he refuses to budge. "Stop flirting, luv, and give Her Majesty a bit o' time to explain everything."

Mary's balled fist swings, only to be caught by Brom.

"Finn," my father says, "what the hell is going on?" His ruddy face is considerably paler beneath his beard, just like it was the day we discovered our mother's Timeline was destroyed with her in it.

My mouth is dry. My stomach bottomed out. I ask Mary, "Did you tell him anything about what happened before you left Koppenberg?"

Brom's sharp, "Tell me what?" fires off at the same time Mary stamps her foot and shrieks, "You have better not failed me, Finn Van Brunt!"

"We, uh, thought it best not to say anything." A flush steals across the A.D.'s neck. "All we said was that you were still searching for the Piper. Best not to cause a colossal panic amongst the masses." He crosses his arms, mustering enough courage to meet my father's intense fury. It's a miracle he doesn't collapse in a pile of ash. "But then, the bastard brainwashed Wen into bombing the Institute, and it was assumed he was in New York, or nearby, so. . ." His shrug is tight and defensive.

Brom rounds on me. "I want an immediate explanation."

I glance at Alice, who steps around the table, toward me. "The A.D. and Mary were sent back to the Institute with a book that we suspected was important. The rest of us, save Grymsdyke, were captured."

Mary's fight drains away as she ceases thrashing about. Brom releases her arm, the blood leaching once more from his face. I tell the story behind what happened to Victor, then Alice and me, as simply and unemotionally as possible, which is damn hard. In the end, it's a woefully piss-poor summation, but too many memories still hold a hazy sheen to them.

Mary's steps are wobbly. "Victor is here, though? Being tended to by doctors?"

"I'm sorry." The black hole within me roars hungrily. "I'm so sorry."

"This is not your fault." Alice is in front of me, as if she knows I'm at risk of spiraling furthering into the vat of forgetfulness. "You bear no responsibility toward these fiends' actions." She fills Brom in on the rest of the details, and those bright Van Brunt eyes move up and down my body, searching for wounds that now live within the black hole inside me. All I see is Mary, crying.

What's between my brother and Mary is real, too. His pain is her pain.

Only family, including Alice and Mary, head to the medical wing. Fresh paint covers the walls, and the aroma of bleach is strong. Puttering about are more doctors than I originally assumed would be present. New instruments line the walls, along with temporary tables, undoubtedly brought in from various Timelines associated with these men and women. One that lives in New York and moonlights for the Society as needed over the years goes over the litany of Victor's ailments and miracles for us. While he's kind, especially to Mary, who cannot keep her focus off of my brother, each new unknown is a blade through skin and muscle. No one can explain how there are four different people's DNA found in his body, including a blue eye and a black leg. There are no conclusive explanations as to why his bones fail to show any grafts or pins on x-rays, or as to why there are no signs of atrophy in his muscles.

"I know it sounds crazy," Dr. Addu says to us, his head bobbing up and down thoughtfully, "but if we hadn't done DNA testing, I would have sworn this is the body he was born with." He gives Brom Victor's chart. "We ran every test twice." He nods toward the others in the room. "We have some calls in to other specialists who we're hoping will come as soon as possible. I must admit, it's a bit of a scientific mystery we have here on our hands."

The paper beneath Brom's fingers crinkle. "He's in a coma?"

"Medically induced." Dr. Addu leans against a counter, lips puckered. "The drug is wearing off, though." His quiet snort of laughter is in no way indicative of humor. "How in the hell somebody in medieval

Germany got ahold of such a drug is beyond me." He throws his hands up. "Victor ought to wake up within the next twenty-four hours. I wish I could give you a more precise timeframe, but if I didn't know better, I'd say he's under magical influences."

My brother is no longer in the rudimentary icebox we found him in. Instead, he's on a bed, hooked up to dozens of machines.

"We think whoever did this tried to jimmy up a poor man's cryogenic system," Dr. Addu continues. "While drugged, they kept his body temperature down to maintain stasis. They obviously have had some kind of medical training."

"Why?" Mary's question is little more than a whisper.

Addu squints behind his thick glasses. "Well, the clean grafting is close to miraculous, and then there's—"

"No." She wraps her arms around herself like a blanket. "Why would someone do this to him?"

"Oh! That I honestly don't know." It's said kindly, though. "There's a whole lot about this situation that's just baffling, which, given the parameters that the Society is working within, is understandable. More testing and observation are needed before any real conclusions can be drawn." His mustache lowers as he leans in toward Brom. "If I were you, I'd work whatever ties you have and find Victor an excellent psychologist before he wakes up. He's going to need one, don't you think?"

Mary's fingers curl around my bicep, digging through the cloth and into my skin. "You were gone for four days."

When I tell her, "I know," I want to punch my fist through the repaired wall closest to me.

Four days of no protocol.

There must be a similar maw within Mary, too, one that eats up her sarcasm, or even her sense of self, because the woman who leads me over to my brother is a mere shell of the one I've known for years. Our black holes grow and merge together into a singular beast, swallowing all of the sound in the room. Time ceases moving as Mary traces each row of stitches drawn upon my brother.

She asks one of the doctors to show us his eyes. The first one peeled back is familiar brown, one that used to sparkle with mischief or mania. The second is a watery blue.

Mary tugs on her sleeves until the fabric covers her hands. "When I was a child, in India, I was my mother's dirty secret—her ugly, nasty, mean-spirited daughter. Then the cholera outbreak came, killing my parents and my Ayah. Everyone else died or fled. Nobody came looking for me. Nobody remembered me. The only companion I had was a small snake. I don't normally talk about this, you know." She rubs her sleeve-covered fists together. "I was found entirely by accident before I, too, could contract the disease." When she presses a kiss against my cheek, I'm afraid to touch this unfamiliar frail woman before me. "Thank you for remembering him." And then she drifts out of the room.

Alice touches my shoulder. "I'll go. She shouldn't be alone, not after a shock such as this." Before she leaves, though, she pulls me into her arms.

I am selfish, because I don't want to let go, not even for Mary.

After she leaves, my father drags a chair over and sits down next to Victor. He takes his son's hand—his real hand—and clutches it like it's the line we need to hold on to this man we both love.

"I'm sorry," I say again. "I'm so damn sorry, Dad."

I'm engulfed in another hug as he holds the both of us. "Never say that. I love you, son. You did what you could. I am so thankful for your safety, and that you are home. Both my boys are, and that is what matters."

In my father's arms, next to my brother, I cry.

Our family is broken, but we're still holding on. And we'll keep doing so.

LIFE AND DEATH

ALICE

D UE TO A RATHER questionably decadent serving of absinthe, Mary does not fight me as I steer her toward my bed. She refused to sleep in her own, citing the presence of a pillow that, *"reeks like Victor."* By her choice, little was spoken about her love over the past pair of hours. She interrogated me about both my and Finn's fates, but refused to hear anything about Victor other than Finn's slaying of his tormentor. That detail brought out the absinthe spoons and fountain, and a bottle absconded earlier from a visit to a Nineteenth-Century Timeline.

Wherever it came from, her version of the green fairy was much tamer than Wonderland's.

"Ima glad yer no' dead." She yanks on my hair, tripping over her own feet as we cross the threshold into my room.

She is lucky to have a fistful of minimal strands. "I thank you for the concern. I am pleased I am not dead, either."

"An' Finn. Though. . ." An unladylike belch that reeks of anise fans my face. I fail to hold back my gag. "Sucks 'bout the torture." She jerks out of my grip and plops face down on my bed.

"What *sucks* is your use of such an uncouth modern slang word." I wrangle her boots off, which is a more daunting task than one might assume, as she pretends to pedal a bicycle whilst singing (garbling?) a muffled song about someone named Daisy who prefers bicycles built for two.

It requires much cajoling to guide her beneath the covers. I then bring round the waste bin and fetch a glass of water to place upon the nightstand. Light, licorice-y scented snores fill the room.

She deserves her rest.

In the sitting room, I begin a list of known quantities about the Piper and his Chosen. When I note to the mysterious book, I begin a new list: *Leather bound; gilded edges; papyrus or similar make; blank; magic.*

Why is this book important? It must have been—the Piper and the thirteenth Wise Woman placed it on a golden stand in between their thrones. What had the Chosen guarding me referred to it as? A tome?

No. A *codex.*

"If this keeps up, heads will roll," Frau Magrek said.

"They already are," the ancient jailer responded. "What with the chaos over the codex missing, and the convergence near upon us—"

The absent codex prompted anger and, undoubtedly, panic. The Piper departed Koppenberg Mountain to possibly search for it. The Institute was attacked from within, but the codex was hidden within the one room Wendy could no longer enter.

What would I do if I knew an item was safeguarded in an inaccessible location, but still must impossibly obtain? If I did not have enough manpower to lay a proper siege? Fire would do, wouldn't it? Explosions and damage would do quite nicely.

Wendy ultimately failed. She was overtaken and nullified by agents, therefore bringing her reign of terror to an end. What if she was fighting to resist the Piper's lure, just as Sara has? Small, timed explosions were detonated, rather than simply dousing curtains and papers and crafting trails of fire. Wendy was strategic in her placements. No one perished during her attack. According to Jack, not one agent was seriously injured.

She protected her colleagues and loved ones, no matter what anyone else might surmise. Wendy might have wreaked havoc within these walls, but, as one who has lived through warfare all too often, I know the damage could have been exponentially worse.

Wait a golden afternoon moment.

Harry is in the kitchen, arguing with the chef over dish cleaning duties.

"We have a dishwasher!" Monsieur Florent, an older gentleman who trained to become a chef for the Society after a run-in with the law in his Timeline, throws up his hands. "There is no need for you to do this!"

The translator, a soft-spoken German woman by the name of Charlotte, patiently conveys this to Harry. In return, the former servant holds a stack of dirty dishes closer to his chest. "It is no trouble."

Florent bangs on a stainless-steel-covered machine. "This is a dishwasher. It will clean the dishes for us! Simply put in the dirty dishes!" Charlotte rapidly converts this as the chef wrenches open the door. Before she is finished, Florent snatches the plates from Harry's hands and slots them between thin white pegs. The door clicks closed and a button pushed. "Vóila! In an hour, they will be spotless."

As Charlotte tells him this, Harry warily eyes the machine, as if it will spit the dishes back out at us like a catapult.

I withhold my amusement and offering greetings instead.

Florent's smile stretches wide. "Ah! Mademoiselle Alice. Might you want some of those tarts you favor? I baked some today, just in case."

"You are too kind." And I am too weak to refuse what he offers, especially since they are rather tasty. "Harry, might I have a word with you?"

"Yes!" Florent shoves a few tarts into Harry's hands, too. "I shall finish up in here while you two enjoy your late-night treat."

With that, I take Harry's arm so we might be shooed away from the kitchen, back into the dining room. Charlotte joins us as conversation flows much more quickly when I must not hunt for words.

Harry asks, "How may I help you, my lady?"

It is wondrous what a mere day of freedom can do to a person, although I am fully cognizant of how so much of his helpfulness, the busyness, are necessary for maintaining a hold on sanity. "I have a problem, Harry, and I am hoping you might offer me counsel on how to solve it."

His lined face wrinkles even further as Charlotte conveys this. "Me, my lady?"

We sit at an empty table. The dining room's lights have dimmed; its music quieted. "All I require is knowledge. Nothing more."

When he savors his tart, it's as if he fears it may be the last to ever pass his lips. "I am happy to share what I know about Koppenberg."

"And I appreciate that." I modulate my tone so that it is soothing rather than demanding. "I am specifically interested in what you may know about the book—or codex—that sat in between the thrones."

After Charlotte translates this, the remaining tart languishes upon the table, forgotten as shadows once more descend upon Harry. Lips white, his attention darts around the room.

"You are safe. Do not fear punishment for speaking, as there will be none. Nor will there be any if you choose to hold silent."

He licks his lips, catching tart crumbs in the corners, chin quivering. "The debased are forbidden to speak of the holy Codex of Life and Death."

Before I can argue, Charlotte swiftly reminds Harry that no one is debased, let alone him.

"Is that what the Chosen call it?" I press. "The Codex of Life and Death?"

His nod is jerky. The quivering spreads.

Charlotte says to me, "Although I am certain you are in need of answers, remember this is a person who has suffered greatly."

I do not allow my irritation to show. "That is true, and I grieve for such atrocities. However, there is a madman and his cult who have the power to destroy Timelines running amuck, and time is not our friend."

Harry asks, "Did I do something wrong, my lady?"

I smile gently. "Of course not. May I ask what is it that makes the Codex of Life and Death holy?"

"I do not know much, my lady." He wrings his bony hands so much so that the skin stretches back and forth like ancient, tanned leather too thin for usefulness. "The Lord and Lady of the Mountain call it so, and that to touch it without permission is to court a fate worse than death." His stares at the half-eaten tart. "Those who do so enter the dungeons to never return."

I think of the young man I encountered in that foul place, and of how he begged for death's release.

"The Codex speaks to the Lord and Lady, and they in turn preach to the Chosen. The debased are not permitted to hear its secrets, or enter the hall when its rapture is called forth."

Its rapture. Not the Piper's.

I ask, "To whom do the Chosen owe their allegiance? The Piper and the thirteenth Wise Woman, or to the Codex?"

"They are the Lord and Lady's disciples." His lanky hair swings across his brow. "The Codex belongs solely to the Lord and Lady of the Mountain."

"Do you know how to read the book?" I press gently. "Or perhaps coax it to share its secrets?"

His entire frame droops. "No, my lady. I cannot read at all."

"Perhaps you can learn now, if you like. There is always time to learn to read." He smiles when Charlotte conveys this. "I thank you for answering my questions, Harry. Shall we take the others some tarts, as well? Do you think they would like that?"

We three pester Florent for more desserts, and he grumbles good naturally before packing a basket filled with more than mere tarts.

Good food, he often tells the Society, is not a privilege that only the fat and wealthy ought to enjoy. It ought and should be enjoyed by everyone.

Finn and Van Brunt are seated next to Victor's bed, cell phones out, folders and papers strewn haphazardly across their laps and the floor. When Finn notices my approach, he yawns behind the crook of his elbow. "Is Mary all right?"

"She's asleep in my bed. Has there been any change?"

Finn stands, stretching his arms high above his head. A small swath of skin peeks out between shirt and jeans. "Some spikes in his brainwaves, which the doctors consider a good sign, but that's about it."

Once again, I must trust in the impossible. I must believe that Victor will wake.

When Van Brunt also yawns, stooped in his chair, he attempts to hide his exhaustion behind papers. That quickly changes as soon as I reveal the contents of my conversation with Harry. Within seconds, he types a message to the Librarian, informing her to expect us in the Museum within a quarter of an hour. A quick conference with Dr. Addu follows before we're off to descend into the bowels of the Institute for the second time in a day.

The Librarian peers through an overly large magnifying glass at the spine of the book. "The Codex of Life and Death, you say?"

"Have you heard of it?" Van Brunt queries. We are all hovered around her desk—and the Codex.

It presents as so benign, despite its gilded edges, as nothing more than an antique book touched by time and use.

One of the Librarian's blue eyes appears ginormous behind the warped glass. "Not specifically."

Finn pulls out his cell phone and taps upon the screen. A moment later, he holds it out for us to see. Pictured are Egyptian figures and hieroglyphics. "What about the *Book of the Dead*?"

A smirk tugs at one corner of the Librarian's mouth as she sets the magnifying glass down. "Certainly, one would think of such an association, considering the name."

Finn opens the Codex to one of its many blank pages. "Not to mention the pages are reminiscent of papyrus."

"No single text of the *Book of the Dead* exists outside of movies, unfortunately." The Librarian rings for Jack to bring down a fresh pot of tea. "It is, however, mentioned in surviving scrolls, but if there ever was a canonical *Book of the Dead*, it has long been lost. Most of what *was* written were upon objects, rather than scrolls anyway."

"Could not this be it?" I prompt. "If it is, in fact, missing—"

She shakes her head, effectively silencing my argument. "Try as you might, this is not papyrus. It's similar, but whatever plant was used is not native to this world." She taps a finger against her plump lips. "Egyptians did not bind their books. Although, I certainly cannot rule out that these pages weren't bound at a much later date. Nevertheless, the *Book of the Dead* consisted of so-called spells and instructions on how to lead a soul into the afterlife. It served funerary functions."

I dig my heels in. "How can you be certain that this does not?"

"Because of what your slave described." She plants her hands down upon either side of the book, managing once more to loom over me despite being shorter. "Think, Alice. What do we know about the Piper and his actions? He is choosing which Timelines to destroy and which ones to leave be, possibly due to influence from this book. He has assembled an army of devoted followers who move in and out of rapture, a state we now know is associated with the Codex. It is considered a holy book, and while the *Book of the Dead* could be dubbed as such, it certainly did not discuss ways to bring about the destruction of life. Instead, it focused on how to ensure the dead found comfort in the afterlife. Can we honestly say that the Piper offers such considerations for those he destroys?"

She may be maddening, but the enigmatic lady makes an excellent point.

"As Harry aptly told you, this is the Codex of Life and Death, and we must assume that it consists of both stages of existence." She sweeps out a hand, knocking several unrelated books onto the ground before whirling to face the other direction, her face contorting into something . . . *monstrous*. Something craggy and hideous.

I stumble back a step, startled enough to instinctively reach for a weapon.

What did I just witness?

A quick glance shows neither Van Brunt nor Finn alarmed. In fact, Van Brunt rounds the desk, his view of her face clear. "You are not omnipotent, old friend, no matter how much you may wish otherwise."

Rue riddles her chuckle. When she angles her head toward him, I find smooth skin, blue eyes, the same beautiful face I have known for nearly a year. "My ego does not accept defeat well, even if temporary."

Had I imagined the whole thing?

As Van Brunt encourages her to keep trying, Finn flips through the pages of the Codex, confusion drawing fresh lines by the second. He brushes across the textured surfaces—not horizontally, but vertically. Up and down, up and down. And then, a flurry of blinking has him jerking away. He rubs his eyes, wincing.

I touch his arm. "Are you all right?"

He startles, as if he hadn't remembered I was still standing next to him. The Librarian and Van Brunt quiet, turning to face us.

I snatch a disposable tissue from the Librarian's desk and hold it to his nose. "You're bleeding."

He takes the tissue from me, the confusion lines on his forehead doubling. "It's nothing. Just a nosebleed."

"May I ask as to why you were running your fingers up and down in the Codex?"

Finn throws away the tissue; the blood has slowed. He shakes his head. "It's the damndest thing but . . . for a moment there, I thought I saw something."

Quick as the Dodo in the Caucus race, the Librarian's attention hones in on Finn. "Such as?"

He squints, staring at the pages once more. "I don't know. Something glowing and golden, but really faint." He shakes his head again, and another thin stream of blood snakes from his nostril. I pass over another tissue.

There is nothing upon the Codex's pages, faint or otherwise.

"Do you still see them?" the Librarian presses.

He dabs at his nose with a fresh tissue. "No. I must be tired."

She tries again. "Could it have been words? Pictographs?"

When he doesn't answer, I say, "Whatever they were, they are situated vertically, not horizontally. Correct?"

Finn winces so hard that he drops the bloody tissue.

The Librarian swiftly skirts around her desk and snatches Finn's chin to crane his head toward her. Despite his nose continuing to bleed, he's startled enough to allow it. Outraged at her misplaced sense of propriety, I hand over another tissue and reach to knock her hand away—only to have Van Brunt stop me.

She stares up at the man I love, her countenance terrifyingly serious, as she angles his head left and right. Finn snaps, "What the hell are you doing?"

As if he's on fire, she lets go of Finn. Before another word is said, Van Brunt's phone chirps. He reads the message and announces, "Victor's eyes have opened."

DESPAIR AND RESENTMENT

FINN

CAN BEST DESCRIBE THE blue-green and brown balefully focusing into the distance as eerie as all hell.

"Victor?" Dr. Addu flashes a penlight in front of my brother's face. "Can you hear me?"

His head totters in an attempted nod, like it's perched atop a coil rather than a solid neck. Eyelids lower and flutter. Cracked lips are sloppily licked as he attempts to focus on the doctor, on the people standing around him, Brom and me included.

His mouth forms a silent oh.

Dr. Addu pulls his stethoscope off his neck and inserts the buds into his ears. He presses the pad against Victor's chest and listens for several seconds. "Are you in any pain?"

Victor smacks his lips together, his tongue clumsy, as if it were two times too big for his mouth. Suddenly, the door to the medical wing flies open and Alice and Mary barrel through it.

"Victor?" Mary rushes the bed. She seizes the hand closest to where she lands. "You scared me, you big lout, staying asleep as you have!"

His attention wavers toward her, tongue lolling.

"What's wrong with him?" she demands of Dr. Addu. "Why is he acting like this?"

Brom says quietly, "Ms. Lennox, please allow the doctor to finish his checkup. There will be time enough for questions later."

"Victor." The doctor reclaims my brother's attention. "Are you in any pain?"

"Pain?" Mary's voice could shatter glass, it's so shrill. "Alice, go to my lab, fetch the morphine."

Alice does no such thing as Victor's dark eyebrows pull down even farther.

He wobbles a no. *No pain.*

Thank God.

"I'm going to do a few tests, Victor," Dr. Addu continues. "Just to check your reflexes."

The bed is adjusted, so Victor is upright rather than prone. Despite his bobble head tendencies, he does not topple over. Brom and I ready ourselves on either side of him, just in case.

Addu pricks the fingers of hand and arm we are certain are Victor's. My brother jolts, annoyance flashing across his face. The other hand is pricked, and he registers pain in it, too. Both feet are tested. He has feeling in both, which blows my mind, considering I know damn well one of those legs isn't his. Addu tests every bit of Victor's body that has been determined to be foreign, and yet my brother feels every single prick. How is this possible? Like Alice and me, he was only in the mountain for a few days. How can nerves connect, muscles knit together, and bones mend seamlessly in such a short time? Transplants are tricky, and often require time to take. Oftentimes, they are rejected. Victor's patchwork before us acts as if it is the body he was born with.

His hearing is checked. His vision, too. Addu even brings out that rubber hammer doctors use for knees. More blood is taken. Dozens of yes or no questions are asked, checking for comprehension. Although clearly confused and often annoyed, Victor does not resist any of it.

As Addu confers with his colleagues, Mary morphs into an unfamiliar mothering figure who cannot sit still. She plumps Victor's pillow, not once, but three times. She adjusts his shirt and tucks in the sheets "just the way Victor prefers"—tight on the sides, but loose on the end, so he can stick his feet out if needed. She dabs at the corner of his mouth, wiping away saliva. She coos to him in the gentlest tone I've ever heard Mary Lennox use.

Each time Brom or I come in too close, she shoos us back.

Victor warily follows her actions the entire time. As the minutes pass, his head grows steadier, his focus less imbalanced. Hands and feet twitch in what appears to be an effort to move. His lips pull together and contort as a visible frustration mounts.

When Mary adjusts the sheet for a second time, ensuring a penny could bounce off of its taut surface, Victor catches hold of her shirt.

She ceases tucking. Her face lights up. "Yes, my darling?"

He screws his face up, mouth moving. Mary is so entranced that, when we all close in, she doesn't push us away.

His first attempted word is little more than a slur. I say, "Take it easy, okay? There's no need to rush," but Mary hushes me.

"Talk to me, darling." She wipes away more drool. "Is there something you need?"

He takes a deep breath. As if it's the hardest thing he's ever done, Victor says, "Gee hway."

Mary leans in closer. "What's that?"

Suddenly, Victor lets go of her shirt and snatches at her hair. "Gee hway!" The volume increases significantly. His mismatched eyes blaze. "GEE HWAY!"

Mary yelps and jerks away, straight into Alice. A sizable chunk of her hair remains tangled in her boyfriend's fist, like it's a hard-won trophy.

"Victor!" Brom grabs hold of my brother's wrist. "What are you doing?"

Dr. Addu and a few other doctors rush toward the bed as I translate what Victor's saying.

Gee hway.

Get away.

If eyes were capable of burning holes, there would be two tunnels straight through Mary. "GEE HWAY BEESH!" he howls. And then Victor screams, just flat out screams like his singular goal is to break every window in the Institute.

"Somebody bring a sedative!" one of the doctors yells.

Victor thrashes upon the bed, swinging clumsy yet rigid arms and fists out to make contact with whomever and whatever comes too close. He gnashes his teeth, he yowls until spittle streaks down his chin. He kicks one of the doctors so hard the guy doubles over. All the while, he refuses to let go of Mary's hair, let alone stop glaring at her.

Brom and I do our best to pin him down as Addu prepares the sedative. Victor continues to shout, hurling what I assume are garbled insults at Mary. Alice partially shields Mary with her body, but I can see exactly what Victor's actions are doing to her. Her face is white, her limbs slack. There are no snarky or bitchy comebacks.

Brom catches my attention, and it's clear he's thinking exactly what I am: *Too much time has passed between protocol dosages.*

Mania has finally completely claimed my brother.

Armed with a pill or two from Addu, Alice escorts Mary back to her apartment. Even after Victor quieted, Mary said nothing. She didn't cry, either. I wasn't even sure that was *Mary* who Alice led away.

Addu loops his stethoscope around his neck. "You two look as if you need some stiff drinks."

A nasty scratch tears across my father's cheek. "As do you," Brom says.

"He'll be out for a few hours." Addu rubs the bridge of his nose.

"Until then, go have those drinks. Get some rest. We need to keep things calm for Victor. Maybe there was too much stimuli. Let's ease him in to this new reality he's woken up to."

Get away, bitch.

I thank the doctor who bandaged my hand (*appreciate the bite, bro!*) and stand up. On the other side of the bed, Brom remains seated. "Wendy didn't destroy all of your bottles of scotch," I say. "I'm thinking now's the perfect time to have some."

He massages the back of his neck, clearly torn.

"The docs here will let us know if there are any changes. You're no good to anyone if you're exhausted."

My brother had said nearly the same thing to me once, after the boojum was removed from Alice's back. Just thinking about it makes me want to howl alongside Victor. Does he know something is wrong? Can he tell? Is he trapped inside his mind and body, screaming to be let free?

Brom finally stands up. He pulls me closer, hugging me while simultaneously patting my back. "You are right, as always."

I don't take comfort or pride in such a statement, though.

When the sedatives wear off, Mary doesn't return to the medical wing. It's for the best, because aggressive is a mild word for Victor's behavior. A psychologist arrives, but even her gentle questions rile him up. He bites. He steals more hair. The doctors strap him to the bed, which only infuriates somebody already manic. One calls for another round of sedatives, but the psychologist insists she wants to talk to him as is.

I think I want to throttle her just as much as my brother does.

Brom and I don't hover. We position ourselves across the room, afraid to overwhelm but still desperate to hear what's going on. Our father crosses his arms so tightly, it's a miracle he can breathe.

He may be alternating between shouting and maniacally laughing as the psychologist settles in a chair just out of arm's reach, but Victor's speech is improving at an unbelievable rate. Within five minutes of constant shouting, I can understand all too well everything he's saying.

I'm a bastard, because, as I listen to him, I wish I couldn't.

The psychologist turns on a small recorder. "Victor, I'm Dr.—"

"I don't give a bloody flying shite who you are!" He lobs a massive wad of phlegm at her. She's stone-cold amazing, because when it lands right on her face, she doesn't even flinch. A tissue is quickly passed over, and she wipes it off as if it were nothing more than sweat from the midday sun. Victor yanks against his restraints. "Let me go, you bloody wankers!"

A tense sigh rumbles out of Brom.

Unfazed, the psychologist asks, "Do you know where you are?"

He seethes, tongue no longer fat and loose, "I'm not an idiot. I have a Ph.D!"

Victor never throws his title at anyone. He doesn't even like colleagues to call him *doctor*.

Her smile is mild. "I didn't ask about college degrees. I asked if you know where you are."

Something in him changes. He shrugs, relaxing against the raised bed. "In the Institute."

The psychologist crosses her legs. "Do you remember your full name?"

"Victor Frankenstein Van Brunt." He lifts up his fingers, although he can't raise his hand or arm, and pretends to study his nails. "I don't give a shite what your name is, though, *shrink*."

Tension rolls off of Brom in tangible waves.

As if she hadn't even heard the last part, the psychologist asks, "What are the last memories you have before today?"

He leers. "Wouldn't you like to know?"

"Do you have any memories from Koppenberg Mountain?"

"You're a bloody moron."

"Are you in any pain?"

"How many times do I need to answer that?" He glances around at the dispersed crowd in the room. "Is no one listening?"

"Do any of your bones ache?" the psychologist presses, albeit conversationally. "Does anything itch?"

"If you're asking if I want to relieve an itch with you, sorry." His laugh is ugly. "You're too much of a cow."

I thrust out an arm to stop Brom from doing anything rash.

"Why did you attack Mary earlier?"

His lips curl distastefully. "Wouldn't leave me alone."

"Do you know who Mary is?"

A long, suffering, exaggerated sigh blasts out. "She's the prissy bitch who tries to tell me what to do all the time."

"Is she nothing more than that?"

"Is that not enough?" He leers once more. "Fine. She's somebody I shag upon occasion."

Christ.

He tilts his head to the side. "They're coming, you know."

The psychologist leans forward. "Who's coming?"

A sneer twists his mouth. "You know who they are. You've got one hanging on your shoulder. *Traitor*."

She doesn't bother to verify his claim. "Can you describe who you see over my shoulder?"

"You'll deserve what you get, nosy bitch." All of a sudden, he convulses as he yanks against his restraints. "Let me out of here, you arseholes! I'm not going to die in here because you're all too stupid to see! He'll find me, and then she'll kill me!" He stares right at Brom, right at me, still thrashing up a storm. "Don't let her kill me! She's going to put a worm in my ear and it'll eat my brains until I'm nothing but their puppet!"

Raising her voice above his, the psychologist asks, "Who will do that, Victor? Whom are you so scared of?"

His screams transition into sobs. After ten minutes of getting no-where, the psychologist finally allows Dr. Addu to administer another round of sedatives.

When the needle slides into his skin, Victor howls. Those mis-matched eyes of his laser in on us. "Don't turn your backs on me.

Don't let me go into the darkness! Please, Dad! Finn!"

Brom finally speaks. He tells his eldest child, "I won't, son. I promise."

It's something I promise, too.

FOUR LADIES & A BOOK

ALICE

BRING ALICE AND COME *to the interrogation room.*

Mary is already shrugging on a sweater as I finish reading the message the Librarian just sent to Mary's phone. My sweater, to be precise, but I do not point this small fact out.

She barks, "What are we waiting for?"

Off with her head.

Hackles rise upon my back, but I allow this, too. After all, it isn't every day when one's great love rips a good chunk of her hair out. Mary refuses to discuss what happened in the medical wing, though, and I respect her enough not to push.

Together, we make our way down to the interrogation room, to where the Librarian waits alongside a blindfolded and earplug-wearing Sara Carrisford and, more astonishingly, a similarly restrained

Grethel Bunting. Both are docile in their beds—indeed, light snores emit from the Piper's lieutenant.

Mary must share my surprise, as she motions toward the John and Paul School for the Gifted's former head mistress. "I'd almost forgot about this one."

"Unfortunately for her, I have not." The Librarian turns away from a small rolling cart filled with books, syringes, and vials. How very curious. "You took long enough."

There's the Librarian I know. I refuse to rise to her jab at misperceived tardiness. "Why have you summoned us?"

"Since our discussion about the Codex of Life and Death, I've thought about it quite a bit." She pats the tome resting at the top of the stack of books. "More specifically, over how we can unlock its secrets, considering I cannot see its words."

I very nearly roll my eyes. Has defeat worn her down so much that she is deigned to regurgitate information we already know?

"I considered what your debased Harry told you," the Librarian continues.

I am cool with my response. "Do not refer to him as such."

"He is unable to read the book, though, being debased," she says, as if I hadn't issued the veiled threat. "And I wondered . . . is that merely because he is illiterate? Or because he was forbidden to do so?" She taps her lips. "Or is it because he legitimately cannot see the words in order to read?"

"Perhaps you ought to show him the book." There's an eagerness to Mary, one forced and undoubtedly mixed with gratitude for a worthy distraction.

"I did." The Librarian raps her fingers across the leather cover. "While he is illiterate, as is common for a slave or a non-educated man from his Timeline, he is able to identity the difference between letters and pictures. I tested the theory with several of the debased in residence."

I grit my teeth, my fingers clenching the folds of my skirts.

"None saw any words in the Codex. Isn't that intriguing?" The Librarian's smile leaves me uneasy. "But it did leave me wondering if someone who isn't debased could read the book. Someone Chosen."

I grudgingly appreciate her connecting of the dots. "Someone like Sara or Grethel Bunting."

"Exactly." She pats a pair of syringes on the table. "Mary, I requisitioned some of your truth serum. Shall we see what these ladies know about the Codex?"

I step in front of Sara. "I will not allow any torture to befall this woman."

Half of the Librarian's mouth stretches upward. "But you will allow it for the other?"

I think back to the day I met Grethel Bunting, and of how rude she was, and of how she attempted to use her set of pipes against Van Brunt, Jack, and myself. She was ruthless, remorseless.

I have no idea if she willingly allowed herself to become Chosen. As one of the assumed original Hamelin children whom the Piper kidnapped, there is a small chance she was swayed at a young age. But decades have passed, and deeds completed. Her complicity in the Piper's villainy is assured.

Sara, though. . . She is fighting the rapture. Her only sin was to fall in love with the wrong person. She made no willing choice, and has continued to rebel.

I stand my ground. "You will have to go through me in order to lay a single hand upon Sara Carrisford."

A rich, throaty laugh is the Librarian's response.

Mary snorts. "No one is threatening Little Miss Princess. Heaven forbid she be treated with anything other than a pair of her finest kid gloves." She selects one of the syringes. "Let's start with Sara, so you can save all your glorious wrath for the hag in the other chair."

The bed is activated so that Sara reclines rather than lies prone. I steady her arm to ready it for Mary. The only reaction she offers us is a slight grimace the moment needle pierces skin. We wait a minute before removing the earplugs and sleep mask.

Green-gray eyes blink against the bright overhead lights.

The Librarian maintains her distance, although I fear more for amusement than worry of threats. "Hello, Sara."

Finn's former partner maintains her focus on the three of us rather than glancing around the room. "You should not have removed those. We cannot risk him finding me." A hitch splits her tone. "I cannot risk hurting anyone else."

"We need your help." I lay my hand upon one of her restrained arms. "We would not go against your wishes otherwise."

Her lower lip trembles. "I will, of course, offer any assistance I may."

Mary snorts once more, but tries to disguise it with a cough. I simply do not have time to deal with her childish dislike of this woman, though. I fire off a warning glance before returning my focus on Sara.

"May I ask . . . are they all right? The people you brought through the doorway?" Sara queries. "Please tell me that no one retaliated against the one who stabbed me. She was only scared. With me being who I am, it is only natural."

"Ugh, now she's a martyr," Mary mutters.

I shift my body to block Mary from Sara's line of sight. "Grymsdyke wished to avenge you. I think he is rather taken with you, although he insists he will still happily bite you upon your request."

She laughs quietly. "He is a dear."

I will refrain from telling him this, as no assassin wishes to be thought of as such a sweet thing.

"All is well with everyone. Have no fears." My smile fades. "What can you tell us about the Codex of Life and Death, the tome that sat between the Piper and thirteenth Wise Woman's thrones in Koppenberg Mountain?"

Her brows furrow as she considers my query. "It is their Bible, only . . . it holds no religious stories. It's also like a ledger."

"Well, that makes perfect sense," Mary mutters.

"Do you recall what is in it? Or any of the text?" the Librarian asks.

"Most of my recollections are hazy," Sara murmurs, "but I believe it tells the first story."

"You said it had no stories," Mary unhelpfully points out.

"Religious stories, no—at least any like I have ever heard or read. There are no mentions of gods or goddesses." Sara licks her lips. "What lies within the Codex's pages is the first story, the one that—" She winces as blood begins to trickle from her nose. "I . . . I . . . I can't be sure, but I think it hails from the first Timeline. Maybe here? Or. . ."

The blood flows thicker, and I rip off a piece of her gown in order to press it against her nose. "Perhaps you ought to rest a moment."

She shakes her head, wincing as if her head fiercely aches. Her words are muffled. "Or gave birth to the first Timeline."

With my free hand, I grapple with one of her restraints. Sara's fingers fumble for mine. "Alice, please. Leave me be. I cannot allow myself to be his puppet."

The Librarian joins us by the bed. "Respect her wishes." To Sara, she asks, "Do you remember any of the story?"

"Just snatches. They have a very dream-like quality to them."

The bit of cloth I've used to stem her nosebleed is soaked through. I quietly ask Mary to obtain some gauze and ice, as well as a painkiller to counter whatever torture the Piper inflicts upon those who tell his secrets. My request annoys her, but she swiftly leaves the room.

"Anything will help," the Librarian cajoles. "Any detail, no matter how small. Think about it while we wait for Mary to return."

It only takes our colleague a few minutes to do so. Gauze is stuffed up Sara's nostril; I press an icepack against the outside. Another shot is administered, this one morphine.

Shortly, Sara relaxes even farther into her bed, eyes glazed. "I'm ready to tell you what I remember." Her voice is light, dreamy even.

Mary pulls out her phone. "We should record this."

"There was Darkness before anything else," Sara says. "It was rich and thick, all encompassing. Darkness ruled its domain with utter ferocity. Nothing was allowed to penetrate the velvet of nothingness. There were no sounds, no sensations, and, most of all, no light. For many millennia, this pleased Darkness." Her eyes flutter closed. "It was Darkness' choice to bring about change. It tore itself into two, and together, the two halves shaped themselves into whatever they wished." A smile plays across her lips. "In the dark, anything can be anything. Or it can be nothing at all."

Mary rolls her eyes. "Well, now. We better make room in the philosophy section for Sara Carrisford, shouldn't we? Watch out, Aristotle."

Before I can say anything, the Librarian snaps, "That is more than enough out of you, young lady."

Well, now, indeed.

Sara continues, "Darkness can even be a story, if it likes."

The Librarian asks, "What kind of story?"

"All stories. Although, if Darkness is done with a story, it can do that, too."

"This makes no sense," Mary mutters. "Darkness as a storyteller? What about authors?"

Although the question was surely angled toward the Librarian and myself, Sara is the one to answer it. "Authors, the blessed ones, take Darkness and make it into something more." Her eyes flutter open. "But the truly powerful, the ones who control life and death . . . They are the ones who take something and make it nothing. That is all of the tale that I remember."

Mary crosses her arms. "Fat lot that did."

"Did the book speak to the Piper or the witch?" the Librarian asks.

"Speak?" Sara's head tilts to the side; she squints. "With spoken language?" She titters quietly. "The Codex of Life and Death is not an audio book." A long sign lifts her chest. "I miss those, by the way. Funny what things you take a liking to in the Twenty-First Century."

The Librarian flips through the Codex, stopping at a random page in the middle. She holds it before Sara. "What do you see?"

A soft smile lifts the corners of Sara's mouth.

Goose pimples race across my arms. *She sees something.*

"You have it sideways," Sara says dreamily.

Mary, the Librarian, and I exchange puzzlement, but the Librarian rotates the book. "Is this better?" she asks.

"Pretty golden words. I can't read them, though. Don't know the language."

Gold.

A lengthy yawn and the closing of eyes delay any further comment.

A tiny rivulet of blood seeps past the gauze.

"How much morphine did you administer?" I chide Mary. "She's on the verge of sleep."

Her arms tighten around her chest. "She was bleeding like someone was squeezing her bloody brains out. She still is! I figured she needed a decent dose."

"Rest now," the Librarian says in possibly the gentlest voice I have ever heard her use. "You have been of great help to us, Sara." She passes Mary the padded sleep mask and earplugs. "We have our confirmation, ladies."

Fear takes hold of my heart, squeezing out a rapid pace. "Finn saw gold upon these pages."

"What?" Mary snaps her head up from tending Sara. "He saw something?"

"I am aware of that." The Librarian marches over to me, teetering in her high heels. "Alice, what do you know of Finn's time in Koppenberg?"

"He was tortured repeatedly." Shame and anger beat against my ribcage. "One of my jailers remarked his eyes turned black a few times, but it never lasted, and was only ever momentary. He fought back. He never fully succumbed to the rapture. He managed to eradicate a number of Chosen." Blood rushes from my face, leaving me dizzy. "I—I dreamed I was in Wonderland. I could not remember the Society, or the Piper. I could not remember his face."

"This is not the time to blame yourself," the Librarian snaps. "You are strong, but even you cannot fight against powerful magic."

"The twelfth Wise Woman told me that as long as my love held true, the poison in his veins would remain nullified." I grab her arm, desperate for her guidance for once. "Do you understand? *Days passed during which I did not remember him.*"

"But you did remember him." She peels me away like a bandage. "You are allowing the Piper and his witch to cultivate doubt. This is not you, Alice. Remember who you are."

I am the Queen of Diamonds, but I am also a woman in love.

The Librarian's lips thin. "Do you know if Finn interacted with the witch?"

"He never specifically mentioned such an encounter." I rub my own lips. "After I found him, there were times he acted strangely. It was as if he was speaking to someone who wasn't present—or at least," I say, gazing at the Codex's blank pages, "someone I could not see myself."

Who or what did he see?

The Librarian's blue eyes intensify. "What did he talk about?"

"It was the other side of conversations." I shake my head, desperate to reclaim memories from a time best buried and forgotten. "He directed us to where Victor was. Whether he knew, or had heard, I did not ask him. He had a fever. His wounds were infected." More fiercely, "I refuse to allow him to succumb."

She wipes the back of a hand across her forehead. "True love only carries a pair so far." Once more, my hackles rise—only to deflate just as quickly when she adds, "Are you sure he made no specific mention of the witch?"

"No," I say, but then stop. Finn did not say so, but Sara did.

"If he goes back to her. . ."

She was terrified of the prospect.

I look to her now, this woman who protected Finn in Koppenberg and who risked suffering today to reveal all that she knew. "Sara said something that I did not hold on to tightly." The temperature in the room chills considerably. "She feared what might happen if Finn was to visit an unnamed woman once more. I cannot help but now surmise she meant the thirteenth Wise Woman."

Mary snarls. "And of course, we have no idea what she did to him, which makes it all the worse!"

For a moment, shadows flock to the Librarian. She bares her teeth: white and sharper than they ought to be. A small hiss precedes, "Sooka!" before she snatches another hypodermic needle. "Let us suck the hag dry of her secrets."

Neither Mary nor I move, let alone speak for several bewildering seconds. But then Mary asks slowly, "Are you a vampire?"

The Librarian hands her the full syringe. "Tick-tock, ladies."

Tick-tock, indeed.

Four hours and three syringe-fulls of truth serum and one dose of adrenaline later, Grethel Bunting is allowed to return to oblivion. She needs it, as she frothed and raged at us the entire time. Her time at the Institute has done little to calm her sour attitude, and while she grudgingly answered our questions, fighting each response as if it were her last, she also hurled multitudes of threats and insults. Toward the end, she panted as if she had run all the way across the continent.

The rest of us are equally exhausted, although for different reasons.

Mary lounges on Bunting's bed, oblivious to the woman drooling behind her. "We need to tell the others as soon as possible."

The Librarian taps away on her cell phone. "An hour will do. Mary, see to informing the others of the meeting. You might want to freshen up." She wrinkles her nose. "Vomit is not the loveliest of perfumes."

Mary pats Bunting's leg before standing up. "Oh, but there you're wrong. To me, it smells like Traitorous Bitch Who Got What Was Coming to Her by Spilling Her Guts—and that, ladies, is a glorious smell."

As she departs, the Librarian tidies up the numerous syringes and bottles littering the rolling cart. I take Sara's hand and squeeze it lightly. She shifts in the bed, still languishing in morphine dreams.

"Jack will be in soon to ensure these ladies are taken care of."

I let go of Sara's hand and smooth her covers. "What we are putting Sara through seems more akin to torture."

"Despite what your overactive imagination is concocting, none of us here are dispassionate toward her situation." The Librarian slips the Codex into a leather satchel. "Jack provides her the luxury of movies and television via special glasses. She enjoys music, too." She nods at Bunting. "This one receives the same benefits, although I wonder if it's appreciated."

"Perhaps Sara might have some of these so-called audio books?"

"I'll make a note of it." She leads us out of the door. "Alice, I would ask that you do not bother Finn with our suspicions that the Chosen can read the Codex. Not yet, at least."

I'm surprised frost does not coat the walls. "I refuse to hide anything from him."

"What if the knowledge triggered rapture? Would you be willing to suppress sharing then?"

The floor beneath me rises up, halting my steps. "Will it?"

"I have no idea. Anything is possible, as you well know. Allow me this evening to. . ." One of her infuriating smiles comes out to play. "Ruminate on the situation. All that is required of you is to remain close to him."

"I am not his nanny, and I refuse to ever act as such."

"No one is asking you to do so. I simply suggested you stay close to him tonight. How is this different than most evenings? One would think this would pose no problem, and would be welcome, considering how often you two indulge in carnal—"

"Enough." My face burns. What in the world has come over this infernal enigma of a woman? "You go too far with that, which is none of your business."

Her lightheartedness solidifies into something hard and unforgiving. "When it concerns the protection of Timelines, it damn well *is* my business, and there is never *going too far*." Her voice is granite, her eyes fire. "Don't ever think differently."

COMPROMISED

FINN

"SOME STORIES HAVE FINITE ends, you cow."

My head is throbbing, and the ibuprofen I took the hour before isn't helping much. Granted, neither is listening to Grethel Bunting shriek and curse on Mary's recordings like some kind of possessed banshee.

My mind and heart are still in the medical wing. With my brother. With my mother.

. . . My mother?

"Don't give up, Finn."

Alice nudges over a glass of water when she notices me massaging my temple.

"Does the Codex tell which stories should be ended?" the Librarian asks from Mary's recording.

"You are such idiots! *A book that talks*. Honestly." I have no trouble imagining the woman sneering.

"What specifically is written in the Codex of Life and Death?" the Librarian asks.

Howls serve as Bunting's answer for nearly a minute. Then, panting, she says, "The closest thing I can relate it to is a card catalogue of all stories."

"Does it tell the first story?" Mary asks.

"Aren't you the little-miss-know-it-all?" The hacking of phlegm is all too obvious. I wonder if Mary smacked her when Bunting let it fly.

"Is that a yes?" Alice presses.

"*Yes*."

"Does the Piper ever add to the book?" the Librarian asks.

Choking sounds follow. Eventually, Bunting hisses, "Yes."

"Did you see him do so?"

"I was blessed once to witness it."

"What specifically does he write?"

It's clear she struggled against answering. "He logs which stories must and do come to an end."

After a long moment, the Librarian follows up with, "Does he base this on what is already written in the Codex?"

When Bunting calls the Librarian a particularly nasty name, blaming her for delaying her attendance at the convergence, Mary fast-forwards the recording, informing us the next ten minutes offer no pertinent information. "The truth serum was wearing off," she says. "We had to pump her full of another dose." She clicks the recording back on. Bunting wheezes, "The Lord and Lady dictate which stories lasted past their expiration date."

"What does that mean, expiration date?" Mary asks.

Bunting snaps, "Are you truly so stupid that you do not understand what that means?"

Mary smiles as she fast-forwards a bit more of the recording. "The serum needed time to adjust."

Once the recording resumes, Bunting is panting. "Some stories are not worthy of continuation."

"What are the qualifications to determining such worthiness?" Alice asks coldly.

"The Lord and Lady never saw fit to inform me."

"If you had to guess," Alice presses on the recording, "what would you surmise are the qualifications?"

Hissing, screeching, and sobbing fill the next minute before Bunting eventually answers. "Some of us wondered if the Lord and Lady did not tolerate worlds where magic did not exist."

My eyes fly to Brom's. While he never personally witnessed any magic in his original Timeline, there were several stories within *The Sketch Book of Geoffrey Crayon, Gent.* that are questionable. Ghosts are mentioned in several of the tales, although Brom always scoffed at the veracity of the tales.

"Worlds without magic," Bunting continues, "are pointless anyway."

"You, yourself, do not possess magic," Mary points out.

A pregnant pause grows. "Don't I?"

"Do you?" Mary is clearly startled.

Bunting didn't even fight her next answer. "Enough."

"What kind of magic?"

"The kind," Bunting sneers, "a whelp like you could only dream of." Her sniff sounds like the tearing of paper. "Your story has no magic, Mary Lennox. None. At. All."

"Mine does." A sharpness slices across Alice's word. "So let us ask, why was my Timeline targeted?"

"Was it?" Bunting grunts. "If I had to guess, it's because you are a bitch who deserves to be forgotten."

Several minutes of bickering between Mary and Bunting ensue.

"What does the Piper use to write whatever it is he does in the Codex of Life and Death?" Clearly frustrated, Alice breaks into the spat. "Does he utilize a special instrument?"

Bunting mimics, *"Does he utilize a special instrument?"*

"How does the Piper log the information about which Timelines he wishes to destroy?" the Librarian snaps.

"He writes in the Codex."

Further questioning goes nowhere. The Librarian's hiss of frustration is audible across the recording. "Why can some people see what is in the Codex of Life and Death and others cannot?"

"Those who are blessed can." Bunting's pride is all too evident. "Those who are Chosen."

Wait . . . what?

The Librarian reaches for the recording. Brom says, "Let it run."

She glowers. On the recording, she is saying, "How?"

"The Lady's great magic has allowed the Chosen, those who carry her magic within their blood and bones, to have the ability to see what others cannot."

I . . . I thought I saw something earlier today. Didn't I? Faint golden splotches.

"Can you read what is in the Codex?" the Librarian presses. "Tell me what it says."

Fresh choking sounds become more pronounced. Mary rasps, "Oh, for goodness' sake, she's turning blue. How bloody convenient! I'll go get some adrenaline."

Stationed at the front of the conference room, the Librarian wrangles the recorder away from my father and turns it off. "Whatever preventions the Piper laid upon his followers to guarantee their silence are maddeningly effective."

Sara talked, though. We heard snippets from her conversation before Buntings. I'm damn proud of her for continuing to fight.

"So we still have no idea what the book says, other than it tells a story about darkness and lists . . . Timelines?" I'm pretty sure my father has a raging headache, too, after the afternoon we've had. Victor woke up long before any of the doctors thought he would, ripping through his restraints as if they were tissue paper.

A good portion of the newly cleaned and refurbished medical wing is once more destroyed.

"We do know that it is important to the Piper." When Alice leans forward, her chair creaks. "And therefore imperative to keep from falling back into his hands. You heard what Bunting said—he wants it for the convergence."

Which must just chap the Piper's ass something fierce.

"And yet, we're still unsure about what exactly the convergence entails," the A.D. points out. "Except that a bunch of crazy Chosen are to attend."

"It's unlikely to occur in Koppenberg," Mary muses. A thick scarf twists around her neck. I simultaneously want and don't want to see just how bad my brother hurt her. "If the explosions did what we hope they did, there shouldn't be a lot of space left for it." A wicked smile curves her lips. "Or a lot of attendees."

So far this evening, Mary is acting like nothing happened earlier. Like my brother didn't rip out more than her hair and grind his heel all over it. Like he didn't try to silence her forever.

I'm envious, actually. I don't know if I can just turn an internal switch and ignore what I've seen and heard today. Victor's fury barrels through my skull, like he's right next to me.

"Don't let me go. Promise me, Finn!"

"Without Koppenberg, or the school in Connecticut," Henry Fleming asks, "where would they go?"

"Do we still have eyes on the Piper's Manhattan apartment?" Alice asks.

"Don't turn your backs on me. Don't let me go into the darkness."

Mr. Holgrave says, "Yes. We've bugged the school. I've been checking in every other hour to see if anything pops up."

"Although mīn hërzeliep *is prone to exaggeration, in this case, I can see that you are exactly as described."*

Although he's clearly hanging overhead, it feels as if Grymsdyke just danced across my back, only to brush his fiery hairs across my brain as these words whisper throughout my mind.

It's not Victor's voice I'm hearing.

It's . . . it's. . .

"Are there any connections we can make to Timelines other than 1816/18GRI-GT," Franklin Blake is asking. "Perhaps one of the other Grimm Timelines?"

"I normally do not indulge such pettiness, but there are times

when a müeterlīn *must consider the whims of a temperamental* juncfrouwe*."*

I squeeze my eyes shut, my headache is so intense. If someone were to saw open my skull, I'm positive they would find tiny monsters with ice picks hacking away at pink tissue.

"Such a scōnī *as you will do nicely for* mīn tohter . . ."

The light is too bright. Everyone's voices are too loud. The metallic tang of blood drips down the back of my throat.

The sound of my chair scraping, then clattering backward as I lurch out of it, stills the room.

"Sorry. I need to—" I wipe at my nose; blood once more stains my hand. I stumble away from the table, toward the door. I don't make it to the trashcan before I drop to my knees and lose the contents of my stomach.

The monsters in my skull hack away with a renewed sense of fervor.

Alice is immediately by my side. I groan, "I must have eaten something bad. I'm sorry, I—"

Have I eaten today?

"There is no need to apologize." She wraps her arms around me. "Perhaps you ought to lay down and rest."

I ought to be listening to what everyone has to say. I ought to be hunting the Piper down.

He hates worlds without magic. That's . . . countless Timelines.

Wait. But what about 1886STE-JH? Or is that a more scientific Timeline?

I fold my hands around my head and squeeze as hard as I can, and let her lead me out of the room.

A cool washcloth presses against my forehead. "You have a fever. I've sent for one of the doctors."

I can barely see Alice as she says this. Hell, I can barely think, the pain is so intense.

"Do not bother fighting it. I know what was done by mīn swëster. *I know how to work around it. She was* senfte *with you. That is her way. I am not her,* mīn scōnī. *"*

I fumble for her hand. "Alice. . ."

She knits her fingers into mine, anchoring me. "I'm here."

"She—" Bile shoots up my throat, but I manage to keep it at bay. It burns like hell when I swallow it back down. "She did something to me."

Alice's grip tightens. "Whom do you speak of?"

"I—I'm starting to remember bits and pieces." I dive beneath a wave of nausea as I roll onto my side, toward Alice. "From Koppenberg. My mom—"

"*Katrina* did something to you?"

I wince at her quickness. "No. But she was there. Jim, too."

A pause. "In the mountain?"

There's no disbelief, no skepticism. Just a request for clarification. "Yes. They protected me. Helped." My mom was there. Jim! How is that even possible? "They couldn't go with me when I was with her. At least, I don't remember them there. I don't remember much anyway. They told me to not tell anyone they were there."

"Whom, love?"

"I think she doesn't want me to remember. Every time I do . . . Damn, this headache is brutal. I've never had one like this before."

An arm loops around me, folding me closer. "You speak of the thirteenth Wise Woman."

I honestly wonder if my scalp is bleeding. If my skull is, in fact, breaking apart. My confirmation is little more than a whisper.

The way she holds on to me, it's like she's afraid the thirteenth Wise Woman will just up and appear in my bedroom just by calling her name, like the world's most insane game of Bloody Mary. "Do you know what she did to you?"

I don't, and that's the most terrifying part of it all.

"Do not fight to remember any more right now. Just rest."

"Alice—"

"Finn, I beg you do not argue with me. You have a fever. I cannot bear to think of what might happen to your body if you continue struggling. I have seen firsthand what Sara Carrisford goes through in her efforts. You have witnessed what befalls Wendy."

Wendy has seizures. I supposedly had a Grand Mal seizure when we left the mountain. Sara . . . She gets headaches, right? Nosebleeds, too.

Despite the agony, I frantically shuffle through the puzzle pieces I have. Bunting could see the words in the Codex. Could Sara? I'd lay down money that she could—and did. There was nothing during the meeting that said one way or another. I didn't see specific words, but there was that one moment I wondered if gold shimmered on those pages.

I'm compromised.

I am a liability to the team and the mission. Any moment I could go rogue.

I lower the washcloth across my eyes as Alice calls the Librarian. Have I done anything out of the ordinary? Are there gaps? *Yes.* I don't remember the seizure or the minutes leading up to it. I didn't remember Katrina or Jim until tonight. How could I forget hallucinating about my mother and my best friend for three days straight?

Was I hallucinating?

Jesus, it hurts to even think about it. I had my mom back. I had Jim.

I've lost them all over again.

Only fragments of the thirteenth Wise Woman are present. I can remember being tortured, of knives and hot pokers, but not what the Piper's partner did.

Something wipes across my nose. "You're bleeding again."

Just like Sara. Does she develop fevers, too?

"You're thinking about it, aren't you?" Hard diamonds edge Alice's frustration. "Son of a Jabberwocky! Stubborn man. Cease this foolishness at once."

"Your bedside manner isn't the best today."

My crack apparently goes over as well as a visit from the Queen of Hearts, because when I remove the washcloth, Alice's glare is just as painful as the monsters in my skull.

She dips the washcloth into a bowl of cool water and wrings it out. "The Librarian will be here shortly."

"Don't tell me anything more about the mission or any findings."

She lays the washcloth back upon my forehead. "You act as if you are in rapture. Stop being so maudlin."

"I refuse to risk anyone—"

"You aren't." The set of her mouth dares me to contradict her assertion.

"You yourself pointed out the comparisons to Sara and Wendy."

"In relation to how those who attempt to reveal secrets are punished." She flattens a hand against my stomach, over where lines of her love trace pictures across my torso. "Neither Sara nor Wendy have this. They did not have the magic of the twelfth Wise Woman." The tension straining the lines of her body eases a fraction. "Or the courage of the goose."

Could Katrina and Jim have been due to the twelfth Wise Woman's spell?

"I saw something in the Codex, Alice."

"By your own admission, you saw only faint golden marks—no words, no pictures, nothing substantial. And certainly not for anything more than a moment at best."

"But—"

"I certainly hope that, by now, you would understand that if I truly believed you to be at risk, I would not hide it from you." She blows out a harsh burst of agitation through her nose. "However, I do believe you in that the thirteenth Wise Woman did something. Allow those who love you to focus on determining what that was and how to counter it."

I tell her the truth. I say, "There isn't time."

"Clearly, the fever has left you addled as a bowl of mush."

Huh? "Every day—hell, every hour that goes by, the Piper slips further away from us. I need to go join Sara or Wendy somewhere, so that—"

"Throwing yourself upon the sword is beneath you." Flinty sparks charge the air between us.

The door to my bedroom swings open. The Librarian coughs politely. "I see I am just in time."

"How convenient that you are so punctual," Alice snaps. "Unlike the rest of us."

The Librarian brushes off the dig and converges on the bed. "You discussed it with him."

Discussed what?

It's Alice's turn to ignore a stab of disapproval. "I believe I clearly stated that I am no nursemaid, and that he is no risk."

The Librarian stares down at me. Thankfully, the nausea is lessening by the second, as is the pain. "Perhaps you are right. Even still, we cannot allow the presence to fester."

I set aside the washcloth and pull myself into a sitting position. "Don't talk about these things in front of me. I refuse to have any information they can dig out of my head."

The Librarian waves a hand at me. "Goodness. Who would have thought you to be so dramatic?" To Alice, she says, "Any solutions that I have researched are not . . . optimal."

Standing up sends my head straight onto a roller coaster. Contradicting my very last statement, I mutter. "I'm right here."

Her blue eyes practically twinkle as they laser in on me. "Make up your mind, Finn. We do not have time for you to teeter back and forth between nativity and determination, fever or no."

I literally bite my tongue in response.

"He doesn't require a doctor," the Librarian informs Alice. "The less he tries to remember the specifics, the less the witch's influence will plague him. What he needs is rest and plenty of distractions to keep his mind off of that which will cause him harm." She frowns. "I don't know what will happen if someone like Finn or Sara were to push the boundaries of the spell too far. Would they fall into rapture? Fall into a coma? Would their brains melt? Would they become soulless? Would they disappear entirely? Would they instantly become murderers, intent on killing everyone in their path?"

Alice blanches. Hell, I think I do, too.

"It's best not to push such things." The Librarian reaches up, patting me awkwardly on my shoulder. "Be a good boy and let your girlfriend distract you, hmm?"

It might be my fever, but I'm pretty sure Alice growls. I know I do.

To Alice, she says, "As I requested earlier, allow me the evening to determine the best course of action." She heads toward the doorway. "Your stubbornness, my dear, is not always an endearing quality. I certainly hope that, when the time comes, you will concede to do as asked rather than fight against reason."

Once she's gone, I ask, "What the hell is she talking about?"

Thankfully, Alice doesn't taunt me about my contradictions. "She requested I withhold our suspicions."

"She was right." I pause. "You knew I was compromised."

"I hardly see how you are *compromised*. That said, it was not hard to assume that the thirteenth Wise Woman had done something to you," she says flatly. "You were able to see something in the Codex, after all."

"Why are you so certain I won't fall into rapture?"

"I already explained this."

"I appreciate the support, but—"

The planes of her face harden. "I am not a romantic, Finn. Nor am I the sort to allow my emotions to dictate my actions. Lest you forget, I am the Queen of Diamonds, and I once had armies at my beck and call and the lives of thousands of people to consider on a daily basis. I am not rash, nor am I prone to exaggeration." Tight lines dart around her lips. "I walked away from everything and everyone I loved in order to ascertain my people's welfare. If you believe that I am deluding myself about whether or not you will become one of the Chosen, then that is your mistake. Allow me to say this once, and only once. If there comes a time in which I believe you to be a liability, I will not hesitate to ensure the Society's safety by locating a secure location for you to reside within until I can figure out how to reverse the change."

It's a surprise that I still have skin attached to my body. "I'm behaving like an ass, aren't I?"

Her smile is still cool. "You have a fever, brought on by magic. It has been my experience that many reasonable men become the opposite during illnesses."

"How very sexist of you."

She herds me toward the bed. "Lay down before you fall prey to the vapors."

Once the washcloth is placed on my forehead again, and I grudgingly accept her assistance in removing my shoes, drowsiness settles in. Alice lies beside me, holding my hand, and I'm reminded of Katrina doing the same when I caught the flu shortly after moving to New York. The entire situation was so foreign, and I didn't quite know how to accept the comfort. I was stiff; she was loving and patient.

I wanted to run. I was so certain she would find me lacking just like everyone else did. She didn't, though. She didn't push me, or expect me to be anything other than I was.

I shift, wrapping an arm around Alice's waist. I hold on to her, not wanting to let go, not wanting to run, until darkness comes for me.

The sound of glass shattering jerks me upright. The room is dark, the sheets tangling my legs damp. I fumble for the light, but a strong hand grips my wrist.

"Shite. Sorry. I thought. . ."

Adrenaline surges past my grogginess. "Victor?"

The bed groans as he sinks down on the mattress next to me. "Tried to get you a drink. Thought you might be thirsty. Ended up breaking the bloody cup."

He sounds so rational, and it worries me even more than his erratic behavior. Victor was tortured, too. Could he have seen the thirteenth Wise Woman? Could he be at risk of rapture? I can't tell, not with the lights out.

My brother cannot be one of the fucking Chosen. He can't.

"What are you doing here?" My question is a piece of sand paper, thinned from too much use.

His silhouette is inky black against the stale gray of an airless room, but I still can make out his lack of hair. "Overheard one of those prats in the lab talking about you, before the Librarian told them to not come. Needed to see for myself how you are."

His voice is rougher, less polished, like a spoon that once slipped down into the running garbage disposal and now threatens to cut the lips of those who use it.

"It's only a fever—"

He cuts me off, as if I haven't said anything at all. "He'll know that I'm gone."

Shafts of clarity cut through the fog of fever. The last time I saw my brother, he was in restraints.

I keep my tone as neutral as possible for one firing on one cylinder. "Dr. Addu?"

Victor springs off the bed; something loud clatters to the floor. "Fuck that prat." Another unseen item bangs against the hardwood floors. The swarm of black mass blurs, and suddenly, hot breath steams in my face. "*He'll* know. He'll kill you if he finds you, and I won't be able to stop him. He'll kill all of you, because no one says no to what he wants."

My gag reflex kicks into gear. "The Piper—"

He swirls away. "Won't do anything." Another crash. "Dammit, keep up, will you?"

I nearly spill toward the ground when I roll over, but my big brother is there to catch me. "You're useless like this. She got to you, didn't she?" He snatches the lamp next to the bed and hurls it against the wall.

I grab a gun out of a nearby drawer.

I angle it toward him just as he tears one of my pillows clean in half. "You better calm the hell down right now."

In a flash, he's pressed himself up against the barrel, arms high in the air. "Do it."

Before I can say anything, let alone do anything, he wrenches away. In his wake, a chair is forcefully kicked across the room, most likely broken. A blaze of light flares, and I hurry to follow him in the bathroom.

Victor stands before the mirror, mismatched eyes focused and yet dead all at once as they fixate on the image before him.

One brown, one blue.

He snarls at the reflection. "It's *his* eye. I—I didn't—"

A fist flies, shattering the mirror. Victor's roars echo off the tile and through the newly formed holes he keeps punching in the walls. *"A family's sin is a stain that cannot be washed away!"*

Eye update: one brown, one black.

I tackle him to the ground. His bellow rattles the glass shards to rain down upon us.

"You've got to calm down!" Goddamn, he is strong—stronger than he's ever been. "Victor, if you don't, I'm going to have to—"

Any remaining words fall into a blinding void of searing pain when he slams his head against mine. "I AM NOT VICTOR!"

I manage a decent slug to his jaw, which only serves to infuriate him. When gnashing teeth close in on me, I knee my brother, or whomever he thinks he is, in the nuts.

"Get off Finn this instant."

Victor's thrashing slows down to about eighty-miles-per-hour. He sneers, "This isn't your concern, *Your Majesty.*"

But he rolls off of me, scrambling toward the shower. The blue eye remains black as a captured sliver of glass angles our way.

Alice steps into the demolished bathroom. "Everyone is looking for you, Victor."

Grymsdyke scuttles in behind her, crawling up onto the ceiling.

Suddenly, Victor slams his head back against the shower door. A loud crack grows visible as hairline fractures run throughout the newly bloody frosted glass.

The black eye fades to blue once more. "He'll know I'm gone. I can't keep you safe if I don't go back."

Grymsdyke positions himself directly over Victor.

"Believe me," Alice says coldly, "the entire Institute is aware of your escape. You are lucky that none of your victims died."

I can't focus on what she's saying, though. I reach for my brother. "Who will know?"

The glass quivers in his hand even as beads of crimson drip toward the floor. "Finn?"

I ignore Alice's protestations as I creep toward him. "It's me, big bro. It's Finn."

Beads transition into a thin sluice of blood that alarms me. He says plaintively, "He'll know."

"Whom are you scared of?"

He shakes his head, skin ashy white. The glass shifts, now hovering over the swatch of skin and the blue veins of the opposite wrist. "Never told me his name. Didn't need one."

"Put the glass down, Victor."

"You need to kill me, Finn. Kill me or take me back."

I ease down in front of him. "Do you mean . . . the creature? Like the one from 1818SHE-F?"

His plea is as hoarse as my own. "A family's sin is a stain that cannot be washed away."

I wrap my hand around the one that holds the sharp shard of glass. My brother jerks, as if shocked by static electricity. "He's dead, Victor. I killed him."

Brown and blue-green eyes fasten upon me in what I can only describe as pure horror.

He doesn't fight me when I tug away the glass. "Right after that, we blew up Koppenberg Mountain with a shitton of gunpowder. He can't hurt you or anyone else again. I made sure of that."

His bloody hand clamps down over mine. "What did you do?"

I refuse to wince over the strength of his grip. "Nobody can hurt my family and get away with it."

The back of his head slams into the shower's glass door once more, sending another crack shooting toward the metal frame. He squeezes his eyes shut. "Oh God. She'll know. *They'll* know. Alice—hide him. Now. Before it's too late."

I catch his head before it smacks against the glass a third time.

"It's okay. You're safe. You're home. We'll fix this."

He tears out of my grip just as Brom bursts through the door. Eyes still closed, Victor cries, "You killed their *son*."

A LIGHT, A KISS, & A PRESENT

FINN

A NUMBER OF VICTOR'S DOCTORS suffer from broken bones; a few have concussions. We nearly deplete Mary's stash of healing spray tending the bevy of wounds my brother inflicted during his impromptu escape. Some people apologetically leave the Institute, no doubt fearful of their erratic charge. A few, Dr. Addu included, commit to staying, even when I wouldn't blame them for also running for the hills.

Victor was tranquilized shortly after Brom found us, but is burning through the drugs at an alarming rate in what we all can only hope is a secure room.

"Do you think what Victor said is possible?" Brom is asking the Librarian. We're back in the conference room, assessing damage for what feels like the fiftieth time in a single day.

"I don't know." A hot current crackles through her words. She disapproves of my presence, but worry for my brother overrides anything else. "And it is beginning to piss me off."

A hint of amusement softens Brom's scowl. "Only beginning?"

"The entire situation is wholly unacceptable. It makes me want to—"

"You won't, though." A sharp edge scrapes over Brom's assessment.

"Want and do are entirely different creatures." She drums a harsh beat against the table. "I wish I could offer more, old friend."

"We assumed that the creature was one of the original children from Hamelin," Alice says. "He bore similar physical characteristics, such as rotten teeth and blackened eyes. Perhaps the Piper and thirteenth Wise Woman view these children as their own."

Did the blue eye blacken because they were able to corrupt Victor, or because whoever used to own it was Chosen?

"It's his *eye."*

Could Victor now have one of the *creature's* eyes? I can't remember if its eyes were mismatched when we fought or not.

The monsters in my head root around for their ice picks.

"You two have dispatched a number of Chosen before," the Librarian points out to Alice. "The difference now is that Victor is concerned about retribution over this one."

"He is raving," Alice counters. "It is quite obvious he is not in his right mind, nor has been since returning to the Institute. Many of his statements are suspect."

"Victor was off his protocol for four days," Brom adds quietly. "There is no telling what effects that might have on his mind."

I lean back into my chair. "He has moments of clarity." Moments when he's Victor. Madness or not, my brother is still there, and I will be damned if I don't help him fight his way back.

"Does he, though?" Alice is gentle with her contradiction to my assertion. "Or could that opinion stem from hope rather than reality? Madness comes in many forms and guises, and is utterly seductive when needs be."

I may be losing pieces of my memory, and can't always trust everything I see. But . . . "I believe him."

Brom strokes his beard. "Say we accept that this creature—"

The Librarian interjects, "Let us call him Prometheus."

My father and I both roll our eyes at her not-so-witty attempts at humor. He concedes and continues, "If Prometheus was truly the Piper and thirteenth Wise Woman's child, then where would that put us?"

"The Piper's goal to ascertain the Codex remains unchanged," Alice insists. "He requires it for the convergence."

"Even for the most terrible of parents, a child's death can change one's course, Ms. Reeve. So the question we must ask ourselves is exactly what we must do in order to prepare for such an event."

"We have no proof that the creature was anything other than one of the Chosen," Alice argues. "Besides, what parents would do such an awful thing to their child? He was stitched together like the creature from 1818SHE-F, indicating he was molded, like many of the others, to resemble persons from various Timelines."

"Who is to say that ones such as the Piper and the thirteenth Wise Woman would not do to their own flesh and blood that they did to others?"

Alice's eyes narrow as she hones in on the Librarian. Before she can say anything, the A.D. flings himself through the door, his boots shrieking against the floor. His breathing is harsh, his face flush. "A light turned on in Pfiefer's apartment a few minutes ago."

In the span of a heartbeat, we're all on our feet. Brom says, "Make it a quick report, Mr. Dawkins."

The A.D. bends over, his hands pressed against knees and thighs. "The team watching din't notice anyone out of the ordinary enter the building, but a light doesn't turn on by itself, does it?"

I ask, "What are the bugs indicating?" And then, "There are bugs, right?"

"Ain't got no bugs inside." My father's assistant glances up at me. "Every one we tried to place fizzled out. It's like they've got some kind of anti-surveillance system, although nobody found anything during their sweep shortly after the attack. There are curtains and blinds in the apartment, so we can't even see what's going on in there save the light framing the window."

"Call Dupin," Brom orders. "Have him meet us downstairs in ten."

Phone already out and fingers flying, the A.D. bolts from the room.

Driving in New York is an art, and for a man who grew up in Paris during the Nineteenth Century, C. Auguste Dupin is a master. We make our way across town in blur of dodges, bursts of speed, and miraculous turning of corners that did not end up with the SUV rolling.

Inside the otherwise empty lobby, Dupin ups his game by blowing a handful of powder in the doorman's face. I catch the man as he slumps toward the ground. The A.D. nicks his keys and enters the security room, ready to take out the building's cameras. I drag the sedated doorman in behind him and prop him up in a chair.

Brom hovers in the doorway. "Any sign of the security guard?"

The A.D. flips through the monitors. He taps on one of the grainy screens. "Fifth floor."

"Leave him to me." Dupin shoves his hands in his pockets and heads toward the stairs.

"Since I don't have one of Marianne's viruses," the A.D. says, "I'm going to need to stay here and manually erase the footage." The sharp crack of knuckles juxtaposes against the soft hiss emanating from the screens. "Shut the door on your way out."

Brom, Alice, and I board the elevator. Thanks to Wendy's infernos, our choices of weapons were limited. I've got the gun I've kept stashed by my bed. Alice toys with a pair of daggers tucked beneath her mattress. Brom has a small pistol he always keeps on him.

"I want whoever it is alive," my father says for the fourth time since we left the Institute. He demands answers, and the dead don't always tell their stories effectively.

Alice goes over the layout of the apartment again, and as she does, I sincerely hope that this location doesn't shift and change like Bücherei, Pfiefer's mansion. One day, it housed a mysterious, multi-story labyrinth of a library chocked full with author mementos. The next, it was unoccupied, an empty shell of a house with nothing in it but an old couch and a photograph of Alice and me.

The Piper had been watching us for some time. Is he watching now?

A ding sounds, and the three of us make our way out of the elevator and down the hall toward apartment 1202. Carpet mutes our journey, but the hairs on my arms prick upward at the sheer lack of noise we wade into. No sounds of daily life slip through door cracks, no faint strains of conversations, music, or television. People go to work, true, but it's early enough in the evening that at least some twelfth-floor residents ought to be home.

My father picks 1202's lock so quickly that I worry my fever hasn't subsidized. I require a double take to ensure that it's Brom with me and not the A.D. He extracts a can of spray oil from his coat and applied to the hinges before opening the door.

When I catch his attention, a single brow raised, he winks.

We quietly enter, silently latching the door behind us. The A.D. reported a light came on in this apartment. He was right and wrong all at once—light, yes, but *all* lights are on. Every damn one of them burns brightly.

No one is in sight.

Brom motions toward a hallway, his nod indicating he'll search the office. Alice is to head to the main living area and kitchen, me down the other hallway, toward the bedrooms.

Hardwood floors and rugs are not as generously soundproof as carpet, and as such, each step is slower and more carefully placed. The first bedroom's door is wide open; a quick glance shows no sign of inhabitants. But it's not this room that I'm concerned with. The door of the one farther down the hall is propped shut, leaving just a crack to peek through.

Jackpot.

Directly in my line of sight is the back of a statuesque woman with dark hair twisted up into a bizarre sculpture of sorts. She's dressed in an elaborate red and black dress. At her feet is . . . I think it's a naked man with a burlap bag covering his face. One of the woman's dagger-like high heels digs into his groin area. He doesn't scream, though, even as I watch blood bubble around the golden-tipped heel.

Beyond is an open golden, glowing doorway to an unknown Timeline.

Suddenly, the woman's head lifts and slowly turns. Just as I am about to kick in the door and begin shooting, the shock of her cold, pale face paralyzes me. *Literally*. I could not move or speak even if I wanted to.

Wonderland's Queen of Hearts beams as if she just won the best croquet game ever.

The last time I saw her was at the New York Public Librarian's fundraiser gala. We were hunting the Piper and instead stumbled upon one of Alice's fiercest rivals. Before we could take her into custody, she disappeared into an unknown Timeline's doorway, leading us to assume she was in collusion with the Piper—although how so, none of us knew.

This is the bitch who instructed Sweeney Todd to insert a boojum into the base of Alice's spine, nearly killing the woman I love.

Triumph crawls across Hearts' blood-red lips as she has the audacity to lift a single finger up to signal me to remain quiet. Then she kicks aside the man and strides toward me.

Her metal-tipped heels make no sounds upon the hardwood floors. How can that be?

I struggle to move, to yell, to shoot. I can't even blink. Hell, I'm not even sure I'm breathing.

I have to make this bitch pay for what she's done to Alice.

She slides open the door, and then, just as my muscles tense enough to snap me out of whatever trance I'm in, she presses her body against mine. Her breath slithers across my skin. "Hello, poppet. I have been waiting for you." Sharp nails did into my chin as she angles my face toward hers. "Naughty poppet, taking his time."

I yearn to tell her how sorry I am, how truly sorry, but she merely pats my cheek before pulling me inside the bedroom. The door is locked behind us.

"Do not fret," the Queen coos as I follow where she leads. "No one can hear us in here."

Why would I care if someone were to hear us?

No—that's not right. I care. Don't I? *This isn't right.*

Is it?

I look down and find a man's bleeding body between us. Bloody holes curve into a heart shape across his chest. She'd been torturing this person for some time.

Did he hurt her? *I'll kill him.*

No—no, that's not right, either. He's . . . I know him, don't I?

The Queen drags heavily ringed fingers down my cheek, across my neck. I crave to lean into her touch. "Although I was cautioned against my curiosity, and advised to wait patiently, I wanted to see if it were true." Fingers curve around my throat. "And I am delighted to find that you are just as promised."

Pride bursts from every single one of my nerve endings even as breathing turns difficult. But then the Queen releases me and taps me on my nose. "I had worried, my poppet, that you would have fought more. I was prepared for it."

Why would I fight her? Why would she even think such ridiculous thoughts?

"It's a shame, in a way. I like it when my slaves fight." The Queen reaches down and removes the gun from my hand. I don't see where it goes, but it doesn't matters. If she wants me to shoot for her, I will. If she wants me defenseless, I'll be that, too. Hell, if she wants to shoot me, I'll stand perfectly still. "I wonder . . . which would hurt the Queen of Diamonds more?"

The sensation of someone plucking a guitar string within my head reverberates enough to cause a wince.

"You disappearing tonight, without any notice or indication as to where you go?" the Queen asks. "Or perhaps as she watches you walk away from her with the understanding that there is nothing she can do?" She grips my chin again and leans across the expanse of blood and victim below us. Is she angry with me?

I'm relieved when her ruby lips caress mine. Not angry. *Possessive.*

When she pulls away, the room tilts. Turns hazy, like there's a blaze contained by these walls.

This . . . this isn't right.

"Honestly, I wish to see her face," the Queen of Hearts murmurs. "One of my greatest joys in life so far was watching Diamonds accept her banishment and realize that she would not only lose her reign, Court, and peoples, but also the White King. Their grief was utterly delicious. I pray it will be the same when she comes to understand that you are no longer hers."

That name again. *Diamonds. The Queen of Diamonds.* Another sharp, painful ache behind my temple has me stumbling a step backward.

"Oh, so there is a bit of fight in you, is there?" Fire gleams at me as her lips thin. "Should I punish you, or. . ." She presses her mouth against mine once more, and exhaustion drapes its heavy blankets over my body. Her tongue runs across the seam of my lips, and—

"Finn?"

It's as if a bucket of ice water has crashed down upon me. I blink, and the woman before me morphs back into my enemy.

I hiss, fumbling for my gun, "I am going to make you pay for what you've done to Alice."

She clucks delightedly as she backs into the glowing doorway. *Where the hell is my gun?* "I think it is the other way around, is it not?" And then, Hearts is nothing but a blur of red and black before the door disappears.

"Finn?"

The door pushes open and I stumble into the man on the floor. Alice rushes into the room. "There you are! The rest of the apartment is—"

She stops. Looks at me hard, her eyes slits.

If I didn't know better, I'd say I've just come off the worst drinking bender of all time. I had the Queen of Hearts before me, and she got away.

How in the hell did that happen? And where the hell is my gun?

Brom appears behind Alice. "Who is that on the floor?" He glances up at me. "Why is there red lipstick all over your face?"

I wipe the back of a hand across my mouth. Creamy red stains my skin.

Brom is bending down at my feet, yanking the burlap sack off the man's head. A sense of searing anger, grief, and outrage explodes in my chest. Below me is Otto Lidenbrock.

Someone captured and tortured one of the Collectors' Society's agents.

And there's lipstick on my face, and it isn't Alice's. She isn't wearing any. I don't remember kissing anyone that isn't Alice. What is going on?

The woman I love steps into my line of sight as Brom attempts to wake the former professor. "What did she do to you?"

She. Which she?

"The Queen of Hearts. What did she do to you?"

Brom swears. "He's alive, but needs a doctor immediately. Finn, call 911."

I dig out my phone from my pocket and do as requested. My father asks Alice, "What's this about the Queen of Hearts?"

She motions at the bloody heart carved upon Otto's chest. "I have seen this more times than I would like." More tightly, "The rogue on Finn's face is a color I know to be hers."

The Queen of Hearts . . . kissed me? I am immediately, and thoroughly, ready to purge the little left in my stomach.

When I hang up, Brom asks, "What happened in here, son?"

It scares the shit out of me to admit, "I don't remember."

A TROUBLING REPORT

ALICE

OTTO LIDENBROCK IS ON life support. His injuries are numerous—more than simply the grotesque calling card the Queen of Hearts left behind. One of the Society's doctors snuck in various medicines from different Timelines to the hospital in an effort to help our fallen comrade, but even so, the mood within the Institute is bleak.

"How can you not remember the Queen of freaking Hearts?" Mary snaps at Finn.

I fire off a warning of my own. "Enough."

Since I found him in the Piper's bedroom, a sense of agitated frustration has engulfed Finn. Worse, his fever returned with a vengeance.

"I—I don't—" He clutches his head to stem the raging headache that now grips him.

I temper my frustration in order to remind him, "Don't force the memories. You must relax."

In the car on the ride home, the smell of Hearts' perfume wafted from his skin. He showered as soon as we arrived at the Institute, almost as if he knew that traces of the evil woman lingered on his face and body.

The list of this woman's transgressions grows exponentially. She and I will have a reckoning before the end.

How dare she attack him.

"I agree with Alice," the Librarian says from her perch by the door. "There is no use haranguing Finn when no answers will come."

Mary shoots off my sitting room couch. "Those bastards are taking us out one by one! Wendy, Otto, Finn. Victor." Her nose wrinkles at the catch in her list. "Dammit, even the little princess was attacked. The Chosen won't stop until they've eliminated each and every last one of us, will they?"

The Librarian says quietly, "It seems as much, doesn't?"

Mary storms from the flat, brushing past the Librarian. Within seconds, a door across the hallway slams shut.

"She isn't wrong," the Librarian murmurs. And then she, too, leaves.

Finn pushes the heel of his hand against his forehead. I remind him again to cease forcing the memories.

He says quietly, heartbreakingly, "I'm so damn sorry, Alice."

I twist my hands into my skirt. "You have nothing to be sorry about."

"I kissed someone. Someone who isn't you. I don't—that's—I can't even imagine wanting anyone but you."

I stare straight ahead, refusing to even allow an image of the event to coagulate, lest I immediately charge off with my blades in my fists. "*She* kissed *you,* an unwillingly partner. Of that I have no doubt."

I am torn between wishing to know why, how she managed to tinker with his memory, and wanting to drive a sword through her blackened, evil heart.

"You have a call."

What timing. I must take a deep breath before turning to face Jack. Van Brunt's assistant loiters in my doorway.

"Don't kill the messenger." As he titters, slashing a finger across his throat, a rosy flush steals up his neck. It is then I realize my fingers are tightly curled into hard balls. Frabjous. "Normally, I wouldn't bother you, considering, but. . ." He glances at Finn meaningfully, and the urge to slap him increases. "I think you'll want to take it."

My jaw aches, my teeth push so strongly against one another. "My phone did not ring." Never mind that I do not have it with me. I haven't the slightest where it is.

Finn rises from the couch and drifts into the kitchen. Jack and I follow. "He means there's a transmission from another Timeline." Finn uncorks Mary's bottle of absinthe; green liquid sloshes into a glass. "Yours, I'm guessing. Is this the strongest stuff you have in here?"

I want to knock the crystal out of his hand and simultaneously drink it all myself. As for Jack, the thief hovers at a safe distance, his large feet uncharacteristically shuffling against tile as he twirls short strands of hair around a pair of fingers.

"Mary brought it over." I indulge in another deep inhalation, cursing the windstorm battering the interior of my body and soul.

This strong, intelligent, brave man has been attacked far too many times over the course of our acquaintance. More than once, these actions came from the hands of my past. He has suffered because of knowing and loving me.

"You should go take the call." He attempts a smile, but it doesn't truly grow. "I doubt the White King is reaching out merely to chit-chat."

When I hesitate, he leans forward and kisses my cheek. "Go. I need to talk to Brom, anyway."

And yet, I still hesitate. "I will be back shortly."

His hip props against the counter as he swirls the contents within his glass. His gaze finds mine and holds steady. Tiny shoots sprout within, ones that pray for growth. But then he drinks the entirety of the glass. A kiss on the mouth is offered before he drifts past me, past Jack, and out the door.

A good several inches of air spans between Jack's boots and the floor. "It was just a few pecks, right?"

"I wonder," the Caterpillar said, his hookah dangling between his third and fourth feet, "if all Englanders are as brittle as you."

We were in my study, and it was close to midnight. He had waited until after supper to present me with three-dozen so-called important papers, treatises, and trade offers to go over. The comfort of warm, soft down and even softer blankets beckoned me like a siren perched on rocks, luring lost sailors to a dark home, and yet candles continued to burn brightly and logs within the fireplace crackled merrily.

Lifting my head was enough to elicit a yawn, although I did my best to hide it from him. Not fast enough, for he snapped, "Or as rude."

For the last two hours, as I poured what precious little energy I possessed into those documents after a day spent walking through a handful of villages, ensuring food and supplies were given to those in need, my Grand Advisor gossiped steadily about those within our court and beyond. After a particularly salacious recollection about the Hatter and the King of Hearts (which I wholeheartedly believed, knowing the Hatter), I mentioned that perhaps we ought to remain focused on state business.

"They are called English, not Englanders," I clarified as I scrawled my name across yet another sheet of parchment. "What exactly have I done this evening that has left you to determine I am brittle?"

A burst of smoky question marks blew my way. "You are always so insistent upon protecting others' privacy."

I knew better than to laugh, but I was amused enough to set down my quill and offer my undivided attention.

Not that I allowed him to see my amusement, either.

"When you hear details of others' lives, the bones within you turn to glass." One of his bare feet lifted a goblet of juice, even though another brought his hookah pipe to his lips. "One need only to tap at you to watch you shatter in a horrified transgression of impropriety."

His riddles left me as exhausted as my day had. "I fail to see the comparison."

"You wouldn't." He snorted, exhaling a long stream of smoke, its ripples burbling over rocks. "Your head is a bit unnaturally thick."

When I said nothing, he added, "Your fear of being thought of as impolite. You are a queen, Alice. Holding on to such a fear is ridiculous and dangerous."

"I hardly see how my refusal to indulge in petty gossip is the same—"

He waved off my protestations, the juice in his cup sloshing onto my desk. "Impropriety is not the same thing as knowing when the sharing of information is beneficial." A sneer turned his lips up before they curled back around the pipe.

I said slowly, carefully, "You were gossiping."

A smoky top hat hit me right in the face. As I waved the sweet smoke away, coughing, he snapped, "I was informing you that the Queen of Hearts marked the Hatter for death. Annoying and idiotic as he may be, his death ought to be from his juice, not her battle-axe. Does privacy trump death?"

I once more fail the Caterpillar, for my upbringing could not be erased, at least not entirely. But in this moment, even when death is not suspected, I allow the glass within my bones to soften, to melt into a much more durable, mobile sand.

This is twice I have failed Finn in the span of too little time.

Instead of knocking Jack to the ground, I instead smooth back the golden strands that have fallen from my neglected bun. "Lead the way."

My gait is brisk as I make my way to the control room. Jack apologizes and detours to answer yet another call that sounds upon his cell. Inside, I find Marianne within the control room, clacking upon her laptop. When she notices me, she digs within a nearby tote and extracts a pair of headphones. "I must apologize over how I cannot leave yet," she tells me, "but these miraculous contraptions are noise canceling, so your privacy is assured."

I wonder what the Caterpillar would think of such an invention.

As Marianne adjusts the fuchsia-colored metal and plastic muffs over her ears, I settle into a partially burnt rolling chair before the large monitor. All around us are blackened, scorched reminders of the Piper's fury—and of the injustice Wendy has suffered at his hands.

I claim the tablet nearby and tap upon the hold button. Within a split second, an all-too-familiar face graces the screen, contrary to time and space.

The White King of Wonderland's face is no longer clean-shaven. A careless, adolescent beard darkens his jaw and above his lip; a fresh, pink scar streaks across a gaunt cheek. Dirt and blood cake pale skin.

Time, distance, and acceptance do nothing to quell the ache that tenderizes my heart. My past and Wonderland reach out to touch me for the second time in a single day.

"I was worried that perhaps you would not come."

In my mind, crystal clear, is a floral wreath of white roses. A large, beautiful diamond ring. A ride across the Dark Meadows, where strong arms and easy banter brought a smile to my face and joy to my heart. A promise of safety, of dreams fulfilled.

Dreams are not reality, though.

I say, "The Institute was attacked, and there is much confusion abound."

His nearly white eyes soften and yet narrow as they trace me through pixels and impossibilities. "Are you injured?"

He asks me this, when it is he who has seen better days of health. "I am fine."

"And the others?" He pauses, voice lowering. "The Prince of Adámas? Van Brunt? The doctor? How do they fare?"

A surprising sting surges forward in both eyes and throat. "Our company is together once more, and that is what matters."

Jace bites his lip, his piercing gaze seeing right through me, just as it always has. But he allows me this privacy, an inherited fragility that came with the love of a so-called Englander.

"And you?" My voice is steady, far steadier than the pulse beneath my skin or the muscle within my ribcage.

His head tilts back to reveal a mud-splattered throat. "War is not a kind mistress, my lady. It demands much." Somewhere behind him, in my beloved Wonderland, a boom rings so strongly that a pencil upon the desk before me rattles to the floor. "The price always feels too high."

No matter what, no matter reason or acceptance, part of me still will forever yearn to be there, defending and fighting alongside my people, and his.

"But, let us not talk about that," Jace says. "I have reached out this way for I have news you must hear."

What would a week, nay, a singular span of light and darkness, be like nowadays that did not possess the darkest of news?

"As you know, since I was last in your acquaintance," he says as another boom thunders in the distance, "I have been hunting the Queen of Hearts. I had begun to worry, perhaps, that she had fled to another land, but word arrived just yesterday of a most alarming nature. The citizens of Nobbytown have become unlike themselves— and the few witnesses who escaped such a fate claim that such stark changes have come at the hands of mysterious pipers roaming the streets and pubs."

My inclination to reveal Hearts' recent whereabouts stills on my tongue, as I have surely fallen off a cliff, or the ground beneath me has turned to quicksand.

"These . . . strangers, if you will, are garbed entirely in Hearts regalia specially belonging to the Queen." When Jace rubs a hand across his face, new streaks of dirt and blood form weary pictures. "It cannot be a coincidence, Alice. Wonderland has magic, but I have never seen or heard of this kind."

The Queen of Hearts was in New York several hours ago, molesting Finn. And now . . . "The Chosen are in Wonderland."

"We have been thus far unsuccessful in our attempts to capture and interrogate one of these pipers," Jace continues. "I am determined, though."

Tiny bumps riddle my arms, eliciting a shiver. "Has there been any indication of the Piper himself?"

"I wish I could answer definitively one way or another, my lady. While most of the reports speak of children, there are some of dark-haired gentlemen. If it is the Piper that you seek, I know not."

"Do everything that you can to protect yourself and your troops,

Jace. Do not allow yourself to listen to their music, no matter how determined you are to capture one of these fiends. Promise me this."

His displeasure creases his forehead. "Alice. . ."

"Please." The word is broken, unsteady as the reality I now find myself within. "I cannot do what must be done if he was to get his hands upon you, too."

My emotions rule me. My bones turn to glass, no matter how much I wish or pretend differently, and they shatter all too easily.

What would the Caterpillar say?

Jace's nearly white eyes widen; his lips flatten as they press between his teeth. For many seconds, I scramble to reclaim the glassy shards I just spewed across the control room, to wipe away the feelings coursing down my cheeks.

He asks me, "Where is your prince?"

The dam has been breached. I seal my eyes closed, so I cannot accept compassion I do not deserve.

And yet, a woman cannot maintain the might of a pillar forever. Here, now, faced with the man who has been my confidant for the entirety of my adulthood, I allow myself to momentarily lean against his strength.

I lay bare my shame. "I failed him."

"I find that impossible."

Jace's belief in me, in my convictions and abilities, cannot be tolerated in this instance. "He is physically fine. They have miraculous medicines here, ones that were able to replace skin peeled away in small strips, repair countless lash marks, and soothe a multitude of other injuries that only the truly evil could inflict." A quick glance over my shoulder promises Marianne's focus remains upon her computer. Even still, the words I need to say are herculean to enunciate, to even accept a release into reality, so I merely gasp, adrift. "As Finn was continually tortured, I lay asleep, unmolested. Just today, the Queen of Hearts. . ."

The name of my nemesis commands oily, strong tendrils down and around my throat, it is so bitter upon my tongue.

Jace, however, bears no impediment, as he seizes on the

assumption with alacrity. "What of the Queen of Hearts?"

"She was here, in New York City, within the Piper's Manhattan apartment." There are no daggers to be found, so the twisted chair arms will have to do to still my hands. "I do not know all of what occurred when Finn . . . encountered her," I cannot, will not mention the lip rogue, "but a Society agent was discovered bearing a bloody heart carved into his chest, and Finn lost bits of his memory."

There is no doubt that Hearts manipulated Finn and Lidenbrock for one reason, and one reason only. She wished to send me a message. She wished me pain.

I desire to offer her the same in return.

"Hearts is in your New York?"

"Gone now."

"Alice."

I close my eyes to his compassion and shared outrage, and command the tide I called forth when I began my confessional to recede.

Jace is undeterred.

"I am sorry, deeply sorry, to hear of this, my lady. And as I was not present, although I wish I had been, I may only surmise at all that truly happened during the time since we last spoke. You and Finn share Wonderlandian blood magic. You cannot harbor guilt for sleeping, for his love protected you, just as it has before. And yours. . ." Unbidden grief, scarred yet raw, still has no place to hide when the White King discusses such matters. "Many people do not survive torture, let alone encounters with Hearts. You know this. How often did we witness such devastation inflicted upon innocents?"

Too often.

"Your prince survived, though. And that is what you must hold on to. *He survives* when so many do not. That cannot be sheer happenstance." Quietly, assuredly, "Not when it comes to those with a bond such as yours."

How difficult must it be for the White King to say such things to me? It is nearly unbearable to hear them, even if he is my confidant. Shame stains the logic he provides. "I apologize for turning the conversation toward more delicate matters. We were discussing—"

"These roads that we traverse upon are not easy by any means, for any soul," he continues, and rather than indulge in annoyance for the interruption, I am taken back to so many nights in which we lay in bed, expounding philosophy. "There are times in the dark of night in which I wallow in the belief that ours, in particular, are even more rocky than most. You and I are rulers, my lady. The paths before us are never straight or meant for an easy day's journey. But perhaps it is not even that we are kings and queens—perhaps each person's road travelled is filled with potholes and stones, and we stumble, fall, and right ourselves all the same. We must be considerate of those we love, and even those we do not. We must find our way with others who may share the road with us, for as little as a small slice of time or even years or further. There are periods when we must clear obstacles that block our journey, be them overturned carriages or people. And there are times when those we share our path with branch off and wander away, or even tread parallel to us upon another road."

Stupid, mimsish emotions, refusing to obey my orders, tumble down my cheeks.

"I am well acquainted with your heart, Alice. I often have wondered if I know it better than my own. And thusly, as your . . . friend, your confidant . . . as one who will always be there for you when needed, I ask that you trust in that heart. Trust in the strength of its love. I always have, and I believe your prince does, too. You could not have failed him. The Queen of Diamonds does not fail those she loves. She will fight, kicking and clawing if she must, to protect those she allows to walk beside her. You may have been sleeping while he was tortured, but you woke, did you not?"

I cannot live in a dream world, no matter how alluring it may be, not when there are those in the real world who need me.

Not when my north star was, and is, in danger.

"You woke, and your prince is no longer anyone's prisoner. Hearts is gone, although you must stay on guard. I do not need to have been present to know that you fought your way to your prince, and you made his safety just so."

I open my heart once more: raw, steady, honest. "You were in my dreams, when I was in Koppenberg Mountain, hunting for the Piper. We were in Wonderland, and there was peace."

The White King's smile is wan. His lip is split and caked with dried blood and pus. "And still, you woke."

I woke, because I could not, would not, let Finn go. Not even in a dream. I freely gave him my heart, and he gave me his in return. I have a home in New York, a purpose. A mission.

I say lightly, "You sound like the Sage."

The quiet timbre of his laugh comforts my hardening bones. "Perhaps I do. I visited her many times after you left Wonderland. She and I debate often."

I tsk, grateful to have, after digging so deep into this confessional well, a clear cup of humor. "A Wonderlandian king dares to disagree with the Sage? Treasonous."

"That is neither here nor there." He cups his mouth, mock whispering, "I believe she rather enjoys it."

Of course she does. She is the Sage, is she not?

I inelegantly wipe a sleeve across both cheeks and nose. "So. It appears that the exiled will return to Wonderland yet again."

For the Piper *and* the Queen of Hearts.

The White King's name is bellowed just before the roar of thunder distorts his image upon the screen. "Name the date," he says, "and I will have soldiers meet you at the rabbit hole in order to assure safe passage."

"Much appreciated, but no escort will be necessary. To risk anyone further is unforgivable."

He does not approve, but I am grateful when he does not argue.

"That said, I cannot allow the Piper to move further away from me." Or the Queen of Hearts. "I will begin my journey tomorrow, just before dawn."

I am given directions to his encampment, which is not too far from Nobbytown, as he wishes to monitor the situation and offer shelter to those who may still be able to flee. Afterward, before the White King of Wonderland places a fist over his heart in farewell, I offer one more request.

"Send jubjub birds to the other monarchs, save the Queen of Hearts. I may be exiled, and many desire my head, but it is time for us to convene once more."

REFUSING TO SAY GOODBYE

ALICE

FINN IS NOT WITHIN his flat, nor mine. When I check the infirmary, neither he nor Victor is present. I barrel toward Van Brunt's makeshift office in the conference room, ready to tear Hearts apart with my bare hands.

Instead of my archenemy, I find my breath and my sanity, for Finn, Van Brunt, and the Librarian are hunched over the table, peering at the screen of an open laptop

As the door's groan announces my arrival, Finn glances up. "I was about to call you. We found a solution."

While Finn uses a plural connotation, neither his father nor the Librarian appears pleased by such a statement.

News from Wonderland is momentarily placed to the side. "A solution for. . .?"

"Victor." Shadows cast across his handsome face. "And me."

I cannot bear that Finn feels this way about himself, that his confidence has been shaken thusly. "There is nothing the matter with you."

"There is. I'm compromised, Alice. I know I am. And I'll be damned if I ever let the fucking Queen of Hearts use me against you again, let alone anyone else." He says this plainly, as if these are facts from a book or a lab, facts that cannot be disputed. "I'm nobody's puppet, and I sure as hell refuse to let anybody turn me into something I'm not."

No, he is no puppet. Huckleberry Finn Van Brunt has always embraced who he is, and refused to kowtow to others. His sense of self has long been attractive to me.

Allowing no room for counterargument, he continues, "I saw something in the Codex, even if just momentarily. Like Sara and Wendy, I'm unable to remember certain things without side effects. Everyone needs to set aside their emotions and realize I'm a liability to the Society. Victor isn't the only Van Brunt who the Chosen messed with."

He is right. Rationally, when laid out relentlessly thus, Finn crafts a clear case as to how the Chosen have manipulated him. Why, then, is it so difficult to accept? Why the persistent instinct to deny?

I search for the logic I fought so hard over the past year to maintain. "Nevertheless, I hardly see how the two of your situations are similar."

"The only reason my eyes aren't yet black," he says flatly, "is because of you and our blood magic."

The twelfth Wise Woman claimed as much, too. *"Blood magic is what protects him. Yours and the other's, given freely out of love. Love is the most powerful magic of all."*

Not only my blood flows amongst Finn's, but so does the White King's. His love for me carries over to protect Finn.

"As there is no probability of my love toward you fading, let alone disappearing," I say coolly, "rapture is an impossibility."

He is equally dispassionate when he counters me. "You, yourself, believe in the impossible."

"Not this possibility."

He crosses his arms, his legs spread just enough to match his shoulders. "Magic is unpredictable."

I match his stance, refusing to give any ground. "Concerning love?"

"Concerning whatever they did to me."

I look to his father for some semblance of support, but silence and anguish have cut away pieces of the elder Van Brunt's tongue.

"Victor escaped the medical wing again when we went to the Piper's apartment," Finn says. "He's burning through sedatives as if they are nothing but water. He attacked Holgrave and Jo Bhaer before making his way to Mary's lab, where he bashed away at the door with one of the emergency axes, like Nicholson in the goddamn *Shining* movie. Like he didn't conceptualize that it's made of metal, not wood. Luckily, Blake and a few others were able to tackle him before he did any further damage. Who knows how long it will take before I attack someone, too?"

I have no idea whom Nicholson is, let alone a movie about shining, but I can easily imagine the dread our colleagues experienced during such a tirade. "Mary said nothing earlier."

"Mary," says the Librarian, "was in the Museum with me during Victor's mania. Perhaps it is best we do not inform her of such an incident."

Too much is spinning away from me. From us. "Are Bhaer and Holgrave all right?"

Van Brunt reaches for his large cup of coffee. "Physically, yes."

The Librarian throws her hands up. "Alice, you disappoint me. You have yet to even ask Finn about what these solutions entail."

She is not disappointed, though, not in me at least. Frustration blotches her cheeks as she rounds on Van Brunt. "These treatments are experimental." Deep ridges erupt across her delicate brow. "There is no guarantee of success."

"What other choices are there?" Brom's query is the soft echo of thunder rolling in the distance. "You agreed that both Finn and Victor are risks. Victor is not only that, but he poses an immediate physical threat to those tasked with his care. You have offered no solutions or even ideas about how to overcome what has been done to my sons. Ms. Darling was used as a bomb against us after months of unwittingly passing over intelligence. Ms. Carrisford rightly fears the same after being used to spy on the Institute. Who can claim the same cannot be said of Finn or Victor?"

I bristle at the insinuation, but Finn nods assuredly.

A guttural snarl tears from the Librarian as she swipes a pile of papers off the table. "It is infuriating that I do not yet understand what has been done." Fire warms her skin; ice hardens her eyes. "I have underestimated *eta ved'ma*, which is wholly unacceptable."

Rather than be alarmed at her temper tantrum, an odd sheen of hope alights Van Brunt's eyes. "What if—"

The temperature in the room lowers significantly. I am genuinely surprised frost does not coat the furniture. "Do not think I have not considered it."

The interests grows exponentially as he invades her personal space. "If I were to assume responsibility, if I were to accept a debt—"

"Never." The laptop on the table shudders from the strike of her fist. Both Finn and I involuntarily jerk. "I would not allow that for you, or for them."

Undeterred, Van Brunt continues, "What if it's our best shot?"

"You cannot want that," the Librarian snaps, "and I refuse to allow you to entertain such ideas. The time will come, and I will be ready, but never for that."

Atypical defeat sags Van Brunt's shoulders. Finn says, "Then we have no other choice than the one we've found."

The Librarian's knuckles pop and crackle as her fingers curl in and out of fists.

The flutter of angry, trapped wings scrape against my sensibilities. "What kind of treatment is under consideration?"

"There are a consortium of doctors," Van Brunt says, his face as emotionless as his words as he continues to stare at the Librarian, "who have done much work on mental illnesses."

The Librarian throws her hands up and scoffs.

I glance at the man beside me, but he, in turn, averts his gaze. "While Victor suffers from mental illness, Finn does not."

Finn snaps, "They're in my head," as Van Brunt, kneading the back of his neck, mutters, "Not in the traditional sense."

I might as well be in Wonderland, these answers are so maddening. "Where are these doctors located?"

Finn clears his throat. "Antarctica."

Which might as well be an entirely different Timeline. "If you were to go—"

"We are," Finn says. "It's decided."

My inhalation is sharp. "When?"

"Tonight. Within the hour."

These are more facts he presents—not opinions, but facts that offer no room for debate.

So soon.

The lights overhead flare too brightly; my balance is too precarious. I blurt, "The Piper is in Wonderland. Or at least Chosen are. And they all bear the Queen of Hearts' regalia."

Van Brunt swears violently. Finn pulls away, stalking toward the windows. Building, street, and car lights slash through the velvety darkness. He focuses on the now familiar sight, one a year ago I could not have even imagined in my dreams.

"All the more reason for me to go." His declaration fogs the glass, and I foolishly wish to doodle a picture in the condensation, if only to feel its realness.

I cross the room to join him. "I planned on journeying there tomorrow, but I will delay so that I may accompany you to Antarctica."

"No." He does not turn away from the vista before us. "Go to Wonderland as scheduled. This might be the lead the Society needs."

The hardness in both tone and muscle tells me he will not be journeying with me, though.

The Librarian does not trust the treatment. And while I do not trust the Librarian often, I do know that, if she is uneasy about something, it is for good reason.

"There are others who can go," I say steadily.

The twist of his mouth is grim yet oddly gentle. "None know Wonderland as well as you."

Stubborn, stubborn man.

"Look. I can't be trusted to be near Hearts right now. I'm sorry, Alice. You don't know how bad of a hit this is against my ego, even though we all know you don't need my help to take care of business."

A roll of unwanted chills sweeps across my skin. "We're partners. I will always desire your assistance."

He must feel the same, doesn't he?

"Put together a team, Ms. Reeve." In the glass, I watch the reflection of Van Brunt close the laptop and tuck it beneath his arm. "If all goes as planned, we will meet up with you in Wonderland within a few days. Finn, I'll verify travel arrangements and will meet you on the helicopter pad in a half hour."

Van Brunt stalks from the room. In the glass, the Librarian appears behind us, her reflection more misty than clear. "You are forbidden to die. Is that clear? You will regret defying me if you do."

He chuckles, and she, too, departs.

Everything is happening all too quickly. "What do these doctors do?"

Finn leans his face against the glass, angling it toward me. "I don't know all the particulars. I only heard about them when we got back. They contacted us about gaining some information on the Chosen."

The unbearable sensation of a corset being laced about me grows. "If the Librarian claims their procedures are experimental, perhaps it is best to side with caution."

"I have to try." He takes one of my hands. "Mary was right, you know. The Piper and the Chosen are taking agents out, and as much as it kills me and my pride, I'm one of them. The people here in the Society . . . they're my friends. My family. The Institute is the only place I've ever truly called home. I can't stand on the sidelines if there is a possibility I'll be used against the ones I love. And to be used against *you* again?" Steely determination only fortifies his litany of reasons. "I love you, Alice. You came out of nowhere to shine bright in my sky, and even though it was crazy fast and everything since has been chaotic, you mean the world to me." His warm thumb strokes mine. "If I ever did something to you because of these bastards, I wouldn't be able to live with myself."

Familiar surges of grief born from forced separation bubble up in my throat. "You wouldn't. You could never."

We have true love, after all.

"I'm going to guarantee that."

I cannot allow any questions or concerns to plant seeds of doubt, for I fear my psyche will not accept any outcome other than success. Finn does not deserve a blithering, weak partner who weighs his conscience down with guilt and fear. And I refuse to ever become that person, anyway.

I tell him as steadily as one must in just such a situation, "I journey to the White King's encampment. We will hunt the Chosen down with our armies."

The string tightening his shoulders slackens a bit as he straightens. "Kick their asses, Alice."

My chuckle is soft, a breath of allowed air. "I fear I will never become truly accustomed to these modern-day sayings."

He requests the location, and I draw a map upon a scrap of paper. I fold it into a square and tuck it into his blue jeans' pocket. "Do not lollygag. I require your gun and expertise in battle. Wonderland will need its Diamonds prince."

He bows before pressing a kiss against my knuckles. "Wild horses couldn't keep me away."

"Do not dare bade me goodbye." I pull him closer as the chasm of my past threatens to rupture between us. "This is not farewell. This is merely a momentary separation, nothing more." And then I seal my lips shut to hold back the onslaught all too ready to tumble into that abyss.

All of the hardened lines etching his handsome face melt, first as his brows furrow and then again as they smooth and his mouth falls opens. He laces our fingers together and presses our joined hands against his heart. "You're right. Because I am coming back to you, in just a few days." He kisses the back of my hand. "This isn't the same as what happened with you when you left Wonderland, Alice. Not even close. There's no prophecy here. And even if there were, as long as this means something to you, there is nothing that could keep us apart."

When I indulge in my turn in kissing the back of his hand, I linger, my lips against his tan, warm skin for many heartbeats.

"I wish," he says, "we had more than a half hour."

Being the greedy lady I am, I will always wish for as much time as possible with this man.

When we kiss, I savor his taste. I memorize the feel of his lips against mine, silky and firm and erotic all at once. I commit to memory his grip on my face and in my hair, and the heat of his breath against my mouth.

The Caterpillar told me our hearts are made up of those we know. So many pieces are etched by this man.

Soon, too soon, the sound of a cell phone chirping breaks through our hastily built cocoon. We reluctantly separate. I am aching and trembling and furious and desperate.

I crave another meal of vengeance.

He peruses the message an interloper sent, even as we still hold one another. "They need me to help get Victor to the roof. He's not exactly cooperative." His phone disappears into his pocket, next to the map I drew. "Not that you couldn't hold your own against him, but maybe it's best if you don't come up with."

An explanation is unnecessary. After all, did I not make the same request to the White King during my departure from Wonderland?

"I love you, my north star." He caresses my cheek with his lips.

I kiss him again, meaningfully, deeply, so that there will be no doubt in his mind over how much this will forever mean to me. So he understands that, as binaries, our orbits are interlocked.

I do not threaten him as the Librarian did. I breathe him in and tell him I will see him in a few days' time.

A WITCH

ALICE

"WE MUST TALK."

The Librarian, nursing a cup of tea, perches upon the sofa in my flat's sitting room as if it were her own. As she drinks from a china set that I do not own, I must surmise she had Jack bring the tea setting with her. "Please," I say wryly, "make yourself comfortable."

She does so by motioning for me to sit down upon my own chair and then assuming role of hostess by pouring me a cup of tea.

I would prefer a cup of the Hatter's juice instead.

"Although the timing of the Van Brunts' departure is unfortunate," she says tightly, ensuring I clearly recognize the words she fails to specifically also attach, "you and I have other matters to focus on. Starting with our trip to Wonderland."

The cup is not even a half-inch from my lips before I unceremoniously jerk it away, splattering tea upon my person and furniture. Surely I misheard her. The Librarian is infamous for never leaving the Institute, save for one situation that left the majority of Society members befuddled. "*Our* trip?"

The woman in question tucks her long, glossy hair back from her beautiful face. "Jack, Marianne, and your assassin will do nicely to provide the necessary backup, both in weapons, thievery, fighting, and technology." Her focus lifts away from me, toward the main door. "Wouldn't you agree, Mary?"

A darkened version of my friend and colleague haunts the doorframe. No longer biting and witty, scarves of sorrow wrap tightly around her. She asks, "Are they gone?"

The Librarian busies herself with readying Mary's tea. "Yes."

Mary drifts into the sitting room, eventually situating herself on the couch next to the Librarian. "Good." More loudly and infinitely more fragilely, "Good."

I do not ask if she shares my qualms. Instead, I wonder if Mary fears she has little to lose with Victor undergoing any experimental procedure.

Mary coughs into a hand. "Why Wonderland?"

As she pours milk into Mary's cup, the Librarian motions for me to explain. Emotional or not, I cannot stem the irritation she inspires within me.

"There are reports of a town besieged by pipers bearing the Queen of Hearts' regalia who change them from what they are to something else entirely."

Brown eyes ringed in red stare straight ahead. "That bloody sonofabitch and his minions are hiding in Wonderland."

"It is an excellent possibility."

Arms fold tightly across her chest. "I'm going with you."

"I rather thought that was obvious." The Librarian passes Mary the teacup. "You'll need to ensure two weeks' provisions for three people, considering Wonderland's food and water are addictive to non-natives. While that sounds like a lot, try to pack lightly." Her head cocks to the side. "I assume Grymsdyke will obtain his own food."

I am once more startled. "Two weeks?"

The Librarian slowly savors her drink. "Your Caterpillar is dead, is he not? How many other Wonderlandian poisoners are talented enough to concoct mixtures to allow non-natives to leave?"

"I meant—"

"I will speak with Jack and Marianne," she continues, as if I were not speaking at all. "It's best we leave while it is still dark."

I try another quandary. "Why only three sets of provisions, if there will initially be five of us—with the possibility of six to eight in total, once the Van Brunts return from Antarctica."

Entirely unruffled, the Librarian tops her cup off. "Brom and the boys know better than to expect us to behave as their pack mules."

Mary slowly refocuses. "Who is the fifth in the original party?" She holds out a hand, ticking down fingers. "Me, Alice, Jack, Marianne—"

"And me, which was clearly stated when you entered the room." The Librarian adds a bit of honey. "Mary, you really must snap out of this melancholia. If you continue to be slow-witted, we might as well paint a large target on your back."

Mary immediately tosses her cup and saucer onto the table, splattering tea onto wood and books. "I beg your pardon."

"You will do no such thing. Begging is below you, Mary Lennox. Now clean up this mess. We are in the Institute, not some kind of coastal tavern filled with drunkards and wenches too inebriated to keep their beverages in containers."

Although grumbling, Mary does as asked and fetches paper towels from the kitchen. As she mops up the liquid, the Librarian says, "I have come to realize that, from this point forward, my staying behind is no longer a viable choice. The Society has risked, and at times paid, too much for me to allow this. If or when the time comes for me to also pay the steep costs for my travels, I will be ready to accept it."

I am the most joyous dog with a juicy bone gifted after months of no treats. "What costs?"

"That reminds me." The Librarian sets her saucer and cup onto the silver tray resting on the table. "Mary, I must have a word alone with Alice. Organize our provisions and pack yourself a bag. Do not bother with period clothing. Bring only the necessities; anything else can be obtained in Wonderland. Tell Jack and Marianne to do the same, and then have Jack put out a call to all agents in residence for a mandatory meeting in two hours' time."

Mary is clearly torn about leaving, as she, no doubt, wants answers, too. Muttering beneath her breath, "This is bullshit," she storms out of my flat.

I am not such a trusting soldier, though. "If we are to work together outside of the Institute, I expect answers. Why are we only to bring three provisions?" I prod. "You yourself pointed out the addictiveness of Wonderlandian food."

Finally, her familiar sly smile emerges. "As your White King ensured his blood runs within you, in order to combat such an occurrence, I figured it was time to put his theory to the test. That said, perhaps you ought to take another dose before we leave, just to be on the safe side."

"That takes care of four members of our party. What of the fifth?"

The corners of her lips curl even higher. "Haven't you already guessed?"

Freshly ground dust flakes from my teeth. "Why would *you* not require such precautions?"

"The reason I wished to speak privately with you, Alice, is to impart a bit of essential information concerning my participation in the trip."

Why do I bother asking anything at all?

"It must be you. The others are . . . more sentimental, I think." Slyness melts into something infinitely harder to recognize. "Should the need arise, and you deem it so, do not hesitate to cut off my head."

I—*what?!* Should a Jabberwocky burst through the walls in this moment, I would not be more flabbergasted.

"Burn it within ten minutes of the act," she continues. "I urge you to collect my right femur—sharpen it and it will be far more useful to you than any sword. Only the right. The left will. . ." She pauses. "Well. I trust you know your right from your left."

To ogle another person is entirely impolite, and yet I am doing fantastically so.

"Granted, I hope we will not have to come to such circumstances, but one never knows. It's been a while, and I don't know if the rush will be too strong to resist."

"Who *are* you?" bursts from me so strongly, I am positive she can feel my words in both her right and left femurs.

I expect the Librarian to brush me aside, as always, or even deflect my query with one of her own. Instead, her authoritativeness eases into susurration. "Promises are sacrosanct to me. I made several very important ones years ago, when I, along with a handful of others, agreed to found and join the Collectors' Society. I have sustained those promises, even when they chafed. I chose to do so because of my faith in the Society and its missions. To me, those were far more important than power." Her attention drifts away from me, to somewhere distant as her eyes lose focus on the tangible. "I am not undertaking this sojourn lightly. But to stay in the shadows, when too many suffer. . ." Her eyes glow in an otherworldly way that leaves me uneasy; the smile she offers is unrecognizable for the face I've known for nearly a year. "We must all take a stand, even if the future is unclear." She pauses. "Even if the devil is both inside and out."

Around a dozen Society agents, all of whom deserve a good night's rest but will surely not get one anytime soon, settle into the conference room. Even Kip, our weapons specialist who normally eschews meetings, has come to listen to the Librarian explain away the Van Brunts' absences. As she lectures the group, I cannot help but find the enigmatic woman unexpectedly fragile in appearance. Three new bracelets in gleaming black, red, and white bind bird-like wrists. Her ebony hair is wound into a tight bun, her face is wiped clean of the faint traces of rogue and shadow she normally favors. No longer donning high heels, the Librarian metaphorically recedes closer to earth with sensible boots.

She does not fool me. She is a powerful giant in a child's clothing.

"There is no need to bother Abraham or Finn at this time." The Librarian hands a stack of folders for Jack to pass out. "Henry, you will assume leadership until one or both return."

Fleming, only recently returned from the hospital after keeping vigil over Lidenbrock, his partner and closest friend, sputters. "Why not you? Everyone knows you are the foundation of this place."

On my second day in the Institute, she told me something quite different. *"The Collectors' Society is somewhat like a living organism. Its members act as functioning body parts. If we were to argue that Brom is the brain, then I would follow as the heart."*

Fleming's confusion, however, is matched across the room by all present save those going to Wonderland.

A haughty look that borderlines insulting is leveled over the tip of the Librarian's nose. I would find it comical, if she weren't quite so fierce in appearance. "I can hardly oversee the Institute, let alone the Society, if I am not here."

Mild chaos breaks out, only to be quickly, tightly reined in by the Librarian's stinging clapping of hands.

"Franklin, I expect you to assist Henry, as needed." Blake startles in his seat, as if she snapped at him with a whip rather than mere words. "If necessary, you may contact Jo Bhaer for guidance. Despite the night's injuries, she is aware of the situation."

Mr. Holgrave, himself sporting a black eye, raps his fingers against the table. "First Brom, now you? This is unprecedented."

Promptly ignoring the chatter, she orders everyone to open their folders. "I trust you will continue monitoring all situations concerning the Chosen, as well as the Institute's reconstruction. While catalyst collections are on hold for the unforeseeable future, all communications between our organization and liaisons must remain as it ever has. Inside these dossiers, you will find Abraham's notes concerning your tasks. Expect to find some emails in your inboxes over the next few hours, too."

The conference room's door groans and then sings as it opens. The most ethereal women I have ever laid eyes upon floats in. Rich copper curls, topped by a thin ruby-clad crown, cascade down her snowy velvet-covered shoulders. "Darling," she says in an utterly melodious voice, "forgive me if I am tardy."

The Librarian warmly takes the woman's hands, and they press kisses against one another's cheeks. "Nonsense. Your travel dress is sumptuous. Is it new?"

The woman hugs the Librarian. "Yes. Would you like one? I will have one made for you."

Mary whispers, "What in the bloody hell?"

I must concur with this assessment.

The Librarian ushers the woman to the front of the room, and the queen in me ogles the stranger's lush gown. Tiny pearls and sapphires that mimic her eyes dot the full skirt, forming intricate designs.

"Allow me to introduce Lady Glinda," the Librarian says. "She kindly agreed to take charge of the Museum during my absence."

Blake's eyebrows shoot upward. "Glinda, as in . . . the witch from Oz?"

A titter of interest rolls throughout the room. Clearly, I am the only one who has never heard of the Lady Glinda, let alone of a place named Oz.

I nudge Mary. She writes on the back of her notes: "Oz is a magical land. Some say it's similar to Wonderland in many regards. Very, very popular books and movies."

Lady Glinda's blinding-white teeth flash as she bestows a benevolent smile upon her audience. "The very one. Although I rarely depart my homeland, I gladly did so to aid a good friend."

A quick, surreptitious glance offers me relief that I am not the only one taken aback by such a warm description of the inscrutable Librarian.

"Have no fear." Lady Glinda may be soft spoken, but the company within the conference room hangs upon her words. "I will do everything in my power to maintain the safety of all within the Museum."

"As if anyone would have doubts." The Librarian clasps the woman's arm. "Come. Meet the fine women and men who have dedicated their lives to the safety and alliances of all Timelines."

Mary and I watch in perverse fascination as the Librarian and Lady Glinda take stock of each and every agent present. Only once the majority departs, and those planning on traveling to Wonderland are all who remain, do Mary and I receive our introductions.

Grymsdyke snuggling (snuggling!) contentedly in the crook of an elbow, the Lady Glinda touches my cheek before kissing my forehead. I fear I ape a statue. "What a strong, beautiful queen you are. I have heard much about you from our shared friend."

I nearly choke on my response. I have many names for the Librarian, but friend is not one I would readily use. "I wish I could claim the same."

Her laugh is a wind chime tinkle in a warm summer breeze. "The MA is not known for sharing details of its members."

Fond amusement curves the Librarian's lips upward. "Thank goodness for small favors."

"What is the MA?" Mary asks.

"The Magical Alliance, which is an utterly inane, unofficial designation, but we comrades find it droll enough to keep using it." Lady Glinda glides over to one of the windows as the rest of us attempt to process this latest bit of information. "What a world you have found yourself, my friend. You must miss the simplicity of nature."

"There is too much stone," Grymsdyke grumbles, from the crook of her arm, "and not enough trees."

Lady Glinda strokes his bristly fur as if he were none more than a mere kitten, and his hair was not prone to causing fire ants to invade one's skin.

"I have grown used to the changes." The Librarian neatly stacks her notes. "Although, may I hope for your sake that Oz never evolves into this."

So many questions erupt in a firestorm within my mind.

Lady Glinda turns away from the window. "I have been meaning to ask . . . Any success in retrieving Scheherazade's veil?"

"Not yet." A frightful scowl mars the Librarian's beauty. "I maintain hope that it will be. I trust our agents to eventually locate it."

"And we all trust you—Schehera, especially. You can understand her concern, though." Lady Glinda lifts Grymsdyke and presses kisses on the top of his head. Even I, as fond of the assassin as I am, would never to dare such affection. And yet, he *purrs* in response.

The world has truly gone topsy-turvy. What kind of woman is this?

Mary elbows me. "Scheherazade's veil . . . Wasn't that the mission that sent Finn back to Bücherei?"

If that were the case, does the Librarian perhaps fear something might have happened to the veil? Might it be a catalyst?

"Of course," the Librarian is saying. "If only there was a way to test her Timeline without it, though."

Lady Glinda turns her liquid gaze toward the Librarian. "Allow me to be frank for a moment. I am uneasy about this trip—and I am not the only one. This unregulated witch—"

The Librarian's laugh, while indulgent, borders on harsh, too. "Before you say it, let me formally reject any and all help toward my person. In these dire times, all that can must endeavor to protect vulnerable Timelines until the Society collects their catalysts. That is where help is most needed."

Glinda passes Grymsdyke to Jack. The thief awkwardly allows my assassin to climb his arm. "Of course. That is undisputed. I am merely pointing out that if this witch is as powerful as we assume, surely it cannot hurt to—"

The Librarian holds up a hand. "Allow me this, my friend, and offer me your luck. Now that I have a better understanding of our opponents, the time has come for me to leave the library."

Jack, Marianne, Mary, and I remain fastened to the extraordinarily revealing discussion unfolding before us. Grymsdyke, the little brute, has fallen back asleep in the crook of Jack's neck.

"There is nothing to prove," the lady from Oz stubbornly insists.

Which naturally leads me to wonder what, exactly, the Librarian wishes to prove.

"Your heart has always been wide and forgiving, Glinda." The Librarian pats her friend's cheek. "There is no need to slap a fresh coat of paint over what we all know to be truth. I do not run away from the past. I carry it with me to this day, and will do so until the end. I am as I ever was."

"Are any of us perpetually steady, with nary a misstep, stumble, or quiver?" Lady Glinda queries. "Do any of us allow ourselves to stay in a box, unmoving, devoid of thought and choice, afraid and unable to breathe as we make our way through life? This is not the way the worlds work. This is not how magic works. I, and those who know you, am well aware of your facets and embrace them. The Society's leaders have always been wise in their steady, unbending faith in your abilities and intentions as well."

A bit of the Librarian's formidability thaws. "That is because *their* intentions have been satisfactory."

"As surely are those from these fine folk." Lady Glinda angles her head toward us.

The Librarian lifts a brow. "They are still here, aren't they?"

Wind chime laughter drifts through the room once more. "It has been delightful meeting you all, although I wish it could have been under kinder circumstances. I offer you my blessings for a safe journey. The Timelines place themselves within your hands." She links an arm though the Librarian's. "Now. Let us trek to your Museum, so I might become better acquainted with it."

Before she and Glinda walk through the door, the Librarian calls out, "We leave within the hour. Be ready."

"What a delightful witch." If I didn't know better, I'd say that my fiercest assassin sounds dreamy in his yawning assessment of the Lady Glinda.

Mary marches over to Jack. "Tell us everything you know about this MA."

His eyes widen significantly. "I never heard of 'em until just now!"

She jabs a finger against his left collarbone. "You are Brom's assistant."

He holds his hands aloft. "I swear I ain't heard of this group before. I din't even know that the Librarian knew anybody from Oz, let alone Glinda! I mean, excepting that we have the silver slipper catalysts and, well, okay, a liaison, too, but—"

"They were *friendly.*" From Mary, the assessment sounds like a curse rather than an observation. "They *hugged.* When have any of you ever seen the Librarian hug anyone, let alone refer to anyone other than Brom as her friend?"

"Surely, everyone requires affection," Marianne offers.

I focus less upon hugging and more upon another important revelation. "If she belongs to the unofficial, so-called Magical Alliance," I muse, "we now have proof that the Librarian does possess some level of magical abilities that might very well explain her uncanny knowledge."

"But who could she be?" Mary asks. "A witch like Glinda? Quick. Let's make a list of all the witches and sorceresses we know throughout the Timelines."

"This entire conversation is indelicate." Marianne slams her laptop closed and proceeds to clutch it to her chest. "Discussing our colleague as if she were fodder for a gossip magazine."

"Oh, come off your high horse, Miss Georgian manners," Mary snaps. "Even you must have been dying to know who she really is. For goodness' sake, no one, save Brom, even knows her given name, let alone if she is from a Timeline or not. Why must we all be an open book when she is allowed her privacy?"

Hearing Mary issue this defense is amusing and satisfying all at once. I have been banging this drum for some time now, and no one else was bothered enough to agree until this day.

Marianne stiffens as she enters an absurdly nonviolent standoff with Mary. "It is none of our business."

"Of course it is." Mary's scowl contorts. "More now than ever. We're heading into Wonderland, and *she's* coming with us. None of us have been in the field with her before. You heard her just now. She was hinting about some kind of nasty past, wasn't she? Who knows if we can truly trust her?"

Should the need arise, and you deem it so, do not hesitate to cut off my head.

"We can trust that she is loyal to the Society," I say. "And while I have long questioned her identity and motives, I do believe her when she insists her intent lies within the safety of Timelines."

There is that word again, associated with the Librarian: *intent*.

Mary remains miffed, but she offers no counterargument.

"We have less than an hour before we depart for Wonderland." I give them no quarter. "Not only are we tasked with hunting down any Chosen present, we will be hunting for the Queen of Hearts. I do not know what you have read or heard about her in all of these ridiculous stories about Wonderland, but I can assure you that she is utterly lethal, especially when in possession of her battle-axe. In addition to this, the war between the Courts is going badly. We cannot enter such a fray divided, not if we wish to achieve any level of success. If any of you do not think you can work properly with the others, I beg you to remain at the Institute. I refuse to act as your governess whilst in Wonderland."

Indignation burns Mary's face. Marianne's chin, however, drops. Jack beams as if he was presented with a shiny award.

"I do not know what we will face. I cannot know if we will be successful. Nobbytown's citizens have fallen prey to these suspected Chosen. I am still an exiled queen, and there are many who will gladly take my head to a number of monarchs. This is not your standard mission, where a catalyst must be stolen. We are hunting those who play God and maker, who wish to destroy worlds. Who wish to destroy us. Fighting between ourselves will only hasten their goals."

Jack drops to a knee. He snatches my hand and manages to press a kiss against my knuckles before I yank it away. "I'll follow you anywhere, Your Highness."

"It's Majesty, you fool." But Mary's temper has lessened considerably. "I'm not kissing your hand, Alice, even if you are right."

I clap her shoulder. "I would never ask you to. Come. Let us finish our preparations. Wonderland awaits."

TORTURE

FINN

"**G**ET. YOUR. HANDS. OFF OF ME!"

When neither Brom nor I do so, Victor's renewed fury drums an ugly beat against my heart. How is he still going? How is he not hoarse?

My eardrums throb, but I refuse to put in plugs, even though the co-pilot offered them an hour after we left New York City by private plane. Confined to the small bedroom, Victor shouted the entire flight to Miami. Once the plane gassed up, he broke free and wrenched open the exit door. Brom and I barely managed to tackle him before he jumped. Our departure was delayed as a sedative was ordered, but he destroyed that, too, before we could even inject the damn stuff. Then, once he saw the stash of protocol we brought, he crushed half of that supply.

The bedroom, we discovered, was trashed.

His foreign eye continues to shift between blue and black. He cries, he screams, he pleads, he begs. He alternates between sounding reasonable and like a stranger.

It killed Brom to have Victor restrained again, but after a number of well-placed threats and punches, it was necessary. Neither of us could physically restrain him the entire flight to Santiago, Chile, and by the time we gassed up again and were on our way to Punta Arenas, I never wanted to sedate my brother more—even if just to shut him the hell up.

"It's okay, son," Brom says as he attempts to offer Victor a drink of water.

"They're *coming!*" Victor strains against the cuffs holding him to his seat. "You're going to get us all killed, you stupid prick! LET ME GO! I'll kill you, do you hear me? I'll kill all of you before I let them get to you!"

I can't handle the helplessness in our father's eyes any better than the same feeling raging about in the pit of my stomach.

Victor's mania is worse than I've ever seen before. Worse than I ever thought was possible.

I attempt to coax him away from Victor. "We're almost to Puerto Williams."

Gnashing teeth nearly sink into Brom's hand, but I yank him back just in time. We hover nearby, reluctant to stray too far from Victor more for sentimentality and worry rather than practicality.

The trip from Puerto Williams to the research station in Antarctica is just as exhausting as all of the others. By the time we gear up and are escorted into the station, I'm the one out of gas. We're greeted inside by a middle-aged woman and an older man as our escorts attempt to hold on to a thrashing Victor.

The woman, bundled in a wool sweater that nearly reaches her knees, offers my father a hand. A thick silver streak courses through her dark corkscrewed hair. "Mr. Van Brunt, Jane Doen. I cannot tell you how pleased I am to finally meet you in person."

It's a carefully chosen pseudonym to protect her identity within the station.

Victor suddenly shouts, "What if she's one of them? You idiots! Can't you see? *Look* at how the spirits hover around her. She's under their control!"

I can't help but wonder if he actually sees something we can't with that creepy eye of his.

Doing his best not to acknowledge this latest outburst, my father says, "Please, it's as I said before. Call me Brom. These are my sons. Finn," he motions to me, and then to my brother, "and Victor."

No pseudonyms for us, and I don't know if that is smart or foolish.

Doen's smile reveals crooked yet pleasing teeth. Something is off about her demeanor, though, like there's a thin veneer hiding something beneath. "Very well. Brom." It's my turn to shake hands with the scientist. Her grip is strong, self-assured. "Finn. It is a pleasure to meet you. I hope you don't mind me admitting that *Adventures of Huckleberry Finn* was one of the first books in English that I read when I first came to this Timeline. I suppose I hold it in affectionate regards for that reason."

I'm dying to ask, *"And just what Timeline did you come from?"* But I don't. One of the rules for coming here was that we don't push for personal information. Shady? Oh, yes. "It's good to meet you," I say anyway. "Thanks for allowing us to come on such short notice."

"They're going to cut me open." Victor struggles to escape his escorts' hold. "Like butchers. They're going to steal me right out of this body. Blood on your hands!" When that gets no reaction, he sags. "Dad, Dad." His voice drops, turns reasonable, even. "You aren't really going to let them dig into Finn's head, are you? Don't let them hurt him." To me, "Finn, let me—let me protect you. Who knows what these butchers are going to do?"

He has a point.

What we *don't* have is another choice. "It'll be okay," I tell him, and he resumes thrashing. One of the escorts leans in too close and gets his nose nearly bitten off.

Dr. Doen motions to her colleague as several men run in to aid my brother's escorts. "Allow me to introduce Dr. Jean Biche. His work in psychiatry and neurology is outstanding. We are thrilled to have him here for a few months."

It's another carefully chosen pseudonym.

Brom and I shake this doctor's hand, too. While his grip is not as strong as Doen's, it's still filled with confidence. "What a pleasure it is to meet the Van Brunt family. Allow me to thank you for all that you do for," his voice drops to a whisper, "Timelines."

"You must be exhausted," Doen says. "Let's get you settled and then we'll discuss your situations."

An hour later, Brom and I are in a viewing deck located behind a glass window separating us from a small, clean laboratory. Victor is strapped to a large chair—or is it bed? It looks like a chair-bed, to be honest. He's entirely out of control: screaming and cursing and generally scaring the shit out of anyone who dares to come close. One of the guys who helped secure him to the chair lost a chunk of his ear, another a piece of his cheek. Worse, Victor spat the pieces back, taunting the men.

I don't think I've ever prayed so hard as I have today. *This has to work. Please, God. Let this work.*

Doen and Biche are part of a medical research consortium whose members hail from dozens of Timelines. Shadowy, at times possibly unethical, the group strives toward cutting-edge practices they hope will better the inhabitants of different Timelines but occasionally come at the cost, too. Human trials, from Brom's report during the flights over, are not uncommon. Deaths from failed drug trials or operations aren't, either. And not just a couple deaths, but dozens across the years. Hundreds, even. If one counts wars, thousands. Millions. The consortium dabbles in biological weapons as well as cures, and while a lot of their actions, at least, the ones I read about, rub harshly against my morals, these people are pretty much our only hope right now.

When I'd asked my father why two members of this so far nameless (to me) consortium were holed up in an Antarctic research base, I was unnerved to discover that he really didn't have an answer. Bottom line, it's assumed they've been working on something and wanted to test it out, and felt an isolated base would be the way to go. The fact that they'd stepped out of the shadows to ask us about the Chosen is worrisome, but if they think they've got some kind of solution to rapture, I'm ready to listen. While their true goals here remain a mystery, both researchers have legitimately done some groundbreaking research in neurology and brain studies.

What *kind* of brain studies, I wish I knew. Pushing the envelope and asking Doen and Biche didn't offer any further illumination. Instead, I got a sharply offered reminder that, if I'm interested in their treatments, I must adhere to our agreements. So I shut up. I'm a selfish enough bastard, an idealistic one, too, because both my brother and I are needed in the game during our quest for the Piper, and this is our only shot.

"Do you trust them?" I ask Brom as Doen fills a syringe in the next room. Biche is nearby, fiddling with some kind of machine. Someone is undoubtedly listening in, but as neither of us agreed to not talk to one another about the doctors, I don't give a rat's ass what they think about our conversation.

Arms crossed and feet planted apart, Brom continues to stare through the glass. When he says nothing, I try a different tactic. "How long have you known about this consortium?"

"A while," is his curt answer.

"Why all the secrets?" Maybe it's because of my nerves, but irritation flares hot and bright. "From her objections, it sounds as if the Librarian knows quite a bit about them. You know about everybody. Why are you keeping it from the rest of us?"

More importantly, why are you keeping it from me?

A burst of annoyed air shoots from his nose. "Finn, there are a lot of things about the worlds that aren't cut and dry. Our job at the Society isn't necessarily to serve as watchdogs for different Timeline organizations, especially those comprised of people from multiple Timelines who willingly band together. We are, officially, the record keepers of Timeline designations. We are also responsible for the re-trieval and storage of catalysts. In order to ensure proper records, we maintain communications between Timelines and ourselves. There are certain groups, such as the Janeites, who willingly chose to act as a bloc in its association with the Society. There are others that do not. This group is one of them."

Doen places an IV in Victor's arm. I can't hear his response, but as the glass before us shudders, I have to assume it was harsh.

"That doesn't explain why you haven't told me about this group. Or, hell, any of the others I bet you've kept secret. If you expect me to run the Society one day, I need to know about this shit."

His smile is thin. "You *will* become the next director. There's no if. We all have our roles to play, Finn. This one happens to be yours."

"Then why keep me in the dark?"

Several bags filled with liquid are hung upon an IV stand next to Victor. One of Doen's assistants, the one missing a chunk of his ear, attaches one to the tubing in my brother's arm.

"Despite what you may be thinking, I do not know much about this particular organization, Finn." Brom might as well be made of stone as he watches what the assistants are doing to Victor. "They are far more aware of our existence than we are of theirs." A muscle twitches at the corner of his mouth. "Fringe organizations such as this one typically fall into the Librarian's purview. She has kindly kept me up-to-date on them."

I fully turn toward him as Biche straps my brother's head to the back of the chair. "What purview?"

"When I was younger, and Gulliver held the Society's reins, I was in the same boat as you." The tick twitches once more. "There are . . . promises that must be given to those who give their life to the running of the Society. Promises that cannot be broken without consequences. Promises," he grits out between clenched teeth, "that are sacrosanct. These promises are extracted when an oath is sworn to uphold the Society's mission. You'll make the same someday, and when you do, you'll understand why there are levels of secrecy that are required."

"That's a bullshit answer, Dad, and you know it."

The corner of his mouth lifts. "I might have said the same thing to my mentor more than once." Before I can respond, he continues, "The Society's relationship with the Librarian is . . . complex. While I have no doubts about her loyalty, and in fact consider her to be a valued friend and colleague, she is not necessarily beholden to the same rules as the rest of us. She willingly chooses to keep tabs on various organizations, so that the Society is unofficially informed of their existences in the case that if any of them threaten the safety of catalysts, we can attend matters."

Dr. Doen inserts the nib of a golden-filled syringe into Victor's IV.

"Is she not beholden to the same promises or oaths you are? Or the rest of us?"

He considers this for a long moment as one of the assistants in the other room shave the remaining bits of hair covering Victor's scalp. Will they be shaving my head, too? I mean, I'm not really a vain bastard, but I've also never considered going bald.

"Yes and no."

I sigh. "Another bullshit answer."

"And yet," he says mildly, "it is the best I can provide."

I met the Librarian a few days after I first came to the Institute. She was mysterious, beautiful, and surprisingly kind to a punk-ass kid like me. I liked that she didn't have any expectations, nor did she try to mold me into something I wasn't cut out to be, like how Aunt Polly or the Widow Douglas and her sister did. She and Katrina were close, sharing daily tea and biscuits together. Brom joined them occasionally, and when he did, he would drag Victor and me along with him for what they would call family time.

But that was it. The Librarian was inexplicably *family*.

I was sixteen when I first asked her what Timeline she was from. She laughed and clucked me under the chin, telling me that someday, I'd know—but that particular day wasn't *someday* yet. There were always whispers going around the Institute, where folks tried to figure out who she was, but none of the guesses stuck. Over the years, I've heard people call her a rani, a queen, a princess, a djinn, a psychic, and/or a runaway slave. Her ability to know things that others didn't spooked nearly everyone, but as it also always benefitted them, she was excused.

The Librarian cried over Katrina's death and locked herself into the Museum for over a week. Afterward, she nearly smothered Victor and me with questions about our health and mental states. She assigned herself as the official Brom-watcher, ensuring he ate enough, got enough sleep, and took care of himself.

She never ages. Her hair remains ebony, her face remains unlined. She has never let her anger touch any person within the Society. She has never failed us on any mission.

I've always been able to see why Alice is suspicious of the Librarian, but . . . she's been family, even if it shook me up to discover Brom knows what her real name is.

"There is time for answers," Brom says quietly. "Right now, let's get our boy back."

Victor's ceased thrashing about. He's struggling to keep his eyes from drooping, but he's losing. Doen waits until they shut completely before injecting not one but ten more pre-prepared multicolored syringes into his IV.

Shit, can a person even handle all of that?

Biche brings over a rolling cart holding the machine he'd been fiddling with earlier. It's not too big, maybe the size of a fishing tackle box. He extracts what appears to be a pair of earbuds, plugs them into the machine, flips a switch, and then inserts them into Victor's ears.

My blood goes cold. Will I be going through this, too?

One of the assistants uses these godawful medieval-looking clamps to pry Victor's eyes open so they can stay that way. Another washes down the top of his head with rubbing alcohol and then adds a small coating of a clear jelly. I nearly lose my lunch when two large electrodes bearing needles are inserted into his skull.

"Are these guys scientists or torturers?!"

Brom grabs my arm before I do something stupid, like wrench the damn door open. "Let them finish. If they don't . . . We don't know what might happen."

"Are you fucking kidding me?" It's an explosion, and rude as hell to say to one's father, but I can't help it. "They just rammed spikes into his brain! They just injected him with a shitton of drugs!"

"They had a reason," he says, as if he's trying to convince himself of it, too, "or they wouldn't have done it."

I watch in horror as Victor's chair is rotated to face two silver pillars stationed near a white wall. Another pair of needles are inserted into the base of his neck, on either side of his spinal column. Doen injects a final syringe into Victor's IV and then signals Biche. An assistant flips off the lights, and suddenly, the silver pillars roar to life. Beams of colored light shoot between them, forming . . . a movie? Pictures waver on the light beams. Flashes and flashes of moving pictures that change so fast, I can't catch what they are.

Jesus. This is some science fiction horror shit if I've ever seen it. These aren't just scientists. These are *mad* scientists.

Victor's body convulses. Blood trickles from the spikes in his skull; smoke sizzles from the machines. My brother's mouth opens into a silent scream.

Two goddamn hours of this torture goes by, with Doen continuing to inject who-the-hell knows what into Victor's IV as Biche rams another electrode into his skull. The assholes and their assistants have clipboards out, taking notes like they aren't brainwashing or doing whatever the hell they're doing to him. They're utterly impassive, even stopping to joke with one another a few times.

I'm going to let them do this to me, aren't I? I'm going to sit in that damn chair, let them pump me full of enough drugs that it's a miracle I don't overdose, and then I'm going to let them ram rods right into my skull and spine. And then I'm going to sit back, convulse, and listen to and watch . . . well, I don't know what.

I stare at the moving pictures, desperate to figure out what they're inserting into my brother's brain.

And it's then that . . . that. . .

I see a flash in the colored blurs of Katrina.

Of me, of our dad.

Of Mary.

Of London, of the Institute in New York.

Of his graduation day from medical school.

They're showing him his life.

"How did they get them?" My voice is hoarse. "Our family's history?"

Brom slides an arm around my shoulders. "The Librarian sent most of them, upon my request, but I also emailed some from my private collection during the flights."

"What is he listening to?"

"Himself." Brom's voice is hoarse, too. "Audio from home movies. Katrina reading him stories. Messages from Mary on his cell phone. You two in that ridiculous Abbott and Costello reenactment back when you were still in high school. A lecture he gave at NYU. He's listening to memories that the mania has obscured."

"Will I be going through the same thing?"

He briefly closes his eyes. "I don't know. I expect so. While we don't have as much information, considering the bulk of your childhood was in your original Timeline, the Librarian and I sent what we could."

"That's all well and good, but how do they plan to counter whatever magic has been used against us?"

"Who says they aren't using magic?"

It's enough to shift my attention away from my brother. "Are you serious?"

"Science, in some Timelines, walks hand in hand with magic. I doubt these doctors would have agreed to your cases if they did not think they could combat magic in some way."

"Magic doesn't work here."

"You're too emotional right now to think straight. Magic is not inherently found within this world. But that does not stop magic from other Timelines from working here. How else could the Piper's music affect us?"

Fine. So they're probably using magic down there. Magic, a shit-ton of drugs, and rods jammed into one's skull.

I take a deep breath. *It's worth it. Magic or no, I refuse to be compromised. Victor didn't get a choice, and neither do I.*

The movies stop. Lights once more illuminate the room. Doen and Biche hover around my brother as the assistants clean him up. Blood streaks his face. A click sounds, and then the thick metal door separating us creaks open.

"Finn?" It's one of the nameless assistants. "Are you ready for prep?"

I squeeze my dad's hand and then follow the woman out the door.

NOBBYTOWN

ALICE

L IFE HAS DESERTED NOBBYTOWN. No laughter or shouting streams from the pubs. Lights fail to illuminate windows. Carriages do not trundle to and fro. No one has lit the street lamps.

The White King described the village's citizens as becoming most unlike themselves, and while I do not doubt his assessment, I cannot help but wonder where exactly these changed souls are.

Are they with Hearts? The Piper? The mere idea of these innocent citizens turned against their wills to become puppets for the Chosen leaves me itching for blades and justice. Nobbytown is under joint Diamonds and White protection, as it straddles both lands. Hearts will pay for daring to subjugate citizens she does not oversee.

Jack smacks his hands against his trousers, desperate to remove all traces of spider webs from our travel through the rabbit hole. Despite his acquaintance with Grymsdyke, he was most alarmed at the presence of thousands of Arachnid guardians swarming the portal between Wonderland and Wales. When we arrived, and the tiny soldiers surrounded us, I wondered if he was close to losing consciousness, his breath heaved so quickly.

Calmer now, he carefully sets one of the heavier bags upon the ground and waves a flashlight about. "No offense, Your Majesty, but your homeland is creepy as all hell."

Even Marianne fails to chide him for such an assessment. Wonderland can be unsettling, true, but daily life in villages such as Nobbytown does not normally fall under such purviews. But now, as early-morning fog rolls across the cobblestone streets, if specters garbed in shrouded, murky robes of despair and memory were to seep through doors, lamenting days of yore, I would not be surprised.

And still, I yearn to comb through each edifice, to uncover the fates of this village's citizens.

A cool hand settles upon my shoulder, startling me away from the eeriness before us. "There's nothing you can do for them here," the Librarian murmurs.

My breath crystalizes in the heavy air. "These are my people."

Or they once were, before I was exiled. Now, in my stead, the White King oversees all of Nobbytown as well as the rest of the Diamonds' region.

"Hope is never entirely lost, not if there are those willing to hold on to it during the darkest times."

A snap of boots upon stone shatters the morning's fragility. Our party whirls toward the disturbance, hands upon weapons. Jack shifts in front of Marianne, one arm protectively blocking her. "Don't worry," he whispers to our technology expert. "I won't let anyone hurt you."

"Oi!" Mary hisses. "What about me?"

Mary may not be talented with swords or revolvers, but she is wickedly clever with poisons. The Caterpillar would have grudgingly approved of her.

Jack winks. "Only got one hand."

Cursing beneath her breath, Mary snatches a dagger from her bag and darts behind me. I hush the squabbling children and direct Marianne and Jack to angle their flashlights in the direction of the emerging footfalls. In their dust-speckled beams, shadows coagulate into a looming figure. Have the Chosen found us so soon?

The Librarian's shoulder brushes against me. A split-second before I hurl my dagger, the long shadow of a pike emerges, followed by the Five of Diamonds.

I nearly throw the dagger anyway.

The White King's pikeman snaps a tight bow before slamming his pike onto the ground. "I am at your service, Your Majesty."

I snatch Jack's flashlight and wave the beam in the soldier's eyes. Despite the bright, artificial light, he does not blink.

The orbs are pink, not black.

I pass the flashlight back before sheathing my dagger. "I believe I clearly informed His Majesty there was no need to send an escort."

He lowers his chin. "As I have sworn a lifelong vow to protect the Queen of Diamonds, I volunteered."

"Bloody hell!" Jack snaps. "You gave us all a heart attack. You might want to not lurk in the shadows like a vampire quite so much, eh?"

"So says the thief," Mary mutters.

"I am a pickpocket, thank you very much." Jack polishes his nails on his coat. "I did my business in broad daylight, I did."

A talented young pikeman sworn to both the White and Diamonds Courts, I became acquainted with the Five of Diamonds during my first return to Wonderland from exile. Hearts card soldiers had raided The Land That Time Forgot, and in our escape, the Five of Diamonds captured both Victor and myself. After a blistering reprimand from the White Nightrider, the lethal soldier became a valuable ally to have around during skirmishes. He even accompanied the White King and Cheshire-Cat to New York City to aid Finn in removing the boojum in my spine.

Annoyed as I may be, I am also not egotistical enough to turn away an excellent pike during wartime, especially whilst Chosen are scampering about. "Report."

He snaps to attention, his massive pike reverberating upon the ground. "During the last four hours, during which I have been stationed at this location, I encountered two degenerate children terrorizing a Sheep family with their pipes. As they bore Hearts, rather than White or Diamonds, insignias, I dispatched the tots."

"Dispatched," Jack repeats.

The Five of Diamonds' pink eyes swivel toward the thief. Rather than narrow, they bug out as the soldier grins all too maniacally.

Jack nudges his revolver in the soldier's direction. "How do we know this lumbering ox ain't one of them now?"

Upon my shoulder, Grymsdyke scoffs. "A pikeman fall prey to the Chosen? How utterly ridiculous. They are much too quick for music."

I motion toward the soldier's pike, which even I, as a queen, dare not touch. "Precious few live to tell the tale against Wonderlandian pikes. I imagine the same can be said for the Chosen. Although, I do wish you might have left one alive for questioning."

The Five of Diamonds bows once more. "I will endeavor to merely maim next time, Your Majesty."

Mary laughs. Marianne chokes a bit. She will need a bit of a tougher hide if she wishes to last more than the day in Wonderland.

Not too far from the rabbit hole, on the outskirts of town, is The Land that Time Forgot. Owned by the Hatter, Hare, and Dormouse, and considered by many to be Wonderland's premier den of sin, indulgences, and raves, I will admit to spending more than one delirious night within the club's walls. Upon my exile, the Hatter stored many of my prized possessions within his network of secretive tunnels beneath the village.

I press up against the sturdy walls of this familiar building, searching for the thrum of music and voices, but The Land That Time Forgot finally lives up to its name.

"The fate of the proprietors?" I ask the Five of Diamonds.

The soldier's attention darts to and fro. "All three luxuriate with the haven of His Majesty's encampment."

"I hope they are not indulging in," Mary's voice drops, *"orgies."*

Grymsdyke shifts upon my shoulder. "Of course they are. That is what they do."

"Well." Mary's sniff is far too loud as she jabs Jack with her flashlight. "I suppose you'll have a grand time with them, won't you?"

If I did not know him better, I might believe the innocence he attempts to convey. "Me?"

"With the amount this one enjoys copulation," Grymsdyke says, "they will be fast friends, if not lovers, within a single day."

Mary clamps a hand across her mouth to contain her howling. I, myself, cough discreetly.

Marianne has the grace to convey bewilderment.

The Five of Diamonds leads our party away from The Land That Time Forgot, angling us toward White lands. The White King's encampment is not far, but as we travel by foot and not horse, and are bogged down by several bags apiece, the journey will require a few hours of travel through blackened woods and meadows. Our sole luxury comes in the form of a goat-drawn cart borrowed from an abandoned Nobbytown house, used to haul Marianne's technological equipment.

Our journey clings to silence. Jack stays close to Marianne whilst Mary strides by me. The Librarian keeps her own pace, the Five of Diamonds scouting ahead. Though I know I ought to be ruminating on places the Hearts may hide, my thoughts are steeped in ice and snow and of doctors who best take care lest I come for vengeance against them, too.

"Where is the snoring?" Grymsdyke scuttles back and forth across my shoulders to survey our surroundings. "Where are the bats? The pigeons scouting for serpents? The spiders dining upon early-morning's offerings?"

I dig myself out of the snow banks and peer more closely at the areas beneath nearby trees where Flowers ought to be dozing. Mary angles her flashlight's beam into the distance and a sickening thud drops within the bit of my belly.

The ground, the Flowers . . . It all has been scorched. Burned alive.

I confiscate the flashlight and rush toward the grove. All along the road, right where the Flowers ought to reside, are ashy patches. Across the road presents the same scene. Backtracking, the same. Forward, the same.

Why?

Why murder these beautiful, harmless Flowers who did nothing but bring joy to countless lives with their songs and beauty?

I round on the Five of Diamonds, now waiting close by. "Does the White King know of these atrocities?"

"His Majesty is aware."

The Librarian brushes past us to step off the road, into the dirt beneath a tree. She squats, intent as she peers down at unknown Flowers' cremated remains. She takes a small bit of the ashes and rubs it between her fingers, head cocked, and then sniffs it.

"If she puts that in her mouth, I will vomit," Mary hisses. "Just you watch."

The Librarian does no such thing. Instead, she rises. "They tried to warn the others."

I block her from stepping back onto the path. "Did the ashes tell you this?"

Her smile is cold. "Get your sharp blades out, Alice. Someone is coming."

Sure enough, the faint snapping of twigs and branches stands out against the dense silence behind the Librarian.

I motion for the rest to get behind me as the Five of Diamonds whirls his pike. The Librarian grabs his arm; amazingly, when his pike whips toward her, she catches it. The pikeman growls.

She growls in return. "I want him alive. Is that clear?"

There is no possible way she could see whomever is in the woods, let alone determine their sex. The thicket is too dense, the light too poor.

Who is she?

The Five of Diamond's looks to me. I nod my assent, and the Librarian releases him. She takes her place by my side.

"This isn't a library," I whisper between clenched teeth, "and there are no books to tangle with. Stay behind me."

Her laugh is quiet and menacing all at once. "I take care of myself."

She tugs something out of her pocket, and when I peer closer, I realize it's a pestle. *Frabjous.* She thinks to fight with kitchen instruments?

She is madder than I thought.

I lift an eyebrow, but the Librarian fails to acknowledge my concern. Instead, she waves an expectant hand, as if to chide me for dallying.

Very well, then.

As the Five of Diamonds stations himself and his pike beyond the tree line, the rest hold still until another crackle floats between the leaves. And then–

The first few notes of a dissonant melody.

I bark at the Five of Diamonds, "Go!" at the same time the others clamp their hands over their ears. Marianne brought earplugs for all, but they are stashed within one of her bags. It is no matter, though, for within seconds, three at the very most, a bloodcurdling scream replaces the music.

Wielding her pestle, the Librarian darts into the tree grove after the Five of Diamonds. I charge after her, my blade at the ready. Not too far away, the Five of Diamonds towers over a gasping, bloody youth.

"You fool! I told you I wanted him alive!"

The Five of Diamonds pokes at one of the gashes inflicted by his whirling pike. He tells the Librarian, "He's alive."

"Not for long." She drops to her knees before the youth, slamming a palm against his chest. "Dammit, I did not want to waste any effort on saving one of these bastards! Alice, go get Mary. We're going to have to stabilize him until we get to the White King's camp."

The Five of Diamonds shoves his pike toward the Librarian. "How dare you speak to the Queen of Diamonds in such a way!"

She swats the weapon away as if it were a Rocking-horse-fly rather than a deadly pike. "I will speak to whomever I like any damn well way I please. Get that thing out of my face before I snap it in half."

Bubbles of blood froth down the youth's chin.

"Leave her be," I order the Five of Diamonds and then sprint to retrieve Mary.

Precious amounts of healing spray are used to tip the youth's scales from dire to stable. As the Five of Diamonds uses his pair of wrist cuffs to secure the youth's hands behind his back, I seethe over the bloody heart stitched into his tunic.

"Think this is one of the Nobbytowners?" Mary asks.

I tear a bit of the youth's tunic off. Luckily, he is still too dazed from his prior injuries to offer much fuss. "Soldier, open his mouth for me."

The Five of Diamonds does so. Within we find blackened, rotting teeth.

"Well, that answers my question," Mary says as I gag our prisoner.

Blessedly, the next hour passes without incident. Apricot rays gleam through the trees just as we reach the crest of the hill overlooking the White King of Wonderland's encampment.

A horn blares as soon as we are spotted. Soldiers peer out of their tents and turn away from their campfires. A cheer lifts to herald the rising of the sun and the official return of the Queen of Diamonds.

HOW TO CATCH A RABBIT

ALICE

FERZ EPONA AND FERZ Eponi, two of the White King's most loyal advisors, greet me as soon as I reach camp. Epona curtsies. "May we just say how wonderful it is to see you, my lady."

"We have ensured that everything is in order for you and," Eponi notes those standing with me, "your party." He bows awkwardly. "Excuse me, my lady." He waddles away, shouting for additional cots to be brought to the main pavilion.

Epona waves an arm toward the large white pavilion holding court in the middle of the encampment. "His Majesty is waiting for you within."

"There is no need to announce us," I assure her, but Epona is nothing if not a creature of decorum. She toddles ahead, desperate to inform the guards of our presence.

Around us, soldiers drop to their knees. Many sing my name. The Diamonds banner flutters alongside the White, and my pride aches fiercely at the familiar sight. "Our queen!" they call. "Our queen has returned to us!"

A Goat breaks ranks and trots forward. Upon his left lapel is a bird, a diamond in its beak. I know this Goat. I know this uniform. "Please, Your Majesty. Allow me to carry your bags."

The White King's pavilion is not too far, but I allow my card soldier his request. Other soldiers and pikemen form lines on either side of the route, pikes raised in the air so that their tips touch. The Diamonds song knits into the chilly, misty air.

I hold my head high.

"Our queen is here to save us from Hearts!"

"Funny," Mary murmurs from just behind me. "I don't think they're talking about the White Queen, do you?"

Before we enter the pavilion, I beat my fist over my chest. The soldiers surrounding us follow, the sound deafening.

Inside the tent, Jack whistles. "Hot damn. You're like Beyoncé around here."

Marianne says, "Oh, Jack," as if *silly creature* were missing. "There is no one like Beyoncé but Beyoncé." She affectionately pats his arm.

Mary stares at her, hard, as if she were a changeling we picked up alongside the road.

One of Marianne's eyebrows twitches high as a smirk emerges.

Ferz Epona has my name announced. I step through the flaps leading to the main room of the pavilion to find the White King of Wonderland waiting before a large table filled with scrolls, maps, and figurines. The Cheshire-Cat perches at the edge of the largest exposed map, batting a small chess figure, as advisors crowd around him.

The White King's eyelashes meet his cheek: a fleeting check of wakefulness. A sigh, quiet and meant only for my ears, curls forth. He strides across the room, hands out. "My lady, you are a most welcome sight."

He is, too, although the display of bruises marring his face leaves me desirous of strong words with the camp's physicians.

For a brief twinkling of time and space, I allow myself to soak in the familiar warmth of his skin against mine.

The familiarity of it all is too raw, though, even now, even a year and forever later. My palm grows cold as proper distance, dictated by decorum, etiquette, and agreed-upon decisions, stretches between us. "I thank you for receiving us at such little notice." I turn my attention to the handful of recognizable faces waiting behind the White King, ones that, both not too long ago and a lifetime ago, I knew as well as those standing behind me.

The White Nightrider, a distinguished Unicorn, bows. "Wonderland welcomes home one of its brightest and most formidable champions."

The company surrounding him follows suit. My heart swells.

The Cheshire-Cat leaps from the table and ambles to where the White King and I are. After he scratches at the White King's legs, Jace picks him up. "Are you sure this is where you want to be, Your Majesty?" the White Grand Advisor asks. "I have a very unsettling feeling about the next few days."

I smile. "I bring you a gift to play with."

The Five of Diamonds makes his entrance, dragging our prisoner behind him. The assembled crowd gasps; some clap.

The Cheshire-Cat's grin is most feral. "You *do* remember what I like best." He springs from the White King's arms and sprints over to the youth. The haze of the attack wearing off, our would-be assailant struggles against his wrist cuffs, garbling assumed insults and/or threats from beneath his gag. The Cat expands to the size of a pony as he loops the youth, sniffing and hissing the whole way.

The Nightrider bellows for guards. The White King says, as the Cat slashes at the youth with unnaturally sharp claws, "I am unsurprised that it takes the Queen of Diamonds and the Collectors' Society to bring in the first live capture." His grim smile eases as he takes in my colleagues. "My apologies for neglecting you too long. You are all most welcome, even if under such unsavory circumstances."

The Cheshire-Cat announces, "This creature is no Wonderlander. It smells entirely too wrong."

Jack eases his backpack off. "We could 'ave told you that, mate."

Mary tells the White King, "All I can say is that there better not be any more SleepMist attacks."

His bow is neat and smooth. "We shall do our best to accommodate."

"Although," she muses, "I will not rule out other poisonous exposures, providing antidotes are readily available. Feel free to share any and all."

Guards arrive, only to remove the Chosen youth to a more secure location. "It's best to let it stew a bit," the Cheshire-Cat announces after the guards depart. "Let it get fat and juicy with worry. Then I will go in and milk all its wicked little secrets."

Jack leans closer to Mary. "If that cat starts talking about baskets and lotion, I'm out of here."

"We," the Librarian announces to the Cheshire-Cat. "*We* shall question the prisoner."

The pupils in the Cheshire-Cat's large yellow eyes expand into cavernous slits. "I do not always play nice."

Not even a beat passes before the Librarian responds. "Neither do I."

Ferz Epona introduces the Society agents to the Wonderlanders present. As there is no time to waste, we immediately get to work. A secondary table is brought for Marianne to set up her technical equipment upon. Whilst Wonderland has no satellites or Internet, our specialist assures us there are many other tools we may utilize to help us with our quarry. The Wonderlanders are fascinated with her laptops and battery-powered generators she guarantees are strong enough to last for a fortnight. All of the Wonderlandian maps are scanned into her databases. "As long as there are those of you willing to supply details of the area and the Queen of Hearts' terrains," Marianne tells to the small crowd gathered 'round, "I shall be able to run search programs."

"We brought a drone," Jack adds. "It's just a little thing, but it might help us track this nasty queen down."

The Nightrider whinnies quietly. "A drone?"

"It's a little robot that flies, but we control it with a remote control," Jack explains. "It spies on things for us."

Ferz Eponi startles. "Your robots are alive?"

The White King pulls me aside as Marianne clarifies a drone's function. "Where is your prince? The doctor? Their absence is worrisome."

The cut his innocent query drags across my heart is neat and clean and stings as if astringent were poured within. And although I exposed the depths of my fears and shames with him the day before, I choose now to brush off his concern as unnecessary, even though I nearly drown in my own. "They were unavoidably detained, but are expected to rendezvous with us within several days."

"I will inform those on watch to be on the outlook." He cracks the knuckles of both hands in succession. "A temporary cease-fire will enact in three days' time when we meet with the other Courts, save Hearts."

Although I had asked him to call such a meeting, part of me was ready to accept refusals from three of the other Courts. "What of the King of Hearts?"

Jace shifts, the leather of his heavy belt creaking. "Intelligence has him at odds with his counterpart, but one never knows." He scrubs a weary hand across his stubbled jaw. "He has agreed to come."

Before us, the Librarian, Nightrider, and Cheshire-Cat pour over maps whilst Mary and Jack interview Jace's advisors for Marianne's search programs. "Any word on Hearts?"

"I have three teams searching, and spies in all Courts on notice, but so far, it is like she has disappeared from Wonderland."

My grunt is indeed unladylike. While it is quite possible the villainess is traipsing about Timeliness, instinct insists she is here. The Chosen bear her insignia. That cannot be by happenstance. "And the White Rabbit?"

Jace folds his arms across his chest. "Interestingly enough, he was spotted at Cor Castle just last night."

"Is he still at the Heart seat?"

"A report via jubjub is expected by nightfall."

If anyone were to know the Queen of Hearts' secrets, it would be the White Rabbit.

Attacking or imprisoning fellow Courts' Grand Advisors is unlawful. Hearts broke this long-held agreement by capturing and executing the Caterpillar. She also kidnapped and tortured the Cheshire-Cat, although, thankfully, he was liberated. How she has failed to pay for those grave sins against the Diamonds and White Courts is unforgiveable.

While I would not stoop so low as execution or torture, I have a right to retribution. But it is more than that. Hearts, as villainous as she is, is a link to the Piper.

The Hearts Court is nearly a day-and-a half- worth of uninterrupted travel from the White King's encampment. If I were to leave now. . .

"I will go with you."

I tilt my head toward Jace, my lips curling in amusement.

"That is what you were plotting, correct?"

"Am I so predictable?"

A quiet chuckle falls into the space between us. "I simply have the honor of knowing you for many years."

"It would be best if you stay here and oversee the drone searches."

He gazes at the cluster of Society agents and Wonderlandian advisors working together. "Matters are well in hand." And then, hushed, "She abducted my Grand Advisor, too. He may still live, but I also have bones to pick."

"Once word gets out, the other Courts will not look kindly upon us. I am fine with such censure, being exiled already, but you—"

"As if I bloody care."

I sigh and chuckle all at once. "Well then. Let us see what Mary has brought in her bag of tricks that will help loosen the Rabbit's tongue."

The acrid sting of smoking torches hazes around the red-sandstone and black-marble monstrosity looming at the base of the Venae Cavae Mountains. Neither the king nor queen's banner flies above the tallest turret, but as a good number of card soldiers and pikemen line the battlements, chances of the White Rabbit's presence remain high.

True to Jace's recent report, the road leading to Cor Castle no longer bears severed heads on spikes. Long a favorite punishment and deterrent of the Queen of Hearts, Jace's army struck the carved posts down whilst liberating the Cheshire-Cat. I hold no illusions about the dungeons' purification, though—queen in residence or no, they are undoubtedly filled to the brim with prisoners both political and indigenous.

The crunch of pebbles upon the cobblestone road alert Jace and me to pair of patrolling card soldiers. For the last half hour, we have lain in ambush, waiting for just such an opportunity. We chose a spot around the first bend leading to the castle, just out of sight of the main guards—and we are not the only ones taking advantage of such circumstances, for our prey removes their helmets and let them drop to the ground once they are no longer in view. The taller of the card soldiers tugs out a flask and savors a long drag.

The other holds out a hand. "It's cold as a witch's tit tonight, it is."

The first belches, wiping his mouth with the back of a gloved hand. "Or Her Majesty's."

The two chortle so loudly they nearly weep. In their distraction, Jace and I creep from beyond the shaped rosebushes, the butts of our blades at the ready. Just as the second soldier drinks from the flask, we simultaneously bash the hilts against the backs of their heads. As the card soldiers crumple to the ground, Jace says, "They could have at least put up a fight."

I hide my smile as I drag the smaller soldier back toward the rosebushes. "Alas, there is no time for a proper fight tonight. It seems a shame it had to be these two, though, doesn't it?"

After all, like us, they apparently bear no love for Hearts.

At first, Jace makes to follow me, but he freezes as reality crashes through the moment. He drags the taller soldier toward the rosebushes on the other side of the road.

I quickly strip the hapless patrolman of his clothes in order to wear them myself. I strap my weapons beneath the large tunic, alongside a small satchel filled with Mary's drugs. I tie the man up, spraying him liberally with SleepMist.

Jace and I slip the helmets on, claim the card soldiers' weapons, and turn back toward the castle.

"Six of Clubs! Two of Spades!" A brawny Gryphon trundles out of the shadowy front gates. "Your check-in was ten minutes ago. If I find out you have been drinking again. . ." He stomps closer, feathers ruffling beneath his armor. Both Jace and I snap to attention, keenly aware of our assumed rolls. My pulse quickens; my hand itches to ready my blade.

The Gryphon crowds our space, his beak clattering as he chirps softly. Although I know the helmets offer a modicum of anonymity, there is always the chance this soldier could suss us out.

We simply do not have time for such a delay.

"Hmm." The Gryphon's dark eyes narrow. "You don't reek of juice." He jerks back, clearly irritated. "Miracles never cease. You may resume your patrol."

"Permission to speak privately, sir."

I am impressed at Jace's spot-on impression of the taller card soldier's intonation.

The Gryphon's head bobs as he chatters some more, his attention riveted on the White King. But then he sighs heavily. "You have three minutes."

The Gryphon leads us into a small office just off of Cor's main entrance. Once I close the door behind us, Jace whips his blade out and slams its butt against the Gryphon's temple. I ready another dose of SleepMist.

The castle is sleepy, with nary a servant to be seen. Much of the furniture is draped with cloth, indicating no one has been in residence for some time. Still, Jace and I unobtrusively make our way down a series of hallways we know will lead to the White Rabbit's offices.

While certainly never a frequent guest, considering the shared animosity between Queen of Hearts and myself, I have visited Cor Castle a number of times during my tenure in Wonderland. Annual balls in each Court are tradition, or at least were, prior to wartime. Spies are tradition, too, as are their reports familiarizing monarchs with their rivals' home bases.

The White Rabbit is a contradiction amongst the Wonderlandian Grand Advisors. Unlike the others, he spends half of his day calm and level-headed, even fearful, whilst the rest utterly deranged. There is no set schedule for such behavior, no identifiable patterns or triggers to rely upon. It is not a solid twelve hours of sanity verses madness, either—both flow in and out of one another like two rivers repeatedly meeting on their way to the ocean.

As we have no idea which Rabbit we shall encounter tonight, it is fortunate Mary brought with her a number of sedatives.

Light spills from an open doorway at the end of the hallway. The White Rabbit employs an entourage of handlers whose sole purpose is to rein in his erratic behavior, meaning they are trained well and are highly effectively. Whilst Grand Advisors, as a whole, are not combat ready, the Rabbit is vicious in his deranged state, his teeth and claws just as effective as any weapon.

It is little wonder that Hearts adores him so.

We linger outside the door, listening for several minutes. I am relieved to overhear the White Rabbit's familiar whiny brogue as he discusses battle plans for several Hearts' regiments with at least two other persons.

I hold up a hand and count down our surprise arrival. I can practically taste Jace's anticipation as he quietly shifts next to me. For so many years, we fought side by side. And here we are again, together, just like old times.

Only there will be no reveling in our victory whilst making love afterward.

We enter the room as nothing more than card soldiers. The White Rabbit is seated at a large desk, scratching a quill across a piece of parchment; a man and woman stand at attention before him. Stationed across the room are two others in a similar stance.

The White Rabbit glances up from his work. His whiskers tug down as he frowns, his pink nose twitching. "Yes?"

Jace taps two fingers upon my back—once, twice. I nod, even as the White Rabbit asks, "Do you have a message or not? We're rather busy, I'm afraid."

Simultaneously, Jace and I pull out the weapons strapped beneath our stolen Hearts tunics. He lunges for the guards stationed near the fireplace, I attack those closest to the White Rabbit. Hearts' Grand Advisor leaps from his chair, shouting for additional guards, just as I kick out at the man. The solider sprawls across the desk, scattering the Rabbit's papers and spilling his inkpot.

The woman snarls, leaping onto my back. Much heavier than expected, as she is fit, I stagger beneath her girth. Is she woman or stone? We crash into the man, still struggling to climb off the Rabbit's desk. He clamps his legs around me, and I become the filling of a Hearts sandwich. The woman claws away at me as the man fumbles for his sword.

The Rabbit screams, "Kill him! Kill the traitor!"

Breath is becoming a luxury. Disagreeable as it is, I plunge my dagger in between the man's legs, right into the soft organs that make or break a man's ability to continue in a fight. He shrieks as warm blood seeps through my gloves; better yet, he immediately releases me in order to attend what is left of his precious manly jewels. I rear back as hard as I can, toppling my barnacle and me onto the ground. Whilst I am undoubtedly lighter than her (anyone but a colossus must be!), being on top, I have my advantages. Still wearing my helmet, I slam my head into hers several times until her grip slackens. I roll off just enough to snatch a fallen book to use to finally knock her senseless.

Jace calls, "He's escaping!"

I spring to my feet and dart out the door. The Rabbit is still in the corridor, shouting up a storm. He is not yet too far away. I dig out a special dart Mary supplied me and send it soaring. When it strikes him in the dead of back, he throws his arms out wide. As if by magic, the Rabbit stops, shudders, and falls face first onto the lacquered floor.

"How dare you mishandle me in such a way!"

Jace stands back, having successfully restrained the White Rabbit with wrist cuffs and to a chair. We are no longer in the Grand Advisor's office, instead choosing a more discreet, less obvious room on a different floor to use for our interrogation.

"You two will lose your heads for such treason!"

The White King of Wonderland tugs off his helmet. "Under whose authority? Yours?"

The Rabbit's pink eyes nearly explode from their sockets when I follow suit. "Your—Your Majesties . . . I . . . I—"

"I imagine," I say coldly, "that you are remembering in vivid detail how your queen kidnapped and abused our valued and trusted Grand Advisors. How she mutilated the Cheshire-Cat. How she executed the Caterpillar and then used his skin to fashion a trophy." I ready one of the two truth serum syringes I brought along for this particular mission. "I wonder how much of a part you were in such decisions."

"N-none at all, Your Majesty." His whiskers twitch violently. "I would never—"

"But you did." Jace bends to check on the knots surrounding the Rabbit's legs and feet.

"You cannot kill me." His ears are rigid at attention. "It is against the law!"

I push aside his cravat and inject the serum into his neck, not particularly caring if my touch is gentle. He thrashes against his bonds, but Jace's work is excellent. Rabid or docile, the White Rabbit will not escape these knots.

I toss the needle aside. "That did not stop your mistress, did it?"

His attention darts between Jace and me. "But—but—but you. . ."

I wait, but he does not finish. I press record on a digital recorder and set it on a table next to him. "For now, we simply wish to talk to you."

His nose scrunches as he warily examines the technology. "T-talk?"

"You will tell us what we wish to know," Jace says, "and if we are satisfied, we will walk out that door without cutting off your tail or skinning you."

The Rabbit blinks several times before his head shakes rapidly. A slow, rabid grin filled with flat yet razor-sharp teeth emerges. "Is that so?"

I ready yet another syringe. "Perhaps."

Jace snatches his long ears and yanks the Rabbit's head to the side. The Grand Advisor gnashes his teeth as I inject yet another needle into the skin beyond the white fur of his neck.

Jace tuts, "Temper, temper."

"She will kill you for this insult."

"Will she?" I ask mildly. "Or will she, perhaps, be more put out at you for allowing us to infiltrate Cor and capture you so easily?"

Spittle flies as the Rabbit shouts, "I have only ever been loyal to Her Majesty!"

My own smile is equally deranged as I spit his words back at him. "Is that so?"

The chair bounces on the ground, so vehement is his last gasps at struggling.

I lean closer, unafraid of his teeth, of his rage. "You see, once upon a time, you did something for *me*. Something that Her Majesty would be most displeased with."

As the sedative takes effect, alarm and confusion reddens his pink eyes.

"You don't remember it because the Caterpillar took your memories from you. Today, I will take more of them from you."

He unwillingly sags in the chair. "I will never betray my queen."

Jace looms over him, his sword in hand. "Where is the Queen of Hearts currently?"

The Rabbit sneers, his fur-covered lip undulating. Defiance quickly gives way to bewildered, angry frustration, though. "The last I heard, she was in the mountain."

For a moment, I am no longer within Cor Castle, but inside Koppenberg's dungeons.

We destroyed that mountain. Those halls, those torture chambers, no longer stand.

"Do you speak of Venae Cavae?" Jace presses.

I repress a shudder and focus once more on the snarling Rabbit before me. His large teeth snap together. "Yes."

The Venae Cavae Mountains are legendary for mining of gold, silver, and a strand of reddish quartz long favored by the Hearts Court.

"She is within the Venae Cavae?" Jace clarifies.

When the Rabbit unwillingly answers in the affirmative, it is more hiss than anything else.

The Piper and the thirteenth Wise Woman resided within a mountain in 1816/18GRI-GT. And now, the Queen of Hearts is said to be hiding within another . . . This is no mere happenstance. It cannot be.

Instinct tells me that if I were to head into the Venae Cavae, I would not only find Hearts but the Piper. Did he trade one mountain for another?

I grab the Rabbit's labels. "Where specifically within the Venae Cavae is the Queen of Hearts?"

He chokes, he froths in rage, he howls in frustration. The White Rabbit does all he can to rebuff my question. But Mary's drug is too seductive, too robust to resist for too long. Salty, bitter tears soak his fur when his resolves breaks. He shudders, and red eyes fade to pink once more.

"Her private residence."

Neither Jace nor I have ever heard of the Queen of Hearts having any other residence than Cor. Our personal house in the tulgey woods was an anomaly amongst Wonderlandian rulers, crafted out of necessity to blur the lines between Courts rather than anything else. None of the other monarchs had separate residences; indeed, once word of its existence spread, the Red Queen publicly mocked the White King and me for livings like peasants in the woods rather than rulers in palaces.

But Hearts constructing a secret lair within the Venae Cavae Mountains? Is that a recent necessity—or one long standing? Is the King of Hearts aware of its presence?

"Why does the Queen of Hearts have a private residence in the mountains?" Jace asks.

"I—I do not know, Your Majesty. She only shared its location recently." His chin meets his chest. "She will kill me for betraying her trust. I am sworn to secrecy. Oh, I am a terrible, terrible Rabbit. I do not deserve to wear the Grand Advisor mantle."

For the next several minutes, Jace extracts specific directions to the hidden dwelling within the Venae Cavae, accessible from the dungeons of Cor Castle, all the while the Rabbit openly weeping and begging us to grant him sanctuary. The hysterics swiftly halt once his alter ego re-emerges, and any requests for clemency transition to threats.

"You will never gain entrance anyway." Leather-clad feet thump upon the floor in a steady beat.

The muffled call of a trumpet fills the chilly air, signaling the changing of the guard. We must be leaving soon. "And why is that?"

His mouth curls into a wicked swirl, showcasing a set of perfect tombstone teeth. "You are not chosen."

Chosen.

Goose pimples frost my skin. I jab a dagger beneath his chin. "Is the Queen of Hearts Chosen?"

The Rabbit's wrists are confined; his legs, too. His head, though, is not, and I realize the error of my ways the moment he jerks forward and impales himself on my dagger. Iron slices through white fur and the soft skin of his throat.

Red rivulets stain his pelt as he gags and chokes and chortles.

Jace snarls, "Son of a Jabberwocky!" as I yank out the blade. I press against the wound, desperate to stem the tide, but the Rabbit's life hemorrhages too quickly from him.

The White King kicks the chair—and the Rabbit's limp body—sprawling across the room. "Coward!"

I gawk at the gory blade at my feet. *The White Rabbit chose death rather than risk Hearts' wrath.*

"If we leave now," Jace says tightly, "we can get down to the dungeons undetected."

"No."

He whirls about, thunderstorms brewing above his head.

"The Rabbit indicated that, in order to access Hearts' lair, they must be Chosen." I pick up the blade and wipe the Rabbit's blood upon a tablecloth. "I have no proof, but I would bet all that I own that the Piper and his minions are within her lair in the Venae Cavae. The two of us alone stand no chance against such an army."

Jace's anger sizzles and crackles, sharp as lightning. "You have so little faith in yourself? In me?"

I shove the blade back into its sheath. Two years ago, I might very well have stormed the Venae Cavae with him without a second thought. Now, though . . . "I have experience and the wisdom to know better than repeating past mistakes. If we two go in alone, and my instincts are correct, our chances of exiting the mountain will be slim to none."

"These villains attacked our people, our lands." The White King quakes as his thunder rebuilds. "You cannot expect me to sit back and ignore their crimes!"

"Do you think I do not crave the same vengeance?" I match him, toe to toe. "Do you forget why I search for the Piper in the first place? He and the Chosen must pay for more than Wonderland. And Hearts. . ." I grapple with the madness desperately clamoring for release. "They will pay, Jace. By God and Wonderland, they will. But I refuse to fail all of those crying out for justice simply because of the allure of rashness."

He pinches his lips together as he stares at me, his breaths hard and resentful.

I am no longer his partner. We are no longer on the same page at all times. The realization is both a relief and heartbreaking all at once.

"In two days, we meet with the rest of the kings and queens. We will lay out Hearts' villainy. If they choose to fight alongside us, our odds of beating such powerful, foreign magic are greatly increased. If they don't, we will have the Diamonds and White armies, alongside the Society, when we make our way back to the Venae Cavae." I grip his shoulders, tethering him to the ground. "We cannot go in blind. We must be smart about this. There is more at stake than either of our prides."

His nod is curt.

He does not hide his disappointment.

WHAT MAKES A MONSTER

ALICE

MARIANNE REQUESTS EVERY MAP of the Venae Cavae Mountain region Jace's men and women can get their hands on. As she, the White King, Jack, Mary, and a number of advisors begin plotting ways in and out of the Queen of Hearts' secret lair, the Librarian pulls me aside to a secondary staging table set up.

"Tell me what you know about the Sage."

Despite stealing a few hours to sleep after the White King and I crossed Hearts land into White territory, exhaustion still beckons me at every turn. I motion for a page to bring a tea serving—a strong one that will fortify me for the coming hours. We journeyed all day, through rain and sleet, to reach the White encampment, and while many welcomed slumber hours ago, I still have much time to go before head may meet pillow.

"Her name is the very definition of her life." I rub the bridge of my nose. "She is one of the ancient pillars of Wonderlandian wisdom."

"Is she a witch?"

Interestingly enough, I do not know the answer to this question. There has never been any associating of that particular word with the Sage, nor has anyone ever referred to her as anything other than what she is called.

The Librarian is thoughtful for several long moments during which I repress the urge to screech for the tea, fearful of collapsing in a frazzled, wearied heap upon the floor. "Send someone for her."

A burst of laughter shoots out of me. "The Sage does not come like a dog. She does not leave her cave. Those who desire her wisdom go to her."

The glare the Librarian levels is insulting at the very least, as if I am a schoolgirl and she an annoyed teacher after a repeated explanation. "Summon her."

The tent flap opens; a card soldier steps through. She offers a sharp bow. "Pardon my interruption, Your Majesties, but the Prince of Adámas and his entourage request an audience."

I stand upright so quickly that my hip rattles the table, toppling strategy pieces to their sides.

Finn. He's here.

But more importantly: *he's alive.*

"Entourage? What entourage?" Mary mutters at the same time the White King says far more calmly than I feel, "Show them in at once."

The card soldier snaps another bow and exits.

Only four days have passed since we last were in one another's presence, yet it feels as if it has been years. Knots tighten throughout my lungs as I step around the table.

"It's about time, isn't it?"

Jack's sentiment is sorely shared. I look to the Librarian, waiting for her own well-placed comment concerning tardiness or the lack of. Instead, I find concern marring her forehead and blue eyes fastened upon the tent flap.

Mary steps beside me, her arm slipping through mine, binding us together. I know not whether she thinks to reassure herself or me—both, most likely.

Marianne abandons her computers. "Surely, by entourage, the soldier referred to the whole of the Van Brunt family."

Mary stiffens, and all of the unspoken yet shared anxiety and fear we two share rear their ugly heads.

If Finn is here, then he must be fine. *They* must be fine.

"What is taking so long?" Mary whispers, strangled by the ghosts of What-ifs haunting us.

The flap shifts, signaling the card soldier's return. My pulse gallops, thundering in my ears, a wild stampede not even remotely close to being under control, as I peer into the darkness behind her. "Your Majesties, I present the Prince of Adámas, Mr. Van Brunt, and Dr. Van Brunt."

The soldier steps to the side just as thunder explodes beyond the canvas walls. And then Finn steps through, and I am a river rushing to his sea.

He is pale—too pale. Purple smudges bruise his shadowed eyes. A knit hat tugs low over his brow and ears; no hair pokes out. He dons a damp, modern puffy coat, jeans, and boots, appearing both utterly out of place in Wonderland and delightfully welcome all at the same time. Van Brunt emerges behind him, similarly dressed. A third figure comes into the light, tall and yet curled into himself, with dark sunglasses hiding his eyes. A knit hat similar to his brother's covers Victor's head. He is unrestrained, and yet the way he carries himself shouts how wary he is of such a fact.

Concern and questions bombard the room, but my focus, my hands, my heart are tethered to Finn's. "You came."

His smile is wan, and the sight of it rumbles within me alongside the storm beyond the canvas walls of the pavilion. "Nothing could have stopped me."

"Are you all right?"

His lower lip tugs between his teeth. His answer takes far too long. "I won't know until," he rubs at the knit hat, "I see her again."

Nearby, Van Brunt is saying to the White King, "I thank you for the assistance you've been providing the Society, as well as the lodging you've provided our agents."

"It is, as always," Jace says, "my honor to assist the Queen of Diamonds and those she works with." He turns to Ferz Eponi. "Ready another tent. Have hot water available, and warm food."

The Ferz bows, and departs. Van Brunt coughs into a fist. "That, too, is greatly appreciated."

Of the three Van Brunts, the elder appears the least altered. While it is obvious he is exhausted, he does not share the stark changes the other two exhibit, nor the careful way they move. Finn's own gestures are slower than normal, almost as if daily acts taken for granted, such as walking, are painful. As for Victor, he remains stationed by the entrance, his arms crossed tightly across his chest, chin tucked into his neck, the dark glasses firmly in place.

"You were sorely missed, old friend," the Librarian tells Van Brunt. "There is much to discuss, but first. . ." Her shrewd eyes narrow upon Victor.

The rest of the room's attention follows. The doctor tilts his head, as though he challenges anyone within to accuse him of resuming recent actions and attitude.

The Society's leader scrubs tiredly at his unkempt beard as he, too, gazes at his eldest son. Rain pounds against canvas as a flash of bright light flares momentarily through the cracks of the entrance.

Victor straightens. His arms slacken by his side, but, just as quickly, he immediately shoves his fists beneath his armpits. "If you're all worried I will go bonkers again. . ." A sneer curls his normally affable mouth. "Good. Stay on your guard."

A pained expression flashes across his father's face. "Victor, please."

"You shouldn't have brought me. You should have left me there, locked away in one of those tanks where I couldn't hurt anyone again." Victor briefly cocks his head in Mary's direction.

"This pity party isn't going to help anyone, least of all you."

I turn, startled, to face Finn. Shadows darken his eyes, his cheeks, as he regards his brother.

Victor counters, "You don't—"

"Don't even finish that," Finn warns. "Because you know I do."

Victor yanks a thumb to his mouth, gnawing on a nail. Whatever fight was in him dissipates. His shoulders sag as he once more curls into himself. "I'm sorry. I just. . ."

Finn tugs the knit hat lower as he approaches his brother. "You have to at least give it a chance."

Victor reaches out an unsteady hand before withdrawing it. Finn grabs hold of it anyway. "I'm not scared of you."

"You should be. I'm a monster, after all." More quietly, "Nothing could change *that*."

Nearby, a tiny, strangled gasp tears from Mary, and for the span of a breath, I wonder if this normally strong woman will finally shatter amongst company. But it is not to be, for she throws her shoulders back, regal as any queen I have ever known, and brings with her storms as she descends upon the doctor. "You are only a monster if you let yourself be, you ridiculous prat."

Her razor-sharp barb slices through the tent. Finn wisely backs away, no doubt concerned about the possibility of collateral damage. "You are a man of three decades' worth of life, and you are behaving as if you are a toddler." Ire—or concern—leaves Mary vibrating before Victor. "Maybe those questionable doctors must have done something right, because you're once more throwing a tantrum over how life is not fair. *Life isn't fair, love.*"

She jabs a finger against the meat beneath his collarbone. "Life hands us some truly shoddy plates, and you just have to take it." Rosy cheeks blossom into scarlet. "But you are *here*, petulant instead of crazed or violent. Isn't that a win?" Several more pokes leave Victor wincing. He opens his mouth, but she deftly silences him whilst snapping, "Furthermore, who gives a flying shite about whether or not you *look* like a monster? Scars mean nothing. Neither do looks, not really, not when people truly know you. You're only a monster if you act like one."

It does not pass notice that the Wonderlanders, including the White King, quietly, and quickly, slip away.

251

Victor snatches her finger—not harshly, not cruelly, but gently, as if it were caressing rather than poking him. And then he slowly slips off his sunglasses.

Behind me, Marianne cries out. Jack swears.

One of Victor's eye sockets, the one that held a foreign, blue orb, is angry red, jagged yet hollow.

He says, "I have more than just scars, Mary."

Mary Lennox is no mimsy, though. She does not recoil at such a gruesome visage, nor does she blanch. Instead, she critically surveys what he presents. "I'm glad it's gone. It wasn't yours. It didn't belong there. You would be better off with a glass eye than anything from the bloody Chosen."

I cannot help but wonder if Victor truly knows this woman, as he gapes at such a response.

"As for the limbs you've acquired. . ." Her dark eyes trail down the length of his stiffly protected body. "Well. I suppose we shall see just whom they belonged to. But as we can't have you limping around, one-armed and single-legged, we will have to make do with what remains. You ought to give serious thought to how some of the Timelines have done smashing work with mechanical limbs and living tissues."

Victor slips the dark sunglasses back on. "You make it sound so easy."

"It is what you want it to be." She motions to the exit behind him. "If you aren't going to make an effort, then turn back around and either edit home or go—I don't know where. Somewhere else. We don't have the time or room to babysit you. People are dying, Victor. People's lives are at risk. We're planning an attack, and we need all the strength we can muster to make it successful. If you aren't able to do that, then we have no need of you."

Through the entire rant, Victor hesitantly reaches toward her. Some of Mary's fire must transfer via an electric current, though, for when this challenge is issued, he grabs hold: firmly, not gingerly.

"I'm sorry," he whispers. "So damn sorry for what I did to you, Mary. I—I wish—"

She cups his face. "Shut up and kiss me already, will you?"

I turn away just in time for Jack to say, "Well, I, for one, am eager to see what kind of robo-eye she's going to find him."

Marianne's sigh is palpable.

"You love me just the way I am, admit it." Jack clucks her beneath the chin, eliciting a rather rosy stain to tint her cheeks.

"I think," the Librarian drawls, "that perhaps any further discussions can wait until sunrise at the earliest. At least, for the majority of the remaining company." She pats Van Brunt's arm. "You and I, old friend, still have plenty to discuss. I've got a prisoner who has told me lots of interesting things I think you'll want to know."

The Society's leader stifles a yawn. "Agreed." He and the Librarian depart to find the White King; Jack and Marianne retire to their tents. As Mary has already whisked Victor away, I lead Finn to my room here in the main pavilion.

Inside, the braziers are lit. A toasty fire emanates from a small metal fire bowl. The room is small, stark, the refuge of sudden arrival and necessity.

Finn wiggles a bag sitting on a collapsible bench at the end of the bed. "They automatically brought my stuff in here." A sly smile emerges. "Princedom has its perks."

I cannot help but chuckle. "I am certain your father and brother are also in possession of their belongings, despite their lack of Wonderlandian titles."

He presses a chilled finger against my lips. "Don't ruin the dream."

I kiss the digit before he pulls away. As I help him out of his damp coat, I consider whether or not to pry about the events of the last few days. For anyone else, manners would assure my silence. But this is Finn, and we have willingly allowed ourselves to be vulnerable to one another.

"If you desire to stay quiet, I will respect your wishes, but I would ask of you to tell me what happened in Antarctica."

Finn tosses his coat over the back of a nearby chair before leading me to the bed. We sit down, hands intertwined together. "Are you sure you want to know?"

Unease scratches against my spine at the doubling of shadows within his eyes.

"A queen must be an excellent actress in times of difficulty."

I glanced up from the scrolls I was studying. The Caterpillar lounged nearby, a bottle of the Hatter's juice dangling from one of his feet, a goblet from another. I rather wished I was drinking a glassful rather than perusing texts dryer than the sands of the Sahara.

"Pardon?"

He slurped the brightly colored drink noisily. "Emotions are liabilities, but especially when visible."

The Caterpillar himself rarely showed any emotion other than irritation. "You cannot expect me to be emotionless forevermore."

He lurched forward, liquid sloshing from both cup and bottle. "Are your ears filled with feathers?" A sneer curled his equivalent of lips. "Obstinate girl, always yet ineffectively attempting to turn my words around."

Correction: irritation and disdain.

I knew that monarchs must rule with their brains, not hearts. It was a rocky lesson to learn, but necessary. "My apologies. You were saying,"—lecturing—*"visible emotions are frowned upon?"*

"Your people look to you for strength."

I waited.

He drained his cup and promptly poured a fresh one. "Cower in fear, and they will follow."

I glanced down at the papers strewn about my desk. They detailed nothing that would inspire fear, let alone anything other than boredom.

Interestingly enough, the very next day, the White Rabbit appeared in my Court, bearing a large hatbox. "A gift from the majestic, generous Queen of Hearts to the Queen of Diamonds." Inside was the head of a kitchen maid, one who once hailed from Hearts' lands but sought asylum in mine.

And now, she wishes to hold sway over Finn.

I damn well *do* want to know every last detail. She and I will battle face to face before she is allowed to even breathe the same air as him again. But rather than rage about, I follow the Caterpillar's years-old piece of advice, masking my worry and frustration. I lean in, savoring his familiar, warm scent, and brush my lips across his. "Partners do not hide such things from one another unless it is necessary."

A hand curls around the back of my neck, tangling within my hair. For many hushed seconds, his forehead merely remains pressed against mine, our lips perilously close to one another. My pulse skitters, as if this were our first kiss rather than the hundredth. And when our mouths do touch, and our tongues, too, I wonder if it will always feel this way.

I pray that it does.

Cool air fills the space between us when he pulls away. His fingers tighten around mine. He stares straight ahead, at the fluttering walls of the storm-shaken tent. "To make a long story short, the scientists, or doctors, I guess, created a," he flashes air quotes, "wall around whatever the thirteenth Wise Woman did to me."

I swallow back the rancorous fear climbing up my throat. "Is it known what she specifically did?"

He chews on his lower lip as he considers my question. "Whatever spell she cast was done in a language that none of the scientists understood, and there wasn't enough time to find a proper translator to figure out the specifics."

"Were you hypnotized?" How else were they to know such a thing?

He rubs a knuckle against the same lip recently abused. "Not so much. At least, I don't think. . ." A sigh finishes the sentence. "I don't even know how to explain it, Alice. Some of it was science. Some of it had to be magic."

Magic.

We learned from the twelfth Wise Woman that such spells cast, at least by her kind, cannot be erased. The intentions within, however, can be altered with opposing magic. "I thought these were doctors, not witches."

"I honestly don't know what the hell they were." His focus falls away, back toward the fluttering wall before us. Voice low yet steady, he proceeds to detail what happened, from the multiple injections to his hair being shaved off. I slowly peel away the damp knit cap as he

255

explains the rods injected into his skull, and when I find soft fuzz instead of soft strands, I wish to both cry and rage. Twin fresh scabs rest upon his crown, ugly, large ones that cannot be comfortable. I gently trace his neck, down to another injection site.

The pain he must have felt. Still feels. I will have to get the healing spray.

"Everything became too much." Finn stays still as I examine the tender flesh around the bruised wounds. "I couldn't even scream. I was paralyzed. They propped my eyes open and I was forced to watch videos and pictures for hours. I listened to audio. I genuinely wondered if at one point, they'd cut open my skull. I thought I might be dead."

A queen must be an excellent actress in times of difficulty.

I can't, though. Not with him.

"When the paralysis took over, my lungs, the movies, the audio, it all stopped." I marvel wildly at how calm he remains when all I wish to do is make my way to Antarctica with a blade. "Then I was put into a sensory deprivation tank. That was. . ." A distance grows between us, wide and deep as an ocean. "At one point, I woke up a room that had some kid in it. A kid who looked like—" His puff of laughter is filled with an undeserved shame I wish to wash away. "I kid you not, Alice, but it looked exactly like I did when I was six or seven. I can't explain it. He just stared at me. Didn't blink, just stared. Neither of us slept or talked. He just stared at me, and I couldn't look away. Then a door opened, breaking our connection. I was back in the sensory deprivation tank. Had I even left? I have no idea. Was it a hallucination?" He shakes his head again. "I haven't slept since."

He rubs a tentative hand across the golden down covering his scalp. He eyes the knit cap in my lap, an unasked question that must rub his ego raw yet serves to break my heart.

I toss the cap aside and climb onto my knees. I lean in. I kiss the space above his ear; the velvety, shorn strands tickle my sensitive skin. Gently, I brush feather-light kisses across the scabs on his skull. I linger as my mouth presses against his forehead, savoring each inhalation of *Finn*. I curl a hand around the base of his head, conscious to not jostle the bruises just below. I lavish more gossamer kisses over each of them. "Are you still in pain?"

His answer is as light as my caresses. "Right now? No."

"This wall." I kiss his cheek, and then the corner of his mouth. "What purpose does it serve?"

Beneath the palm of one of my hands, his heart's march increases. "To slow down or even contain whatever the spell's intentions are."

My kisses trail down to his jawline. "Were these doctors witches?"

He grips my waist. His breath against my skin is deliciously unsteady. "Probably."

We've spoken enough. Finn is alive. He is safe. My partner and my lover is once more by my side. The next day is filled with many terrifying unknowns, but for now, there is nothing to be done about it but embrace the moments we now share together. I smile against his mouth whilst pilfering a line from Mary. "Shut up and kiss me already."

He does, and callooh callay, he takes his sweet time doing so. Beyond the canvas walls a tempest howls and rages, bellowing like a horde of uffish jabberwockies gallumphing about, but the nearby fire bowl is toasty, and the hands curling around me even more so. Finn loses his boots; mine are gone within seconds, too. I remove his flannel shirt; he does the same for my dress. His pants meet the ground, as do my leggings. In the golden firelight, he is beautiful, my own Adonis reanimated by the best kind of magic. Greed and need have me devouring him with all my senses. I cannot get enough of his beauty: of his taste; of the sound of his sighs and moans; of the feel of his skin beneath my own; of the weight of his body against mine. Although I have long committed to memory each freckle, each scar, each dip and curve and muscle that together comprise Huckleberry Finn Van Brunt, I take my time retracing them with both mouth and hands, desiring to stretch this time out until I am blind and insensible with sensation and urgency. And I am not alone in such needs, as Finn paints his own pictures across my skin's canvas, each touch, each kiss and caress more than the sum total of its parts.

He and I, we are more than just partners. More than mere lovers. We are mirror images of one another. We both began life as something different and then willingly chose to change our stories, voluntarily embracing the scope of larger destinies whilst constantly taking into consideration the lives of people we would never meet. We freely place others' needs before our own without thought toward glory or acknowledgement. We risk much. We feel deeply. Our pasts are deep and vast, and, at times, difficult to tread within. We attempt to make our way to the other side anyway. There is sexual chemistry, oh so much of it, but that alone cannot carry us through all that we face. There is shared camaraderie. There is belonging, acceptance.

There is true love.

When Finn pushes into me, and bliss beckons like a sultry siren on nearby rocks, I fight to keep my eyes from closing. I watch my north star as we dance together, marveling at how deeply he resonates within me—not just in my body, but in my soul. I am entirely overwhelmed, and grateful to be so. He moves to kiss away my tears, but I stay him, maintaining the strength of our gaze upon each other.

Euphoria crashes over me first before pulling Finn in its undertow. Afterward, I refuse to let him roll off me, instead savoring the sweet pressure of his weight, the musky scent of our lovemaking, the cooling sweat covering both of us, the gradual slowing of his heartbeat and breath. We compensate by shifting to our sides, still connected, still together, still one.

As I doodle light pictures upon his back, I struggle to coherently piece together the contents of my heart. I fail miserably. I whisper, "I cannot find the proper words in any language or any Timeline to convey the strength of what I feel for you."

I shiver as his large hands languidly trace the length of my body. "You already told me, here in this bed. I heard you loud and clear. I hope you heard me, too."

I did, thank goodness.

I did.

THREE UNEXPECTED GIFTS

FINN

"**I** CANNOT BE THE ONLY one who thinks this is a terrible idea."

I glance across the table at Mary. She's not, of course. I think all of us from the Institute are equally concerned. Today, Alice is set to travel to a so-called neutral location and convene with the rest of the Wonderlandian monarchs. Outside of the White King, none of the other royals are true allies. Alice once said that the White Queen would have no qualms turning her into a doll, and that the Red Queen would gladly crucify her. There was no mention of what the Red King would do, but I can't imagine it would be pleasant, considering the ruling that banished her from Wonderland. And then there's the King of Hearts, who must be a piece of work himself considering he actually *married* his crazy psychotic bitch of a co-regent. Who knows what lengths he'll go to get his hands on Alice?

"After what happened in Koppenberg Mountain," Alice is saying coolly, "we need all the help we can get to battle the Chosen. As the interrogation with the piper we captured on the first day has proven, Hearts is officially aligned with the Chosen, this is now a Wonderlandian problem. And as she is here, on her home turf, we cannot hunt her without informing the others of her crimes."

"You will be a lamb to the slaughter!"

Mary never has been one to know when to shut her mouth.

"The Queen of Diamonds is an excellent swordswoman, nearly unparalleled in skill." The Nightrider's displeasure crackles throughout the dining tent. "The same can be said for the White King. If you are insinuating that Their Majesties cannot maintain the Queen of Diamonds' safety during the summit—"

The A.D. holds up a hand, shocking the unicorn into silence. "Mary is not insulting anyone, let alone your king. She's just worried about our friend facing a pack of loonies."

The Nightrider sputters over his of cup of tea.

"Although inelegant, Ms. Lennox makes a valid point," Brom says. "Will guards be allowed?"

One of the squat, egg-shaped White advisers clears her throat. I think her name is Ferz Epona, but I get her and her twin's names confused at times. "Summits such as these are rare, but certain protocols and comforts are expected. Each monarch may bring their Grand Advisor, their Ferzes, a taste tester, and a member or two of their household. Pikemen and card soldiers may wait a thousand yards away."

I damn well will ensure that I will be the official household representative of the Diamonds Court. While I trust Alice, and have faith in her abilities, she doesn't have to face this firing squad alone. I'm here. I'll stand by her side, just like she's stood by mine.

We'll face this Wonderlandian pit of vipers together.

Brom considers what the Ferz has described. "Are weapons allowed?"

The Ferz's twin swallows a lemon. "Monarchs are never without weapons."

Several of the advisors seated at the table snort in derision, as if what my father asked was the stupidest question ever.

"So Grymsdyke can go?" the A.D. asks.

Hanging from a web in a corner, the Spider rouses from its morning meal of a large mouse. "I am an assassin, not a weapon, thief."

The A.D. pokes at his rehydrated eggs. "What's the difference?"

"As the Diamonds Court is lately overseen by the White Court, who will stand with the Queen of Diamonds?" Marianne asks.

The Cheshire-Cat materializes on a stool next to the White King, in front of a bowl of cream. This morning, he is the size of a toddler. "I will, of—" but the Librarian deftly cuts him off.

"I will fill in as her current Grand Advisor." The look she levels the Cat dares him to contract her.

I try not to crack a smile at chimera of irritated shock, suspicion, and pleasure that flashes across Alice's face.

"You will be busy with the White King," the Librarian continues. "The Queen of Diamonds does not deserve the diminished attention of any advisor."

The Cat's ears flatten. A low growl rumbles from his chest. "Now see here, witch—"

The A.D. stupidly knocks his knife against the table, chanting, "Fight! Fight! Fight!"

A pair of narrowed, blue eyes from the tiny woman sitting to his left shuts the thief right up.

"If we're assigning ourselves roles, then, I suppose I ought to be the bloody taste tester," Mary mutters. "Or at least the sniffer. I'm the only one of this motley lot with the knowhow to figure out antidotes and poisons, and I'll be damned if anybody slips something by me." Her smile is feral. "Maybe I'll be able to pick up a pretty for my collection if I'm lucky."

Alice's consternation softens considerably, even if wariness leaves her silent.

Brom folds his napkin and sets it next to his bowl. "Finn and I will serve as the equivalent of your Ferzes."

"If present in public functions, even if he has no ruling powers," Alice says quietly yet firmly, her attention on my father, "as my official consort, the Prince of Adámas is expected to publicly take his place in his Diamond throne."

I think, had I been drinking the tea in my hands, I just might have choked on it. As it is, a bit sloshes over the side, onto my jeans. She can't be serious, can she? I'm just—I know she gave me a title, but I'm just a hick kid from Missouri. Hell, I'm wearing jeans, another plaid shirt, and that ugly knit hat. I don't look like someone who ought to be on a throne.

"It would be best if you had your guns," the White King is saying to me. "One never knows when an excellent weapon will come in handy during such situations." When I glance down the length at the table and meet his eerie, nearly colorless eyes, I'm taken aback to discover he is utterly unperturbed at the thought of me sitting in one of Wonderland's thrones like I'm his equal. I've never felt less than him before, or uneasy about his kingly status, but I've never had to sit in a throne before, either.

"Victor as the second Diamonds Ferz, then," Brom offers smoothly. My brother says nothing to being anointed as the equivalent of a military advisor. He's still wearing those damn sunglasses, hunched over the table like some goth kid, intent on listening to Bauhaus' whole catalogue before finishing his rehydrated breakfast. "Ms. Brandon and Mr. Dawkins will round out the group as members of the Diamonds' household." The hint of a smile peeps from beneath Brom's mustache and beard. "After all, it isn't a lie."

Alice clears her throat. She fingers the edge of the white bone china plate before her. "If you choose to come, it must be upon your own volition. And it must be with the clear understanding that Wonderland's monarchs may not necessarily act in a way that any of you may be familiar with."

"You can't get rid of us so easily, luv." The A.D. kicks his feet up onto the table, leaning back in his chair, hands behind his head. Several of the Wonderlanders present murmur in outrage over the idiot addressing one of the queens so disrespectfully, even if the sentiment was appreciated.

Marianne takes swift action, snatching his napkin. Using it as a shield, she shoves his feet off the table and then smacks him across the face with the linen. "Your manners leave much to be desired, Jack."

He leers at her. "I make up for it in so many other ways. I can show you, if you like. Take a trip over to the tent with me and we'll have a go around."

As his meaning becomes clear, Marianne legitimately, genuinely turns green. The napkin in her hand becomes less of a weapon and more of a barf bag when she covers her mouth and gags.

Mary cackles brightly. The Librarian and Brom both issue audible sighs.

The Nightrider leans in closer to one of the Ferzes. "Perhaps," he murmurs thoughtfully, "these fellows are more like Wonderlanders than we previously thought."

"I was right, you know."

Alice sets the polishing rag down and holds one of her daggers aloft. It glints, a sharp, clear ray of light in the hazy, misty gray of the morning. The storm has quieted for the time being. "About?"

Mary motions toward a nearby tent, her cheeks scarlet. A large group of men and women lounge before a campfire, drinking tea and who knows what else. Some are sleeping. Others are kissing. Some are—well, some ought to go back into the tent.

Alice barely steals a glance. "Did you talk to the White physician about any antidotes he might have in stock?"

"I cannot believe you guys," Mary hisses. "The A.D. is over there! With the Hatter! Doing—whatever he's doing. Right before we're to leave!"

I'll be damned. She's right. He's smack in between the Hatter and the Hare, his shoulders rubbing against their shirtless ones. Some nubile young lady perches on his lap, sucking on his neck. If I'm not mistaken, her hand is down his pants, too. Or is that the Hatter's hand?

Well, now.

Victor mutters, "I think it's pretty clear what he's doing."

Mary's outrage falters as her attention shifts to my brother. She squeaks, "It's in the *open*."

"Sometimes, Mary," Alice says fondly, "you are a delightful quagmire."

"That . . . that orgy of theirs has gone on nonstop. The whole time you and the White King were gone, it raged on. The A.D. hooked up with them on Day One, just like I predicted." Mary's voice shakes, as if she's telling us the most scandalous story ever. "And that Dormouse fellow. . ." She visibly shudders. "Why didn't you warn me about him?"

Alice laughs. "Ah. You met him, did you?"

Mary's glare could melt glass. "Poor Marianne has been hiding the entire time."

The smile Alice offers turns wicked. "But not you?"

Mary shoves Victor. "You should go get the A.D. Remind him why he's here."

"Sorry, love," He disentangles himself. "I refuse to be the fun police."

He sounds like the Victor I know.

"Is there something the matter?"

We glance up from our weapons to find the White King, his Ferzes, and a page. The military advisers carry two hatboxes on white-velvet pillows while the page teeters beneath a huge box.

"Not at all." Alice stands; I follow.

The White King nods, absently rubbing the back of his neck. "Good, good." He coughs into a fist. "I come bearing gifts, considering the day's events."

Alice tilts her head, a question marring her brow.

"When you requested a meeting with our fellow Courts, I knew that you were well aware of the odds already stacked against you for daring such a public appearance. The Diamonds crown is in New York City, not Wonderland. The Queen of Diamonds deserves a crown as benefitting her legal and rightful place in Wonderland." He opens one of the hatboxes and removes a glittering crown of gold and diamonds. "Immediately after our conversation, I sent riders to Anacites to retrieve several items. Upon their return, I had one of your smiths use some of the hereditary Diamonds jewels to create this for you. He worked day and night to ensure it be ready for today. I know it is not your original crown, but . . . I hoped that, considering it contained your Court's history, it would suffice."

Alice solemnly accepts the crown, her face devoid of any emotion.

"What is Anacites?" Mary asks.

Alice does not look away from the headpiece. "It is the name of the Diamonds palace." The twist of her lips is fragile. "I do not think I am vain to say it is the loveliest of all of Wonderlands Courts."

One of the Ferzes grunts. "Not at all, Your Majesty. Anacites remains unrivaled."

"Your lucky dress is here, if you so wish to wear it." The White King motions toward the large box the page is collapsing beneath.

Alice clears her throat, crown still balanced in her hands. "Your thoughtfulness is much appreciated."

He places a fist over his heart and bows. Alice turns to me. "Will you do the honors?"

I only momentarily ogle the crown she offers before taking it. She does not lower her head when I nestle the gold and jewels into her hair.

When I stand back, she shines brighter than any ray of light.

The White King opens the second hatbox. "While my men were at Anacites, I asked them to retrieve the Adámas crown from the vaults."

The what now?

In his hands is a circlet of gold, dotted with fat diamonds. He passes it to Alice. "I must go and finish readying myself for the day's journey. Prince Finn, I have sent a suit tailored for your Court to your room. There is a specific decorum to our meetings, I am afraid, that we all must adhere to."

Alice dips her chin, too overcome, I think, to say anything else. The Ferzes and page swiftly bow and scuttle off behind their king as he strides back to the main pavilion.

Mary waits until the Wonderlanders are gone before she says, "Well? Aren't you going to put it on?"

Victor snorts. "Yeah. He's going to look smashing: bald with a crown."

Mary smacks his arm. "You're just jealous."

I'm all too aware of the knit hat tugged low over my ears. Of the lack of hair. Of my jeans, of my flannel. Thanks to this morning's application of healing spray, holes and scabs no longer riddle my scalp and neck, but I know what I've been through recently. How I'm not quite whole anymore. But for some odd reason, Alice's smile is wide and genuine, and I can feel it all the way into my soul.

Alice tugs the knit hat off, revealing the scrub of downy gold. She runs a hand across it once, twice, her smile dreamy. Then she settles the crown onto my head, adjusting it so I barely feel its weight, which seems impossible, considering how many large diamonds circle the damn thing.

So quietly, so only I can hear, she whispers against the shell of my ear, "My heart is so full, seeing you wear this."

Mary tells Victor, "What do you mean, bald?! Finn has more hair than you, you big lout!"

KINGS, QUEENS, AND THRONES

FINN

S ITUATED IN THE EXACT center of Wonderland and completely round and carved from polished, gleaming green stone, the Courts' shared yet neutral castle isn't very big. On the ride here, the Nightrider informed me its only purpose is for meetings like today's. The permanent staff, supplied by all four Courts, is minimal and meant more for maintenance than anything else. There are no soldiers or guards, as no one can claim the nameless keep. If a meeting lasts for more than one day, monarchs must bring enough food and staff for their stay.

As for this day, the Nightrider was sure to add, "We'll even send a pair of stable hands along with you all, to take care of the horses."

I'll admit it was bizarre having a comment like that come from a Unicorn.

The inside of the keep resembles an onion and its rings. The outer halls are filled with tapestries representing Wonderland's past and present Courts, as well as pedestals filled with bits of history, such as swords, suits of armors, and books.

Voices waft out of the large hall situated in the dead center of the keep. The Cheshire-Cat leaps into the White King's arms. "How kind that they all came early in order to get a look at the Queen of Diamonds."

Alice says nothing even as she adjusts a pair of blades in her boots.

She is regal and utterly gorgeous in her supposedly lucky dress. Crafted of shimmering raw, royal-blue silk and peppered with enough diamonds to leave me wondering just how heavy the outfit actually is, when Alice walks, the train forms into the shape of a flying bird. It defies proper explanation, but it's safe to say that she and the dress are mesmerizing.

If she were to take flight, I would do my best to try to find a way to fly after her.

"It's best you go in together," the Cat is saying. "We'll want to reinforce the political alliance between the White King and Queen of Diamonds is unchanged and that our Courts are still intertwined, not absorbed as rumors claim." His ears twitch. "If one is to be targeted, both must be." Yellow eyes flick toward me. "You'll want to be careful, boy. You will be of much interest to those within. Never forget that, while you are an asset to the Queen, you are also her greatest liability."

Mary snorts. Jack titters. I don't bother responding to such an asinine observation, but it's clear the White King's Grand Advisor knows he put a paw over the line.

Alice absently scratches the Cat's head. "Finn is more than equipped to handle anything a Wonderlander might throw at him."

The Cat tilts its ear, providing Alice better access to what must be a favorite spot. "You New Yorkers simply follow what His Majesty's attendants do. Do not dally, do not ogle or show fear. Every single person in there loves to devour the weak. You. Witch." His stubby tail twitches toward the Librarian, and I can't help but wonder why she hasn't set him straight for the constant insults. "We will walk immediately behind Their Majesties. Ensure that no one attacks from behind."

"Perhaps I shall carry you, little kitten," the Librarian mewls, "and ensure no one attacks *you* from behind. We can't have you losing any more of your tail, can we?"

His ears flatten as he studies her with his overly large eyes. But then he surprises us all by leaping from the White King's arms to hers.

The A.D. whistles quietly.

One of the Ferzes instructs the door attendant, a portly, elderly Lizard, to announce Alice and Jace. It scrambles to yank open the pair of gilded doors, nearly breaking off its tail in the process.

In a surprisingly gravelly voice, the Lizard shouts, "Presenting His Majesty, the White King. Presenting Her Majesty, the Queen of Diamonds. Presenting His Highness, the Prince of Adámas."

Just before Alice and Jace walk into the room, she loops her arm through mine. Linked together, we step into the belly of the beast, and the inhabitants fall completely silent as their attentions swivel in our direction.

Before us are six sets of thrones arranged like the hands of a clock, each one set ten minutes apart, tapestries and insignias signifying Courtly allegiances. Behind the thrones, various representatives sit upon raised platforms. As for the thrones themselves, four sets are vibrant. The other two are dusty and ignored, as if they exist in a long-forgotten slice of space and time none of the keep's staff are able to access. Partway across the parquet floor, which mimics a humungous chessboard, Jace releases Alice's arm, bows deeply, and pivots toward an empty chair. Alice remains in the middle of the room as he does so, her face devoid of any emotion. Her fingers, though, curl tightly around my bicep, warning me to be on my guard.

The White King's throne is white—white-leather padded seat and backing, white wood, white opals for decoration. In the second throne is an extremely pale, gaunt woman with hair filled with white roses, swathed in a ridiculously voluminous gown of white silk and velvet that billows over the arms of her ornate throne.

Truthfully, she resembles an exploding marshmallow.

At her feet is a white bag with snowy feather spilling from the top. They cover the floor, the bottom of her dress, and the tips of her razor-sharp, white, pointy boots that peek from beneath the silk. In her lap is what appears to be an animal of undistinguishable origin, or at least, what once was an animal. She tugs a needle and thread throughout the graying skin even as her eyes hone dangerously in on Alice, her upper lip curling with scorn.

So this is Jace's counterpart, the White Queen.

Alice subtly tilts her head toward the Librarian, her eyes drifting to the Cheshire-Cat. Without another word, the Librarian strolls over to the White King and passes over her hitchhiker.

Jace says loudly, clearly, "I thank both you and the Queen of Diamonds for the excellent care bestowed upon my most trusted advisor."

The Cheshire-Cat lays his ears back, hissing—not at the Librarian, but at the White Queen. In turn, when her attention snaps from Alice to the Cat, she hisses right back. It's eerie as fuck, but I'll give it to the Cat, who doesn't recoil one bit. After a tense, mini-stare-off, he hops off of Jace's lap, significantly enlarging before positioning himself at his king's feet.

A bonnet-wearing Sheep whispers into the White Queen's ear.

Alice squeezes my arms and we resume our journey past the White thrones, past one of the neglected sets (perhaps the Clubs?) to a pair of lacquered chairs glittering with thousands of diamonds. She settles into the throne on the right, leaving me to drop into the one on the left. It's surprisingly comfortable for something encrusted with gems—the padding, which feels a bit like memory foam, is covered with supple leather. As the White contingency takes its place behind Jace, the rest of our party joins us, positioning themselves on the dais behind where we sit.

Of all the places I've gone, of all the things I've done, I think this is the most surreal.

A Frog, dressed in tails and donning a powdered wig, marches to the middle of the hall. He holds aloft a small golden bell. "So begins the temporary peace between the four Courts of Wonderland." He jiggles the bell, and its peal rings surprisingly loud against the curved walls. The Frog croaks twice and departs.

"Well, well," drawls the man directly before us. Red-haired and bearded, a weird fur stole wrapped around his neck, he lounges with a leg dangling over one chair leg, no doubt to highlight the overly obvious bulge. He twirls the corner of a fantastically styled mustache exactly as a cartoon villain would. Dressed in varying shades of scarlet, cherry, burgundy, brick, and wine, I peg him right away as the Red King. "There had been rumors, of course, of you sneaking into Wonderland like a thief in the night, but I did not actually think you would be so. . ." His overly bright eyes twinkle as he takes Alice in. "Well, brazen to do so, but then, that was naive of me, wasn't it? You, my darling, gorgeous Diamonds, are as brazen as the jabberwocky's tooth is long—and just as sharp, too."

Next to me, Alice leans back in her throne, fiddling with a dagger I've never seen before, one whose hilt is covered with diamonds. I've never seen the smile lifting her lips, either. It's more than a bit wicked, more than a bit mad, to be honest. "How deeply touching it is to hear that you still lust so strongly after me, Red."

The Cat catches my attention, as if to remind me to not show my hand, no matter what the cost.

The Red King's counterpart, a woman with flaming red hair twisted into her ruby laden crown, claps politely. Ringed around her neck is a scarlet Elizabethan collar so stiff, I'm positive it is a weapon in its own right. "Brazen you may be, you also wish for death." And I was right to suspect her collar, because she whips out several shuriken from hidden pockets and readies them.

I'm on my feet, gun in hand. Jace is out of his chair, too, Alice's vorpal blade in his fist. And most surprising of all, the White Queen lurches out of her throne, feathers flying everywhere as she clutches a coiled, white whip.

Jace's counterpart purrs, "You would be the prettiest doll of my collection, little fox. I would comb your hair every night. Put you in a new dress every day."

The Red Queen's laugh is best described as deranged. "Diamonds

271

has long been your dream doll, has she not? I would let you have her if you just step aside. I would not even ask for much, perhaps just a foot for my bandersnatches."

The feathers snow about her as the White Queen drifts closer toward the center of the room. "As much as I have dreamed of the little bird becoming part of my collection, I am afraid today, I must resist. I have entered into an alliance, you see. If you attack Diamonds, you attack *both* Whites. Do you dare to test whether you can withstand us both? We Whites are very good at foxhunts, my sweet kit. I do so love foxes. They are so soft, so wickedly, cleverly soft once I get my hands on them." The whip cracks, knocking one of the ruby shuriken out of the Red Queen's hands. "And Diamonds, as nasty as a little bird as she may be, is so, so good with her knives. She could cut me a lovely pelt as a thank you."

The Red Queen, grinning, walks backward, her focus on the White Queen the entire time. When she reaches the Red King, she extends her bleeding hand . . . and then *he sucks on it.* Jace pays the grotesque scene no attention as he sits back down. Alice merely watches with amusement. The other monarch, who must be the King of Hearts, is too busy allowing one of his attendants to jerk him off in front of everyone to notice the chaos.

Holy shit, these people *are* mad as the proverbial hatters, aren't they?

"I welcome the chase," the Red Queen sing-songs. "For when you fail, my bandersnatches will dine on your fair flesh for days. And your blood will be such a lovely red. Perhaps I'll keep some in my rooms, to use as blush on special occasions."

I sit back down, but do not put away my gun. Instead, I slide it into the space between my leg and chair. Best to keep it close. These people clearly do not play by any rules I'm used to.

"Promises, promises." The White Queen coils the whip even as the Red Queen bounces her remaining shuriken in a hand. "Name the date, little fox, and we shall have our hunt."

"That hunt must wait," Alice interrupts, "for we have other prey to ferret out first."

The other queens pause only a second before sitting back down as if nothing had happened. The White Queen resumes sewing up her animal. The Red Queen picks up a fan covered with naked bodies—both human and animal—and proceeds to cool herself in a leisurely manner, blood dripping down her hand and onto her dress.

Nearby, the Red King stares longingly at the sight.

"Ah, yes," the Red Queen sighs. "There are some charges you wish to bring about concerning Hearts?"

The King of Hearts lifts his head, stilling his attendant. He is effeminate, beautiful, even, his face lean, his hair fair. From what I can tell, there is little muscular definition beneath his tightly laced black and red tunic and pants, reminding me much more of someone used to pleasure rather than work. Ruby hearts glitter upon each tip of his crown. "Are we talking about my counterpart? I want to go on record right now that I have nothing to do with my wife's shenanigans."

"Shenanigans?" Jace inquires tightly, and when I look over at him, his eyes are more enflamed than colorless. I'd seen him look such a way just once before, when I told him about Alice's boojum infestation. "Because of your *wife*, Nobbytown and its residents are altered." He grips the arms of his throne as he leans forward. "Nobbytown is not, and never has been, part of the Hearts' purview. It belongs to White and Diamonds, and we do not take kindly to anyone tainting our people."

The King of Hearts pushes the attendant to the floor. "Now, you have no proof—"

"Ah-ah-ah!" the White Queen sings. She holds up the animal she'd been sewing, shaking it out. The King of Heart blanches. I want to, too, when I finally get a look at its shark-like teeth. "Such a sweet little rath." She snuggles the hideous turtle-pig-shark closer. "I always yearned for a whole pack of raths of my own, but they don't thrive in White territory—or, alas, Diamonds." Her pert nose wrinkles. "Or Red." She brightens. "Just Hearts! And there are so, so many raths in Nobbytown, all bearing these lovely heart brands your wife does so enjoy putting on her possessions." She pauses, nuzzling the rath. "Tell me, little thoroughbred, where did she brand you? I have always been curious. It is on your wee-willy?"

Both she and the Red Queen chortle, as if they weren't threatening one another minutes before.

"I bet it is," the Red King drawls. "Right on the very end."

"Perhaps we ought to ask the Hatter," Alice offers slyly, and even the White King chuckles.

I am actually shocked that the A.D. hasn't cracked a joke about this yet. Somebody must be stepping on his foot.

Suddenly, the King of Hearts stands up and orders his attendant to unlace his trousers. The Red Queen claps her hands in delight. The White Queen smiles beatifically as she sings an entirely nonsensical song about jam. I glance over at Alice and am relieved when I find *her*, the Alice I know and love, peeking out from beneath the madness.

Once the King of Heart's pants are unlaced, he turns around and allows them to fall to the floor. On both buttocks are bright pink-scarred hearts; inside both are the letter M.

"Oh, that's no fun." The Red King sighs. "No fun at all."

As his attendant laces the trousers back up, Alice says, "I have a witness, lest anyone dare to question the White Queen's proof?" None of the other monarchs say anything. She tries again, "Say the word, and I will have the villain brought forth to swear of an alliance between Hearts and foreigners, in efforts to overthrow White and Diamonds citizens."

The Red King yawns.

"Then you accept the first charge?" When none answer, Alice continues, "The second charge I bring against the Queen of Hearts to the council is the use of a boojum."

Save Jace, the rest of the monarchs and attendants, the King of Hearts included, blanch.

"I second the charge," Jace says. "My Grand Advisor and I assisted the Prince of Adámas in extracting the boojum. The perpetrator confessed to receiving it, alongside instructions, from the Queen of Hearts."

"Treason," the White Queen hisses. The Red Queen joins in, and soon, the audience is hissing the same word over and over, a room full of incensed snakes.

"I did not know," the King of Heart cries above the din. "I am a kept man! She does not tell me anything!"

Jesus.

"The use of a boojum carries a death sentence!" the Red King roars. "No one, not monarch, not Sheep, not Walrus, not Rabbit, may use snarks against the living!"

This is getting us nowhere. I know I'm supposed to pretend to be a kept man, too, at least here in Wonderland, but we don't have time for this bag of insanity. I lift my voice and shout, "Everybody, shut the hell up already!"

And I'll be damned, they do.

The Red Queen swivels her dark-brown eyes toward me. "I must say, Diamonds. Your prince is utterly delicious. No wonder you are bearing the loss of White so gracefully. Too bad White is still moping about, his heart breaking near daily." The tip of a pink tongue touches the corner of her mouth. "Perhaps I will have a taste of your prince once this mess is all sorted out. I imagine he is. . ." She lowers her gaze. "Well."

Alice actually laughs at this before baring her teeth. "I would like to see you try."

"Sharp, sharp knives," coos the White Queen. She props the rath up on her lap, making it dance.

Was Alice like this, like *them*, when she lived here full-time? When she was mad and addicted to both food and drink? There have been times when I've interacted with Jace and I've found him unnerving, and his people, too, like their insanity bubbles just beneath the surface, but he's always come off as decidedly more rational than anything else. But is that because of the influence he and Alice have on one another? Are they the only sane monarchs in Wonderland?

Or are they, when fully submersed in this world, just like the rest of them?

It's enough to make my skin crawl, and as I know that Grymsdyke is with the soldiers half a mile away, it's not because a Spider is traveling across me. "We have reason to believe the Queen of Hearts is hiding in the Venae Cavae Mountains directly behind Cor Castle with a group of dangerous psychopaths who have an agenda that we all need to be worried about. So, can you all just focus right now, so we can figure out what we're going to do about it?"

The King of Hearts wobbles to his feet, even as he grips the arms of his throne, as if a ghost was peeling him away. "You are the Prince of Adámas."

An attendant drops a red grape into the Red King's mouth. He mutters, mouth full, "The Diamonds Prince *was* announced, old chap."

The King of Hearts ogles at me—hard. Long. *Fearfully.* "What is your name?"

Alice's answer is swift. "The prince is of my Court. You are not owed such a privilege."

The king sways, his gaze so intense I almost worry he's stripped me bare—not sexually, but in a much more clinical way. He whispers, "F-finn. Is your name *Finn*?"

Both Alice and Jace straighten in their thrones, grappling toward weapons. Behind me, rustling indicates Brom and Victor, possibly the A.D., too, have moved closer.

The King of Hearts staggers toward the middle of the room. Both White monarchs, plus Alice, launch to their feet. I'm up, too, my gun tight in my fist.

Does the Queen of Hearts think to sic her husband on Alice?

I cock my gun. "Don't come any closer."

"She told me you'd come. She—she said—" His neck bobs as he swallows. A flood of noisy tears track down his cheeks. Every muscle is taut yet quivering. "I thought it a dream, I hadn't seen her in. . ." He swallows. Whispers, *"Help me."*

Suddenly, he whips out a dagger, slashing it across his throat. Shouts and cries fill the room as he slumps to the floor, gurgling. An extremely ugly, large-headed woman wearing a ridiculous headdress flings herself at the king, attempting to stem the gushing blood flow with her skirts.

What. The. *Hell?!*

Victor and Brom rush out from behind us, as do Jack and Mary.

The Red monarchs order the crowd back even as they, too, converge on the twitching body. Alice pushes me behind her—her eyes are wild, scared even. "Is she here?" she shouts about the chaos. "Is the Queen of Hearts here?"

If there's an answer, I can't hear it. Sobs and wailing override anything else. *The King of Hearts is dead. The King of Hearts slit his own throat!*

Victor makes his way to the body, but it's clear he's too late.

Alice brandishes the jeweled dagger. "If you are here, Hearts, come out and face me!" She grips my arm, scanning the room.

The White Queen wanders closer to the King of Hearts. "Oh, the poor, poor thoroughbred. His life was short, yet beautiful. He ran fast but couldn't make it to the finish line. He'll make a fine addition to my collection. I will stitch his neck up in just a way the line will be invisible."

The ugly woman clutches the king's newly stilled body close to her large bosom. "A Heart is a Heart, even in death! His Majesty will be interned with all of the other great Heart monarchs."

The White Queen sneers. "Be grateful you are too hideous to join my collection, Duchess."

"Any guesses on who his successor will be?" the Red King asks, as if it hadn't been only mere minutes since the King of Hearts took his last breath. "Can't think of any standouts that come to mind."

The Red Queen jabs the White Queen with her scepter. "Aren't you dallying with someone in the Hearts Court?"

"We should leave," Jace is saying to Alice. "I do not have a good feeling about any of this."

The Cheshire-Cat growls. "Nor should you." He rears back, hopping. "It cannot be."

A hush envelops the room seconds before a weight settles upon my head. Those from the Hearts contingency, formerly weeping uncontrollably, dry their faces and smile.

"I'll be a Jabberwocky's arsehole," the Red King murmurs.

I reach up and feel more than the Adámas crown. There is thick, embellished metal, and, as I drag my fingers up a spire, jeweled hearts.

I turn to Alice, stunned. Her cheeks have lost color; her attention is riveted on the top of my head. Nearby, Jace shares a similar expression, as does everyone else I know.

Because I'm Wonderland's newest crowned King of Hearts—and the newest counterpart of the woman I love's greatest enemy.

PROPHECY, REVISITED

FINN

N O.
There is no way in hell that I am the King of fucking Hearts.
No. Way. In. Hell.

I rip the damn crown off my head and toss it on the floor, uncaring that it's undoubtedly a priceless Wonderlandian antique and what I've done is probably some kind of treason.

Alice watches the crown bounce on the parquet, from a black square to a white one, as if it's an asp, ready to strike at any moment. Bouncing transitions to rolling before it clatters home a few feet away from the newly deceased king.

"This has got to be some kind of sick joke," I tell her. "A mistake."

She doesn't say anything. Doesn't even look at me, just keeps staring at the damn piece of gold.

"Wonderland does not make mistakes." The Red Queen is practically foaming at the mouth, she is so gleeful. "If the crown chose you, then you are its owner and co-ruler of its Court."

Jace focuses on Alice, rather than me when he talks. "Wonderlandian laws of monarchy are indisputable. The only way to abdicate is," his attention slides over to the man in the Duchess' arms, "death, be it natural or unnatural."

The White King's body is taut as any bowstring, ready to fire as he tells me this.

"Whether the crown sits on your head, on the floor, in a musty, dusty, closet, or in the Pool of Tears, little lion," the White Queen says, "you are the King of Hearts."

I scoff. "I'm not even a Wonderlander."

"Neither," says the Red King, "is our darling Queen of Diamonds. And yet a crown chose her, and she is Queen until she dies—even if she is forever exiled."

Exiled.

Shit.

Alice is still, too still, her face so pale, the line of her mouth so grim. She was banished from Wonderland because of a prophecy, one that insisted the Courts were unbalanced, and that if the decks were to shuffle, a great calamity would devastate the land. She didn't have a counterpart, and she was involved with someone from a different Court. It's why she left, why she couldn't be with the White King, even though they deeply loved one another and had been together nearly a decade. She willingly left, because she believed it the right thing to do. She left, and it nearly broke her, but she did it anyway and would do it again without a second thought.

And now . . . she—they—believe I am the King of Hearts. The Courts are still unbalanced with her here. And if she and I stay together. . .

No. No way. *This is not my story.*

I grab her hands in mine. Ask Jace, ask anyone who will listen, "Clear the room."

I don't bother to wait and see what happens. Instead, I cut the space between Alice and me. Will her to forget the crown and instead see my face, my heart. I say, "We will find a way to fix this."

She seals herself into darkness, away from reality. Her breaths are unsteady, and each one splinters another crack across my heart. "There is no way. The prophecy dictating my exile provides no loopholes." Much more quietly. "We—the White King and I searched for months. There was no stone we left unturned. He has since continued to search to no avail."

Huh. I didn't know that.

Nevertheless, I want to tell her that I choose *her*, that I will always choose her, that I know in my heart this is a mistake, that I am no king, especially the King of Hearts, but I also know Alice, as she should, will choose Wonderland.

My destiny is and always will be with the Collectors' Society.

Has she made up her mind to give up so easily? Just . . . just like that, with a crown settling on my head? "This is a mistake. I know it is. I can feel it in my bones." I wish I could elaborate better than that, but how can a deep-settled, inherent knowledge be described anyway else? "This is not who I am supposed to be. I am not the King of Hearts. I am Brom's heir. I've always known that I've been groomed to take over the Society when he retires. So, here, in Wonderland, I am only one thing, and that's the Prince of Adámas. And *that* only comes from your love and nothing else."

Before me, Alice's strength, her glorious, wonderful, admirable strength, crumbles into fine powder. "Wonderland is never wrong."

It's a sucker punch to the gut, and then one to the chin, close to a K.O. if there ever was one.

It's then that I remember the defensive woman who joined the Society nearly a year before, the one who kept me and everyone else at arm's length. The one who had lost her whole world, her assumed destiny, her identity as a queen. She lost Jace, thanks to this fucking prophecy. There's no question she now believes that, within the last quarter hour, she's lost me, too. She's gone through this before, and she is instinctively reverting to protection mode.

I can't blame her, even if what she's doing is unnecessary.

I hold on tighter. I won't let go. "It is this time. I'm not supposed to be the King of Hearts, Alice."

The twist of her mouth is so damn bittersweet. *She doesn't believe me.*

Well, I'm just going to have to prove it, then.

I erase the space between us. Her eyes shine brighter than the Mississippi on a sunny day before she tucks her head against my shoulder. I kiss her forehead. Breathe her in. "Don't give up on us so easily, because I sure as hell am not."

My shirt twists in her fingers as she fights to hold back her denial—or her admission of acceptance.

"We have true love on our side, remember?" My words are for her, and her alone. "Besides, binary stars cannot function without the other. We've faced a lot of obstacles so far, and we've bested all of them. We're still standing, and we're standing together. That isn't going to change."

I feel her swallow against my chest. "This is different. There is no villain to slay, no person to blame or hold accountable. This is a prophecy. *My* prophecy."

"A prophecy," I remind her, "that was written long before you even knew I existed. Long before Alice Liddell's and Huckleberry Finn's stories ever crossed paths. That prophecy has nothing to do with *me*. You have to trust me. I know it seems hard right now, but I'm asking you, Alice. Give me some time to work through this. Show you that I am right."

Her grip on me tightens, digging into my skin. Rather than hurt, I take comfort in just how close she turns into my body, how hard her entire frame shakes. "I want you to be." Her warm, breathy hope seeps through my ridiculous tunic. "So very much."

There is no way I will lose this woman, not without a fight. Not without her explicitly telling me that she is done with me and our relationship.

As much as I want to take her back to our tent and show her how much I love and believe in her, our time is limited. Each minute that ticks by will only compound her belief in this preposterous mistake. I know I am not a king. But how to prove it?

I'm both irritated and a bit relieved to find the other Wonderlandian monarchs still present in the hall, although it appears Jace herded them, alongside the Society agents and Grand Advisors, to the opposite side.

"We've got a Piper to catch," I gently tell Alice, "and the Queen of Hearts, and we also need to figure out what the hell just happened. And I cannot do it without your help, partner."

It takes a few seconds, but she lifts her head. Offers her agreement, even if it comes off as less resolute than what I've become accustomed to.

But still. She's by my side.

The remaining crowd is clustered around the King of Hearts' body. Victor laid his jacket over his face so the gore isn't quite as visible anymore, but a puddle of darkened blood stains the checkered floor.

Alice and I join them. I'm tempted to kick the Hearts crown straight out of the door. "Why would the King of Hearts commit suicide?"

"He wasn't a very clever man." The Red King twirls both sides of his mustache. I'm pretty sure that it's waxed so heavily that, if a wick was inserted, it could serve as a candle. "Or strong." When Jace snorts derisively, the Red King stomps his foot like a petulant child. "Do you have something to say, White?"

Jace's obvious amusement is probably chapping the Red King's ass . . . well, *red*. "As you have yet to fight a single battle, let alone eat a meal by yourself, you are certainly not one to talk."

I snap my fingers. "Focus on the matter at hand. Had the King of Hearts ever shown a predilection toward suicide before?"

For the first time in our acquaintance, I earn a not-so-friendly glare from the White King. "Not to my knowledge. The *former* King of Hearts was renowned for his love of life and all that it offered."

"What is wrong with that?" The Red Queen begins waltzing with an unseen partner, to unheard music. Her steps are formal, her arms outstretched. "He held much love for sex, for food and pleasure, for horse racing and gambling. He would copulate with anything that moved." She swoops past Alice and me, gloved fingers meant for a partners' shoulder trailing instead across ours. "Save his wife."

"Oh, Hearts." The White Queen tut-tuts, petting the partially sewn rath. "So pathetically desperate for feelings he could never give her." The White Queen cocks her head as she glances down at the man's shell. "He married her, but that was as much as he was willing to give. A queen should never beg for love. It is very unseemly. She takes."

The Red Queen circles the White Queen, her shoes tapping out a soft pattern upon the floor. "Did you not beg once, White? Did you not plead with your counterpart to marry you?"

The White Queen lifts the rath's mouth open and hisses for it.

Brom's shadow looms over mine. "His entire demeanor changed once he noticed you, Finn."

I scratch the back of my neck, thankful that someone is staying on topic. "I was announced at the beginning, though."

"He wasn't paying attention to you then. It wasn't until *you* specifically started talking about the Queen of Hearts that he noticed you." My father frowns as he strokes his dark beard. "When he stood up, it seemed very much as if it weren't upon his own volition. And when he took the blade to his throat, his hand shook. There was fear in his eyes. He didn't want to die."

"Who is this?" The Red Queen's dance stops. "How dare this commoner speak in our presence! Why is this hairy nobody here?"

Mary, who had been quietly talking with Victor, Marianne, and the A.D., suddenly pushes forward. "She did not just say that."

The Red Queen snatches up her scepter and jabs it at Mary. There is a ring of needles sticking out around the red-jeweled center.

Alice steps in her line of sight. "These people are here at my bequest."

"*You* should not be here, though." The Red Queen peers down the length of her Romanesque nose at Alice. "Perhaps *you* are the reason the former Hearts is dead. The prophecy is ringing true! Your presence in Wonderland brings with it death and destruction!"

My strong, beautiful Alice, who battles giants and fiends without a second thought, grows smaller right before my eyes. Did she find a DRINK ME bottle without me noticing?

Jace whirls the vorpal blade toward the Red Queen. "Say another word, and your crown, too, will search for a new owner before night falls."

This isn't right. Alice doesn't need him to fight her battles. Hell, she doesn't need me to fight them, either. Alice can eviscerate someone with fewer words than anyone else I know. Even in those early days at the Institute, when she was still finding her footing, she was razor sharp.

Now, though . . . now, Alice whispers, "She is right. I. . ." Her blue eyes, unnaturally glassy, shift uneasily through the small crowd in the hall. "It was hubris, I suppose, believing that the strengths of my convictions would persevere over the prophecy. I thought that because I came to hunt the Piper, Wonderland would overlook my presence, as it did when I came to claim its catalyst." She presses her hand against her mouth as she turns back to me.

It's as if she drank another damn bottle of DRINK ME.

"Don't even go there," I warn.

The Librarian inserts herself between the White King and Alice. "We do not have time for this."

Alice rears back, as if she'd been smartly slapped. Jace growls, the vorpal blade switching targets.

"We all have histories that are not the easiest." Even though I don't think she reaches five feet, somehow the Librarian towers over the small crowd. "Abraham lost his wife, his entire Timeline. Finn and Victor, their mother and family. Finn's childhood was traumatic; Victor's health the same. Shall we go over what they faced at the hands of the Piper and the Chosen?" The Wonderlanders actually dare to try to argue, so she presses on. "Mary's parents died when she was young, and everyone forgot about her, leaving her to die, too. Jack grew up a thief, poor, badly used by a scoundrel,"—the A.D. yelps in protest—"jailed, and sent to Australia as punishment. Marianne's husband died; her father died and her brother cut her off, and a swine broke her heart. Shall I go on, Alice? Is your pain the only one we must focus on?"

The Librarian's touch is heavy, but when Alice's fists curl tightly at her sides, I know my girl found some EAT ME cakes and grew back to her right size.

"This, as we all know, is no game. Crowns, thrones, and all the rest are meaningless as long as Timelines are at risk. The Chosen are wreaking havoc upon Wonderland. We know they are connected to the Queen of Hearts. Turn your focus onto these villains and do what you do best, Alice. Find them and kick their asses."

"Holy shite!" the A.D. crows quietly. "I've never heard her cuss like that."

Marianne swats him, as does Mary. His yelp is satisfying.

The Librarian picks up the Hearts crown. "Oh, and Alice?"

Alice says nothing, but her focus is riveted upon the wily woman.

The Librarian sniffs—sniffs!—the gold and jewels. "I know you revel in your stubbornness, but listen to him, will you?"

"Who are these Chosen who dare to wreak havoc in Wonderland?" the Red King roars. Tapestries and banners flutter as he sends a goblet full of wine soaring through the air. "Why have I not heard of this before?"

The White Queen sidles closer to him, rubbing the rath against his arm. Her gleaming whip is in full view, and if I didn't know better, I would insist that it was alive and begging to be used. "Ah-ah, little bandersnatch, asking such a thing, when for all we know, you are still in league with Hearts."

"Me?" he sputters, spittle frothing in his ginger beard. "With that she-devil?"

The White Queen drags the whip's coils across the Red King's cheek as she circles him. "Did you think her a she-devil when you copulated with her?"

His cheeks violently blend in with his hair.

"When you copulated with her," the White Queen sing-songs, nudging the rath's sharp nuzzle of teeth at the front of his trousers, "for years and years and called her your great love each time your seed spilled out?"

Jace surges forward, snatching the Red King's collar. So fast that they're almost a blur, he has his opponent slammed up against a tapestry, feet dangling off the ground. "How long?"

The Red King spits in Jace's face, which earns him a solid fist just below the left eye. Jace shouts his question, the vorpal blade pointed at the other man's throat.

"What the hell is happening right now?" Mary asks for the majority of the non-natives.

Next to me, Alice pales even impossibly more.

"I am terribly shocked." The Red Queen may say this, but she makes no motion to come to her counterpart's aid. In fact, she yawns—leisurely and lengthily. "I had no idea Red had such terrible taste in bed partners."

Still dangling in Jace's grip, the Red King sneers, his chuckling more wheezing than jeering. This time, the White King slams the butt of the vorpal blade against his other cheek, and it knocks the Red King's head against the wall so hard that, afterward, it lolls like a doll's. Jace releases his hold, and the Red King drops to the ground. His skull bounces twice on the parquet, meaning it'll be some time before he wakes.

Victor darts forward, instinct and the Hippocratic Oath no doubt kicking in, but the White King swings the vorpal blade toward my brother. "Assist him at your own detriment, Doctor."

Ally or no, nobody threatens my brother. Gun out and ready, I tell the White King, "You better back the fuck down."

He doesn't acknowledge me, not even when I cock my gun. The vorpal blade doesn't waver one bit as it closes in on my brother's chest.

Victor holds both hands up. "He could have a concussion."

The tip of blade hits the patch of cloth over Victor's heart. "Then he will be lucky that is the worst of it so far."

Fuck him. I shove the barrel of my gun against the White King's forehead. "Put. The. Sword. Down."

"Don't hesitate, Finn," Mary hisses. "Don't you dare hesitate."

The White Queen snuggles the rath so tightly feathers snow in her wake. She presses up against the other side of the White King. "Oh, my poor little monster, learning now, after all that has happened, that the prophecy concerning shuffled decks could have referred to Red and Hearts, not White and Diamonds!"

"Let us allow cooler heads to prevail." Brom's hands are up, too, as he approaches his eldest son. "Tensions are high right now, but if we all put our weapons down and talk—"

"Our monster doesn't wish for talk, does he, Diamonds?" The White Queen rubs her cheek against Jace's sleeve. "Not when he's like this. He covets blood, not words."

"Put your sword away." I shove the gun harder against the White King's temple. "Victor isn't your enemy. Neither am I—but if you dare to hurt him, I will be."

"Listen to him."

At Alice's quiet demand, Jace swiftly sheaths the vorpal sword. I holster my gun as he staggers several steps back. Without seeking anyone's permission, Victor squats next to the Red King. "Mary, get my bag."

"The Courts were uneven," Alice says. "Do not forget that part of the prophecy."

It's then that I realize that she, too, must have realized that the relationship between the Red King and the Queen of Hearts was more than too many drinks or a one-night stand.

Eight years, I think. Alice and Jace were together for eight years. They planned to spend their lives together, but were forced apart by a prophecy.

And today they learned it might not have referred to them at all, or at least the White King thought it a possibility.

Acid roils in the pit of my stomach. Alice remains quiet, pale, and my world continues to shift off axis.

"You're a right bitch, aren't you?" After handing Victor his bag, Mary is only a foot or so away from the White Queen. She continues hotly, "Was that really the time to reveal that juicy bit of gossip?"

The White Queen regards my friend as if she were a common housefly in need of swatting.

"Didn't you hear a word the Librarian said?" Mary jabs a finger against the White Queen's breastbone, eliciting a nasty hiss. "We don't have time for this petty shit. The Chosen are here! You really are crazy, aren't you?"

The White Queen throws back her arm, her whip uncoiling. Alice darts forward, snatching the vorpal blade right out of Jace's belt, and inserts herself between Mary and the monarch.

"This woman is under my protection, and if a single drop of blood is spilled, I will extract retribution."

She sounds like *Alice*—the Alice I know.

"Do you dare to break our alliance?" the White Queen seethes.

"Over this woman?" Alice queries. "Or any of the people that journeyed here with me? Absolutely. I would die for each and every single one of them without question or thought."

The A.D. clasps his hands over his heart. "I knew she loved me."

"Nobody is breaking any alliances." Thunder rolls throughout the hall as the Librarian comes to stand next to Alice. "Not when we need as much intelligence and cooperation as possible in order to best the Chosen and the Queen of Hearts in her secret lair."

"This again." The Red Queen studies her long, sharp nails. "Why do foreigners care so much about Hearts?"

"Maybe if everyone would shut the hell up and listen instead of going off tangent so much," I snap, patience thin as my remaining hair, "we could tell you."

The Red Queen's smile is vicious. "What a delicious King of Hearts you will make."

"The Prince of Adámas is correct." Alice backs away from the White Queen. "For once, let us put our bickering to the side and come together for Wonderland's sake."

Prince, not king. A small step.

"Are you proposing an alliance?" The Red Queen lifts a glittery eyebrow up. "Is that not moot, considering you are still in exile?"

A much calmer Jace says, "I propose an alliance between the four Courts of Wonderland, along with a ceasefire, so we may hunt down the Queen of Hearts and eradicate the Chosen."

Four Courts.

He expects me, as the King of Hearts, to agree to this.

"Three of us already allied." The White Queen plucks a rose from her hair and offers it to me. "With the King of Hearts, we are four.

What say you, Red?"

Alice snatches the rose and tears out all of the petals.

The Red Queen runs a fingernail, long and blood red, along her chin line. "I cannot speak for my counterpart, considering he is a sack of potatoes."

"No one is asking you to," Jace snaps.

The Red Queen taps on her chin. "Why should I care about Hearts' deeds—or these Chosen?"

"Because these Chosen are turning Wonderlanders into creatures very unlike themselves," Alice says quietly, "who serve a non-Wonderlander."

The Red Queen snorts. "Impossible. Wonderlanders are Wonderlanders. The only non-Wonderlanders to breech our borders have been the Queen of Diamonds and those in her party." She blows me a kiss. "Including our new King of Hearts."

"With magic," the White Queen coos, "nothing is impossible, Red."

This does not move the Red Queen, though—or at least, not entirely. "Say this is true. What do the Chosen have to do with Hearts?"

Alice says flatly, "The Chosen wear Hearts' insignia. It is as I said before. I have a witness who will testify to this."

"Agree to the alliance, and to peace, even temporarily," Jace says, "and we will share all that we know."

"I control only my half of the Red army, lest you forget. His half," she motions to the still unconscious Red King, "will be free to wage war as he sees fit."

"Take his half," the White Queen says. "And when he wakes, tell him he will do as you say, for the good of our fair land. Besides." Her mouth curves so wide, I wonder if she is somehow related to the Cheshire-Cat. "Who better to tell us secrets than Hearts' lover?"

The Red Queen sashays over to where the Hearts crown lies. "I will join your little alliance, agree to peace, and offer my support and armies upon a few conditions."

Jace crosses his arms. "Name them."

She picks up the crown and dusts it off. "The newly chosen King of Hearts agrees to wear his crown, use his title, and rule his armies and lands."

The bitch smiles all too sweetly as she offers me the gold and ruby-clad monstrosity.

I'm just about to tell her where she can go fuck herself when the Librarian takes the offending piece of royal jewelry. She yanks the Adámas circlet off my head and plops on the Hearts crown. "Agreed."

FOUR COURTS UNITED

ALICE

I T IS A MIRACLE that my friends and colleagues from the Institute have not yet run back to the rabbit hole in Nobbytown in order to flee Wonderland. Truthfully, now that I am no longer under the influence of Wonderlandian drugs, I am sorely tempted to do so myself.

Word is sent for all armies, save the Queen of Hearts, to uproot to the Keep. Whilst a formal temporary peace decree is signed by all of the ruling monarchs present, myself and Finn included, official news was not spread to the lands. Hearts is to be kept in the dark at the true extent of our collusion.

She will soon enough know the depth and scope of it.

The Red King is placed under formal Distrust by the rest of the Courts, including his own counterpart, and assigned guards from each to monitor his moves, lest he report back to Hearts. He argues vociferously against the need, but with five votes outweighing his one, he has no leg to stand upon. His only hope is to now prove himself loyal to Wonderland, not Hearts, something he insists he will do with aplomb.

He throws his arms wide open, his head back, a bruised and battered martyr without his cross. "You will all rue the day you doubted where the strength of my loyalties lie!"

The Red Queen grabs hold of his cock. "Here, Red. They have always been here."

He can tell us little about Hearts save her favorite wines and sexual positions.

It takes hours to fully debrief the Wonderlandian monarchs and their Grand Advisors. The bickering and fighting sidetracks Van Brunt and the Librarian so many times that even Marianne takes to shouting. The Chosen piper is brought in, administered truth serum, and forced to tell all what has long been suspected.

The Queen of Hearts is in league with the Chosen. Worse, the youth saw the Piper and Hearts together in Wonderland on more than one occasion. Worse yet was the revelation that a woman matching the thirteenth Wise Woman's appearance was seen in the presence of Hearts and the Piper, too.

She lives.

Both Finn and Victor remain stony with the news.

It isn't until dawn and the Flowers begin their wakeup songs do the Society agents finish conveying all that we know about the Piper and Chosen, via reports, computers (which the White Queen likens to sorcery), and recordings.

The Carpenter, the Red King's Grand Advisor, shucks a fresh batch of oysters. "I find it terribly difficult to believe that Her Majesty would be in collusion with this Piper and his witch."

The Librarian snaps the pencil she'd been toying with in half. "Have you not listened to a word we've said? Or to the prisoner?"

The Carpenter tosses a shell on his plate. "Prisoners can say lots of things when tortured."

The Cheshire-Cat knocks a glass on the table over with his stubby tail. "I barely tortured him. His scratches are minimal, at best."

"We used truth serum," Mary says. "It wasn't torture."

The Carpenter slurps several oysters. "Seems unstable."

"It's science!" Mary sputters.

The Carpenter taps on his nose. "Sorcery, you mean."

Although I know him to be exhausted, Finn leans forward, his elbows against the table, the infernal Hearts crown glittering upon his brow. "Look, both Whites have given you sworn testimony that the pipers in Nobbytown wear the Queen of Hearts regalia. We at the Society have witnessed the Queen of Hearts in the presence of known Chosen figures. You just listened to the questioning of one of the Chosen guaranteeing she's been working with them. So yeah, we're pretty damn certain that she's in league with the Chosen."

The Duchess pours a dash of milk and plops several large sugar cubes into a cup of tea before sliding it Finn's way. "Drink this, Your Majesty. It will help soothe your nerves."

The offensive beverage is ignored. "I get that Wonderland has been self-sufficient and unaware of all of the other worlds and Timelines. Hell, you guys weren't even really aware of even England until the Queen of Diamonds arrived. But you have to pull your heads out of your asses and realize that trillions of innocent people are dying. Whole worlds are disappearing. There is a sick bastard out there who thinks it's his right to choose which worlds flourish and which ones no longer get to go on, and that's not right. If our hunches pan out, and he's hiding with the Queen of Hearts in her secret mountain lair, then we have a chance to put a stop to all of this. We have a chance to bring justice to all of those who are crying out for it. And maybe you all want to just bitch at each other and fight about stupid, pointless things, but here's your chance to do something important. Help us attack Venae Cavae. Help us take down the Queen of Hearts and the Piper. Help us eradicate what's left of the Chosen."

Several of the Grand Advisors politely clap. One deigns to yawn. The Duchess weeps, she is so very proud.

Mustache drooping, the Red King holds up a finger. Finn provides him no room for nonsense. "If you dare ask what's in it for you, so help me, I will lose what little patience I have going for me right now."

The Red King slumps back into his chair, ego as bruised as his face. As long as we have his army, I care not about his tantrums.

"What will happen to Hearts?" The Red Queen picks at her nails with the Carpenter's oyster knife. "How shall she pay for daring to corrupt White and Diamonds citizens?"

"Hearts is guilty of more than crimes against our citizens." The assembled crowd startles at the White King's harsh reminder. For most of the meeting, his silent, festering attention never strayed from the Red King. He would not listen to me when I tried discussing the prophecy with him. "She dared abduct and torture two Grand Advisors. Whilst the Cheshire-Cat was mutilated, the Caterpillar was executed on trumped-up Hearts' charges she had no governance over."

The Red Queen's advisor, the Walrus, harrumphs. The table shifts with his girth as he reaches for both biscuits and oysters; everyone quickly steadies cups, plates, and anything else at risk of toppling over. "Speaking of, word arrived from Cor just yesterday that the White Rabbit was found murdered."

The Sheep reclaims her knitting, her baaing mournful. "Are none of us safe?"

"Nonsense." A song hums as I run a wet finger along the rim of my crystal goblet. "The White Rabbit was not murdered. He committed suicide rather than reveal his secrets to myself and the White King."

Several gasps fill the Keep's hall. The White Queen crawls upon the table to snatch a plate of biscuits, her dress sweeping aside glasses of wine and tea. "Naughty, naughty little bird and monster, keeping secrets from the rest of us."

I snatch my goblet away a mere second before she capsizes it. "He was restrained—"

"Naturally," the Carpenter murmurs, "as ain't nobody can trust the Rabbit."

I continue, as the White Queen settles back into her chair, "—and he was particularly nasty. So I brought out my dagger, and when I asked a question he did not wish to answer under the influence of a truth serum, he chose to impale himself upon said blade."

The Duchess wrings her hands as she turns to Finn. "Oh, Your Majesty. Let me assure you that I am no coward like the Rabbit." Her overly large saucer eyes nearly encompass her face. "Although, if it meant I was to ensure your silence and trust, I would gladly do what must be done."

Several seats away, Mary cackles. "Oh, promise me we can bring her back with us. Please, Finn."

All simpering transitions to fury as the Duchess snarls, "Do not dare to refer to His Majesty so informally!"

Finn pinches the bridge of his nose. I lean closer, my hand upon his knee. *"Breathe."*

"The question now is," the Cheshire-Cat says, batting several empty oyster shells at the Red King, "does the Queen of Hearts know of her Grand Advisor's death?"

The petty child in me wishes I had removed the Rabbit's tail and kept it for a key fob, just to spite her as she did me with the Caterpillar.

"It doesn't matter." The Librarian ducks a mere second before a shell whizzes past. When it strikes the Red King squarely in his bruised eye, he cries out. She ignores his whining. "The only concern any of us ought to have right now is when we launch our attack. Sooner is more favorable than later, as any of the Chosen are free to edit themselves out of Wonderland any time they wish. And if they do, we lose our lead and must start at the beginning once more."

"How long would it take to organize an attack?" Brom asks.

"It is now dawn." The White King accepts a fresh cup of tea from the Walrus. "At your estimates, there are several hundred to possibly one thousand Chosen. Between our four armies, we have more than enough to counter that, meaning we can be selective in who we bring." His gaze traces each and every monarch at the table. "Most of us have sufficient numbers camped here as it is. As we are centrally located, it would take our foot troops at least twelve hours to march to Cor Castle." His attention slides toward Finn. "Will you allow the rest of Wonderland upon your lands and in your Court?"

Although we are barely touching, I can feel the entirety of Finn's muscles tighten at the query. While the Librarian accepted his role as King of Hearts on his behalf, he has done and said nothing to agree other than sign the peace treaty—and even then, he signed with his legal name rather than either Wonderlandian title.

He insists he is not king. For my sanity, for my heart, I must place my trust in his faith.

After several long seconds punctuated by the Red King's snarling at the Cheshire-Cat, Finn grounds out, "I want that bastard caught, and that bitch to pay for everything she's ever done."

The Duchess claps her hands. "I am certain that, with certain considerations, we can ensure the safety of Cor and its—"

"As long as the Piper and Hearts are caught," Finn growls, "I don't give a shit about Cor or anything else."

The Duchess withers in his displeasure. "Yes, well. Yes. Of course. Excellent point, Your Majesty. We must think of the safety of Wonderlanders. We cannot allow these foreigners to come in and hypnotize us, after all."

"The Duchess makes a good point, though." Behind her glasses, the Sheep appears pained to say this. "We must do our best to ensure citizens—Hearts, White, Diamonds, and Red—do not become collateral damage during this battle."

"The quicker we get in and take these bastards out," Jack says, "the better it is for everyone."

Marianne rubs her eyes. "I cannot ensure every soldier on the battlefield has earplugs, though. It simply is impossible. And we cannot possibly consider sending anyone out to confront the Chosen without such protections."

Grymsdyke rouses in his web. "My kind will help."

An absurd fondness for the assassin warms the stone within my chest. "That is much appreciated." I quickly describe to the others the makeshift earplugs he assisted me with whilst we were in Koppenberg Mountain.

An exaggerated shudder rolls across Jack's shoulders. "You want me to stick spider webs in my ears? Are you insane?"

"We shall make a deal, you and I." Grymsdyke drops onto the

table, in front of the thief. "When you succumb to the childlings' dissonant music, I will personally see to it you are put out of your misery."

"You are the stuff nightmares are made out of, you are," Jack says mournfully.

"Are the Tweedles present?" the Cheshire-Cat asks the Sheep.

She peers up from her knitting and snorts. "Naturally."

"Excellent." His ears twitch. "We can use as many assassins as possible in this war." His harvest moon eyes flick toward me. "Will a scheduled battle time for tomorrow morning do for you, Your Majesty?"

Rogue rays of gray-tinged sunshine, which fought their way through storm clouds and lingering night skies, slip through the Keep's slats, warming the room. "It will do quite nicely."

"Oi! Alice! Finn! Get yer lazy arses up! The Librarian needs you."

Finn yanks the blanket over our heads. I curl into his warmth.

Fist meets door once more, rattling it nearly off its hinges. "I know you two are in there! Are you shagging? I'm going to come in! I've got my phone with me!"

"I'm going to kill him," Finn mutters.

I tuck my forehead against his chest. Exhaustion beckons so strongly that I am equally nauseated and limp. "I'll get your gun."

Jack makes good on his threat, for the door creaks open. "What are you two—oi! *Are* you shagging?"

Finn throws back the blanket. He rubs his eyes, the top of his head. I itch to do the same, so I might, too, revel in the downy softness. "Sleeping, asshole. As you should be. What's so important that you let us get . . . hell, it feels like all of five minutes of sleep."

I would argue less than that, what with the Duchess trailing us to the room after the meeting and shouting from beyond the door about the improperness of the King of Hearts and the Queen of Diamonds daring to tempt the prophecy.

"Think of Wonderland!" Her fists pounded an unwelcome nap-time lullaby. "Think of what you are doing to its people! You Majesty, do not tempt another king into ruining our fair land!"

The moment the door closed, Finn tossed the crown across the room. I was in his arms, in his bed. His promises warmed my ear, and I may be the most foolish, idiotic woman to ever live, but I held on to them.

I hold on to them still, these precious, fragile pieces of today and tomorrow.

I walked away from Wonderland before. I will walk away from it again. I left Jace, who remains part of my heart to this day. Duty has always come first for me. It is engrained in my soul, the very fiber of my being.

I put it above all else.

Jack closes the door, smart enough to stay clear of both of our aims. "The Librarian said to come and get you both. So 'ere I am."

I reluctantly, blearily sit up whilst discreetly searching for a rub-bish receptacle in case my stomach truly revolts. "She's a menace."

As I watch Finn tug on his jeans and shirt, I allow myself to cul-tivate a raw, ugly doubt.

I do not believe I can walk away from this man.

Finn and I are led outside of the Keep, into the torrential downpour and howling winds. During our short rest, Wonderland unleashed hell upon the land. Could it guess my secret? Our plans for the next day?

Too warm for snow yet too cold for comfort, a diagonal mixture of sleet and rain batters the hundreds of tents and pavilions stretching as far as the eye can see. It takes less than a minute for mud to coat both boots and clothes. We hurry into a small multi-room tent not too far from the Keep. Inside is warm, though, thanks to a small fire bowl. Van Brunt and the Librarian are hunched over one of Marianne's lap-tops, their shoulders nearly touching.

Finn's father barely spares Jack a glance. "Thank you, Mr. Dawkins. Now, go get some rest."

The thief salutes his boss, spraying rain and mud in a wide arc. "Aye-aye, Captain o'mine." A blast of chilled air sweeps into the tent as he slips back into the storm.

"Ten bucks says he's on his way back to the Hatter's tent," Finn says.

I refuse to take the bet, as I would be out of money very quickly.

The Librarian's yawn only reminds me of the warm bed so recently left behind. So does her frown. "You are not wearing your crown, Finn."

He unconsciously tugs the knit hat lower on his brow. It must be drenched. "It's practically a hurricane outside, and you're worried I'm not wearing a stupid piece of gold on my head?"

She twists her hair back into a bun, securing it with a pencil. "Whether or not you approve, the crown symbolizes part of the agreement with the Courts."

"This is asinine. You know that, right?" Finn slaps the laptop shut. "None of you can seriously believe that I am the fucking King of Hearts."

My breath stills in my chest as I await opinions that normally should not matter.

"Wonderland," the Caterpillar said, "never makes mistakes."

I disappointed him when I could not contain my sneer, but the Queen of Hearts and her miserable fury was beyond irritating for such a sunny day. "Nothing is infallible. How else could it choose such a wretched woman for queen?"

He did not bother with any shapes. He simply blew a faceful of smoke directly at me, erasing my visible disdain.

"Dad." Finn blocks his father from reopening the laptop. "How many years now have you been telling me that my destiny is taking over your position in the Society?"

"That," Brom rumbles quietly, "has and never will change."

Satisfied, Finn releases his technological hostage. "Want to explain why we were dragged out of bed, other than to bitch at me about not wearing the fucking crown?"

The tent flaps rustle. The Librarian says, "We have a guest."

Although I am standing perfectly still when the visitor enters, I fear I will stumble over my own feet. For the eyeless woman dressed in sopping, mud-spattered rags and carrying a walking stick and a bag is none other than the Sage.

"The Sage does not come like a dog. She does not leave her cave. Those who desire her wisdom go to her."

I was wrong, for here she is.

"Are you just going to stand there, Your Majesty?" Wonderland's oracle shakes herself out, exactly as a wet animal would. "Or will you help an old woman to a chair? My feet are weary from the journey you requested."

My feet uproot and I do, in fact, stumble over and offer her my arm. "My apologies. I—"

She slaps a rock into my other hand. The tinge of iron and blood fills my mouth when I bite my tongue.

I lead her to a chair close to the fire bowl. She shoves the walking stick at me, knocking me into another chair. "I am not a Dog, Your Majesty."

The sharp edges of the rock dig into my palm. The urge to pluck my hair is utterly seductive.

The Sage's craggy face swivels; her nose wrinkles. She hisses—more cat than any dog. Hissing transitions to growling. The stick flings wildly about. "Show yourself!"

Finn approaches. "I'm—"

She whips the stick toward him, missing his knee by a mere inch. "Not you!"

Irritated, yet undeterred, Finn continues, "My father and—"

This time, the stick makes contact. Finn jumps as the mud-splattered tip cracks across upon his kneecap. "Not you!"

I grab hold of him before he strikes her. He perches on the arm of my chair, rubbing his sore knee.

The Sage inhales, her shoulders hunched, both hands on the cane. "Show yourself."

The Librarian rounds the table and positions herself next to Finn and myself. "I am here."

The Sage angles her stick across the fire bowl in our direction. The sound she emits is utterly inhuman, a keening cross between wail and growl that sets both teeth and nerves on edge.

I left my daggers in the Keep, Finn the same with his pistol.

"Be at peace," the Librarian says. "No harm will come to you here."

Icy tendrils of unknown fear curl their way into my chest.

A bestial slit slashes across the Sage's face. "It is because of you that the Queen of Diamonds bade me to leave my sanctuary. You dared use one of my own!"

"Take the rock back," the Librarian says, her voice and face the eye of a hurricane, "and let us discuss what is necessary."

A cackle tears from the Sage, one so chillingly nightmarish that it is difficult to remember I once considered the woman benign. "You think to tell me what to do with *my* people? *You* are the trespasser. *How dare you summon me.*"

Unnatural darkness swarms the tent as fresh squalls rattle the walls. "I am one of the trespassers, yes, and a dangerous one, too." Shadows flicker from the fire bowl, throwing images upon the canvas. I fear I am losing my mind or at least dreaming when the outlines of three tall figures loom over the Librarian. "But I am not the one you must be concerned with, *wicce*. Not unless you wish I must be."

"I do not know this word: *wicce*."

Although logs crackle and spit within the fire bowl, chills leaps from the flames.

"I think you do."

The Sage licks her cracked lips. "You cannot—"

"I can," the Librarian says, "and I will if you do not take back the damn rock."

The trio of mysterious shadows shift away from the Librarian and crawl toward the Sage. The old woman fumbles for her drawstring bag, but it falls just out of reach. Cold darkness veins across her face, forming tendrils of curling moss, or mold. Her bravado cowers beneath the covers as she cries out in terror. She grapples for her walking stick, only to deal a stinging rap against the back of my knuckles. The rock skitters to the floor, rolling beneath the fire bowl.

Warmth eases back into the tent. The Librarian drags a chair closer to the Sage, a smile as bright as the fire on her face. "Excellent choice."

Finn massages my hand as I ask, "How did you know the rock ties its holder's tongue?"

"This one reeks of her affinity for the geological." When the Librarian gazes across at the Sage, her gaze is as intense as if she is reading a book the rest of us cannot see. "She lives amongst rocks, seeks guidance amongst stones and boulders, and imbues pebbles with her magic." She presses both pointer fingers to her lips, a sharp steeple tipped with nails. "What else but magic could silence the infamously stubborn Alice Liddell?"

Her point, accurate as it may be, is entirely unwelcome.

The Sage clamors to her feet, rooting around for her bag. "I would be amongst my rocks now, if it weren't for you, vile sorceress."

The Librarian claps her hands, and then I know I am daydreaming, for three disembodied hands appear bearing cups of tea—one for her, one for Van Brunt, and one even for the Sage. "It takes one," the woman I called colleague lifts her cup to her lips, "to know one, my dear. And I prefer *witch*." One corner of her red-stained mouth ticks up. *"Wicce."*

Finn murmurs for the both of us, "Holy shit."

"But that is neither here nor there. There is a much nastier witch who we must concern ourselves with. Sit a spell."

The Sage does so with alacrity.

A pair of the disembodied hands materializes before Finn and me, offering us tea. The Librarian merely nods encouragingly, as if we were small children urged to try a bite of a new food.

Van Brunt stands behind his colleague, sipping his drink as if nothing were amiss.

The Sage lowers her walking stick so she can use both hands to hold tea and saucer. "Fine. You have my attention. But you must first reveal your name, *wicce*. It is only fair, as you know mine."

Nearly a year of puzzling the Librarian out ought to have left me unruffled in such a situation. Yet, now that the moment of truth is upon me, I cannot help but grip Finn's thigh.

If she tells the Sage her name is the Librarian, I may very well rain bloodshed upon this tent.

"Fair enough." The Librarian holds her cup out; one of the mysterious appendages appears to take it and set it on the table. "I go by many names, but the one I think you wish to know is my oldest. I am Baba Yaga."

Baba Yaga. A Russian name for an Indian woman?

The Sage digs several polished stones out of a pocket and rolls them, in succession, across her knuckles. "Crone, snake, goddess, wicked, horror, grandmother." She nods thoughtfully, eyeless face angled as if she can see all of these things in the Librarian's—no, Baba Yaga's face.

Finn clears his throat, once, twice. Says, whispers, *asks*, "You're . . . Baba Yaga?"

The smile the Librarian gifts him is indulgent, affectionate even. "You have never had anything to fear from me, Finn. Your bones are safe from my teeth."

I could swear Grymsdyke was dancing upon my spine once more.

"I wish," she says with a hint of sorrow, "you would not look at me that way, though."

Finn yanks off the hat, wringing it out, at the same time he yanks away his gaze. "You knew?"

Van Brunt requires no clarification from his son. He runs a hand across the Librarian's shoulder before he, too, sits down. "I have known since the day I became director." A trace of amusement influences the corners of his lips. "You are the first of our line who will know before he or she takes office."

Finn lays the small hat near the fire. The muscle between thumb and forefinger twitches.

Unnerved by how shaken he is, I wade into depths I had long wished to dive in. "I apologize, as my knowledge of witches is sorely lacking, but would someone care to illuminate which story Baba Yaga is from?"

"My little, nosy queen." The Librarian's exasperation is more affectionate than anything else, though. "Always asking questions. Always pushing for answers. Because of my fondness for you, I will tell you a secret. I am not from a singular story or Timeline. People have whispered stories about me for. . ." She taps on her lips. "Well, more years than a polite lady ought to admit in public."

The Sage cackles once more. "How is it that Baba Yaga and the Queen of Diamonds are so closely intertwined, and that the Queen bears the *wicce's* protection, yet Her Majesty knows so little of her benefactor?"

Her *protection?*

"My secrets," the Librarian says, smooth as butter scraped across toast, "are my own."

"As is your true face." The Sage hums appreciatively. "Alas, I do not have the power of transformation, not even amongst my rocks. It is a shame, for I, too, could have been a great beauty."

Beauty is not a word often associated with the Sage, physically or personally, although many may find her proclamations equally soothing and distressing. I do not even know if I can term her purely human, with her small, wrinkled face defined solely by nose and mouth and her hair a twisting turret of steel and moss. Her back curves with a pronounced hunch, her limbs are gangly and disproportionate to her torso. When she speaks, it is with leashed winds.

But the Librarian. . .

The Sage motions for one of the Librarian's disembodied hands to hold her tea. Another hands her the ratty drawstring tote she'd tried for so many times. After nearly a full minute's worth of rummaging, she extracts several small stones that she plops into her drink. Several sips later, she smacks her lips blissfully. "Would you like one?"

The Librarian holds out a hand, and the woman who has no eyes grunts. "Suit yourself." She relishes another long, noisy sip. "Incidentally, who is the enchanted foreigner marked by two Wonderlandian queens?"

When Finn makes to toss his untouched drink upon the ground, one of the mysterious appendages deftly grabs hold of it.

The Librarian clears her throat. "He is also under my protection."

"Not yours. Although, you've done a shoddy job of it, eh? Letting that despicable sorceress get ahold of him when his path is so clearly aligned with the Queen of Diamonds."

"You know of the thirteenth Wise Woman?" I ask.

The Sage's nose juts toward me. She sniffs, a bloodhound in search of prey. "The who?"

"The sorceress you spoke of." I grip Finn's hand. His skin is cold, too cold, for the warm tent. "The one who cursed Finn."

Her rotund nose twitches as she takes several exaggeratedly deep breaths. "Ahh, yes. Yes. I see what you mean. There are other spells, aren't there?" The Sage taps the side of her nose as she leans toward the Librarian. "Not yours, though. Now that we know each other, I see yours. I can see the Queen of Diamonds', plain as the day is long. And I can see the sorceress', too, as well as someone else's who tries to shield him. But *this* one . . . yes, yes. It's nasty, isn't it." She inhales deeply, her chest juddering. "There's something about it, though. Something that tastes familiar, but doesn't all at the same time, it does."

Finn's grip turns vise like, but I welcome it. "If you don't mean the thirteenth Wise Woman, then whom do you refer to?"

The Sage swirls her teacup so that the stones clink together. "I am beginning to have an inkling of why I am here, Baba Yaga. Dark magic is afoot in Wonderland. I have been forced to tolerate the abomination for as long as I have, but now. . ." She licks a finger and holds it aloft. "Now true evil embraces its origins."

When the Librarian leans forward, face illuminated by the fire bowl, I do not quite recognize her anymore. Unfamiliar lines grow and recede, eyes darken and lighten, her nose sharpens and softens. "They have purposely kept me blind, and I cannot stand for it any longer. Help me rid the worlds of these plagues, sister."

A broken, jagged excuse for a smile cracks beneath the Sage's nose. "Only if you swear to rid me of my demon."

"Name your price," the Librarian says, "and it will be done."

The Sage dips into her tea, extracting a stone. She sucks on it for several heartbeats before offering it to me. "What I desire most is the sorceress' heart replaced with this. And I wish the Queen of Diamonds to be the one to do it. It is only fitting, eh?"

The rock is small and jagged, black with red streaks throughout.

"Oh, my dear Queen of Diamonds. My apologies." The Sage rubs her thumb across the brightest ruby cord. "I forget, sometimes. I forget how she silenced me with one of my own rocks when she came. A small, petulant girl. I underestimated her." She spits on the rock and it doubles in size. It shifts and groans, its shape contorting into the size of a fist. "Have you, though? I have often wondered. Maybe now that she has dared to come after you in this most painful, personal of ways, you are not so blind anymore."

A thin sheen of sweat breaks out along my hairline. *Marble and red sandstone.* "You speak of the Queen of Hearts."

Teeth I have never seen before sprout within the Sage's mouth, elongating as she hisses and growls.

Finn stands up. "The Queen of Hearts is a witch?"

The Wonderlandian oracle's nails curve into claws. Her jaw stretches, more snout than nose. The rock clacks against her lethal talon. "Take . . . the . . . rock . . . Diamonds."

The words themselves are stones ground between serrated teeth. I have spent hours with the Sage. Jace has, too. For hundreds of years, she has counseled our peoples and rulers.

I do not recognize the beast before me.

I quickly accept her offering.

The teeth and nails and snout retract. The disembodied hand returns the tea to the Sage. She digs out the second stone from the cup and sucks on it. When she offers it to Finn, it remains small. She remains calm.

Once we both have stones, she finishes her tea and then spits upon the fire. "The sorceress is the evilest magic wielder of my acquaintance." She bares a gummy sneer at the Librarian. "Even more evil than you, Baba Yaga."

Over the rim of her cup, the Librarian murmurs, "We'll see."

"How. . ." I stare at the stone in my palm. "Until today, I did not know that Wonderland had witches."

"Keep that safe, Your Majesty." The polished stones reappear, rolling once more across the Sage's knuckles. "I am Wonderland's only native sorceress, and when I die, I will be its last. The one you speak of, though." Her lips curl up, but no teeth are visible. "She was not born here, nor did Wonderland choose her, as it did you. She remains only through the strength of her insidious magic."

The Queen of Hearts is a *witch*.

"Hearts was crowned on her eleventh birthday." I rise from my chair and root around the Librarian's tent for a scrap of paper. Notes must be taken to ensure I am not hallucinating. "Her parents were at the coronation. People from her village."

"Were you there?" the Sage asks.

I knock aside several folders. "No, of course not. I was in England then."

"What are you looking for?" the Librarian asks.

I glare at her. "Hearts' name is Margaret. Her parents are Mortimer and Millie Mason."

"How do you know this?" Van Brunt asks.

"Public records." I hold a pencil aloft, victorious.

One of the disembodied hands snatches it away from me.

The Librarian says, "Sit down, Alice. You are not under the influence of Wonderlandian drugs again. And please remember records can be easily forged."

"How do you know the Queen of Hearts isn't a native?" Van Brunt asks the Sage.

The oracle hisses. "She doesn't smell like a Wonderlander. Doesn't taste like one. The rocks don't recognize her, just like they don't recognize any of you save the Queen of Diamonds." She flips one of the polished rocks up. "*She* was prophesied to become one of our great queens. The other. . ." Her nose wrinkles. "The rocks do not like her one bit. The ground, either. Or the air. *She isn't meant to be here*." She tosses the stones into the air and they hover, a miniature solar system above her head. "What she's doing is unnatural."

The stone in my hand grows warmer. "What is she doing?"

"She's forcing her will on that she has no right over."

She is doing the same as the Piper and the thirteenth Wise Woman. They are forcing their wills on to worlds, determining whether or not they will continue to exist, and the Queen of Hearts is—

"Put the rock in your mouth."

I startle, as it is the size of my fist. The size of a heart.

The size of Hearts' heart.

"No, Your Majesty." The Sage scratches her beak-like nose. "Your lover."

He stares at the small object, so freshly wetted within her own toothless mouth.

"Do you want your answers or not?"

"She cannot hurt you, Finn." There is no amusement, no room for argument when the Librarian says this. "Nor can the rock. Not in here, not while this is marked my domain."

"Only," the Sage grumbles, "because you hid yourself from me."

Finn places the rock on his tongue like a child with a sugar cube, waiting for it to melt. The Sage climbs out of her chair, knees creaking. I am aware of every step she takes toward Finn, every move of her fingers, every turn of the stones around her head.

The three shadows reappear.

"Be a good lad and open wide." She stands on her tiptoes and reaches one of her gangly arms up, its ball and joint sockets abnormally large and wieldy. She plucks the stone from his mouth and then, quick as a heartbeat, sucks it in between her lips.

After several minutes, she spits it out into her drawstring bag. "It is as I thought."

Finn asks tightly, "Meaning?"

"She is forcing her will on that which she does not rightfully have say over." She waves a gnarled hand at him. "Case in point: you." Her tongue clicks against the roof of her mouth. "Her magic, her anger, corrupts Wonderland. You must be careful of the Queen of Hearts, Your Majesty. Her hatred of you has grown too difficult for even her own to control any longer."

"You speak in circles." I am irrevocably finished with these maddening women and their verbal games. I am not a circus performer, leaping through blazing hoops alongside tigers simply to reach a dangling prize at the end. "If you have something of pertinence to share, do so. If not, get out of my way. Tomorrow, if Wonderland smiles upon us, I will face the Queen of Hearts, alongside other truly evil magicians. I refuse to waste my time attempting to pry answers out of you—or any of you—anymore."

The Librarian holds her teacup aloft.

Knees bowing and creaking like branches in nearby trees during the morning's storm, the Sage totters before me. "The sorceress has claimed your lover as her own, Your Majesty, with the help of another magic wielder. Their magics are strong, stronger than my own, stronger than any I know of. Not even your strength can save him."

Finn says, "Bullshit. This is—this is bullshit. And pointless, because we need to focus on the Chosen and the Piper, not some stupid love spell. I've already taken care of that."

The Sage licks a finger before plucking one of her stone planets from the miniature orbit circling her head. "What she has cast is more than just love. This is revenge, lad. She will own you, body and soul. You will be a tool for her, the strongest yet to wield against her enemies. The spell is nearly complete. Once the planetary convergence occurs tonight, then—"

Van Brunt, the Librarian, and I simultaneously stand up. Along with Finn, we all shout, *"Convergence?"*

The Sage plucks another stone from above her head, tucking it in her tote. "Well, more like align, but yes. Mercury, Venus, Mars, Jupiter, and Saturn will form a line across the sky from twilight to sunup."

Van Brunt thrusts his teacup out; one of the disembodied hands takes it. "It's ten o'clock in the morning now. If it takes twelve hours to march to Cor Castle. . ."

Finn grabs hold of his hat. "Then we better move our timeline up."

"Wait." The Sage reaches out for the Librarian. "Sister. We must talk. Our deal."

"Go," the witch now known as Baba Yaga tells me.

CORCASTLE

FINN

T WELVE HOURS OF TRAVEL are cut down to eleven, simply through the sheer stamina, will, and badassery of Wonderlandian soldiers. Granted, a special poison is administered, one that helps overcome exhaustion, but still. After the Sage's bombshell, it took the White King less than two hours to mobilize the armies, and, more importantly, the other Wonderlandian monarchs. Once we brought them to the Librarian's tent to consult with the Sage, and she confirmed what she had told us about the Queen of Hearts, the rest were out for foreign blood.

"This is our land," the White Queen told the others. Her whip coiled around her arm, pearly white and serpentine, was ready to strike at the slightest movement, but for the first time in our short acquaintance, she was more rational than maniacal. "These are our peoples.

Wonderland has and always will choose what is best for it. To use alien magic to change the order of life is a perversion. It is a crime against nature. *Our* nature."

Reasonable discussion went downhill from there, but all centered around the need to destroy Hearts. To get to her, the Wonderlandian monarchs are more than happy to mow down any and all Chosen that step into their paths—which is fine by me.

During the journey, an army of Spiders works overtime to spin as many earplugs as possible for the card soldiers and pikemen. Brom and I have no worries about the Chosen anymore. It's only a matter of time before Wonderland brings them to their ancient knees. But the Queen of Hearts was seen with the Piper *and* the thirteenth Wise Woman. If Hearts is an actual witch, and she is aligned with the couple from hell, I don't know how even an army as talented as the one I'm promised is at my back will take them down.

Even if Baba Yaga is on our side.

Talk about a mind fuck.

I'd heard stories of her, of course. The Widow Douglas and her sister told me a few, and then in college, in one of my folklore classes, I read about her. The infamous Baba Yaga was the most feared of all Russian witches. She dwelled in a house built upon chicken legs and traveled in a mortar and pestle, like it was a damn boat she could paddle through forests in. She punished those who ventured to demand favors. Occasionally, she rewarded the kindhearted and generous. She was a cannibal and a trickster, a benefactress and a grandmother. She was a boogeyman and a goddess rolled into one. She didn't hail from a singular collection of stories—instead, her fame arose from years of people never forgetting her name and deeds.

Baba Yaga helped found the Collectors' Society.

I still didn't know why, and the eleven hours of travel left no time to ask questions. Each minute is devoted to revising our attack plans.

The Sage chose not to journey to Cor. Before we departed, she spit on a few more rocks and bequeathed them to Baba Yaga. "I will not beckon Death's scythe. I watch life, not destroy it."

When we reach the Hearts' stronghold, the rain has lessened to a mere shower. Everyone is clammy, soaked straight through. The clatter of teeth rattles through the ranks. As we crest the hill, black and red turrets peek out of smoke and clouds. Card soldiers and pikemen from all four Courts take another dose of their poisons, ensuring their effectiveness for battle.

I'm tempted to steal a dose for myself.

The Hearts soldiers lining Cor's battlements crowd along the carved stone pillars, ogling the thousands of soldiers flooding the path, gardens, and forests before them. *This isn't my castle,* I can't help but think. I feel no loyalty toward it, no interest in learning its secrets other than how to get to Hearts. At the main gate, pikemen ready their weapons, but the Queen's patrolling card soldiers almost look lost as they shuffle back and forth in an effort to figure out where they ought to be.

Our troops pull away from the front to reveal the cluster of Wonderlandian monarchs. All, save the Queen of Hearts and recently deceased King of Hearts, are present.

A burly Gryphon pushes his way past his pikemen. "What is the meaning of this? Who dares invade Hearts territory?"

The Red Queen slips a shuriken from her ridiculous Elizabethan collar and flicks it toward him. The jeweled star strikes the soldier between his eyes. He crumples to the ground as she pulls out a second. "How dare this commoner speak to us in such an insolent manner."

The Queen of Hearts' soldiers' unease spreads like an ugly disease, visibly hopping from one to the next. Just twenty-four hours before, the entirety of Wonderland was at war with one another. Now, all of the Courts, save their queen's, are banded together at their gates?

Jace nudges his white stallion forward. Garbed entirely in white that somehow managed to not become transparent in the rain, his crown glints in the torchlight held by nearby soldiers. "If your loyalty remains with Wonderland—and Wonderland alone—our fight is not with you. We will give you five minutes to lay down your arms and revoke your allegiance to the sorceress, or we will cut you down where you stand."

A young card soldier has the audacity to yell, "What sorceress do you speak of, Your Majesty?"

The Red Queen readies her shuriken, but Alice snatches it from her before it flies free. The youth darts behind a large pikeman, quivering so hard his knees knock together, just like in a cartoon.

"The Queen of Hearts," the White Queen trills, "is no Wonderlander. She is a sorceress, come from another land, and is defiling our home and people with evil magic! She stole her crown. Wonderland did not give it to her! We will take it back, so our homeland may give it to its rightful owner!"

A deafening cheer lifts around us, crashing through the dense fog. If the Chosen didn't know we were here yet, they do now.

"Pardon my questioning, Your Majesty," the youth continues, hands gripped on the pikeman's shoulders, "but isn't the Queen of Diamonds a foreigner, too?"

I'll give it to the kid. He's got balls of steel.

Fury mottles the Red Queen's delicate features. Her eyes cut to Alice. "I cannot believe I am forced to say this."

Alice lifts both eyebrows, amused.

The Red Queen looks as if she's swallowed a whole lemon. She shouts, "The Queen of Diamonds was rightfully chosen by Wonderland. She was prophesied. The sorceress calling herself Hearts was not."

The youth ogles the monarchs, and then the vast army before him. He emerges from the safety of the pikeman, his sword clattering upon the wet wood of the drawbridge. "I am a proud Wonderlander. My family has lived in the Hearts lands for generations. If what you say is true, Your Majesty, we deserve our rightful queen."

The majority follow suit, either dropping their weapons and leaving or coming to join our side, but the so-called victory is hollow. These soldiers aren't our enemy. Hell, they're nothing but window dressing. They're decoys. The point is proven when hundreds of new faces take their places on the battlement and in front of the gate. Many are children, some are still youths. Their smugness showcases painful sets of rotten teeth. The rest are clearly Wonderlanders: Goats, Unicorns, Lions, pikemen, and others, their eyes black and soulless, their weapons farming tools or kitchen utensils.

The Queen of Hearts insignia decorate each lapel.

How many Wonderlanders has Hearts corrupted?

Jace signals the for the battle horn. The moment metal touches lips it's yanked away, though. Soldiers spill from the castle and from the sides—real combatants, card soldiers and pikemen, all black-eyed and wearing Hearts' insignia.

Jace pulls his horse back, swearing. "She allowed the Chosen to convert her entire army."

Our odds on the battlefield just got a whole lot lousier.

A horn blows, long and clear. A second horn trills, three notes high before jumping around. Our soldiers stuff their ears with their silken earplugs and shift into formation. Those of us readying ourselves to fight our way into Cor fit Marianne's special communicators into our ears.

The White Queen stands in her stirrups, roses tangling in her hair. She traded her billowing gowns for white-leather breeches and coat: a glowing, insane angel of death. She holds her whip aloft as the pipers on the battlements lift their flutes to their lips. She unleashes her coil, snapping it through the air, sharp and high, just as lightning strikes the southern turret.

The heavens weep for Wonderland's civil war. Soldiers from both sides crash into one another, swords flashing in the dim torchlight. All of the Wonderlandian monarchs surge into the fray, even the Red King, still surrounded by his guard.

No mercy is offered from either side.

Static hisses in my ear. "I will clear you a path."

I look over at Jace and nod. He urges his horse forward, rearing up to trample a non-friendly Hearts' pikeman. Watery red mixes into the mud on the White King's snowy coat. His stallion sustains some damage from the pike's spurs, but shows no signs of slowing down when Jace shoots a pink flare soaring into the sky.

A team of elite soldiers from all four Courts peels away from the fracas. Bloodshed is a tame way of describing what they do as they, the White King, and the White Queen slowly carve a passageway for Alice and me. Brom, the A.D., and Baba Yaga, whom I don't know if I can ever just call the Librarian again, are close behind. The rest of the Society team is on and around the battlefield. Marianne and Mary are manning computers set up in a small tent not too far away; Victor is providing coverage for their safety. He may be one eye down, but I still trust him over just about anyone to take out targets when it counts.

After I shoot a pikeman, I peer up into the sky. There are too many angry, murky clouds to see the planets lined up. We weren't able to pick out any during the journey, and it set Baba Yaga's teeth on edge. She kept muttering, "I should have known."

The thing is, there's a spell on me that comes into effect during the convergence. Does Victor? More importantly, we know that the Piper called his followers to Koppenberg for the convergence, but why? What did—does—he and the thirteenth Wise Woman have planned?

There are too many variables to leave me feeling easy about any of this. What if the so-called wall breaks?

Alice kicks back a card soldier, her daggers dripping the blood of her enemy in the rain. Grymsdyke scuttles back on her shoulder, fresh from his latest kill. I push on the button in my right ear. "It's taking too long."

"The Hearts' soldiers are clustered at the front," Jace snaps. In the distance, I watch as he tears his hand away from his ear in order to slam the vorpal blade straight through a man's skull. A pair of men, dressed in identical White uniforms, move completely in sync as they take down six soldiers. "We are presented with a living wall. Be patient. We will get you through, Your Majesty."

Alice catches my attention, but loses it just as quickly when I shoot a pikeman charging her.

Bodies pile up before we make our way to the gate. Entering isn't any easier. Junior pipers mingle with Hearts soldiers, and our elite team is halved by the time we gain the upper hand.

"I will hold the hall," Jace tells us. "Hurry." And then, to Alice, "Stay safe."

She presses her fist against her heart. "Stay safe."

Half of the team, including the twin assassins Alice tells me are the Tweedles, follows Alice, Brom, Baba Yaga, and me as we weave through the corridors. Both Alice and I did our best to memorize the route to the dungeons during the journey here, and it pays off when we find the stairs leading into Cor's bowels with no difficulty.

Alice warned us that the cells would be filled, and her instincts were spot on. The stench alone nearly drives me back up the stairs. After the Tweedles and Grymsdyke take out the few guards at the entrance with hardly any exertion, the A.D. nicks a ring of keys off one of the deceased men's belts. Broken men and women wail and scream from behind the bars, undoubtedly begging us to let them out. But when the A.D. moves to the first cell, Alice pulls him back.

She taps on her earpiece. "We do not know if any are Chosen."

I don't hear his response, but I can imagine it wasn't pretty. I refocus him, telling him to get the drone ready. He crouches down and removes the small plane from his backpack, along with a video monitoring system.

It only takes a minute or two to get the drone in the air. Many of the prisoners press their faces against the bars, terror gripping the already frightened. None of our Wonderlandian soldiers pay the technology any attention, though. The Tweedles spend their time standing perfectly still, as if they are wax figures. The A.D. sends the drone down the hallway and around the bend, sticking close to the ceiling. Marianne reworked it to be quiet, undetectable by human ears. If Hearts has some other kinds of guards down here, though, maybe Dogs or something. . .

I crowd the thief as I peer down at the screen. So far, only darkness and the faint orange blur of occasional torches appear. But after the drone creeps around another corner, we find what we're looking for: a dozen pikemen and a pair of pipers standing before a closed door, their blank stares made even eerier by their black eyes.

"This is only the entrance," Alice says. "There could be more— many more—beyond the doorway."

"Some doors open to other doors," Grymsdyke says unhelpfully.

I take inventory of the two-dozen soldiers still with us. They've got to be beat after what it took just to get this far, even though the stimulant poison must still be coursing through their system.

Alice touches my arm. "We have to finish this before the last planet shifts into place."

None of Marianne's computers knew exactly when that would be, as she didn't load any astronomy programs ahead of time. The Sage mentioned something about dawn, but it's anyone's guess right now.

We reload our guns and clips and check our weapons. The soldiers take another small shot of the poison after the A.D. fills them in on the dozen soldiers. The Tweedles knock their heads together. As I'm loading my holsters, Baba Yaga pulls Alice to the side, which is unnecessary, as all our earpieces are linked.

"Do you remember what you agreed to?"

What agreement?

Alice shoves a pair of daggers into her boots. "Yes."

But Baba Yaga blocks her from rejoining us. "Do not be persuaded by Abraham's sentimentality, if it comes to that. Is that clear?"

I don't have to be a lip reader to know that my dad is pissed at that comment. Baba Yaga heads over to where he is. She says for all of us to hear, "I must break my promise now."

His large hands engulf her small ones, tan skin covering tawny. She is so tiny next to him, a dwarf to his giant. When he speaks, none of us can hear, as he doesn't activate his earpiece. She reaches for his face, and he has to stoop. They hug, and it's a real one, a friendly one, and I'm taken back to years of watching Katrina and the Librarian hugging. They were such good friends. The best kind. And now she's hugging another good friend, and we don't know what the hell is about to happen tonight. By morning, we could all be dead. The world as we know it could be over.

Baba Yaga wipes her eyes when she pulls away. She crouches, legs tucked beneath her, and pulls out a mortar and a pestle. Several items from her pockets are added to the worn, stone bowl. She grinds as she chants, occasionally spitting into the mixture. Shadows crawl down the walls, shrouding the already gloomy dungeon. She dips the pestle into the bowl and touches her tongue to it. A burst of blackness blinds me and, when it clears, the woman I met on my first day in the Institute is no longer with us. In her place is an elderly woman, stooped and gray-haired, her face heavily lined and her nose sharp as a beak.

Narrowed, wicked eyes laser in on all of us as she sweeps the room.

My skin crawls as her magic pulses from every pour.

The real Baba Yaga has joined our party.

If any of the others have a comment, I don't hear it. For once, the A.D. is tactful enough to not blast his shitty opinions out on full volume. None of the Wonderlandian soldiers even blink, but then, they're probably used to seeing bizarre shit all the time anyway.

Baba Yaga tucks her mortar and pestle into a bag tied to her waist. She taps on her earpiece. "It's time."

Brom nods, slipping a rifle into a holster on his back. The A.D. sends the drone back down the hallways. Once we find nothing changed, Brom signals the soldiers. He tells his assistant, "Stay here."

The A.D. reaches up to tap on his earpiece, his face screwed up like he wants to argue, but, faster than the blink of an eye, Baba Yaga darts over to where he is and shoves him down into a chair I'm not so sure was there just a few seconds before. One of those terrifying disembodied hands materializes with the drone scanner.

Chances are, the thief just crapped his pants. Maybe I did, too.

I keep my gun out. Alice has her blade. We follow the soldiers down the hallway, Brom and Baba Yaga bringing up the rear. The skirmish with the guards and pipers is bloody and brutal, but thankfully quick. I have to give it to the Tweedles—they're damn effective. And I particularly appreciate the piper's frustration when their music does nothing to anyone in our party.

I appreciate the bullet I put through one of their brains even more.

The tunnel leading from Cor to Hearts' secret lair is narrow and unlit, its coarse walls and uneven, rocky ground slowing our pace. We pass out a handful of small flashlights to soldiers in both front and back, but the darkness devours the thin beams. The drone whizzes overhead, an opaque shadow barely distinguishable from the low-hanging roof.

In front of me, Brom taps on his earpiece. He whispers, "Report."

Jack's voice hisses in my ear, "The tunnel continues for approximately half a mile before a light source appears, AVB."

Alice lifts her hand to her ear. "Is the light coming from a door?"

The A.D. is quiet for several heartbeats. "It appears so, AL. Or is it AR? Or maybe even QOD?"

Alice's hand drops back to her side.

"Are there any guards?" I murmur.

"None visible, FVB."

It doesn't make sense. "Get the drone as close as possible."

Several more minutes pass. "No guards as far as I can see, FVB."

Alice and I exchange an uneasy look.

"What about security measures?" I ask. The Piper, as Gabe Lygari and Gabriel Pfiefer, lived in modern-day New York City. A number of his minions did, as well. He would have had access to plenty of technology. Hell, there were things that didn't make sense back at Koppenberg Mountain, such as the medical equipment Victor was hooked up to. "Lasers?" I prod. "Video cameras? Trip wires?"

Suddenly—*"Bloody fucking hell!"*

Brom halts, one hand reaching for the rifle. "Report, Mr. Dawkins."

"You ain't going to believe me, bossman!"

Alice glances about us as my father whispers, "Try me."

Our Wonderlandian soldiers ready their weapons, instantly shifting into defensive stances. Grymsdyke moves from Alice's arm to mine.

"That open door—I just had a good look at it." The thief's voice crackles in my ear. "And it looks like the one we saw at John and Paul School for the Gifted, which is what Her Majesty said the door at the Piper's fancy library looked like, right? I saw it in 1816/18GRI-GT. She was right."

Alice's nails dig into the meat of my arm, her eyes finding mine.

"That's *this* door. The same one. It's a big door, too. Like, really big. And ugly—I mean, there's a lot of ugly stuff on it, violent stuff. I'm a lover at heart, you know. I'm not into this kind of grotesque art."

Brom snaps, "Get to the point, Mr. Dawkins."

"Well, I snuck the drone inside, just a peek, since the door was open, and . . . and that's a library in there, AVB. I think it's *the* library."

How is Bücherei in Wonderland? Last we saw, it'd been in 1816/18GRI-GT, and even that'd been a mind fuck.

A squealing sound, so incredibly painful that I see and hear stars, blows out my right eardrum. Before the same can happen to the other side, I yank out both earpieces to find every member of our party doing the same. Even the Wonderlandian soldiers, wincing, remove their spiderweb earpieces.

"What just happened?" one of the Tweedles asks. Is it Dee? Dum? I can't tell them apart.

No one answers, because all of the Wonderlandian soldiers drop to the ground like windup toys whose keys have stopped turning.

"That is . . . unexpected," Grymsdyke comments. "What was it that the thief saw with his demonic flying machine?"

An impossibility.

Blood dripping from his ear, my father drops to the ground next to one of the soldiers. He presses two fingers against the man's neck. "He's dead."

Alice whisper-sings our fallen comrades a song for safe travels to the journeylands.

How did they die so quickly? Was it the thirteenth Wise Woman? Hearts? How could they take out a team of elite soldiers without even touching them?

I hurl the burnt, useless bits of technology I dug out of my ears against the wall. "Somebody inside the library must have seen the drone."

Alice peers into the gloom behind us. "Jack."

"Mr. Dawkins has a highly developed sense of self-preservation." Brom wipes the blood on his face and ear with a handkerchief. "Do not concern yourself with his welfare, Alice."

She softens just a bit. As my dad and Baba Yaga collect the flashlights they can find, I use the back of my sleeve to dab the blood from her ear. "Why the smile?"

She reciprocates in kind. My ear feels like it's on fire, or like TNT exploded in it, or possibly both. I tilt my good ear toward her to hear. "Your father called me Alice."

She kisses me before I can ask what that means.

Baba Yaga blocks the passage, her gray hair matted against the blood on her face. "The thirteenth Wise Woman is mine. Is that clear?"

Alice counters, "Hearts is mine."

Which leaves the Piper to my dad, and me, which is exactly how it should be, considering that bastard orchestrated Katrina's death. Only . . . "Victor ought to be here, too."

Brom neatly folds his bloody handkerchief and stuffs it back into a pocket. "Someone needs to protect Ms. Lennox and Ms. Brandon."

"There are thousands of soldiers out there who could have done it."

He grabs his rifle. "He would never allow a stranger to protect Ms. Brandon, let alone Ms. Lennox." Fine, that's true. "And there are those on the battlefield who will need him far more than we will." One-handed, he pumps the rifle's chamber. "And, selfishly. . ." My father clamps a hand on my shoulder. It's warm and large, covering most of my well-defined muscle. "I cannot bear the thought of all of the Van Brunts gone."

I'm not insulted. Brom is a realist. There's an excellent chance we're not walking out of Bücherei alive. There are two witches in there and the fucking Pied Piper of Hamelin. Who knows who else could be hiding inside?

"You made the right choice," I tell him.

THE CONVERGENCE

FINN

BÜCHEREI IS EXACTLY AS I remember it. Three stories high with mosaicked floors depicting monstrous scenes from various fairy tales and legends, the library is stuffed with countless priceless books. Dozens of glass cases filled with author paraphernalia pepper the galley; above us, glowing eyes stare down from nightmarish frescos of crashing waves, dark forests, and eerie caves.

"Our guests have arrived! You don't know how long I have waited for this moment."

Over by a small cart filled with bottles of wines and liqueurs is the Piper. He's dressed in a sharp tuxedo, his hair immaculately combed and gelled back. "Champagne?" He holds a drink aloft. "It's an excellent vintage that I've saved just for this occasion. Brandy?" He clicks his tongue. "No, I seem to remember that Abraham Van Brunt and his kin are scotch men." He cups his mouth, shifting slightly to the right. "Melantha! Our guests are finally here. Do you remember if we brought any scotch?"

A voice *made* of whiskey answers, rich with a heavy German accent, "Alas, my love, we do not have any in stock. Nasty stuff, scotch." A pause. "Margaret! Did you bring any?"

Alice readies her dagger. Both Brom and I have our guns pointed. The Spider on my shoulder hisses. The Piper chuckles when he notes our intensity. "Whoa, whoa. None of that right now. Not when we've gone to all this trouble. It's the convergence!" He flashes jazz hands. "It's time to celebrate and have drinks, not," he waves dismissively while sipping his champagne, "well, ruining the floor and all. I had hoped to celebrate with a much larger crowd, but as you . . . people," he side eyes us, "keep shooting at them and blowing them up, you'll have to do. Witnesses are always lovely to have at grand events."

Alice throws her dagger anyway. The son of a bitch catches it between two fingers a split hair before it sliced open an eye.

The Piper tosses the blade onto the drink cart. "You know, Alice. I tried. I really, really tried to talk Margaret out of this whole vengeance quest. Your feistiness is refreshing amongst a sea of *yes men*." An infuriating leer slicks across his mouth. "You and I could have had some fun together. That first night together was exhilarating."

"We could still have some fun together," Alice counters. "I can make you pay for all of the atrocities you have committed."

A woman with flaming-red hair strolls out onto one of the second-story balconies. She's dressed in an elaborate red and black gown that looks more sci-fi than anything else. I know her, unfortunately. I know the cruel twist of her blood-red lips. I know how her brown eyes are fathomless. I sat at her feet, chained, and felt her hands twist into my soul.

The thirteenth Wise Woman chides the Piper in a language I don't know. When he scowls, she adds in English, "You were warned, my darling. Too bad you do not listen to your *tohter.*" Those dark pits of despair zero in on me. "I am very vexed with you, *mīn scōnī.* Ruining my beautiful mountain and running off without even as much as a goodbye kiss."

She takes hold of a railing and winds down a curved ladder.

Brom nudges me and we both fire at the Piper. The bastard somehow sidesteps both our bullets, which end up destroying medieval manuscripts.

"Those," the Piper says irritably, "cost me a fortune."

I glance around. Where is Baba Yaga?

I fire again to the same end. Grymsdyke leaps off of me, his silk flying behind him. Alice charges the Piper, only to freeze midway, her blade glittering in the bright Tiffany lamps spread out throughout the library. And then, I'm paralyzed, too—and as I can't see any movement out of the corner of my eye, I fear my father has fallen to the same fate. Grymsdyke hangs in the air.

The thirteenth Wise Woman saunters past Alice, to me. "I told you he would come."

The Piper shrugs. "Where is Margaret?"

"Taking her time, as always." The Wise Woman lifts the crown off my head and runs her fingers across what's left of my hair. "Where is your mane, *mīn scōnī?*" She leans closer, her skin perilously close to my own. I drown in the smell of belladonna and decay. "What happened in here?" She taps on my forehead, and then on the spot where one of the rods was inserted into my skull. "Who did this to you?"

The Piper finishes his glass of champagne. He strolls over to where Grymsdyke hangs in the air and plucks the assassin like a flower. "What are you jabbering on about, my love?"

The thirteenth Wise Woman drapes her arms over my shoulders, and my stomach instantly revolts. I am back in Koppenberg Mountain, at her feet. Pain, it seems, can be more than a memory. Her pain, at least. "This one has been naughty. I'll have to cleanse him."

"Margaret will be displeased." The Piper drops Grymsdyke to the ground and crushes him with his well-polished shoe. I just about lose my goddamn mind at the bitter crunch that follows. He may have been a spider, but Grymsdyke deserved better. He was fierce, strong, and loyal.

He was a friend.

The bastard who just killed him scrapes the heel of his shoe on the drink cart and pours another glass and drinks half of it straightaway. Bits of brown and blue hair and blood smear the floor; chunks drip from the cart. *Jesus.* Alice has to see this, standing where she is. I have no doubts her fury and grief are just as venomous as mine.

The Piper says nonchalantly, like he didn't just murder a member of our team, "You know how she is about these things."

The Wise Woman hums as she lays her head on my shoulder.

I am going to make that asshole pay for what he just did.

He nudges his glass toward her. "She gets that from you, you know."

"Tell me, *mīn scōnī.*" The Wise Woman's breath tickles my aching ear. Fire ants invade my ear canal. "Did you enjoy the blood of *mīn sun* on your hands?" Her own tighten on my shoulders, digging past muscle and into the bone. "Was it payment for agreeing to give you to *mīn tohter?*"

"Melantha."

The Piper's warning is a sharp crack of a shot, but she doesn't release me. His stride eats up the distance between us before he physically wrenches her away. He slams the crown back down upon my head, and I'm pretty damn sure it cuts into my scalp. "Margaret chose this one. She went to all the trouble to crown him. *You* will leave him alone. She has plans, remember?"

She crowned me. Not Wonderland.

A witch crowned me. I wasn't chosen.

The thirteenth Wise Woman—Melantha—growls as she whirls away. "You coddle her too much."

He backhands her so hard, she sprawls a good three, four feet across the floor. She wipes the blood from the corner of her mouth with the back of her hand, the tip of her tongue erasing the rest. But rather than fight back, she laughs delightedly.

"Before we sleep, my love," she says, "You will scream for mercy."

He moves out of my line of sight. "Make it hurt, darling. Make me bleed."

"Enough of your disgusting public displays of foreplay. What will our guests think?"

I can't see her, but I know the Queen of Hearts' voice. I will every muscle, every joint in my body to break free, for my trigger finger to flinch.

"Margaret!" The sharp slap of well-heeled loafers on mosaics sounds behind us. "We were just discussing you."

"Müeterlīn!" Hearts brushes past me, icy fingers trailing down my arm and across the barrel of my gun. She stops at Alice, hands on her couture-swathed hips. "I told you that this bitch is mine."

Melantha presents a cheek for Hearts. Two dutiful kisses are offered. "She still lives, does she not?" Hot coals glow upon Hearts' face. *"Mīn tohter,* you must reconsider the man, though. I understand your reasoning, for it is sound—"

The Piper reemerges to pour himself a third glass of champagne.

"But," Melantha continues, "can you not think of your *bruoder?"*

Bruoder. Brother?

Hearts yanks Alice's hair out of its tight bun and twists the strands into what must be painful coils. "What's done is done." She yanks the dagger out of Alice's immobile grip and slices off one of the golden chunks. My vision hazes red. "I will cut her up and stitch her back together in his honor."

Where the fuck is Baba Yaga?! Why is she letting this happen?

"You are all focusing on the wrong things anyway." The Piper wanders over to join them, still hovering around Alice. He lifts one of the intact coils and sniffs it. "The convergence is upon us. All that we have worked so hard toward for so long will be permanent in the annals of history."

Hearts saws off another chunk of Alice's hair. Bile stings in the back of my mouth. "What *you* have worked so hard toward. This is not my game, *Vater."*

He slaps the dagger away. It clatters onto the ground, a few specks of red beading below it. "It is not a game, Margaret. This is about reconstructing the worlds to fulfill your mother's vision. Those without magic come to fear us, daughter. They hunt our kind down. They butcher our peoples. They burn them on pyres. The more worlds that inherently reject magic, the more dangerous it is for the rest of us."

Hearts presses the back of her hand against her forehead. "Oh, so noble." She laughs bitterly. "I wonder if they believe it, if they think you have sound reasoning behind your actions." She leans against Alice, a long fingernail digging into the woman I love's injured ear. "Not that you deserve it, Diamonds, but I will tell you an ugly secret. There are not always wondrous reasons behind my parents' madness, nor are there extensive, reasonable experiences that lead them to their deeds. I suppose I inherited this from them."

Her dark hair presses against Alice's blonde. "I despise you. I despise your smugness, your stubbornness, and the way you always act so infuriatingly noble. It wasn't fair, not fair at all that you could come into Wonderland and be so utterly accepted while I had to force the land to give me what I wanted. This is my world. I chose it. They gave it to *me*. It was *my* birthday gift." She pushes Alice to the ground.

I do not know how I stay in one piece.

"Was there something specific you did to me?" Hearts pets Alice's mangled hair. Streaks of red mix in with the gold. *Can she breathe?* Black splotches of panic burst in my bones. "I honestly cannot remember. It does not matter, though." She presses a kiss in the golden strands, leaving behind a ruby lipstain. "I will destroy you anyway, just as my parents destroy anything they dislike, too. For no good reason at all. Because it makes us feel good. The power of life and death *feels* good. And as I am a goddess, I am allowed such rights."

The Piper's sigh is audible. "That is overly simplistic, Margaret."

These three are a family. The Queen of Hearts is the Pied Piper of Hamelin's and the thirteenth Wise Woman's *daughter*. The sister of the creature who tortured my brother.

"I apologize, *Vater*. You destroy worlds because you find their stories unworthy of your good opinion. You create armies because *mīn müeterlīn* adores chaos." She grabs a handful of Alice's dress and inserts the blade. "You cultivate followers to carry out your deeds, all the while finding it hilarious that they offer blind obedience without any knowledge as to why." She tears off the chunk of dress, revealing

Alice's pale back.

He turns toward the shelves behind him. "I've read the most interesting op-ed pieces lately, decrying the romance book industry. Many critics feel that such books are junk food, rather than quality meals to be savored. We should turn our eye toward these pieces of so-called literature."

Wait—what? No, really.

What. The. Actual. FUCK?

This piece of shit has been deleting Timelines because . . . because he doesn't like the original books the Timelines were based one?

Could the reason be so simple? So asinine? So . . . petty? Were all of those trillions of lives snuffed out due to this jackass' book snobbery? Because he felt the story wasn't good enough, so their lives weren't, too? Did he create a whole group of people to carry out his deeds simply because . . . he could? Because he gets off on power? On death?

My mother died because this asshole didn't like her story.

Rage like I have never felt before explodes throughout me.

"Next, you will be jabbering on about the 'quality' of Young Adult books." Hearts collects one of Alice's shorn strands and stands up. "Leave me and Wonderland alone and you and mother can go and do whatever you like to the rest of the worlds. Create your magical utopia. Bathe in the bloodshed. Collect your souls. Do whatever it is you do."

Melantha steps beside her husband. "All of this is moot if we do not reclaim the Codex."

"While we do not need the Codex for the convergence to work," the Piper wraps his hand around her throat, "we'll get our book back. Before you kill Abraham Van Brunt, ensure you get its location. We must log in our deletions and changes, or they don't count."

"I still do not understand how anyone else hasn't written in that book before," Hearts muses.

The Piper's smile is ugly and filled with false pride. "It was waiting for *me*."

The room dims, and the fucking trio of horrors give a startled glance around. Blood surges through my veins, and with it, movement.

I fire. I fire again. Brom is right there with me, shooting. This time, the Piper isn't too fast, and we pump his body with our lead.

Out of the corner of my eye, I watch Alice roll and jump up, tugging twin daggers out of her boot. Hearts launches herself at Alice at the same time a black mass churns toward the thirteenth Wise Woman.

Even though we've clearly hit him several times, the Piper manages to break free toward one of the staircases. Brom and I follow suit. The fucker tugs out a set of pipes from his tux pocket.

I cock my gun again.

"You go high," my dad says as the Piper climbs, "and I'll go low."

Brom pumps his rifle as I aim at the Piper's head. *BAM. PFFT.* Brom rips into the psychopath's knee at the same time I lay one into the base of his skull.

The pipes drop over the railing first, splintering as they hit the hard, mosaicked floor. Then, its owner follows, face first. When the Piper hits the ground, Brom slams a boot onto his face. "This," he snarls, "is for the love of my life." He pumps the rifle again, lines up the shot, and cleanly shoots that bastard straight into his heart.

I turn in time to watch Alice slam Hearts into a shelf of books. Volumes from all three stories rain down upon them. "Help her." Brom kicks the Piper away. "I'll go help the Librarian."

I don't bother to look around to even see where Baba Yaga is.

Somehow, Hearts has gotten hold of the biggest damn battle-ax I have ever seen. It slices through the air, whistling as it barely misses Alice. The woman I love drops and rolls, snatching a fallen dagger.

She calls out, "The bag, Finn!"

I spring back over to where I'd dropped it earlier. Inside is the Sage's rock. I wait until Alice sends Hearts sprawling to send a warning shot. It grazes the bitch's cheek, leaving a nice burn mark. Hearts rears back, giving me enough time to toss the stone to Alice.

Hearts lunges for me, much faster than I expected she could be. She grabs hold of my shirt and twists, tugging me close. Her chubby fingers circle my wrist and lock on tight.

Everything blurs.

No. No. They—*they fixed this.*

"Finn, move!" the Queen of Diamonds barks. No—Alice. It's *Alice*.

The Queen of Hearts yanks me up against her chest, the battle-axe crossing in front of us. "This time, my King of Hearts will not stray."

"Wonderland did not choose him," the Queen of Diamonds is saying. "You forced this choice upon the land. He does not want it."

King of Hearts.

"Is that true, poppet?" The Queen of Hearts leans her head against mine. "Do you not want to be my king?"

I stare at the Queen of Diamonds, at the blood on her dress and face. At her uneven hair, at the strange rock in her hand.

Above her, a star appears. It's bright and beckons me home.

North star.

"Shoot her, poppet. Just enough to incapacitate our enemy. We don't want her dead yet, though. The Queen of Diamonds hasn't suffered enough yet."

Another star appears. They orbit one another, strong and bright, their pull undeniable.

Binaries.

I aim my gun at the Queen of Diamonds. She stands perfectly still, her back straight, her head held high.

She tells me, "I believe in you."

I spin around and jab the gun into Hearts' side, right where I know her kidney is. I pull the trigger and say, "I'm not the fucking King of Hearts. And you're the enemy, bitch."

The battle-axe clatters to the ground. I step back just in time to watch Hearts collapse, clutching her side. She's instantly pale, too weak to even cry or yell.

Alice darts forward, knife at the ready.

She stops, though. Grabs hold of the crown on my head and tosses it across the room. I tell her, "See? I told you so."

"Is this how it will be for the rest of our life together? I doubt one small thing, and you lord it over me?"

"As long as it's the rest of our lives," I say, "I don't care about the rest."

She kisses me: hot, intense, and far too short. Then she drops to the ground, fingers upon the queen's neck. "Hearts is dead."

"Of course she's dead. I shot her in the damn kidney."

She takes a deep breath and nods. And then she carves.

"Brom?" The galley is empty, save Alice, Hearts, and me. "Baba Yaga?"

No one answers.

I rush over to where the Piper's body fell, where my dad plugged a huge bullet into his heart.

It's not there. *He's* not there.

"Brom?" I cup my hands, scanning the galley. "Brom, answer me, dammit!"

Alice wipes her hands off on a bar towel from the drink cart. "They went after the thirteenth Wise Woman."

"The Piper's gone, too."

She immediately darts back over to Hearts, but the dead queen is exactly where we left her. The Sage's rock peeks out from the hole in her chest.

Alice would make a terrible surgeon, by the way. But she's a damn fine executioner, because she claims Hearts' battle-axe and, with one swing, severs the former queen's head from its body. The mosaics below shatter. Her crown disappears.

"Unless she can resurrect her brother in order to reattach her head," Alice says grimly, "this one will stay put."

Darkness swarms the galley. I grab Alice's hand and pull her behind one of the staircases. In one blink of an eye, Hearts is before us. In the next, Baba Yaga and the thirteenth Wise Woman are attacking one another.

Where did they come from?

When Alice moves to join the fray, I hold her back. I remind her, whisper soft, of our promise to Baba Yaga, to not interfere.

The thirteenth Wise Woman shrieks in fury, tearing at Baba Yaga's robes. "How dare you hide from me! How dare you infiltrate my home!"

Baba Yaga swings her pestle, slamming it into the Wise Woman's brow. The air between the women crackles, blue-white sparks flashing. Russian chanting fills the galley, growing louder and louder until my already aching ear is more than ringing—it's bleeding anew. Horns curl out of the thirteenth Wise Woman's head as she breathes fire, but Baba Yaga's pestle grows larger, heavier. *Stronger*. When she swings it the last time, it's the size of a baseball bat. The thirteenth Wise Woman hits the ground, half of her head caved in. Soon, her skull is completely shattered.

Even Alice has to look away.

Baba Yaga continues to beat the shit out of the thirteen Wise Woman. Just pummels Melantha into something that no longer resembles anything. She chants in Russian the entire time, beating and swearing and chanting, the pestle as gory as her dress and everything else within spitting distance.

When she's done, Baba Yaga's narrow eyes cut through the gloom into the small space behind the stairs where Alice and I are hiding. She knew we were here the entire time. "Where is Brom?"

We step out, but the room doesn't grow any lighter. Neither of us come any closer, though, not while she holds her enormous, bloody pestle. I say, "I hoped he was with you."

Her face, white as the full moon, crumples in horror. Her attention swings toward the ceiling, toward the third floor. "Don't you dare!"

Her threat is too late. My father's body hits the ground not a full second later. I collapse at his side. Jesus, there's so much blood.

I grab his face. I love this face. It's so damn strong and kind all at once. "Dad. Dad, talk to me."

"It takes more than bullets to kill me," the Piper calls from above.

I fumble for his pulse, but . . . but there's so much blood. My fingers slip and slide against his slick skin. "Dad. Brom. *Abraham*. Answer me."

Baba Yaga's shriek shatters every window.

"If you think I will show any mercy after what you have done to my family," the Piper says, "and to my people, I beg you to let go of such foolish hopes now. You wanted a reason for villainy? *You've given me one.*"

Why does my dad feel so cold? Katrina always joked that Brom is a heater. It could be freezing outside and all she'd need was him and a blanket. "Dad. Please don't leave me. I need you. Victor needs you."

I can't. . .

Jim.

Katrina.

Grymsdyke.

Brom.

"Finn, I need you to move," Alice is saying. "Take your father and move. Find shelter on the other side of the room"

A storm of black and gray swirls by me, dripping blood and gore up the stairs.

"Dammit, Finn!" Alice grabs hold of my shoulder. "I know it is difficult, but you must move now. Take your father over to the other side of the room. *Now.*"

Katrina and Brom read to each other at the breakfast table. Victor thought it was weird, preferring to eat in silence. I loved listening to them, though, loved how they were genuinely interested in what the other had to say.

I hook my arms under his and pull.

The last time we all ate breakfast together was a few mornings before she went to visit Opa. Mary joined us that day, which was nice because it meant Victor wouldn't be so snarky to our parents. When Mary was around, she stole all the sarcasm, leaving none for anyone else. Katrina found an article about a couple that died in bed together, on the same day. She'd found it romantic. My father was noncommittal. The rest of us thought it morbid.

"To be with the one you love when you die?" Katrina said. "To not be alone when you enter the unknown? What a gift."

She had *died alone, away from my father, away from Victor and me. I don't know if she was with Opa or not. I like to think she had*

335

been.

"You're not going to die here," I tell my father. "This isn't the end of your story. This isn't how Brom Bones goes out. You're the fucking Headless Horseman. You go out in a blaze of glory. This isn't—"

Bücherei explodes around us.

THE DEBT

ALICE

BEFORE I AM ABLE to even open my eyes, sharp pain, the sharpest, cruelest kind I have never felt until this moment, wicks the air cleanly from my lungs. And then, when I manage a breath, I am seized by a coughing fit. Blurry, blackened dust and ash sparkle around me—and if it were not accompanied by rubble and destruction, it would be beautiful. But the remnants of Bücherei replace what was once a splendid space, revealing chaos amongst former grandeur.

I am on my stomach, my hips and legs beneath a large chunk of broken fresco which, only minutes prior, hung above me. Pain does not radiate from my lower half, though; in fact, I cannot feel anything below my waist—not from what must surely be broken bones and numerous cuts, nor the weight of the plaster and stone. No, what pierces each breath originates where my crown once sat.

I reach up and gently prod what is left of my matted, mutilated hair. When I pull away a shaking hand, it is painted with sticky crimson.

Blinking does little to clear my field of vision. Bücherei, or what is left of it, is dark, dark as the swath of clouded night sky visible overhead.

Is it finished? Is the Piper dead?

I cannot see him to know if the risks I just took are worth it.

"Finn?" Dust and stone have weakened my voice. "Finn?" Several seconds that last more than the span between birthdays stretch forth. My heart pounds frantically. "Finn?"

"Here." His sweet confirmation is too hushed for my liking, too faint. Too much like it hurts to speak. "What happened?"

The compulsion to break down nearly mummifies me. I am not so fanciful to assume I am all right. That much is obvious. I cannot feel my legs; there is too much blood seeping on the floor around me, soaking my dress. What nearly shatters my composure, though, is the stark terror that he is the same or worse off. "Where are you? I cannot—" Another glance is stolen, craning my neck as much as my pinned body will allow. Greedy pain suctions my strength away as black spots dash across my eyes. "Did you find a space place for you and Van Brunt?"

At least, I think I say these things, but goodness, are words hard to get out.

"Think I'm . . . behind you, maybe."

My chin scrapes against jagged bits of stone as I shift my head to the other side. The glowing eyes of mysterious beasts hidden by bushes and caves stare back at me. I cannot twist my neck enough to ascertain how massive this piece of the ceiling is, but it stretches into the darkness far enough that it might as well be a wall.

"Marianne gave me a small bomb as a last resort. It was in my bag. The situation rapidly descended into such a state. How do you fare?" I ask, I beg, I fear, I hope.

Too much time lapses. Madness whispers in my ear. I keep my focus on the chipped, ruined paintings before me. Dimmed eyes judge me for my failures. Dark waves and bits of caves beckon me to let go and accept the hand I've been dealt.

He answers me, and, as if on cue, raindrops splatter across my face. He says, "Can you see the Piper? Is he . . . finally taken care of?"

I choke back a sob. Well, then. Finn is likely as injured as I am, but refuses to disclose it just as I did.

I tell him, "I do not know."

The roar of cannons briefly lights up the sky above us. We have broken through the mountain, into the clean space of Wonderlandian air. Our friends, our colleagues and loved ones, are still combating the hordes of Chosen beyond these battered walls. No one will come for us, not any time soon, at least. And even if they did, would there be anything left to save? No healing spray can tend these injuries.

"I love you," Finn says. "I will always love you. I'm here with you, Alice. I'm with you until the end, and then beyond."

My lips press together. My eyes seal closed. My heart bleeds just as surely as any Wonderlanders. I reach out, fumbling for the wall, desperate for a connection we are unfairly denied as we undoubtedly drift closer to our last sleep, our final goodbyes.

Oh, how I despise goodbyes—and this, the worst one of all.

I find a crack, though. And in that crack, I find his hand. He searched for me, too. "You have my heart, my loyalty, my trust, and my hopes and dreams. You are and always will be my north star, Huckleberry Finn Van Brunt."

One always imagines embracing death gracefully, as if it were an old friend, ready to lead you home. It might be on a field of battle, pride and honor carrying last thoughts. It might be in bed, a gentle farewell after the width and breadth of a life lived. It might be suddenly, tragically, inexplicably, too quick for any proper reaction.

I never considered that I would cry as my life ebbed violently from my body—not so much for my own loss, but for that of a bright future with a loving man cut short, and for the same man who reminded me, in so many strong, wonderful ways, that life and purpose could go on, even when sometimes it felt too hard to believe in such hope. For the uncertainty over whether or not my actions tonight and over the last year have ensured that all Timelines are now safe from the Piper and his quest to reshape the worlds to meet his vision. For leaving Wonderland behind once more—this time, more permanently than ever before.

And yet, here I am, tears mixing freely with dust, dirt, and rain. I am ready to pay the price for what is right. I have always been ready to do so.

I just never imagined that those I love would also pay such a steep cost.

My fingers, my palm, press against the chipping paint and plaster. If only I could hold Finn this one last time, if only I could assure myself that there wasn't something more I could do for him, to save him, to save all of those fighting outside, those living blissfully unaware in their Timelines, those suffering here in Wonderland from the Queen of Hearts' wrath.

Save him. Save them. Save them all.

A conversation several days old scratches its way forward, of when Van Brunt begged the Librarian to save Finn and Victor, but she refused, unwilling to allow the grieving father to assume any debt toward such a feat. That was when she was merely another agent within the Society, the so-called heart, as she once dubbed herself, of its inner workings. But she is more than that, is she not? She is Baba Yaga, a great witch capable of both terrible and wondrous magic. She vanquished the thirteenth Wise Woman.

Could she. . .?

My inhalation is sharp and shuddery, and yet the strength I was so recently lamenting steels what's left of my shattered body. I whisper, I call for Baba Yaga.

Only a second, perhaps two pass before the rustling of fabric draws my attention. Dirt and rocks scrape the already bleeding cut on my chin as I angle my head toward where a staircase once spiraled upward. Inky darkness hides the source of the sound, and it isn't until more cannon blasts briefly illuminate the sky do I see what appears to be an old woman hunched over a body on the second-story landing. But then the skies fade black once more, and I am left wondering if my mind is playing tricks on me, if I am only seeing what I wish to be there.

I have nothing to lose, though. I lick my filthy lips and hoarsely ask if whoever is present to make herself known.

The rustling of cloth and the scratching of sharp pebbles against tile mix with Finn's weak query of whom I am talking to.

"You beckoned me, did you not?"

It is not the voice that shook the skies during the battle between Baba Yaga and the thirteenth Wise Woman. Instead, it is familiar, irritating, and oh-so-welcome all at once.

It is the Librarian's voice.

The strength of my emotions hitches in my chest. I tell her, "You are late."

Her laugh is melodious. "It is a good thing I like you, Alice Liddell. Did I ever tell you that you remind me of my goddaughter? Her name was Vasilisa. She had a sweeter temperament than you, though."

Small bits of stone dig into my cheek. "Is—is that the Piper you were examining?"

"Yes." More rustling. "He still lives. He is unconscious. This one is tricky. His soul does not want to let go."

Son of a Jabberwocky.

Somewhere behind me, Finn swears softly.

"If he succumbs," the Librarian—Baba Yaga—says, "it will mean nothing. The Codex remains, and with the Piper's additions, the convergence will see to their permanence."

The Codex. Where is the infernal book?

"Both of your times are short," the witch murmurs. "Too short. The battle beyond these shattered walls is not going the way we hoped. The Chosen have many tricks up their sleeves. Too many have fallen. Too many are corrupted. Our friends are falling. Soon, none will stand."

It is not the weight of stone that silences both Finn and me. I close my eyes, unable to control the onslaught of emotions threatening to drown me.

We failed.

Words thick and broken all at once, I throw every last bit of my strength into one last hand of cards. "I will pay any price required to ensure this is not the end of the worlds' stories."

The pressure of his fingers on mine breaks pieces of my heart away. "Alice, no."

"Any price?" Amusement drips from Baba Yaga's query.

I do not hesitate. "Yes."

Winds whip up, scattering dust and rubble to shred exposed skin. And then a light appears next to Baba Yaga, courtesy of a glowing skull resting in a disembodied hand. Another blazing skull and hand materialize, and then another to make three in all. On the outskirts of the golden ring thrown off by the skulls, three dark figures appear, forming a semi-circle. I cannot see their faces, nor anything other than shades of white, red, and black coloring their long coats.

Baba Yaga's skin is a map of time, her spine curled from years and toil. She holds a mortar and a pestle, and she is fearsome to behold.

"Alice . . . What—" A coughing fit envelopes Finn. "What is going on? What are the lights?"

"Rest, Finn. Conserve what little of your strength remains. Pray, if you must. Hold tight to your father, for he was a good man. The best of men. He was my friend. I owe him—and your mother—much." Baba Yaga crouches next to the Piper's prone body once more. "We women have work to do."

A shiver runs down what little of my freezing spine I can still feel.

One of the hands floats closer, depositing a skull near where I lay. Flames burn from the eye sockets and the open maw of bone and teeth. Before a breath is fully inhaled, it returns to where Baba Yaga looms over the Piper's body, its fingers yanking on the fiend's hair until his head lifts.

Eyes creak open; when the Piper gasps, blood bubbles from his lips. Baba Yaga dips her pestle in the fresh red like she was readying to paint a picture rather than work magic—providing, of course, that is what she is doing.

"Couldn't have you sleeping the whole time, could we?" Baba Yaga asks, seeming as though she's inquiring merely about the weather and nothing more.

He licks his lips, eyes glittering like hard sapphires in the skulls' lights. When he speaks, his physical pain is evident. "Erasing your worlds will be too merciful for you."

Another skull is placed upon the ground, and that particular disembodied hand smacks across his face so hard that it echoes throughout the chamber.

"What was that?" Finn inquires slowly.

Just desserts, I think.

Baba Yaga runs her wet pestle alongside the rim of her mortar. "You never did take to instructions well, did you, Finn? Rest. That's an order."

He says, "But—"

I squeeze his fingers, and he quiets.

She throws me a familiar, sly smile, and it is jarring, finding it upon such a wrinkled, cruel-looking face. "It is a good thing I like him so much, too." She pauses. "Are you sure this is what you want, Alice? Are you sure you are ready to pay the steepest of all of the prices you've ever been asked for?"

A fat raindrop splatters right into the eye facing the sky. I blink rapidly as her image wavers before me. "If it means the—" It is my turn to fall prey to a coughing fit. My ribs protest, jabbing cruelly into my fragile lungs. *I do not have much time.* "If the safety of the Timelines . . . of Wonderland . . . of—of Finn, my loved ones are assured. . ." *Jace.* Another small round of coughs saps even more of the little amount of strength I have. "I will pay any price you demand."

From behind me, "No—let me. I'll pay it. Alice—" But speaking is too difficult for Finn, too, as a sharp groan dissolves away his efforts.

I wish I could see him. Hold more than his fingers this one last time.

"You think you can undo what I have done? I am the master of life and death, not you!" the Piper snarls, but one of the hands clamps over his mouth.

Baba Yaga's hard eyes press me even further against the broken floor. "I will not ask again. There will be no turning back."

I offer as cool of a smile I can muster. "Then don't ask."

Baba Yaga straightens as much as her curved, ancient spine allows and trundles down to where I lie pinned. As she crouches, she snaps, "Bring me the Codex."

The Piper mumbles from beneath the disembodied hand, his chin unnaturally high from his hair nearly being pulled out.

The third hand deposits its skull close to Baba Yaga and then disappears. She settles next to me, her joints creaking loudly. "This body," she sighs, "was never my favorite."

And then, she is beautiful once more, her hair luxurious and black, her skin unmarked by time.

I ask, "Why Indian? Why not Russian?"

"A long time ago," she taps the pestle against the mortar, "I knew a woman. She was a good ally. I wear this face in her honor." She pulls a beautiful veil out from behind her. "This is for another ally. I do not let those I trust down, Alice."

Raindrops blur my vision. "Why did you set aside your magic?"

"I came to realize that sometimes it is better to safeguard than destroy. I don't think everyone learned that lessen yet. Magic is like a drug, Alice. The more you use it, the more you want to. It was best to leave it behind in order to serve the Society." She taps the pestle against the bowl. "What do you know of the Codex, Alice?"

Is she funning me? Her knowledge of the text and mine are the same. After all, we journeyed together toward the discovery. And surely she is aware of the effort it takes for me to speak as the blood pooling beneath me enlarges. She cannot expect me to merely mimic back what she already knows. But as I lift my eyes from the mortar and pestle in her bony hands, I find somber expectation reinforcing her worn face.

My answer is slow, painful, each syllable the equivalent of a day's worth of fighting on the battlefield. "It names the first story, and of the stories to come and go since. It is a bibliography of Timelines."

She continues to absently tap the pestle against the stone mortar. "What else?"

What else is there? "Magic imbues it."

She leans closer. "What else?"

344

Rivulets of dirty water trace down my nose, dripping onto the ground. What more does she wish to know? I cannot personally read the infernal text, but from what others have said. . .

My wet lashes blur my vision. "It can be altered. Or edited. The Piper . . . he wrote in it." Puzzle pieces fall before me. "His writing must be different than the rest. Hearts said no one else had written in it."

Baba Yaga's thin lips curve upward, but there is no kindness, no pride to be found—only savagery.

I mentally shove the pieces together. "His entries are not natural, not to the Codex."

She taps her nose.

"His entries," I murmur slowly as the pieces finally match and form a picture, "should not count. He wanted to change what he should have no right over. All because he could. There was no true reason, no good logic behind his actions."

As if on cue, the third disembodied hand materializes, the Codex clutched between its fingers. I have no idea where it came from. Baba Yaga takes the tome from the hand and sets it directly before my face. And then she stills, glittering, hard eyes focused uncomfortably on mine.

The Piper's entries should not exist, but they do. He wrote within the Codex, even though not a single other creature has ever done so before him. He defaced the pages with his wishes, his distorted belief in what the world ought to resemble.

He played God, judge, and jury. He took it upon himself to write endings he had no right to. He was the ultimate critic, the final author.

I do not know who owns the book, or who started it. It could have been Sara's Darkness—but I know it should not have been the Piper's.

I fumble for the book, flipping the cover open. As before, the papyrus-like pages remain empty to me, their secrets locked away.

It was meant to be this way, wasn't it? The Codex was never meant to be read, let alone edited. If what he told his followers was true, it serves only as a record of the worlds' stories and lives. Records are impartial. They offer information, nothing else. Had the Piper and the thirteenth Wise Woman not found the Codex, nor found the magic necessary to illuminate its entries, it would continue to serve such a function. But they did find it, and they and the Chosen are able to read what ought to be hidden, what ought to remain lost to the power hungry.

I stare at the blank pages inches away from my face, considering these facts.

"What would happen," I ask slowly, "if one was to tear out the pages the Piper added. If we did so before the planets complete their alignment?"

Frantic, muffled anger surfaces across the hall. I ignore it, maintaining my focus on the witch before me.

"I honestly do not know," she says. "But a logical guess says what was written upon them would no longer be part of the Codex, wouldn't it?"

To continue that line of thinking, it might also mean that whatever changes he brought about would disappear, as if they never occurred in the first place. His legacy would be erased. All the Timelines he destroyed would be whole once more. All of the destruction, all of the deaths, all of the horror *gone*.

Wiped clean from the record, including the day's events.

According to the Collectors' Society, the Piper and the thirteenth Wise Woman began destroying catalysts several years ago. One could assume that they were in possession of the Codex for either months to a year or so before that—or possibly longer. To know for sure would be to find the first page that bears his handwriting. In order to do that. . .

I would need to be Chosen, or develop the ability to fall into rapture.

I do not have the time to do so, though. The transitional spell requires a full day to complete, and I have, at the most, hours, if not minutes.

How, then, if—

Victor.

Victor possessed a piece of one of the Chosen, did he not? *The creature's eye.* The part that was always Victor Frankenstein Van Brunt remained so, even as it struggled to fight off that already tainted. The eye no longer remains, not after Antarctica, but for the time it was with him, he fell in and out of rapture.

Which means he would have been able to see the words within the Codex.

Can I ask for such a thing? Dare I? Does Baba Yaga even have the magic necessary to complete such a feat?

I ask, "Are you able to tear the pages out?"

There is not even a hint of a sly smile when she shakes her head. "Why?"

"I am no hero."

She is no villain, either. Of that, I am sure. Or rather, she is both benefactress and punisher, complicit upon intent, her own history filled with deeds on both sides of the spectrum.

"What is it you wish from me?" Baba Yaga prods after a drawn-out lapse falls between us.

Swallowing is painful. My choice is not. My price, my debt, comes at losing part of myself, even as I drift toward death. "I ask for you to switch one of my eyes for one of the Piper's."

"Alice, no—you can't—" Finn calls out before a coughing fit shatters his latest protestations.

Baba Yaga's pestle changes then, elongating, its edges uneven in serration. One of the disembodied hands grabs my chin, steadying my head. Another, the one muffling the Piper, appears and wrenches open the eye that faces upward.

Finn calls my name, and the sound of it, of his dear voice, solid-ifies my resolve. So does the Piper's loudly voiced fury and threats.

I tell Baba Yaga, "The Piper and the Chosen will not write our endings. Not today. Not ever. Not as long as I can do something about it."

Her beak-like nose fills my peripheral vision. "This will be extremely painful."

I never thought it wouldn't.

She is not kind when she shoves the pestle-blade between my eye and socket, nor is she gentle as she digs out my eyeball. I scream, the agony more piercing than her pestle-blade. I may not feel the destruction of my legs, but this consumes every last working nerve ending in my body. Blackness swamps me, and I am unsure if it comes from the lack of vision or from teetering on the edge of unconsciousness.

My cheek hits the ground once more as the hands disappear. I yearn to cry. I fear I do. Can tears fall from a bloody, empty socket?

Finn continues to call my name, but I cannot answer. I cannot do anything but lay in the rubble and dust and dirt, bleeding from far too many places. I am dizzy, I am scared. And yet, all at the same time, I am entirely resolute.

Another scream rips through the air, one crafted from deranged rage. More threats pour out of the Piper just as surely as blood, but I cannot see him. All I can see is a slice of the Codex, and even that is blurred.

I do not know how long it takes before the witch returns by my side. All three hands hold on to my head, my body. I ask thickly, "What—" but Baba Yaga wastes no time in explanations. She shoves what I assume to be the Piper's stolen eyeball into my bleeding, empty, damaged socket, and I lose my breath.

She chants in Russian. What she says, I do not understand. Lightning sears through my blood, through the broken bones that try to hold me together. Darkness beckons, but I do not allow myself to succumb. Not yet.

She taps the mortar against my eye, and all of that blood of the Piper's she put in it earlier drips down upon my face. Just as quickly, she removes the stone bowl.

I blink.

I blink.

I see.

The hands release me. Two lift the Codex so that my eye—*the Piper's eye*—can take in full pages. I want to laugh, hysterically even, as golden, glittering text fills my field of vision. Slowly, upon my request, the third hand flips through the pages, one by one. Although I cannot read what is written, it is not difficult to recognize patterns and similarities between the entries. Everything is neat yet elegant.

Orderly.

But then it changes. The script, while still cultured in appearance, becomes familiar. It's High German, the old kind, the kind that both the Piper and the thirteenth Wise Woman would have spoken in their youths. I motion for the hand to continue flipping, so that I can be assured of each and every single page that bears his mark—and also so that I can determine that there are none from the Codex itself.

Something occurs to me. Something that cools my already chilling blood.

I whisper, "Does history repeat itself?"

Baba Yaga studies me for a long moment. "I do not know."

Selfish worries rear their ugly heads. If I tear out these pages, if they become nothing, if they no longer exist . . . what does that mean for the love and home I found with Finn Van Brunt? The Collectors' Society? Will the last year mean nothing? Will we find one another again? The idea of losing him and our love forever is unbearable, even if I never knew the difference once the slate was wiped clean. He is part of me. I am part of him. He is my north star.

We are binaries.

Everything we have gone through together, everything we mean to one another, has helped shape the woman I am today. To consider we may not be a second time around stills my resolve.

What if the Piper and the thirteenth Woman begin their reign of terror anew? What if we are meant to play this hideous game out time and time again?

As if he hears the worries that line the walls of my heart, Finn's fingers press against mine. His voice is softer, less robust. He is fading, just as I am. "Don't ever think there is a reality in which true love isn't real, in which we don't find one another, Alice. It couldn't happen, not even if a butterfly causes a hurricane."

I have no idea what that last part means, let alone how he knows what fears have stilled my hands. I glance over at Baba Yaga, who, in turn, continues to steadily stare at me.

I think of what Mother Holle told us not too long ago: *True love works in mysterious ways.* I choose to believe it, to hold steadfast in faith that it will win out—even if a tiny butterfly can somehow miraculously create a maelstrom.

I suck in a painful, sharp breath. Across the room, the Piper orders me to stop, to admit defeat, to know that what is done is done. He is a god. I am nothing. It's too late, that the convergence is here. I am not strong enough to be a master of life and death.

Although part of me, his part, wishes to obey, the other knows I am damn well strong enough to stand between him and his horrors.

I flip through the pages bearing his handwriting. Deliberately, unhurriedly, I began to tear the sheets out of the Codex. Ashes flutter about me—from the pages, from the sky, from Bücherei, from the books, from the lumps of stone pining me to the ground.

The whole world crumbles like sandcastles at high tide. Stars above melt. The moon peeking from behind dark clouds showers the sky as it transitions from ball to sands within an hourglass. The floor beneath me softens, and I wonder if it will support my weight just long enough to finish the task. Baba Yaga chants in Russian, waving her pestle over the Codex. I have no idea what she is saying, nor what she is doing, but I keep to the mission at hand. I hold on to Finn, to maintain the connection between us, even as all that is around us disappears into nothingness. I refuse to believe he is ash, too, or accept his grip has slackened.

Bits of ashes flake from Baba Yaga's face, fluttering in the wind. Her voice dims as colors bleed from her hair, from her skin and clothes. The pestle touches my forehead in benediction, then she throws open her arms and allows herself to disintegrate.

Before the last of the Pipers' pages is fully released from the Codex and the world, I say, "I love you, Finn Van Brunt. Come find and recruit me. I will be waiting for you."

One last tug, and the loose sheets soften to dust in my grip. And then there is nothing.

THE PLEASANCE ASYLUM

ALICE

T HE CEILING ABOVE ME is a mysterious map of cracks and chipped paint, nearly undecipherable in origins or destinations. Voids unsettle me, though, so night after night, as I stare up at it, tracing the moonbeams that flit in between hills and valleys, I assign them my own designations. There, that bump? It's Gibraltar. That chunk? The Himalayas. The deep groove near the Southeast corner of the room? The Great Wall of China. The smooth patch nearly dead center is the Pleasance Asylum, which is vastly amusing to me.

I shy away from the splattering of flakes in the Northwest quadrant, though. Those ones, whose ridges grow on nearly a daily basis, are far too easy to decipher. I made the mistake of telling Dr. Featheringstone this during a fit of delirium, and he's not forgotten it. In fact, he's asked me about them again, just now, and he's waiting patiently for my answer.

"They're flakes of paint," I tell him. "Created from age and lack of upkeep."

As he chuckles softly, the thick mustache that hides his lip twitches. "Always the literal one."

I keep my eyes on his face rather than in the area he's quizzing me about. It taunts me though, just over his left shoulder. "Why shouldn't I be? Word games are silly and are best left for children or the elderly who seek to hold on to their wit." The muscle inside my chest works in overtime as I tell him this. He's heard my ravings, and knows my struggles.

"And you are no longer a child?"

I lean back in the still wooden chair, delighting in how its discomfort bites into my bones. "I hardly think a woman of twenty-five is a child, Doctor."

In direct opposition to his faint yet genuine smile, pudgy fingers stroke his bushy mustache downward. "Many ladies of your standing are long married with family."

Hey says many when he means *most*. I smooth the stubborn wrinkles on my gray skirt. "It's a little hard to meet prospective suitors in. . ." I glance around the room, eyes careful not to settle too long above his head. "A fine establishment such as yours."

Neither of us mention where'd I'd been before here, or what I'd seen and done and experienced.

Another chuckle rumbles out of him. "Too true, dear. But you will not be at the Pleasance much longer. What then?"

My fingers knot tightly together in my lap. "I imagine I will be sent to rusticate at our family's summer house near the seaside. Perhaps I will find a nice stableboy to court me, and by the ripe age of twenty-six, we will be living out our bliss amongst seashells, ponies, and hay."

Featheringstone sighs, his face transforming into a look I could sketch from memory, it's given so often to me when I offer up an answer he doesn't like. I call it Disappointed Featheringstone.

My eyes drift to the one window in the room. "I am still not positive my release is the wisest course of action."

"You've been here for over half a year," the doctor says. "Most people in your position would be clamoring to taste freedom."

A thin smile surfaces. That's the problem. I've had a taste of freedom, true freedom, and I'm loathe to accept anything other than such.

"You are in good health," he continues. "Your need for confinement is gone. Your nightmares have decreased significantly." His chair creaks beneath his significant girth as he leans forward. "It is time for you to resume your life, Alice. You cannot do that here at the asylum. You are, as you pointed out, twenty-five years old. You still have many years of experiences ahead of you."

I have many years of experiences behind me, too.

"Perhaps I ought to become a nurse," I muse, keeping the edge of my sarcasm soft enough to not wound. "What a story mine would be: patient to nurse, a grand example of life dedicated to the Pleasance."

"I think nursing school is a grand idea." His ruddy face alights. "There are several reputable ones in London you could attend."

It's my turn to give him a patented look, the one he affectionately calls Unamused Alice.

"Your father has sent word he will come to escort you home at the end of the week."

Unamused Alice transitions to Curmudgeonly Alice.

Featheringstone stands up, glancing up at my past before shuffling over to pat me on my shoulder. He is a nice man, whose intentions for his wards are sincere. It's for this I both appreciate and resent him. An old schoolmate of my father's, he was selected upon my return sorely for this purpose. Too many horror stories about hellish asylums and nefarious doctors rage about England, but my father knew his friend would treat me with kid gloves. While the Pleasance may be physically showing its age, it's amongst the most sought after when it comes to those in the upper class due to its gentle hand and discreet employees.

Sometimes I wish my father hadn't been so kind. It might have been easier had he thrown me into one of the hellholes, where I could have gotten lost amongst the insane.

Mandatory strolls are required of all patients at the Pleasance as, Dr. Featheringstone believes, "fresh air is the tonic to many ails." At first, I was resistant to such outings, preferring to stay in my snug room with the door closed, but after several tours with the good doctor and a team of nurses and orderlies, I determined he perhaps had a point. There is a nice pond that is home to a family of ducks, a small grove of trees, and a handful of boring, quiet gardens that house no red roses after the good doctor had requested them removed. Worn dirt paths lined with benches connect the Pleasance's outdoor pleasures, and one can experience everything in as little as a half hour. We patients are never left to our own devices during these Fresh Air Hours, though. Nurses and orderlies mingle amongst the residents, setting up tables for games of checkers, chess, or croquet, although I naturally recuse myself from such frivolity.

Half a year in, and I am still a stranger to most of the folk here. That was by my choice; many of the residents did their best to welcome me into the fold, but I was determined to keep my distance out of early fear of spies.

There is nowhere you could go in which we could not find you, little bird.

"A letter, my lady."

My head snaps up sharply to find one of the orderlies standing over me, an envelope in his hand. I eye the object warily; outside of my parents, whom I requested not to write to me during my stay, no one else of my acquaintance knows I'm here. "There is no need to be so formal with me. We are at an asylum after all."

I think his name is Edward, but it could easily be Edwin, too. Or perhaps even Edmund. A mere incline of the head is given, but I highly doubt my bitterly voiced suggestion means anything to him. The staff here is the epitome of propriety.

I don't want what he has to offer. "Toss it into the fire."

His smile is patient and kind, one borne of tempered familiarity. "Dr. Featheringstone has already previewed its contents." The open flap is jiggled. "Would you like me to open it as well?"

I sigh and set my sketch pad on the bench next to me. The ducklings in the distance scatter across the pond, leaving me without subject to capture. "Go ahead and read it aloud."

A slim piece of paper is extracted. Through the afternoon's golden sunlight, I can determine less than a quarter of the sheet is filled with thin, spidery calligraphy. *"Dear madam,"* E reads, modulating his voice so it sounds very dignified, indeed. *"It is my great hope that I may come and speak to you tomorrow afternoon about a matter of great importance. Yours sincerely, Abraham Van Brunt."*

"That's it?" I ask once the paper is refolded.

"Yes, my lady."

What a curious letter. "I am unacquainted with an Abraham Van Brunt," I tell the orderly. And then, as I reclaim my sketch pad, "I suppose Dr. Featheringstone has already sent off a missive telling him not to bother coming round."

Naturally, he does not know whether or not the doctor did just such a thing. "Would you like the letter, my lady?"

I'm already turning back toward the pond. "No. Please burn it."

The crunch of twigs informs me of his retreat, allowing me to reclaim my solitude. The ducks long gone, I spend my time perfecting the tufts of grass and reeds growing at water's edge on today's landscape.

Alice.

I focus harder, my charcoal furiously scraping across the paper until I remember I don't want to do anything furiously. Not any more, at least.

Alice.

I close my eyes, focusing on the red and orange kaleidoscopes that dance across my lids.

Alice?

The paper in my hand crumples as easily as my heart. I leave it behind on the bench when I make my way back inside, because I'm positive there was an H etched into it. And to think that Featheringstone is convinced I'm sane.

I haven't been sane in over six years.

POLITE SOCIETY

ALICE

"**T**RY TO KEEP AN open mind, hm?"

I'm sitting in Dr. Featheringstone's ode-to-wood office, my hands folded primly across my lap. "Do my parents know about this?"

The corners of his mustache twitch upward. "As you've pointed out numerous times in the past, Alice, you are not a child. There was no need to inform your father about this as he is not your legal guardian."

My smile is tight. "If that's the case, then I must insist you turn the gentleman away at the door. I simply do not have the inclination to entertain a visitor today."

The good doctor is undeterred. "Since arriving at the Pleasance, you have spent very little time conversing with anyone outside of myself and the staff."

I nod vigorously.

"But Alice, none of us live in a vacuum. Mr. Van Brunt's visit could be an excellent chance for you to practice your conversation skills."

"Do you find my ability to converse lacking, Doctor?"

He chuckles softly, no doubt remembering how I wasn't chatty with anyone, himself included, for the first month of my stay. To be fair, it was difficult to carry on an invigorating discussion when one is shaking so hard from withdrawals they fear they might shatter into thousands of painful pieces before a single word can be uttered. Plus, there was the tawdry truth of how once I did open up, I raved liked a lunatic about things no normal person could imagine being true.

"Certainly not," he says to me. "But as I must stay at the Pleasance and you must go forth into the world, it will do you good to practice on a somebody new."

"Then send in one of the orderlies. Or one of the nurses. I'll happily chat with a staff member."

One of his bushy, out-of-control eyebrows lifts high into his forehead.

"There are people out there who are quite content being solitary," I point out. "Who do not need to converse with anybody but themselves and their dogs."

He sets his pen down. "What about cats?"

Rigor mortis sets in ever so briefly at this question.

"Your father said you were quite fond of cats growing up. There was one in particular that you favored. Dinah, was it not?"

"I'm—" I have to clear my throat. "Lately, I wonder if perhaps I'm more of a dog person after all."

The mustache hides nothing. I'm patently aware of how the corners of his mouth turn downward. "Nonetheless, Alice, I'm afraid I must insist you allow an audience with Mr. Van Brunt."

Irritable Alice emerges. "Do you know this gentleman?"

"I do. He and I go way back."

"As far as you and my father?"

"Not that far." The frown gives way to another soft chuckle. "But far enough. He would not come here to talk to you if he did not have something important to say."

"How do you know it's him?" I ask. "How do you know the missive was not forged?"

Concern fills his dark eyes.

I push my advantage. He must be wondering if I've gone mad again. "What if it's one of the Courts? Or their assassins?"

Fingers tap against the felt mat guarding the top of the wooden desk as he studies me. Just as I feel victory is within my grasp, he says, "You will take the meeting, Alice. Hear Mr. Van Brunt out."

I slump back into the padded chair. I don't wear defeat well.

A new note arrives late into the night, accompanied by a carriage. My mother has taken ill. Dr. Featheringstone needs not to say it, but we both are aware Henry Liddell would not send for me if he did not believe his wife's situation serious.

An orderly packs my belongings whilst I ready myself to re-enter English society—not as a queen, but merely as Alice.

Do I even know who that woman is any longer? My stay at the Pleasance has not brought me any closer to her. Rather, I am someone in between, someone lost without a purpose.

When I arrive in London, I am too late to bid my mother farewell. Setting aside my own grief and losses cultivated over the last year of life, I insert myself as the lady of my father's house as he succumbs to his sorrow. Filial duty accepts no other response. There is no talk of my recent stay at the Pleasance. If the servants know of my history, they do not dare mention it in my presence. There is no discussion of my six-year absence. My reappearance draws no outward suspicion from the staff, although it does raise some discreet eyebrows from society.

I care not a whit. My focus remains on the task at hand. I am the one who takes charge of ensuring my mother is laid to rest in her favorite gown, and that her hair is immaculate. I am the one to oversee her memorial and to converse with our guests, as my father cannot be roused to do so. I handpick the flowers and arrange for payment of both headstone and burial plot. I do not wallow on Wonderland and what once was. There is precious little time to do so, and for that I am grateful. Even in the late of night, as sleep folds me in its arms, I fail to dream of all I have lost. In the weeks and then months that pass, I rule the household as I did my palace at Court, and soon, the Liddell homestead is in tiptop shape. When it is time for my father to return to work at University, and he cannot because grief refuses to leave him be, I am the one to arrange for an extended leave of absence.

When the weather warms, I arrange to close up the London residence. The greatest city in the Western world has nothing to offers us. We Liddells will make our way to our summer home on the Welsh coast.

As our carriage trundles westward toward Penmorfa, my father says to me, his voice as quiet as his zest for life, "You are a good girl, Alice, to care for your papa so."

Girl.

I am a woman of twenty-six. A displaced queen who once ruled a mighty land and fought bravely with a fierce sword. Now I am a nursemaid.

I kiss his cheek and pat his hand. I tuck a blanket around his lap.

We must take what life gives us, the Caterpillar once said. *And you, particularly, as a Queen, must take it and make it worthy of yourself.*

I sent word for staff to be hired and to clean and air the house out, as my mother's maid shared that it had been some time since anyone had used it last. The housekeeper did an excellent job, for everything is exactly as it ought to be.

I take my father's arm as our trunks are carried in. "Let us take a stroll down to the waterline." The air is soft and tangy, the roar of the waves pleasantly loud. My father walks slower than I remember, as if when my mother died, she took part of him with her. Or did he lose himself during my absence?

For weeks, our days replicate themselves at a steady, unvaried pace. We stroll the same paths, look at the same seashells. We read by the fireplace, we dine at the same table. The monotonous routine comforts him. I go to town while he dozes with his papers, inserting myself into society, all the while struggling to both fill the hollowness and combat the agitation threatening to shred my skin off all at once. I allow myself to cultivate a few new acquaintances. Although they term me dear friend, and agree to go to regular teas, I cannot find it within me to find the same empathy. I engage in small talk, and when ladies discuss advantageous marriages, I want to gouge my eyes out with the butter knives upon the table.

I fought in wars. I defended my peoples. I created schools of high learning. My lover was a king.

I remind myself: *This is what ladies do here.*

I even reluctantly allow a few men to call upon me, which inordinately pleases my father—or at least pleases him as much as one whose joy drained away can be. One man attempts to steal a kiss, and I punch him squarely in the nose.

He does not call on me again.

One afternoon, as my father naps, I hike up the hills behind the house, up to where the shrouded, sleepy hole a hypnotized White Rabbit crafted me lies. I do not wander too close. I am weak, after all. I am an addict not a year from her last hit. It was foolish of me to come to Wales, but I suppose I figured both my father and I needed comfort in days such as these.

I lower myself into the long, wavy grass and gaze at the rocks and hidden hole in the distance. My fingers curl tightly into fists, until my nails dig into my palms and draw blood. I do not cry, though. I cannot. Something within me is broken.

Is this all there is to life?

The sun makes love to the horizon. I release my fingers and rise. It is time to ensure my father's dinner reaches the table.

On a perfectly ordinary afternoon, after arriving home from another dull tea and marriage talk, I find my father slumped in his favorite chair, a picture of my mother in one hand. The cook is in town, shopping. The gardener is outside tending his plants, as the sun is miraculously shining. It is the maid's day off.

I lower myself onto the bench before him, eyes dry yet stinging. My chest heaves. He does not appear to be in pain.

Only a broken heart, which is perhaps the worst pain of all.

What little purpose I had is now gone.

Bleakness unlike any I have ever known stretches out before me, vast and far as the eye can see. I pluck strands of my hair out, one at a time, until a soft pile grows in my lap.

When I am assured that my voice will not crack, I make my way outside and ask the gardener to fetch the town doctor. And then I head inside and begin a list of all of the things I must do in the coming days and weeks.

THE ASHBURY'S BALL

ALICE

PLEASE COME TONIGHT. *I have to see you.*

There is a plaintive whine, a desperation to Leopold's note, one increasingly all the more evident lately, even in written form. Despite the circumstances, it isn't attractive in the slightest.

Sometimes, I wonder if I left my physical heart in Wonderland alongside my crown.

I fold the unsigned note and tuck it into a desk drawer, massaging my forehead. I already planned on attending Lord and Lady Ashbury's ball tonight, although a lingering headache tempts me to send late regrets.

A knock on my door brings a maid bearing a bouquet of primroses. "These just arrived. They came with no note, Miss Alice, but aren't they pretty?" She fusses with the leaves after she situates the vase on a table.

She knows just as well as I do who sent the flowers. It isn't exactly the first time the Prince of England sent me a bouquet, and since his mother issued her stringent edict, his deliveries have doubled.

I thank Edwina, and she leaves. I stare at the flowers, simple flowers who have no faces or voices, and wonder why I cannot be bothered to feel anything other than mild pleasure or irritation toward them.

I tug a stem from the vase and rub the petals against my cheek. Against the pads of my fingers.

Feel something, dammit.

I toss the poesy into the wastebin.

I first met Leopold when I was collecting my father's personal items from his office at Oxford. The prince was finishing his education, and I suppose it was comforting to make the acquaintance of a learned man who did not care about trivial matters. Or, at least, in those early days, he did not portray himself in such a way. He was charming and intelligent, and I was egotistically blinded by his crown, assuming him an equal. Our conversations were political, not superficial. We argued good-naturedly for hours. We debated, and not once did we discuss advantageous marriages or horse racing. For months, we danced around the friendship we built, and for the first time since I returned from Wonderland, I almost felt as if I'd come close to finding a bit of myself.

Leopold took me for a boat ride on a cool yet sunny afternoon. Willow trees wept all around us. He kissed me, oars still in hand. His lips were gentle against mine, smooth and closed. I felt nothing except mild pleasure, but I accepted it, because Leopold was a flash of light in the bleakness before me. Soon, he informed his mother he was in love with a commoner—at least to his knowledge—and his mother, the grand Queen Victoria, informed him he must discard me immediately.

At first, I bristled, incensed at her proclamation. She dare find me, the Queen of Diamonds, unfit for her son?

And then it came, slowly, then quickly, a dam crumbling beneath a torrent of a storm: I had been ready to settle. I, the Queen of Diamonds, who knew the strength and beauty of true love, almost settled with a man whom I shared no viable chemistry with. Someone who did not hold my heart, because I would never think to willingly give it to him.

Would I tear apart England to be with him?

I knew the answer. I did not even have to take time to consider it.

I will go to the ball tonight, to tell him in person that his mother is right. He deserves his happy ending. My affections for him are true enough for those wishes.

The crush of the crowd leaves beads of sweat tracing paths down my neck less than a quarter of an hour after arrival. Leopold has his spies looking for me, so the moment I'm spotted, I am escorted to a private balcony upstairs.

He is quite handsome tonight, fashionable and the epitome of every English lady's dream. I curtsy; the moment the door shuts behind the servant who showed me the way, Leopold rushes over to take hold of my hands. "Sweet, lovely Alice. You are a divine sight tonight. I was worried you might not show." The prince presses several kisses upon the palms of my hands, an action that would send most ladies downstairs swooning straight to the ground.

My spine, instead, stiffens in resolve. "Leo, we must talk."

Another kiss is offered, against the inside of a wrist. Surely another swoon-worthy moment for any other woman. He deserves better than me, better than a woman whose heart and purpose were carved out by a prophecy.

"I truly feel that if Mother meets you, she will change her mind."

I squeeze his hands and then gently extract myself. I step away, steeling myself against the confusion and hurt before me. "Her Majesty desires the best for you, for England."

Betrayal adds to the mix of his messy emotions. "I should know my own heart!"

As do I. Part of me wants to tell him my story, explain how it is I came to be this person. Part of me will miss this prince. While I know he is not my match, that we are not meant to be, he is a soul that I like very much.

I *will* miss him. At times, I believe I will miss him quite keenly.

I tell him a lesson I have learned most painfully. "As a royal, sometimes you must put crown above heart."

Leo gapes, outrage staining the pale skin peeking from his collar. "I am willing to break with the crown for you. With the queen."

I tell him calmly, "I refuse to allow you to do that."

If he believes he can intimidate me into changing my mind by staring at me the way he is, sizzling me with an intensity I have never seen from him before, he is sorely mistaken. I have faced more belligerent monarchs than him before. I have sacrificed greater.

I will not settle. I am worth more than that.

I close the space between us, reaching up to touch his smooth cheek. I press a kiss against it, inhaling the musky smell of his expensive cologne. No Bread-and-butter-flies search for flowers within my chest. No tears spill down my cheeks. I do not even wish to pull my hair out. "I will always think of you with great fondness, Leo. I hope you will do the same for me."

He whispers, "I love you, Alice. This cannot be how our story ends."

I walk through the doors and back down the stairs.

I do not leave the ball. I do, however, find a waiter with champagne and have myself a glass. And then I allow myself to be pulled into several conversations by several nitwits who discuss their marriage prospects and carefully avoid asking about mine, long accepting I am unavoidably now a spinster, or better yet, as the gossip mill is churning, soon to be Prince Leopold's mistress. Painfully polite gentlemen request to dance with me, and each time I am on the dance floor, I can feel the weight of Leo's eyes.

It is better this way.

My head pounds. The volume in the room is deafening. I escape to the dessert table in search of sweets and possibly punch, and while there, I map out exit routes. Just as I am reaching for a crème puff, someone knocks into me, tipping my plate to the ground.

"My sincerest apologies," a rich, warm voice says as a tawny-haired gentleman bends to clean up the fallen food.

"You need not do that," I tell him at the same moment a waiter rushes forward to assume the job.

The gentleman straightens, his cheeks flushed just the slightest. And . . . frabjous. I am certain my own have pinked just a teeny bit, because heavens, is the man before me handsome. Tall and sandy-haired, eyes an alluring shade somewhere between blue and gray, he smiles at me winsomely yet ruefully all at once. "I've never been to a ball so crowded." He holds up his hands. "That's no excuse, though. You have my sincerest apologies for knocking into you, Miss. . .?"

"Liddell." I offer a cool smile, even though my pulse skips a beat. "Miss Alice Liddell."

If I am not mistaken, the corners of his mouth lift a bit higher. "Miss Liddell, I am delighted to make your acquaintance, even if it is under such poor circumstances. My name is Finn Van Brunt."

Finn. I like the name.

He bows; I curtsy. I ask, reluctant to move away yet, "You are American?"

He leads us to the side of the table, away from the guests desperate for Lady Ashbury's decadent crème puffs. "I am. Is it that obvious?"

It is, although I do not tell him this. "Which part are you from, if I may be so bold to ask?"

"Originally Missouri, but I live in New York now."

I use the moment to peruse him. His suit is impeccable—dark and tailored, not as flashy as so many of the other gentlemen's. His collar is snowy white. He doesn't stand rigidly, not the way Society dictates. Everything about him is done so assuredly, as if he knows himself and is comfortable with that person.

I am envious and intrigued all at once.

"And now you are in London," I muse lightly, curiosity burning throughout my veins like a wildfire throughout the Dark Meadows during summer, "attending the Ashbury's ball."

"I'm in town for business," he confirms, his blue-gray eyes holding me to where I stand. A moment passes, but then he leans in and says quietly, almost naughtily, "May I tell you a secret?"

I ought to place a proper amount of space between us, but goodness, does this gentleman smell frabjous. Is that mint? "Is it scandalous or worthy?"

He accepts a drink from a passing waiter; I do the same. I ignore inquisitive eyes discreetly studying us from all around the room. *The Ice Queen and the American Stranger.* "Earlier today, I very nearly went home when my partner left. You see, work wasn't going the way we'd wanted. This particular assignment has been been. . ." He presses his lips together, amused. "Let's just say it's been a hell of job that's really tested my patience for several years."

I say mildly, "Mr. Van Brunt, I am terribly scandalized at your use of profanity in polite society."

He sips his champagne slowly, eyes never leaving mine. "Should I stop telling my secret?"

"Oh no." I, too, take a sip. "If you do, I might be forced to do something drastic. Perhaps the vapors might take hold. And then you will feel obliged to finish, your guilt will be so heavy."

He laughs then, and it is so lovely that I cannot help but to wish to laugh, too. Really laugh, in just such a way I have not done in too long.

"You don't look like the sort of lady who partakes in the vapors."

"You are right. Nevertheless, you must continue."

He nods, and takes another sip of his champagne. "My partner wanted to head home. But I had a feeling that despite all of my . . . challenges over the last few years, this day was different. So I came here, to this ball."

As he finishes his drink, I murmur, "That is a terrible story, with an unsatisfying end. You would be a wretched author."

This, too, amuses him. And his mirth, I realize, makes him . . . attractive.

I am stunned.

"Would you dance with me, Miss Liddell?"

I am ashamed to admit that no answer emerges.

"I promise you that, while I am an American, my mother did her best to make sure I'm not an embarrassment on the dance floor."

I fight for words. For clarity. The Bread-and-butter-flies found their flowers after all. "Oh, she has, has she?"

I am attracted to someone. Me. I am attracted to a stranger. Well over a year after I was exiled from Wonderland, and I meet an American of all people at the Ashbury's ball.

"She loves to dance, and throws parties all the time," he's saying. "My brother and I took dance lessons for years." He holds out a hand. Not an arm, but a hand.

And still, I hesitate.

My heart is in Wonderland, isn't it? I left it with my crown.

"While we dance," he says, his voice lowering, eyes still holding mine, "I'll tell you a better story. One I think you will like." The hand stretches closer, alluring. "Are you ready for an adventure, Alice?"

My heart skips as I stare into those blue-gray eyes.

I take hold of his hand.

EPILOGUE

FINN

"**N**O, NO. NOT LIKE that." I set the bucket down and stand behind Alice. I reach up and grab one of the apples clustered on the low-hanging branch. "You twist and then pull. You never just try to yank it off the tree."

She leans back against me, smelling like apple blossoms even though they're long gone. It's a gorgeous fall day. The air is crisp, with just a hint of fog rolling through Opa's apple grove. New York in the fall, no matter what Timeline or century, is incomparable.

"Like this?" She twists and tugs an apple, and it gives way with no resistance.

I kiss the base of her throat. "Exactly."

She drops the fruit into the bucket and turns around, her arms curving around me. Her lips brush across mine, and my pulse jumps.

Two years after our first meeting, and each touch, each day, feels just as intense as the very beginning. "Remind me how long we can stay? Please say forever. At least for right now, in this moment, say forever."

After the last year's heavy rotation of catalyst collections, we are more than due for a vacation. Even now, even though she's obviously blissful at my Opa's farm, I wish it could be somewhere else, somewhere where it's just the two of us. But my mother wouldn't take no for an answer. She patted my cheek, like I was sixteen rather than nearly thirty, and said, "Your grandfather's birthday is a family tradition, Finn. We spend it in Sleepy Hollow."

I kiss Alice as leaves float on the gentle, perfumed breeze around us. I whisper against her mouth, "We can stay forever."

She touches my cheek, her lips lingering on the spot her fingers marked. "Now tell me what the Librarian gave you before we left the Institute."

I definitely can think of better things to discuss than work. "Details on our next assignment. Or at least, what she considered to be details. It's going to be . . . different."

Interest piqued, she pulls away and wraps her brown sweater tighter across her shoulders. Although she originally hails from Victorian England, it is always jarring to see her wearing anything other than Twenty-First-Century clothing. "How so?"

I collect our bucket and we stroll down the vast grove, back toward Baltus Van Tassel's house. "She wants us to find a book."

She tucks her arm in mine, her head resting on my shoulder. "Why is this *different?*"

How to explain? "The Librarian said our mark was a special book that would probably have empty pages. She doesn't even know what Timeline it'd be in, but it's critical we find it so it can be protected. What's really intriguing is that she added it would allow us to remember the past."

"Sounds like typical Librarian mumbo-jumbo mysticism."

I pause, wondering if I'll sound crazy with the next part. But I tell Alice anyway. "I get the impression she was referring to us specifically."

"You and I?"

I nod, our heads sliding comfortably together.

"I wasn't aware we've forgotten anything." She squeezes my arm. "Although, I must say, when we first met, it was as if I were coming home. It still feels that way, as if I've always known you. Perhaps we knew and loved one another in a past life. It would explain a lot of things."

"Like?"

She considers this. "Remember when you and Victor had too much to drink on that one mission, and you got the tattoo on your chest. I told you it was eerily, yet beautifully, familiar."

I chuckle. "To be fair, it's the Queen of Diamonds insignia, so I would think it'd be familiar."

She snorts. "Do you remember when we were on a mission, and we were sleeping beneath the stars? That was the first time we called one another north star—at the same time, to boot. That cannot be mere coincidence."

Okay, yes, that was a bit miraculous.

Alice hums. "I think I will help your mother make pies tonight."

I try, I really do, but a derisive laugh falls out of me anyway at her sudden change of topic. "Why would you do that to yourself?"

"It could be fun."

In the distance, Mary and Victor sneak out of the barn, brushing hay off their clothes. Katrina asked them to pick apples, too, but the barn proved too alluring.

I don't want a quickie with Alice in a barn. I plan on spending all night making love to my warrior queen.

"Fun for you is practicing with your daggers, not baking pies," I say. "Since when are you interested in the culinary arts?"

She hums serenely again. The sound is utterly addictive. "A lady can have many interests."

I kiss her forehead, wanting more than that but taking what I can get when I know we are needed back at the house. Supper must be close. "Bake away. Just don't kill my mom."

My brother and his lady love head back into the main house. Alice asks as she watches them, "Do you think he'll ever man up and put her out of her misery?"

"Look at you, using all that Twenty-First-Century slang."

She pats my arm. "My point remains. I adore Mary, but if I have to listen to the marriage spiel one more time, I may use my daggers on her. There is more to conversation than marriage prospects. Why do so many people fail to understand this?"

I know Victor loves Mary. She is the love of his life, just like Alice is mine. But he's got a lot of demons, and I don't know he can ever truly exorcise them, even for her.

"Forget about them," I say. "Let's focus on us."

She stops, arm still linked through mine.

I set the bucket down again. I'd been thinking about this for a long time. Two years, actually. I knew pretty quickly after we met I was in love with Alice Liddell. I'd searched for her for years, and when I finally found her . . . well, it was like she said. I had come home.

Two years prior to our first meeting, the Librarian explained she had a mission specifically for me. Her spiel concluded with, "The Wonderland stories are very popular, so it's important we collect the catalyst and preserve the Timeline."

There were hundreds, thousands of popular stories, all equally deserving protection. I'd heard of Alice in Wonderland—I mean, who hadn't? Disney made sure everyone did.

I'd said, "I've already got a pretty full schedule. Maybe you can give the assignment to someone else?"

She'd laughed as if I'd talked nonsense. "No, Finn. It has to be you. Find Alice Liddell. Don't give up until you do. She's the only one who can get us into Wonderland in order to collect its catalyst." Her smile was sly and knowing and unsettling all at once. "Offer her a position at the Society. She'll be a valuable addition to our organization."

At first, I hunted for Alice because I'd been assigned to find her. I thought it'd take a few months at the most. When more time ticked by, the search became a compulsion I couldn't let go of. I had to find her. I had to *know* her. I couldn't explain it better than that. I read her stories. I interviewed people she knew in England. She was a ghost, one Sara was tired of trying to find. "Why is this so important?" she'd complain. "There are lots of other Timelines we could be working with."

I would remind her the assignment was a directive straight from the Librarian, but it was more than that. Alice, herself, was more than that, even though I hadn't even laid eyes upon her.

The day of the Ashbury's ball in England a couple years ago, my former partner informed me she was done searching. I understood her frustration. I accepted her defeat. For one brief, dark moment, I contemplated giving up, too. But then I got a pain in my chest that doubled me over, struggling to find breath. Not three seconds later, a text appeared on my phone.

It was from the Librarian. *Don't you dare give up.*

I went to the ball.

The Alice Liddell I met was nothing like the books or the person anyone told me about. She was . . . *Alice*, which was infinitely better. She claims she felt like she'd always known me, but I felt that and more, and it wasn't because I'd researched the hell out of her. When I first laid eyes upon her, standing by the dessert table in a heartbreakingly gorgeous gown, my chest and torso burned again—not painfully, but in *pleasure*.

Helpless to do anything else, I was sucked into her orbit, my gravitational pull immediately tying itself to hers.

I asked her to join the Society. She travelled to New York with me that very night.

We took our time getting to know one another. She wasn't a cartoon character-- Alice revealed herself to be a kickass queen who didn't take shit from anyone. Her heart is a mile wide and fathomless, and if you earn her trust, she will go to the mat for you, no questions asked. Her past was rough, and when she let me in and told me about it, I saw her. I told her about my past, and she saw me.

She's more than my partner. I never believed in true love before Alice, but I do now.

Maybe she's on to something with the past life business. How else can I explain the depths of what I feel for her?

The sun is setting, orange and red watercolors staining the horizon to match the season. I ought to be nervous, my palms sweating at the very least. But I'm not.

I'm just sure.

I lay a hand against her cheek, and she leans into it. Golden strands break free of her bun and dance across her face.

She says, "Somebody ought to write a story about Alice Liddell and Huckleberry Finn falling in love and spending their lives together. It would be my favorite." She pauses. "It *is* my favorite, and will always remain so." She chuckles ruefully. "Dammit, Finn. We are speaking of marriage prospects. I do this willingly, only for you."

My strong queen, beating me to the punch.

Many minutes are spent kissing. Goddamn, can this woman kiss. It's dark when air becomes a necessity. Stars twinkle overhead. The Milky Way blazes a path across the sky. I tell her, "Let's write the story together."

She sighs contentedly and links her arm through mine again. "Poor Mary. Think she'll try to poison me for getting a Van Brunt brother to propose first?"

My laughter crystalizes in the dusk. "Technically, you proposed. But, probably." Chances are, Mary will shit a brick and never let my brother live it down, especially considering they've been together much longer than me and Alice.

"I wonder if we were married in our past lives."

"If we weren't at least together," I say, "I'd have been the biggest idiot."

She hums contentedly. "Your mother will be so pleased."

That's an understatement. She adores Alice. Feisty, strong-willed women are her cup of tea.

As if on cue, my parents are on the porch, their waving illuminated by the lights in the windows. "I want to bake pie," Katrina calls. "Hurry up with those apples!"

We resume our journey back to the house. "Now," the love of my life says, "tell me more about this book we are supposed to track down, the one that will tell us about our forgotten past. How can she expect us to do so, if she cannot supply a Timeline?"

"You know the Librarian—"

"She's a menace," Alice snaps. But there's no heat behind her words. Her head rests upon my shoulder once more. "You were saying? About the book? I'm intrigued."

"I'm not sure if it's a catalyst or not," I admit, "but she's put a priority on it being found. You and I are to dedicate as much time as it takes to find it."

"What if it takes a year?"

"Then it takes a year."

"Five years?"

I smile. "All the time we need."

"I find it difficult to believe that Van Brunt would agree to take his two best agents out of the field in order to search for a single book."

"You know," I say, as we reach the steps, "you can call him by his name. He's going to be your dad, too."

She kisses my cheek, aware of what I've just said and who I've just said it to. Katrina immediately barks, "What was that I just heard? Did—" My mother's face alights as she grabs hold of my father. "Oh, Finn. Alice!" She holds out her arms. "Welcome to the family."

I shake my father's hand. There's time to talk about mysterious books tomorrow.

A BIBLIOGRAPHY

Curious as to who was featured or mentioned within *The Lost Codex*? Here's a list of some of the people and the books they came from.

Abraham Van Brunt (AKA Brom Bones); Katrina (Van Tassel) Van Brunt
Featured in the short story *The Legend of Sleepy Hollow*, found within *The Sketch Book of Geoffrey Crayon, Gent.* by Washington Irving

Alice (Reeve) Liddel; Grymsdyke; the White King; the White Queen; the Mad Hatter; the Hare; the Caterpillar; the Cheshire-Cat; the Queen of Hearts; the King of Hearts; the Red Queen; the Red King; the Sheep; the Walrus; the Carpenter; the White Rabbit; the Duchess; the Jabberwocky; various other Wonderlandian animals & peoples
Both from and loosely based upon *Alice's Adventures in Wonderland* by Lewis Carroll
Through the Looking-Glass, and What Alice Found There by Lewis Carroll
The Hunting of the Snark by Lewis Carroll

Harry, the Wise Women; the Golden Goose; Grethel; Mr. Pfriem
Both from and loosely based upon characters found within fairy-tales in *Children's and Household Tales* by The Grimm Brothers, including:
The Blue Light
Clever Grethel
The Golden Goose
Lazy Henry
Little Briar-Rose (Sleeping Beauty)
Master Pfriem
Mother Holle
The Young Giant

C. Auguste Dupin

The Murders of the Rue Morgue by Edgar Allan Poe
The Mystery of Marie Rogêt by Edgar Allan Poe
The Purloined Letter by Edgar Allan Poe

Charlotte

The Sorrows of Young Werther by Johann Wolfgang von Goethe

Florent

The Belly of Paris by Émile Zola

Franklin Blake

The Moonstone by Wilkie Collins

Glinda

The Wonderful Wizard of Oz by L. Frank Baum
The Marvelous Land of Oz by L. Frank Baum
Ozma of Oz by L. Frank Baum
The Road to Oz by L. Frank Baum
The Emerald City of Oz by L. Frank Baum
Tik-Tok of Oz by L. Frank Baum
The Scarecrow of Oz by L. Frank Baum
Rinkitink of Oz by L. Frank Baum
The Lost Princess of Oz by L. Frank Baum
Glinda of Oz by L. Frank Baum
The Royal Book of Oz by L. Frank Baum

Gwendolyn Peterson (AKA Wendy Darling); Peter Pan

Based loosely upon *Peter and Wendy* by J. M. Barrie

Henry Fleming

Red Badge of Courage by Stephen Crane

Mr. Holgrave

House of the Seven Gables by Nathaniel Hawthorne

Huckleberry Finn; Jim
The Adventures of Tom Sawyer by Mark Twain
Adventures of Huckleberry Finn by Mark Twain
Tom Sawyer Abroad by Mark Twain
Tom Sawyer, Detective by Mark Twain

Jack Dawkins (AKA The Artful Dodger); Fagin
Oliver Twist by Charles Dickens

Josephine (Jo) Bhaer
Little Women by Louisa May Alcott
Little Men by Lousia May Alcott
Jo's Boys by Lousia May Alcott

Marianne (Dashwood) Brandon
Sense and Sensibility by Jane Austen

Mary Lennox
The Secret Garden by Frances Hodgson Burnett

The Pied Piper of Hamelin; various children
Featured in the fairy-tale *The Pied Piper of Hamelin*, found within *German Tales* by The Grimm Brothers

Professor Otto Lindenbrock
Journey to the Center of the Earth by Jules Verne

Sara (Crewe) Carrisford
Both from and loosely based upon *A Little Princess* by Frances Hodgson Burnett

Sweeney Patrick Todd; Rosemary Nellie Lovett
Based loosely upon *A String of Pearls: A Romance*, most likely written by James Malcolm Rymer and Thomas Peckett Prest

<u>Victor Frankenstein Jr.; Victor Frankenstein; the Creature</u>
Both from and based loosely upon *Frankenstein; or, The Modern Prometheus* by Mary Shelley

ACKNOWLEDGEMENTS

Those in the Society would argue with me saying this is the end of the story, because life goes on after the last sentence. However, I must thank all the people who helped make this journey with Alice and company possible. Suzie Townsend, your belief in this series (and me) has made all the difference. Sara Stricker, I truly appreciate all you've done for these books. To my editor Kristina Circelli, thank you for being with Alice and me every step of the way with these books. The Hatter sends his love. Victoria Alday, is there nothing you can't do? Hugs and love are sent your way for designing yet another masterpiece of a cover. Stacey Blake, formatting goddess, you always make my books so lovely. Appreciation goes out to my publicist Jessica Estep for getting the word out.

Evelyn Torres and Samantha Modi, you have been my rocks. I love you both. Thanks for keeping this gal sane and on track, as well for all your feedback. Cherisse Nadal, Ashley Bodette, Natalie Gisness, and Amber Shepherd, please know I am deeply grateful for the time, feedback, and love you gave to the earliest incarnations of this story.

To my wonderful peers Amy Bartol, Rachel Higginson, Shelly Crane, Daisy Prescott, Stacey Marie Brown, Chelsea Fine, and Andrea Johnston, I value your friendship and support so much. Dishing our craft together is one of my fave things to do.

To the fab members of the Lyons Pride, there are few words that can sum up what your support means to me. (in alphabetical order) Alexandra, Amber, Amy, Ana, Andi, Andrea, Ashley, Ashley, Autumn, Brandi, Camille, Candice, Candy, Cherisse, Christina Lynne, Courtney, Cynthia, Daniela, Debra, Eunice, Ivey, Jamie, Jenni, Jenn, Jessica, Jessica, JoAnna, Jodie, Jothee, Karen, Kate, Kathryn, Keleigh, Kelli, Kelly, Kerry, Kiana, Kiersten, Kristina, Lauren, Lindsey, Lissa, Maria, Meaghan, Megan, Meredith, Nicole, Nikka, Nina, Peggy, Rachel, Rebecca, Saman, Samantha, Sarah Jane, Shawna, Sheena, Shelbi,

Stephanie, Tracy, Tina Lynne, Tricia, Vilma, Whitney, Yael, and all the rest . . . you are all beyond fabulous. Cheers!

Jon, north star and binary of my very own, how could I write this without you in my corner, or as my sounding board? Thank you for all the glasses of wine, the meals, and the love you gave me while I was writing. Hugs and love go out to my sons for not only tolerating their mom being locked away writing so much, but for also listening to crazy plot points and encouraging me to go for them. I treasure your imaginations, boys. Don't ever let them disappear. To my parents and mother-in-law, to my friends and family who have supported me, you are greatly appreciated.

Finally, for everyone who has ever wondered what happens to characters after the last word, who has ever dreamed of a place like the Collectors' Society, I hope you have enjoyed this journey as much as I have writing it. Thank for coming along.

ALSO BY HEATHER LYONS

The ultimate, full-color guide to the Collectors' Society series . . .

". . . a fantastic in depth look inside the Society and agents that we've come to love."
-Amazon review

CLASSIFIED MATERIAL

If you are reading this dossier, you have been granted Level Three clearance within the Collectors' Society. Included in these pages are snippets from multiple key agent files as well as those on persons of interest. Please keep in mind that this compendium is considered highly sensitive and is illegal to share with anyone outside of your clearance. It is not to be removed from the Institute.

Happy reading!

-The Librarian

For those previously introduced to the mysterious Collectors' Society and their mission, eager to discover more, The Collectors' Society Encyclopedia is the perfect full-color companion piece to the series. Within are detailed entries elaborating upon the various agents and employees as well as the key villains suspected of targeting and destroying Timelines. Backstories, relationships, secrets, and clues are revealed alongside a thorough bibliography of important Timelines and their designations. Profiles are also included of the Institute in New York City as well as Wonderland. Society fans and lovers of classic literature will undoubtedly delight in unraveling the secrets that lay within these pages.

Enjoy the rest of the Collectors' Society series . . .

"Each of us here has a story, but it may not be the one you think you know . . ."

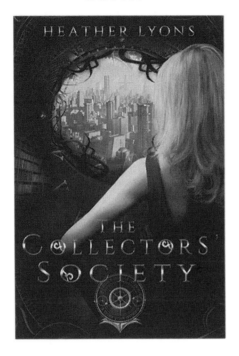

"The most unique, fascinating, wondrous book I've read in a very
long time!
I was glued to every page."
*-Shelly Crane, New York Times bestselling author of Significance and
Wide Awake*

*From the author of the Fate series and The Deep End of the Sea
comes a fantastical romantic adventure that has Alice tumbling down
the strangest rabbit hole yet.*

After years in Wonderland, Alice has returned to England as an adult,
desperate to reclaim sanity and control over her life. An enigmatic
gentleman with an intriguing job offer too tempting to resist changes
her plans for a calm existence, though. Soon, she's whisked to New

York and initiated into the Collectors' Society, a secret organization whose members confirm that famous stories are anything but straightforward and that what she knows about the world is only a fraction of the truth.

It's there she discovers villains are afoot—ones who want to shelve the lives of countless beings. Assigned to work with the mysterious and alluring Finn, Alice and the rest of the Collectors' Society race against a doomsday clock in order to prevent further destruction . . . but will they make it before all their endings are erased?

The series continues with . . .

"This is not a series for fantasy lovers or new adult lovers.
This is a series for all book lovers."
-Book Briefs

Sometimes, the rabbit hole is deeper than expected . . .

Alice Reeve and Finn Van Brunt have tumbled into a life of secrets.
Some secrets they share, such as their employment by the clandestine
organization known as The Collectors' Society. Other secrets they
carry within them, fighting to keep buried the things that could
change everything they think they know.

On the hunt for an elusive villain who is hell-bent on destroying
legacies, Alice, Finn, and the rest of the Society are desperate to
unravel the mysteries surrounding them. But the farther they spiral
down this rabbit hole, the deeper they fall into secrets that will test
their loyalties and pit them against enemies both new and old.

Secrets, they come to find, can reveal the deadliest of truths.

"If I could give a book a million golden stars, it would be this one."
-Typical Distractions

After years spent in Wonderland, Alice Reeve learned the impossible was quite possible after all. She thought she left such fantastical realities behind when she finally returned to England.

Now Alice has become a member of the clandestine Collectors' Society, and the impossible has found her again in the form of an elusive villain set on erasing entire worlds. As she and the rest of the Society race to bring this mysterious murderer to justice, the fight becomes painfully personal.

Lives are being lost. Loved ones are shattered or irrevocably altered. Each step closer Alice gets to the shadowy man she hunts, the more secrets she unravels, only to reveal chilling truths. If she wants to win this war and save millions of lives, Alice must once more embrace the impossible and make the unimaginable, imaginable.

Sometimes, the rabbit hole leads to terrifying places.

An enthralling mythological romance two thousand years in the making . . .

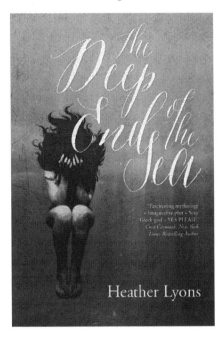

"Heather Lyons's *The Deep End of the Sea* is a radiant, imaginative romance that breathes new life into popular mythology while successfully tackling the issue of sexual assault. Lyons is a deft storyteller whose engaging prose will surprise readers at every turn. Readers will have no trouble sympathizing with Medusa, who is funny, endearing and courageous all at once. The romance between her and Hermes is passionate, sweet and utterly engrossing. This is a must read!" *–RT Book Reviews*

What if all the legends you've learned were wrong?

Brutally attacked by one god and unfairly cursed by another she faithfully served, Medusa has spent the last two thousand years living out her punishment on an enchanted isle in the Aegean Sea. A far cry from the monster legends depict, she's spent her time educating herself, gardening, and desperately trying to frighten away adventure seekers who occasionally end up, much to her dismay, as statues when they manage to catch her off guard. As time marches on without her, Medusa wishes for nothing more than to be given a second chance at a life stolen away at far too young an age.

But then comes a day when Hermes, one of the few friends she still has and the only deity she trusts, petitions the rest of the gods and goddesses to reverse the curse. Thus begins a journey toward healing and redemption, of reclaiming a life after tragedy, and of just how powerful friendship and love can be—because sometimes, you have to sink in the deep end of the sea before you can rise back up again.

The magical first book of the Fate series . . .

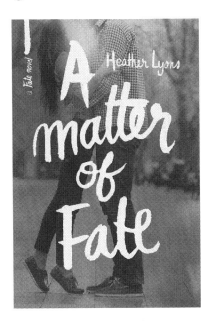

"Love, love, love this book! Such a fun and exciting premise. Full of teenage angst and heartache with a big helping of magic and enchantment. Can't wait to read the rest of this awesome series! Not to mention. . . TWO hot boys to swoon over." —*Elizabeth Lee, author of Where There's Smoke*

Chloe Lilywhite struggles with all the normal problems of a typical seventeen-year-old high school student. Only, Chloe isn't a normal teenage girl. She's a Magical, part of a secret race of beings who influence the universe. More importantly, she's a Creator, which means Fate mapped out her destiny long ago, from her college choice, to where she will live, to even her job. While her friends and relatives relish their future roles, Chloe resents the lack of say in her life, especially when she learns she's to be guarded against a vengeful group of beings bent on wiping out her kind. Their number one target? Chloe, of course.

That's nothing compared to the boy trouble she's gotten herself into.

Because a guy she's literally dreamed of and loved her entire life, one she never knew truly existed, shows up in her math class, and with him comes a twin brother she finds herself inexplicably drawn to.

Chloe's once unyielding path now has a lot more choices than she ever thought possible.

Follow Chloe's story in the rest of the Fate series books . . .

"Heather Lyons' writing is an addiction. . .and like all addictions. I. Need. More."
–#1 New York Times Best Selling Author Rachel Van Dyken

"Enthralling fantasy with romance that will leave you breathless, the Fate Series is a must read!" –Alyssa Rose Ivy, author of the Crescent Chronicles

Fans of *The Royal We* will not want to miss this epic love story!

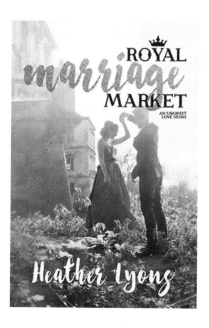

"The perfect royal romance." —Nichole Chase,
***NYT* bestselling author**

"Heather Lyons has officially charmed me. Royal Marriage Market is an indulgent read that will have you flipping pages until the very end."
—R.S. Grey, *USA TODAY* best-selling author

Every decade, the world's monarchs and their heirs secretly convene to discuss global politics and social issues—and arrange marriages between kingdoms.

Elsa may be the Hereditary Princess of Vattenguldia, but she finds the entire situation archaic and unsavory. While she wants what's best for her country, she isn't about to jump into an unwanted relationship— let alone a marriage—with a virtual stranger. Of course, her feelings matter little to her parents, whose wheeling and dealings over trade pacts and alliances achieved at her expense begin the moment they set foot in California for the Summit. So when a blindingly handsome royal runs into her, she doesn't hesitate to tell him there's no way she's marrying him.

Christian is all too happy to agree: no marriage. As the Hereditary Grand Duke of Aiboland, his main goal is to get through the summit without a bride being foisted on him. Which is why he suggests they help each other field potential intendeds. As Christian slowly gets to know Elsa, though, he realizes they have a lot more in common than just their feelings about the Royal Marriage Market. Only he can't fall for her, because royal or not, they're not meant for each other.

Elsa and Christian will have to evaluate matters of the heart verses those of state and crown, and decide whether or not tradition trumps love.

Read on for a sneak peak of the first chapter of

ROYAL Marriage MARKET!

CHAPTER 1

ELSA

Whenever I am faced with my full name in print, strung out in letters and words like clothes whipping on a line, my visceral reaction is the same had somebody raked rusty nails down a dusty chalkboard. Years of careful practice were cultivated in order to prevent me from physically recoiling at the sight or sound of *Elsa Victoria Evelyn Sofia Marie*.

Most girls are given a first and a middle name—two middle names, perhaps, if the parents are feisty or bound by family tradition. Or even a hyphenated first name, such as Lily-Anne or Ella-Mae. My name, the one my parents bestowed upon me, the one that informs the world who and what I am, is three bloody names too long and hangs around me like a noose rather than the garland surely envisioned. "You are a princess," my mother rationalized when I queried as to why she and my father went vindictively bonkers come naming time.

Fair enough, but my sister (also a princess) has only three names: Isabelle Madeleine Rose. Still lengthy, but far more tolerable. Even my father, the illustrious Prince Gustav IV of Vattenguldia, does not lay claim to so many names; his tops out at four. Indeed, no one in my acquaintance—royal or no—possesses such a lengthy appellation.

Just me.

"You are the Hereditary Princess of Vattenguldia," my mother clarified when pressed further. "Someday, you'll be sovereign over our great land."

Sovereigns apparently have hideously long names, even in tiny principalities like ours that rest in relative, yet fairly wealthy, obscurity in the Northern Baltic Sea. I often wonder if I will be as cruel when I have my own children, if I will saddle them with a name so convoluted and extensive that air must be drawn in between syllables. I like to think not, but the truth is, I'm partial to tradition, especially when it pertains to the throne in Vattenguldia.

Correction: most traditions. Because I am most certainly not in favor of the one my father's private secretary is delivering to me.

By letter from the Secretary of the Monarchs' Council to allow a formal invitation to be extended to Her Royal Highness The Hereditary Princess of Vattenguldia Elsa Victoria Evelyn Sofia Marie.

Sighing, I extract the surprisingly heavy missive from Bittner's age-spotted hands, like a bomb expert under the gun to sever the correct wire or risk the entire building disintegrating around them. Which, considering what waits within, might be a preferable situation. "Gee, thanks."

His smile would be best described as a shit-eating smirk, only that would make me sound uncouth and not very princess-like, or so my parents claim. They've taken it upon themselves to attempt to rein in my so-called foul and inappropriate language as "sovereigns, let alone Hereditary Princesses, do not speak like common sailors." It ought to be mentioned they do not personally know any sailors; the ones I have met working in our shipping industry are quite articulate.

An audible thunk sounds when the envelope hits my writing desk. "Has my father seen this yet?"

"I delivered His Serene Highness's shortly before I came up here." That's to be expected. "Upon viewing it, did he uncork a bottle of his finest champagne?" Bittner's exceedingly perfect manners prohibit him from acknowledging this was most likely the case, so he instead says in the crisp, cool, yet distinctive voice of his that would render him perfect to narrate movie trailers, "Prince Gustav was most amenable to receiving his invitation."

I can only imagine. A whole week set aside for hobnobbing with his peers? He's probably frothing at the mouth over the prospect of getting the hell out of the country and away from my mother.

I eye the envelope on my desk, envisioning a baby asp inside, ready to strike the moment I release its apocalyptical contents. "I suppose he will insist upon us attending." Which is inane of me to say, because there is no doubt my father's orders for packing and travel have already been issued. Whether or not we attend has never been up for question, because royals never decline attendance to this particular event.

I wait until Bittner departs before I pick the invitation back up. I have an appointment at a favorite local children's hospital within the hour, so it is now or never. As my silver letter opener hisses quietly through the paper, I remind myself that none of this would be a problem right now if I were already married. Still single at twenty-eight years old, I am considered one of the most eligible women in the world. Being the next in line to a throne, even an insignificant one, will do that to a lady. It's not so much that I despise the thought of marriage, because I do not. Done right, it is an alluring temptation that could provide comfort and companionship in a life such as mine, only none of my experiences so far have led to anything close to persuading me to join my monstrosity of a name and family baggage to another's. Finding the right person to share my life is no easy task; my last few efforts at romantic entanglements all blew up in my face.

Most recently, I made the mistake of fancying decided to sex up a former schoolmate—in public, no less. The press had a field day when Nils and Trinnie were photographed groping one another upon the slopes while I was skiing elsewhere. Much to my chagrin, *Popular Swedish Count Cheats On Vattenguldian Princess—Will They Weather This Storm?* ran in local newspapers, glossies, and on television for weeks. Pre-Nils, there was Theo and his fervent yet wholly unexpected decision that the church was a better fit for him than a palace. Pre-Theo, there was my teenage crush Casper, who wasn't even an option. None of the other gents in my history are worth a mention.

Why do you have to be so picky? my mother often laments. And that amuses and disheartens all at once, because one would assume Her Serene Highness would wish the Hereditary Princess to marry a man of upstanding character. Personally, I would never term a lady who found her arsehole of a boyfriend *en flagrante* with her so-called friend and summarily dumped their cheating arses from her inner circle picky, though. That was pure practicality.

Although I am sincerely grateful—perhaps relieved is a better word—over extracting myself from such relationships before serious damage could occur, part of me rues not getting engaged (even temporarily) to some nice local before the madhouse of horrors known as the Decennial Summit were to commence. I naively assumed I had time. Time to fall in love. Time to find somebody on my own. Time to grow into my role in the principality.

Yet, time is nearly at an end, because the Royal Marriage Market (or as the unfortunately unattached like myself often refer to it, the RMM) is close at hand.

Irritability skitters down my spine when I finally rip the papers out of the envelope.

Lord Shrewsbury,
on behalf of
the Monarch Council,
requests the pleasure of your company
at the Decennial Summit
at Hearst Castle, beginning 23rd of April

I lean back in my chair, staring at the words in front of me until they fully sink in. Three days? THREE BLOODY DAYS before His Serene Highness and fellow royal cronies go hard-core, full-press in their quest to ensure my ilk and I are popping out sanctioned heirs in the very foreseeable future?

An inner Doomsday clock roars to life, each second a searing reminder of the utter tragedy that lies ahead. A mild panic attack settles into my lungs and chest, and I am gasping like a dying fish as I claw hungrily for air.

Calm down, Elsa. You are a Hereditary Princess. You will act like a Hereditary Princess. You do not let anything touch you. Not even this.

I focus on the details of the missive, ones to bottleneck my fears escaping in wide berths down to a manageable load. I breathe in and out. Fine-tune my focus until it is honed laser sharp upon the silver words clutched within my hands. Deep breath in. *Twenty-third of April*. Deep breath out. *Hearst Castle*. Deep breath—

Hearst Castle?

I mentally flip through the names of palaces and castles inhabited by fellow royals throughout Europe. Maybe it's . . . no. Maybe . . . not that one, either. I move on to various seats of nobility, combing through name after name, but none match. In a fit of annoyance, I relent and open my laptop.

The results come in fast. Hearst Castle *is not a real castle*. At least, not a European one and certainly never inhabited by royalty. Technically, it is a mansion in California, surrounded by several guesthouses.

Sonofabitch.

I click on one of the links and read up on the location. It was previously owned by someone in the newspaper business, a rich and influential man, which I suppose makes him the equivalent of American royalty. Currently, the building is a United States Historical Landmark and open to the public on a daily basis.

I nearly shred the invitation as I grapple to take all this in. The Monarch Council wishes to send the entirety of the world's reigning sovereigns and many of their heirs to a popular tourist destination in California?

Has the MC gone insane?

I storm out of my suite in a righteous fit of indignation, gripping the linen in my fist. Propriety dictates I call ahead, or knock at the very least, but as there are precious few days between the Decennial Summit and my freedom, I bypass manners and decorum and wrench the door to my father's office open. Bittner is in there with His Serene Highness, but that matters little. He has worked for the House of Vasa long enough to know just about everything there is to our quirks, including my occasional warm-to-the-touch temperament that flares to life during the most inconvenient times. Like right now, when I am so upset I can barely unfurl my fingers from the invitation to shake it properly in my father's face.

"My word, Elsa. You appear quite vexed." My father is smooth as butter as he smiles faintly up at me. "Bittner, I wonder what in the world could inspire Her Highness to lose sight of her manners."

Before Bittner can respond (not that I think he would), I slap the paper down onto the antique desk that dominates the room. "Is this a joke?"

Although I guarantee he already knows what I have brought to him, His Serene Highness slides on his reading spectacles and peers downward. "I hoped you'd finally gotten over your . . ." His lips purse as he most likely attempts to assign the most diplomatic phrasing he can to what he considers my ravings. "*Hesitancy* over the Summit. You knew that it was coming at some point this year."

Not only The Prince of Vattenguldia, but the Prince of Tact—because I'll admit to offering (behind closed doors, of course) my sincere feelings concerning the Decennial Summit on more than one occasion. I must clarify that it is not the Summit that has me in fits, it is the infamous RMM. Because, for nearly five hundred years now, alliances forged through arranged marriages concocted at a Summit hosted every decade have often overshadowed legitimate diplomatic work achieved. In essence, single heirs older than twenty-five rarely depart the Summit unattached. Both male and female are lambs to the slaughter.

It is a tradition I desire no part of, one I cannot find it in my heart to embrace.

But that terrifying, archaic possibility is neither here nor there at the moment. The Prince knows my view on this, and, as he sharply pointed out the last time I attempted a debate, I've had my say. Currently, I have other battles to fight. Calming oxygen floods my lungs while I slip on a cool smile. "Not that." I tap on the paper. *"This."*

Dark blue eyes, so much like my own, squint behind his reading spectacles. "I'm afraid I'm not—"

"Do you know where Hearst Castle is?"

His bushy eyebrows rise ever so slightly, aging caterpillars whose micro- movements illustrate volumes of emotion.

Shite. I barked at him; father or no, he is still my sovereign and deserves my respect. Another deep breath is required for me to continue. "My apologies." I assume a more respective, ladylike stance, one hand folded over the other in front of me. "I simply wish to know if you are aware of pertinent details of the location?"

As he leans back, the creaking of a chair sounds in the surprisingly modest yet elegant personal office.

"It's a bloody tourist destination in the United States!"

At this, a small, choking cough escapes Bittner. I quickly apologize again. If I don't get myself under control, Hereditary Princess or no, I'll find myself on the other side of the door in no time.

My father's fingers form a steeple in front of his face, long fingers once elegant and now marked by time and arthritis. "I am well aware of what Hearst Castle is and where it is located, Elsa."

Ah. Of course he is. After all, he serves upon the Monarch Council, although in a much reduced capacity nowadays, what with two heart attacks in three years. Still, I never would have thought my father this naïve about sending so many monarchs and their heirs to such a public location. "What about terrorists?"

When I was younger and lost control of my emotions, my father reminded me that such passion does no monarch any favors. *The key to being an effective sovereign is to remain calm and clear-headed. Never make crucial decisions or arguments when your emotions get the better of you. Productivity and goodness cannot stem organically through heightened feelings, even if crafted under the best of intentions.*

It is a lesson I fail to prove mastered, for another lift of eyebrow is meant to remind me continued outbursts will not be tolerated. "Terrorists?"

"I am concerned about safety logistics that might arise during the

Summit. While most of our kingdoms and principalities are constitutional monarchies, it would still be devastating if something were to happen to any of the royals present. What if someone were to catch wind of the Summit? Target us?"

A tiny smile bends one half of his thin lips. "Someone like a terrorist?"

"I cannot possibly be the only one to believe it is a monumentally terrible idea to convene every monarch in the world, alongside their heirs, in a single location, let alone such a public one."

"And yet, we have convened every decade for centuries without incident, Elsa. Nary a terrorist attack, let alone a single act of crime, has ever touched us during a Decennial Summit."

He's right. For all our romantic failings in the press, royals are exceedingly excellent at keeping their shite locked down tight. Even still, I cannot let this go. "Respectfully, my point stands in consideration of twenty-first century politics. There are many countries whose citizens wish to abolish monarchies, viewing them as archaic and unnecessary in light of democracy and socialism. The Summit is an excellent opportunity for the disgruntled to—"

"Are you sure your true concern hinges on our safety?" His tongue clicks quietly in reproach. "Or, is it more likely you are fretting over the RMM?"

Well, yes, but . . . "I am simply saying—" "Must I remind you that your mother and I were betrothed at the RMM?" It is a far cry from a selling point. My parents, brought together by politics, are no love match. Other than myself, Isabelle, and Vattenguldia, they have little to nothing in common and do not speak unless in public or necessity dictates more than a written note or a message sent via their private secretaries. As much as it disgusts me to contemplate, I am fairly confident words were not even spoken during the conception of their children. A note was most likely written and delivered: *Let's make an heir. Eight o'clock tonight, my room. Best to be drunk beforehand.*

So, yes. Maybe my mother has a valid point. Perhaps I am picky, because I desire that, if and when I attach my life to another's, it will be to someone I can at least talk to. And like as well as respect. Is it so wrong that I would not mind a storybook tale? Not the horrible bits—no poisoned apples or sleeping spells. I do not even require a prince, let alone a charming one. My life is one of service. Responsibility. Importance. When the day comes and I assume the throne, I simply wish somebody I love to be in my corner. And if I cannot find that, I would rather not marry.

I tell my father, "I am well aware of that, sir."

He slips off his reading spectacles and sets them on the desk. "Let me assure you every precaution will be taken to secure the location. At this very moment, Hearst Castle is closed to the public for renovations and restorations, and is not scheduled to reopen to the public for another two months. While the location is news to you today, the MC has worked closely with the American government for nearly two years to ensure the Summit goes off without a hitch."

His words, so crisp and no-nonsense, leave no door open for dissention.

"I am sure you are curious as to why Hearst Castle was chosen," he continues. "Of that, I will indulge you. After much discussion, the MC decided it best to meet on neutral ground. The United States is a good choice. While we could have easily taken over a hotel, many feel an event such as the Decennial Summit deserves something special. Hearst Castle and its history fit the bill."

I am beating my head against a wall. "It is no longer in use as a residence!" "Another fact I am also aware of, Elsa." It is a soft jab; he is informing me that none of my arguments carry any weight in his mind. I want to argue: It's a tourist trap. He would counter: I've already addressed that issue. I want to argue: From what I saw on the website, it is not a very big venue for such a large party. He would argue: That's part of its allure. I want to argue: Where will everyone sleep? We have employees to think of, too. Will we all be in tents? He would argue: You worry too much. It will be taken care of. I want to argue: Please do not force me to be part of the RMM. He would argue: The House of Vasa lives and dies by tradition. But none of this is said. There is no need, not when the outcome is so easily predicted. Instead, I remain silent in my defeat as he reclaims his pen. "You'd best hurry if you are to make your appointment this afternoon. I know the children would be sorely disappointed if you missed story time."

Translation: You are dismissed.

I am at the door when he adds, "Please let your sister know she will be expected to accompany us. There is vital business I must attend to at the Summit, and I will need my girls with me."

At first I am stunned, but that is foolish of me. Of course Isabelle is to come. She is an attractive bargaining chip, after all.

Three days. There are three days until we journey to California. Three days until the Royal Marriage Market opens its doors after being shuttered for ten years.

Three days until life as I know it will change, whether I wish it so or not.

ABOUT THE AUTHOR

photo @Regina Wamba of Mae I Design and Photography

Heather Lyons is known for writing epic, heartfelt love stories often with a fantastical twist. From Young Adult to New Adult to Adult novels—one commonality in all her books is the touching, and sometimes heart-wrenching, romance. In addition to writing, she's also been an archaeologist and a teacher. She and her husband and children live in sunny Southern California and are currently working their way through every cupcakery she can find.

Website: www.heatherlyons.net

Facebook: www.facebook.com/heatherlyonsbooks

Twitter: www.twitter.com/hymheather

Goodreads:
www.goodreads.com/author/show/6552446.Heather_Lyons

Stay up to date with Heather by subscribing to her newsletter:
eepurl.com/2Lkij